Glowing reviews for *Take Me In*

(*Amazon:* reader) '**Captivating page.** Such a fantastic story, full of twists and turns, that have your emotions doing the same. The main characters are warm and wonderful and have you laughing and then crying within the blink of an eye. The underlying theme of cross generational love is told with humour and drama. A fantastic read.'

(*Goodreads:* Libby) 'Wow! I absolutely loved this book from cover to cover. It made me realise on how lucky I am to have all I do in my life and how much there is to be missed should I no longer be here anymore. Absolutely beautiful and thought provoking. What an incredible debut novel! Would recommend this book to anyone (and already have done!)'

(*Goodreads:* AmyAmyAmy) '**Brilliant! A clear 6/5!** One of my favourite books of the year and I've already bought it for friends for Xmas and have a queue of others waiting to borrow it. I sincerely hope that you have got someone looking at making this into a TV series?! The way you deal with DV is sensitive, empathetic and still positive, such a hard balance. Can't wait to read your next one...'

(*Amazon:* Monica) '**Dark funny mystery with a big heart.** A gripping read; bright characters, vivid places, dark humour and weighty themes are weaved and balanced together brilliantly. Touching and funny. A debut to be proud of.'

Praise for *Sleeping Partners*:

I didn't think this book could possibly be as good as Take Me Instead BUT it is. I loved it. So many twists and turns. Well done, again. (Linda, Portobello)

I loved that this book was set in Fife. I knew all the places and living in a small village, I could identify with all the residents of Duneden. An authentic, funny drama about the ups and downs of family and village life. (Liz, Fife)

My wife recommended Faye's last book to me. Not usually my genre but I thoroughly enjoyed it. She asked me to try this one. Wasn't disappointed. An author with a great sense of humour. (David, Perth)

You can't help but root for Jennifer when she takes over The Maltings. Just as you think everything is going well for her, along comes the chapter, The Day Everything Changed. I did not see that coming. Fabulously endearing characters; flawed, funny and (sometimes) scary. (Anne, Broxburn)

I didn't want the book to end. The characters were so real that I felt as if I was saying cheerio to good friends. I hope there is another book about Duneden coming soon. (Sandra, Freuchie)

Thank you, Faye, for another great read. The first paragraph is an eye opener and I knew immediately that a good story was about to unfold. I wasn't disappointed. Funny yet emotional. Lots of laughs, gasps and tears. What more could you want? (Gillian, Kinross)

About the Author

Faye Stevenson grew up in an East Lothian mining community. She graduated with a teaching diploma at Moray House College, Edinburgh. As well as teaching, she helped her husband run the family businesses in hospitality for thirty years. Now in semi-retirement, she has returned to her love of writing.

Her debut novel *Take Me Instead* has received fantastic reviews from readers all over the world.

SLEEPING PARTNERS

Faye Stevenson

First published in 2024 by Faye Stevenson

Publishing services provided by Lumphanan Press
www.lumphananpress.co.uk

Front cover photography by Mark Stevenson
www.markstevensonphotography.com

© Faye Stevenson 2024

Faye Stevenson has asserted her right to be identified as the author of this Work
in accordance with the Copyright, Design and Patents Act 1988.

To all my family and friends.
Your support has been invaluable.

The best-laid schemes o' mice an' men
Gang aft agley,
An' lea'e us nought but grief an' pain,
For promis'd joy!

Robert Burns (1785)

PROLOGUE

Thursday 23rd June 1983

Afternoon

Jennifer Cameron should have booted her husband's balls right up his bare, betraying, hairy arse. Bastard! Instead, she lurked in the shadows and watched, holding her breath for fear of being caught. The thumping of her heart squeezed through her parched throat and settled in her head.

Thump, thump, thump.

Mark Cameron's pale buttocks pumped in and out of the splayed knees on the pool table.

Pump, pump, pump.

The female looked uncomfortable. She supported her upper body on her elbows. Her neck strained to hold her head in position and her chin was protruding. Jennifer couldn't fathom why she was remotely interested in Roxanne's comfort, considering what was unfolding before her.

Mark cradled her arse as it hung over the edge of the table.

In and out. In and out. He had plenty to hold on to.

His beige chinos shimmied around his ankles. A pair of burgundy knickers were trapped beneath one of his shoes. His head was tilted back too, making his brown hair appear longer than normal. Roxanne, with her long blonde locks, was far too young for him. Or should have been.

How could he have repaid her loyalty in this way? Jennifer had given up everything for him – moved away from friends and from family. For what? So that he could shag a wee girl half his age!

Jennifer backed slowly out of the lounge bar, her eyes transfixed on Roxanne's red, wedged sandals digging into her husband's exposed flesh. The lack of oxygen made her giddy. Moving backwards was precarious but she needed to make sure that she had not been seen. As soon as she was in the corridor, she made for the back entrance of their village pub. Each carefully planted tip-toe pounded her body.

A bright, narrow shaft of sunshine cut through the double doors that Jennifer had left ajar.

'Don't squeak! Please don't squeak,' she whispered, squeezing her way through the gap.

She was shaking. Her left hand supported her right hand, as she pushed the large key into the oval hole. There was a knack in lining up both doors before locking them. Jennifer lifted one of the heavy, black doors by the handle, pulled it quietly into position, and turned the key. It worked first time. She thanked God. She pressed her back and shoulders against the stone building and dared to breath. The relief was painful. She closed her eyes to think.

If she told no-one then no-one would know. But she knew. And would always know.

It was over. There was no going back. But not yet. Jennifer needed revenge.

ONE

Eighteen months earlier: January 1982

'When will we be there?' asked six-year-old Emma for the umpteenth time.

'Not long.' Her dad had a smug grin on his face.

'At least another hour,' answered her mother truthfully.

'We'll see,' laughed Mark.

Jennifer stared at her husband. He was unusually chirpy considering it was pissing down with rain and they'd had to have their picnic sitting in the car. He was up to something.

Their journey to St Andrews had been two-fold. Mark had a disgruntled customer he had to pacify and, for weeks, he had been promising the girls a trip to the Fife seaside resort.

It had been a miserable weekend, weatherwise, and Mark had dismissed Jennifer's earlier suggestion to abandon their plans, stay at home in Edinburgh, and head there another day. Who goes to St Andrews in winter?

Jennifer had learned that it was less hassle to appease her husband when he was in a certain mood or he would sulk for days. He was her third petulant child. This was also a side that others rarely witnessed. Mark portrayed himself to friends and colleagues as a congenial, happy-go-lucky kind of guy. Good company and always cracking jokes. Like many comedians, his frivolity was hard to maintain.

The rain rattled off the car. Jennifer thought that the windscreen wipers might actually snap under the strain. She leaned over her seat and handed her squabbling twosome a packet of chocolate buttons, just as the car turned off the A914.

'Where are we going now?' She was curious.

'Duneden.'

'What for?'

Without answering, the car pulled up in front of a large sandstone building. Mark turned into a parking area at the side of it.

'Everybody out!' he ordered.

'For Heaven's sake!'

'Out!' That tone again.

Jennifer zipped up her navy cagoule and pulled the hood tight around her auburn hair before bracing herself. A gale force wind pummelled her skinny body. An umbrella was never an option. Unperturbed, a smirking Mark ushered Jennifer and the girls round to the back of the building. They stood on the gravel as he tried a couple of keys in the big double doors. Behind them, a green lawn swept down to a river at the bottom of the garden. At first, Jennifer assumed the small hotel was one of G&B's customers. Gordon and Blair Brewery had several pubs and hotels that were leased to landlords. It was part of Mark's remit to monitor them as well as supervising the sales teams.

'Welcome to our new home and business,' he sang.

The two girls and their mother stood in the dark hallway. Puddles formed on the floor around their wellies as the rain dripped off their waterproofs. The sour stench of stale beer and abandonment scorched Jennifer's nostrils

'Say something,' he urged.

'You have got to be kiddin' me?' Jennifer flashed a look at

Mark, glanced at the girls then settled her incredulous gaze on her husband again.

The girls were as gobsmacked as their mother.

'I don't want to move,' wailed Emma.

Wee Katie was too young to comprehend but not too young to grasp that something seismic had been dropped. She drowned out her sister.

'For fuck's sake. I thought you'd all be happy,' shouted their dad.

'You should have warned me,' snarled Jennifer.

*

'Is he having a mid-life crisis?' asked Grace Thomson. 'Ellen Matthew's son-in law had one. Got a tattoo right across his shoulders. Bought a Harley Davies (Jennifer didn't correct her mother. She never listened anyway) and buggered off to America to drive from one side to the other. Poor wee Mary. Never got over it. Took to the drink.'

'It's nothing like that, Mum. But he should have discussed it with me first.' Jennifer couldn't help defending Mark. It was okay for her to openly criticise her husband but not for anyone else. Particularly her mother who had an opinion on everybody and everything.

Jennifer's parents lived in Port Seton, a small coastal town in East Lothian. Fife was on the opposite side of the Firth of Forth: a stretch of water that separated the two coastlines.

'I can't bring myself to tell Hannah.'

Hannah was an eighty-six-year-old widow who Jennifer cleaned for. They had become great friends. Jennifer did much more than cleaning; she looked out for her. Although, if you asked Hannah, she would say that she looked out for Jennifer.

Grace twisted her face. 'Your dad says that you can see Falkland Hill from the harbour. Is that no' near you?'

Jennifer stood at the window of the neat council house and stared forlornly in the direction of Duneden; not that she could see anything except another row of houses. She sighed, 'Not too far. Close to St Andrews.'

'Me an' your dad stayed at a caravan in St Andrews for our honeymoon. On a cliff top. Bloody freezing.' Grace rubbed her hands together as if to warm them up. She deliberately didn't mention Hannah.

Grace rarely enquired about Hannah. She hated to admit it but she was a wee bit jealous of her relationship with Jennifer. Even her husband, Jimmy, helped out with some light gardening for the communal areas surrounding Hannah's flat. Fair enough, it brought in a few extra pennies. Cash in hand. Hannah was lucky to have someone like Jennifer run after her hand and foot.

If it hadn't been for Mark (Grace could feel the scowl on her face deepening), Jennifer would have had a secure job and earning a decent wage. But no. He whisked her off her feet, to God knows where, and returned with more than they bargained for. As much as she loathed the snobby Camerons (Mark's parents), they hadn't sanctioned their travels either. You could tell that Jennifer hadn't the right credentials for their son. Not that they would dare say it in front of Grace but the implication hovered during the few meet-ups the families had. However, Grace couldn't deny that the pair of them had made it work. They'd seemed besotted with each other and those two gorgeous daughters of theirs completed the family unit.

*

The following ten weeks had passed in a blur. Their house in Liberton, Edinburgh, had sold within days of being put on the market and Jennifer was now dishing out instructions to her brother, her dad and the removal men as to where things should go in The Maltings. Her mother was keeping the girls for a chunk of the Easter holidays to allow Jennifer time to clean and organise the rooms the family would need. Humphing furniture up to their living area was not easy due to the sharp left and right turns three quarters of the way up. Several times the men wobbled on the awkward narrow steps at the turns.

Mark was busy setting up the bar in the lounge when two women appeared. Jennifer assumed it was more folk dropping in for a nosey. Plenty had already. After a good few minutes, she realised they were still there. She tried to eavesdrop whilst directing all the men. The tall, slim, dark-haired woman seemed to be doing all the talking. The shorter, dumpier one jumped in occasionally but stood back, allowing the better looking of the two to control the negotiations. Next thing, Mark was shaking their hands then the women whipped off their jackets and got stuck in to washing the glasses.

In the hallway at the bottom of the stairs, Jennifer caught her husband's eye and pulled a 'what's going on' face. With a tilt of his head, he smiled and summoned Jennifer through to the lounge.

Everything pertaining to the running of the business was on ground floor level; the lounge, games area, the function suite, kitchen and toilets. The living quarters were upstairs to the left and as far as Jennifer could make out, an unused residential area to the right. The bedrooms there had been used mostly for storage.

'Jen, this is Angie and her cousin, Maureen. Our first employees. Ladies, this is my wife, Jen.'

It would have been nice to have been consulted, thought Jennifer. She knew her tight smile would be perceived in the wrong way. She had no truck with the two women but Mark was on a very sticky wicket since he had sprung all this on her.

'A bit of advice,' snapped Jennifer. 'The actual room needs scrubbed from top to bottom before any glasses.'

The snipe was aimed at her husband but Angie threw up her arms in self-defence. 'Whoa! Only following instructions from the boss.'

Jennifer clocked immediately from her tone that Angie was no shrinking violet.

'Well, as am the cleaner, I'll get started on that *FIRST* then.' Maureen rolled her eyes at Angie.

'You'll need piping hot, soapy water,' Jennifer warned her. 'The nicotine has seeped into the walls like tar.' She pointed to the wall behind the pool table. 'You can see where I started last week.' Although the wall had been thoroughly washed down, streaks of dirty brown were still visible. 'I'll paint the room as soon as I'm organised upstairs.'

It wasn't the only room that required a deep clean. The whole place had been sadly neglected. Jennifer felt her body dissolve into the manky, sticky carpet at the prospect of what lay ahead.

'Aye, am used to hot water. Am takin' it that ye huv safety steps. Am no' standin' on a chair.'

Jennifer smiled. She doubted a chair could take Maureen's weight.

Seconds later, Mark stormed up the stairs behind his wife.

Maureen stared into her cousin's face. 'I dinnae think a can work for her.'

'Beggars can't be choosers,' hissed Angie. 'It's on our doorstep. We can walk here in minutes. Anyway, she's right. This is a shit hole. I'd be cleaning everywhere else before the bar. So would you.'

'Hhhmmm. I suppose.'

Mark grabbed Jennifer by the arm. 'What the fuck was that.'

'What?'

'You know fine well, WHAT? Don't go pissing off the staff, Jen. We need the locals on board and from what I can tell those two know nearly everybody in the village. They've got good contacts and I'll need all the contacts I can get.'

Jennifer walked away.

'Where are you going?'

'To find safety ladders. Obviously.'

TWO

Thursday 23rd June 1983

Morning

Jennifer silenced her alarm before it woke up everyone else in the flat. Mark barely stirred as she slipped out of bed. She quickly checked on her two young girls then jumped in the shower. The hot spray soothed her tense shoulders. Her fingers massaged the citrus shampoo into her scalp. She relaxed; it was so good. Her hair hung over her wrists all the way down to her elbows as she allowed the water to rinse the lather from her fingers and her long hair.

Once out of the shower, she upped her pace. She rubbed her body with her husband's towel. The hairdryer blasted out hot, dry air. Beads of sweat trickled down her back. The hot weather showed no sign of ebbing – an unaccustomed heat wave, especially for the Central Belt of Scotland. She bent forward from her waist. Her slim legs were straight and her auburn hair skimmed the tiles of the bathroom floor. She brushed and smoothed out her long mane from the nape of her neck to the top of her head. As she gripped the coil of hair with her left hand, the fingers from her right hand twisted a black band around what now resembled a fox's tail. When it was tight enough, she stood up and shook her head. Red-chestnut curls flicked her shoulders and slid down her back.

She looked in the mirror. *A bit severe but it'll have to do,* she thought.

To soften the look, she tugged a few strands from above her ear and curled them around her finger. Jennifer pulled on a green sleeveless blouse and tucked it into skin-tight jeans, cropped above the ankle. She would have to put make-up on later; not that she needed to. Her skin was flawless. She slipped on a pair of trainers that had seen better days and made her way downstairs to open up the pub.

All the windows and the wide, double doors at the back of the building were flung open to allow fresh air to flood in. The acrid smell of last night, a mixture of cigarettes and beer, clung to everything. In the past, it would have made her gag. Jennifer loathed smoking but it was an occupational hazard that she had forced herself to tolerate. Not that she was an anti-smoking zealot but she dreaded the thought of a fag end smoldering undetected. Fire was her biggest fear. They had to sleep above that dump. She insisted that all her staff double check each area of the pub before locking up at night. If she could, she would check it all again.

She sat on the back door step with a strong coffee and kicked off her ancient trainers, flexing her bare feet and long toes. She held the mug to her lips. Jennifer loved that first luxurious sip – her caffeine fix – and the first of many in a day. It was only six-thirty but the heat from the sun bathed her body. The young mum closed her eyes and smiled into the orangey glow burning into her face. She stretched out her legs, surveyed the beer garden and planned how to set everything up for the evening's birthday bash.

A full year and a half had passed since Mark had purchased The Maltings without Jennifer's consent. She was absolutely livid. Taking on a rundown pub, miles from her beloved Edinburgh and her small cohort of close friendships, was way down at the bottom of her list of priorities for her wee family.

She didn't have many friends now, apart from Fiona, her bestie from primary school, and her two old cronies, Hannah and Fergal, and she pondered for a moment if that was her fault or Mark's. Probably both. She'd always felt that Mark was enough for her.

The outlook from the back door of The Maltings was breathtaking. A wide expanse of green grass sloped gently down to the River Eden. It had only recently been mown and set up as a proper beer garden. On the opposite bank, Malcolm Patterson's orchard complemented the view. Malcolm came into The Maltings most evenings. Usually later on. The jury was out on him. Jennifer found him too touchy feely for her liking, erring on sleazy.

Jennifer rubbed the well-worn step with the palm of her hand. It was warm to the touch. She wondered how many other women, over the century, had sat there contemplating their futures. She knew she had spent most of the year smarting when she should have been putting more energy into building the business and enjoying it with Mark. It was as if a fog had enveloped her and she couldn't find a way out. It hadn't helped her build good relationships in the village either. That would be no relationships; entirely of her own making.

The crunching of gravel on the driveway shook her from her reverie and she winced at the phlegmy coughing winging its way round the corner. She enjoyed the solitude of her mornings.

Maureen, The Maltings cleaner and general dog's body, cringed when she saw the boss's wife sunbathing on the back doorstep. She'd been hoping to get in and out again before anyone else was down. Mark entrusted her and Angie with a back door key. Maureen often rocked up early. She was an early riser. She preferred to prepare all the packed lunches for her brood before she took her mum and dad's dog for a walk. It wasn't a total surprise to see Jen who, for some reason, had shown more interest in the place in the last few months than she had ever done.

She gritted her teeth. 'Mornin'.' Christ, she hoped she sounded bubbly enough.

'You're early,' cried Jennifer, failing to disguise her displeasure.

'I need to buy somethin' to wear the night so I came in early. Big day for us,' explained Maureen with a fake cheery grin. There was no pleasing her sour-faced boss. 'I'm so excited. I'll be back before lunches though. So, I'll jist bash on.'

Maureen was aware that Jen was peering at her fleshy bits causing her to pull a washed-out tee shirt down over her belly. It was futile. A two-inch gap between her jeans and the tee shirt revealed a generous layer of flab hanging over her belt.

At least I'm fucking happy, smirked Maureen before sauntering off.

Really? thought Jennifer. *She's hardly an asset to us.*

Jennifer had an image of Maureen squeezed into a way-too-tight outfit for her size and age at this evening's celebrations. She tried to work out how old Maureen was. She looked at least fifty but could only be in her early forties. It was all that smoking, she mused. It had destroyed her voice and her face. And five boys in quick succession hadn't helped.

Unbeknown to Maureen, Jennifer had constantly urged Mark to dock her wages an hour each day because she spent more time on fag breaks and gossiping than working, but Mark had managed to talk her round. He stressed that Maureen was thorough and quick and, like Angie, she was prepared to help out at short notice. Deep down, Jennifer acknowledged that it was true yet it irked her that she, Mrs Mark Cameron, was the butt of her cleaner's tittle-tattle with the whole of Duneden.

Angie, on the other hand, was an unlikely ally of Jennifer's. She was a versatile cook and a thoroughly competent barmaid. And a good listener. They had more in common than perhaps Jennifer was willing to concede. Jennifer kind of liked her and she hoped that it was reciprocated. Plus, her girls adored Angie's daughter who was a regular overnight visitor. Jennifer busied herself in the kitchen and the gantry, making notes of everything that she had in stock, while Maureen chirpily belted out her own version of the lyrics to every song playing on the radio.

'I'll get started again... then I'll water Willie's plants. I'll check the kitchen's okay before I go,' called Maureen to her boss who was heading to the cellar to clean out the beer lines. 'I'll be back for 11.30!'

Jennifer glanced over her shoulder but didn't reply. Sometimes, she wondered if she had any clout. The staff appeared to pick and choose their hours as they saw fit and her opinion didn't seem to matter. If she complained to Mark, he would shrug it off.

Jennifer used to be so nervous about the pipes. The hissing of the gas would freak her out. Old Sandy Lawson who owned the pub long before them had been a great help. Angie had arranged for him to pop in and show her and Jennifer what to do. Mark was too impatient. (No surprise there.) Sandy talked them through it and made it look so easy. It was really, as long as you were careful. As soon as the gas was turned off, the barrels were disconnected and the correct amount of cleaning fluid was cautiously measured out and flushed through the pipes. Jennifer's hands used to tremble constantly. No matter how careful she tried to be, too many good jeans and tops were peppered with tiny splash burns. Items that she couldn't afford to replace. With the chemicals resting in the system, it gave her at least half an hour to put out all the empty bottles.

Not long after the pub had been reopened, Agnes Dunn, next door, complained to the police that the noise of the bottles crashing into the recycling bins kept her awake at night. Any reports to the police, however trivial, didn't look good when the licence was due for renewal. Mark, with his usual charm, assured Agnes it wouldn't happen again. Jennifer hoped that 7.30am wasn't too early to start the clattering but there was no time later.

When the bottles were sorted, the purple fluid was purged through each line with several pints of water and when they ran clear, the barrels were reconnected. The lager pipes had already been cleaned out earlier in the week because of the unusually hot weather. Pristine lines ensured that the beer, lager and cider were served at their best as dirty pipes could spoil the taste and were a haven for bacteria.

Jennifer had so much to do that she felt a migraine was coming on. She sat at the bar with a coffee and wrote a to-do list. *When a Man Loves a Woman* was playing on the radio for a second time that morning.

girls to school
check cash n carry order
get room sorted for Andrew and his girlfriend
phone mum/Andrew/florist

<pre>
            tidy
    clothes for girls/me on beds
    lunches/buffet/beer garden
         pick up Katie
         pick up flowers
           get ready
         smile!!!!!!!!!!!
</pre>

Jennifer hated The Maltings. She hated Duneden. She hated the person she had become.

THREE

Thankfully Jen hadn't seemed too put out when Maureen had asked for some time off to go shopping. Made a change! Maureen had her eye on a new top she'd tried on last week in River Island. She should've bought it when she had the chance because, now, she would have to nip down to Kirkcaldy before lunches.

Maureen rarely treated herself to new clothes. She preferred to spend it on her house or on her five beautiful boys. Her only ambition had been to get married and have babies and she'd achieved that. Maureen was as happy as a pig in shit with her lot.

She was as excited as everyone else in the village. It had been a year since the pub reopened and Mark wanted to celebrate with a family barbecue in the Beer Garden, followed by a karaoke. The pub had made a huge difference to the village. It had become a focal point again; a meeting place for young and old alike. It would be a busy evening and Maureen was a big part of it. She made a coffee and lit her third ciggie of the morning. Her cleaning routine rarely changed.

First the Gents then the Ladies.

The lounge bar and the pool room.

The back room – if it had been used (which was hardly ever).

All the corridors and the back and front entrances.

A coffee break at the front door (usually with Angie) but not today. No time.

Lastly, a quick surface clean of the kitchen before service begins.

She shouted out to Jen, who had been out at the bottle bank, to let her know her intentions. What was the dirty look for? Maureen couldn't fathom Jen out. She always smoked outdoors. She knew that Jen preferred her not to smoke in the pub while working, so she didn't. Maureen didn't allow smoking in her own house unless she was well and truly rat-arsed and had no recollection of it, so she chose not to do it in other people's homes (unless they couldn't give a toss). Jen had never actually said anything directly but she had that smug way of looking at you when she wasn't pleased; her face would twist into a long thin smile. Aye, she was a smug cow right enough. There was no getting away from it, Jen was hard work. Maureen loved her wee job in The Maltings. Thank God, Mark made up for Jen's churlishness. He was a good laugh – in spite of his posh voice.

The back doorway out to the beer garden and the front entrance were finished off before Maureen's coffee break. It gave her the chance to sit at the front bench and catch up on all the gossip with whoever happened to be passing the front door – which was often given that The Maltings was near the centre of the village on Main Street, next to the only shop, which housed the Post Office. Not forgetting that Maureen and Angie were related to half the population in Duneden.

'That's me awa to do Willie's tubs,' she called to Jen who was through in the cellar cleaning the pipes. She stubbed out her cigarette, knowing full well that frozen features would deliberately ignore her.

She picked off all the dead heads from the hanging baskets

and from the window boxes. Willie had filled all the planters with plants cultivated in their own greenhouse and Maureen had to admit they were bloody gorgeous: a profusion of red, orange and white geraniums, along with colourful petunias and lobelia spilled over every single one of them. Horticulture was Willie's passion. He spent every spare second, when he wasn't working, tending to his garden and his greenhouses. Most of the flowers had been planted in the early spring but the Mediterranean conditions had helped to keep them going. Willie had tons of trays with young plants ready to replace them when required.

Maureen had a wee blether with a few of the old codgers ambling along to the shop for their morning paper. Most had a comment to make about Willie's handiwork.

Right on cue, Willie passed in his works van, slowed down, and let out a sharp wolf-whistle.

'The flowers, not you!' he chuckled.

'Fuck off!' replied Maureen laughing and she slopped her bucket of water over his wheels. 'You two are later than usual. Been sleeping off the drink?'

Joe Blakeley, Willie's boss, was sitting in the passenger's seat; very green about the gills. Joe and his brother Tam owned a successful building firm. Joe was the grafter and Tam had the brains. Joe was the more handsome of the two. At six foot three, he was much taller than his brother. In his neighbourhood, Joe was regarded as a catch; single, good looking and it would be assumed, not short of cash. The short sleeves of his grey tee-shirt cut into the muscles of his upper arms, emphasising his toned physique. His black hair and chiselled square looks meant that he was never short of admirers or willing partners. He'd had numerous girlfriends and more one-night stands than he could ever recall yet a long-term relationship had eluded him. As he was never done telling Maureen and Willie, it was all he wanted.

'Anyway, what time did you sneak in last night?'

'Maureen! Ye ken fine what time I got in.' Willie jumped out of the car and whispered to his wife, 'Don't you be repeatin' anything I told ye last night. Too much whisky.'

'My lips are sealed.' Maureen assured him; miming a zip being closed shut across her mouth. Although, she couldn't wait to discuss it all with Angie later.

The first thing Willie had told Maureen as he'd rolled into their bedroom and onto their bed was the juicy revelations shared by everyone in the pub that night. Discussing openly in a bar in Duneden, with others in Duneden, who you would like to shag given the chance and who you have shagged and every minute detail into the bargain, is a big no-no. At the first opportunity, it WILL be used against you.

Willie missed out his own fantasies but was happy to tell Maureen about everyone else's: Joe's in particular. Maureen had said that it didn't come as a surprise.

Maureen poked her head through the open window. 'Christ's sake, Joe, you look like shite!'

'I feel shite,' he moaned.

'A long lie for you and me tomorrow though!' teased Willie, raising his eyebrows before jumping back into the van.

'Do you two horny buggers mind?' Joe rolled his eyes in mock horror.

With a huge grin, Maureen sauntered back in. She stopped and checked her newly dyed, brown hair in the long mirror in the hallway. She'd done it herself last night. She rubbed the top of her head with her fingertips. The colour was looking good.

Maybe a wee bit too rusty at the roots but it'll wash out. Her shoulder length hair was always tied up at work. She stood and surveyed the lounge bar as she always did to ensure everything was clean enough and to envisage the changes she would make to the place if she had the chance. She would definitely open up the lounge and the pool room (a large recess at the far-right hand side of the lounge) to make one, big, socialising area.

It's depressing in here, she thought.

It was a dark room – devoid of natural light. The old, wooden shutters at the large bay window beyond the pool table were always half-closed. Brown, heavy velvet curtains overwhelmed the three small windows on the other wall. Even the bottle-green, psychedelic carpet sucked the life out of the place. She couldn't understand why Mark had spent so much money on an expensive new bar when the old bar was perfectly functional. New furnishings would have had more impact and been much more practical. But what would a mere cleaner know?

And, if I looked like her, Maureen was staring at Jen who was darting between the bar and the cellar, *I'd give myself a bloody good shake and take a bit more interest in what's going on around here. Hopeless, grumpy cow.*

Most of the staff felt the same. They much preferred Mark and his easy-going ways.

Maureen checked the clock. She had just enough time to see to her boys then nip down to Kirkcaldy and back before helping Angie with the lunches and the sandwiches for later. She was in the mood to get bladdered tonight and her new batch of sloe gin was beckoning.

FOUR

Angie sprinted along the road to the shop. She'd spent too long passing the time of day with one of her neighbours and she was running late – a common drawback if you lived in a small village. Angie spotted Willie as she walked into Duneden Stores.

'Sobered up, Ang?' he laughed.

'Get to fuck,' she replied.

Despite the fact it was baking hot outside, Angie Lennie was wearing black jeans, tucked into long black boots. Her black vest (ninety per cent of Angie's wardrobe was black) was more in keeping. Her pixie-cropped hair matched her clothes perfectly.

Willie laughed. He was used to Angie's sharp tongue. Joe Blakeley came into view.

'You look like shite!' she yelled at Joe. Angie beamed. She liked tall men. She herself was tall and slim.

'So I've been told. I feel like it,' he answered feebly.

What should have been a quick drink before tea-time had turned into a late-night session for a group of regulars at The Maltings. Joe visibly cringed.

As if sensing what he had been thinking, Willie slapped his back, 'Forget it, we all said more than we should have last night. Too much alcohol and too much bravado. Isn't that right, Angie?'

'It'll be the talk of Duneden tonight,' moaned Joe. 'No harm,

Willie, but if you or Angie tell Maureen, the whole fuckin' place will know!'

Willie's face flushed again. 'Who cares? We were all rat-arsed. Everybody said something stupid last night even Angie... and she wasn't drinking that much!'

Joe gave Willie that 'really?' look. It was well known that Angie could knock a few back during a shift if she wanted to.

'You didn't, Willie. You said that nobody comes close to your Maureen. Fuck me, you made me blush at your bedtime gymnastics!'

'Who said anythin' about bedtime?' sniggered Willie. 'Maureen'd huv my balls if she knew!'

Joe held his head. It hurt when he laughed.

'Leave me out of it. I was working ya cheeky, fat bastard.' Angie bent down to scan the confectionary for something for her mum and Bethany.

Willie's reference to his and Maureen's sex life made Angie smile. They may not have been the most glamorous of couples but she was envious of Willie's relationship with her cousin. They had a lovely home and five boys that any parents would be proud of.

It was unfair of Angie to call Willie fat. He was not fat. Willie may have looked short next to Joe but most blokes did. Willie had a stocky build. His thick, stubby neck was squeezed between a ruddy, round face and large, burly shoulders. For as long as Angie could remember, Willie had been bald – the shoulder length, blond hair in his wedding photographs, long gone. He was the joker in the group. If Willie was in your company at night, you were guaranteed an entertaining evening. Maureen was a lucky woman. Willie would insist that he was the fortunate one.

'Four white rolls, please... well fired.'

Angie paid for a newspaper, the rolls, a packet of mints and two fudges. The shop assistant reminded Angie that a video was long overdue for return and hadn't been paid for.

'I've no' rented a video for ages!' replied Angie.

She checked Angie's rental records. 'It's *The Fox and the Hound*. A new Disney one, I think.'

Angie said she would check with her mother.

'See you tonight?' she called to Willie as she was leaving.

A chorus of 'ayes' and 'yeses', 'of course' and 'we'll be there' echoed throughout the shop. Nearly everyone intended to join in the shenanigans later that evening.

Most mornings, Angie Lennie bought fresh rolls and a newspaper to take to her ma. She was the only daughter. Unlike Angie, her two older, married brothers had done well for themselves. The one in London had prospered during the rapid growth of the telecommunications industry and the other, an insurance consultant, lived in one of the executive houses on Kinnoull Hill in Perth, while her shitless, witless, younger brother languished on the generosity of the state and her mother. Angie made it her business to protect her mother from her youngest child.

'Morning, Miss Lennie!' boomed a voice that Angie knew only too well. Her heart sank to her knees.

Malcolm Patterson leaned against the door of his black Range Rover. His eyes bored deep into Angie's as if he was desperate to gauge what she was thinking. He had the first parking space as you turn off the road and into The Maltings' car park. He wore a beige suit and an open-neck brown, silk shirt: a more casual business look than his normal city attire. His blond hair was combed back over his head to disguise the small bare patch poking through at the top. Regular games of squash, cricket and golf meant he was lean and fit for a man who had just turned fifty-two.

'See you didn't drive last night? Makes a change.' There was a heavy tone of sarcasm in Angie's voice.

'I'm a law-abiding citizen, Angie, as well you know!' There was a threat lurking in Malcolm's retort.

'Don't I know?' Their disdainful looks locked until she had passed Malcolm by.

'See you this evening,' he called to Angie.

'I'm sure you will,' replied Angie as she forced herself to walk more purposefully than her usual gait.

Angie felt uneasy. She had crossed a line last night. She had allowed a flippant, drunken remark to goad her into reminding Malcolm that she had something on him. It was well known that you crossed Malcolm Patterson at your peril. She'd been a barmaid for years. Why hadn't she kept her trap shut? Worse still, she had intimated that she had gleaned more from their weekend tryst than she actually had. All she really knew was that Malcolm Patterson was not who he said he was. When someone, obviously from his past, had bumped into them in Newcastle and spoken with them, Malcolm was emphatic that the down-and-out was mistaken.

Angie walked through the unkempt front garden and round the side of the grey, pebble-dash council house. If you stood at Joyce Lennie's front gate you could almost make out the Calsco brewery sign at the gable end of The Maltings.

'It's me,' bawled Angie, as she stepped through her mother's back door – never locked even at night. The key had been lost years ago and had never been replaced.

She caught her mother, Joyce, stuffing her purse into the

pocket of her apron. Her brother, David, pulled away from her and turned to look out the window. Angie knew the score.

'The bairn's had her breakfast and she's watchin' the end o' a video David got for her last night,' explained Joyce. 'I was giving him the money for it before he takes it back today.'

Angie said nothing. She popped through to the living room to kiss Bethany and to check that her daughter's school bag was ready. She'd been sleeping over at her granny's. Bethany was engrossed in the Disney classic and barely acknowledged her mother.

On her return, David flopped onto a chair and put his feet on the kitchen table whereupon his sister swiped them off. Her brother was woefully thin; all arms and legs. He'd had the same pale, gaunt expression since his late teens – yellowing eyes sunken in to hollow cheeks. He never looked clean. Brown and broken teeth didn't help and he never appeared to have shaved.

'Did you rent that video out in my name?' she barked at her brother. 'Don't you ever,' and she poked David's arm with every word she forced, 'ever... do... that... again!'

'Is that all the thanks I get for getting my niece a wee gift?'

'It was *MY* effin' money! And you... you lying, little shit-bag. You got it last weekend when you had your own effin' half-wits for the night. So don't you dare make out it was for Bethany.'

David thought about taking a swing at his sister but remembered how scary Angie could be. Also, his arm was aching and the mood that she was in, she could do some serious damage.

Angie instantly regretted calling her niece and nephews half-wits. They were decent kids in spite of their upbringing. She poured hot water from the kettle into the teapot then left the pot to stew on a warm ring on the cooker. Two cups were placed on the table. She scooped two teaspoons of sugar into her mother's bone china mug.

'Three for me, Angela,' David suggested hopefully.

'Of what?' asked Angie.

'Fuck off, Ang!'

Joyce intervened. 'Enough the two of you!' Then she added, 'David's going down to the Jobcentre today.'

'For what?' snipped Angie, 'To wait for his pal to come out?'

'It's better money than your wages,' David snapped back.

'I get more than you!' Not much more, she was loath to agree. But there were perks; extras that didn't have to be declared to the Tax Man or the Benefit Office.

'Can't ye try, Angela, for me?'

'Sorry, Ma, but he's a prick always has been, always will be.'

Angie looked at her mother, weary beyond her years, and felt guilty; not for her reaction towards her good-for-nothing brother but for the angst the Lennie sibling rivalry brought her mother. Joyce had been widowed for almost twelve years. For twelve years, she had supported one of her three sons and her only daughter, financially and emotionally, when they ought to have been supporting her. The older brothers had abandoned their mother long ago as if somehow their father's failings had been her fault. Neither brother communicated with each other or the rest of the family. They both had the means to help their mother should she really need it. The eldest had claimed that he didn't grudge his mother a penny but knew she would only hand it over to David. Angie couldn't disagree. She'd banned her Duneden brother from entering her house years ago. You'd trust a flock of magpies before that thieving bastard.

Angie's father had been an alcoholic and an aggressive drunk. That was why Angie's two older brothers had left home at the first opportunity. Unfortunately, David had inherited his father's addictive gene – except his wasn't alcohol. When he was between partners, which was frequently, he stayed with Joyce. She regularly moaned that if her husband had been alive today things would be different. They would have been a lot worse but no one was prepared to disillusion Joyce.

Angie planted a kiss on the top of her mother's grey hair, tinged nicotine yellow at the front. 'Thanks for having Bethany tonight.'

Joyce Lennie had Bethany most days and sometimes David's three if she was on speaking terms with their mothers or when the courts allowed David access to them. Even the two little ones from The Maltings insisted on calling her 'Granny Joyce'. Joyce was tall, like Angie, and her fine structured features hinted that she had been a beautiful woman in her day.

'Why don't you come to the party tonight? Stevie Wilson's on the karaoke and Jen's two are staying up,' coaxed Angie.

Joyce sighed and shook her head. She poured herself more of the strong brew then stopped.

'To hell wi' it, I think I will come, for a wee while.'

That made Angie feel much better. Or less guilty.

FIVE

'See you this evening,' Malcolm had called to Angie.

'I'm sure you will,' she had replied.

Malcolm had felt her sneer ripple through his bones. After slipping into his car, he watched his former mistress cross the road in his rear-view mirror.

'Bitch! Why couldn't she just meet some gullible sod and leave? Somebody out there must want more than a good shag!'

He thumped the steering wheel with the palms of both hands. It had been a long time since he and Angie had strayed into his past. He had annoyed her last night, unintentionally, and she had retaliated. A trivial comment. He couldn't even remember what he had said but Angie had kicked back. She made it clear to him, and him alone, that she had not forgotten.

When she barked, 'Another whisky, Sid? Or... have you had enough Mr. Rose?' The others laughed.

'Sid? Is that for Sidney the one-eyed-snake?' Willie joked.

Fortunately, everyone else was more interested in what Joe was sharing about his sex life than digesting what Angie was snarling at the other end of the bar.

'That'll be Sid short for Cyril,' hissed Angie as she stretched over the bar, her nose almost touching Malcolm's. 'Cyril Rose, a snake in the grass.'

'Fuck!' And what alarmed him more was that Angie seemed

to hint that she knew why he had once been known as Cyril Rose. His former pals had called him Sid (it's what folk from his neck of the woods would shorten Cyril to).

He'd sat at the end of the bar, sipping his Lagavulin, and watched Angie as she pretended to engage with the rest of the punters. Angie had the power to reduce him to a salivating wreck. He still hankered for her. She was as sensual as ever. A tall beauty with black hair. He poured over that particular conversation on that particular weekend trying to recall what else Angie might have overheard.

Malcolm owned a large, detached Victorian house, a short walk from Duneden and The Maltings. The grounds and gardens were equally impressive. He threw lavish parties and knew who to invite. His business and connections were well established. His wife Doreen and his daughter Roxanne wanted for nothing. Doreen may have had her own demons to confront and Roxanne was yet to map out some kind of career but apart from that, life was good. Malcolm had taken Angie's compliance for granted. It was time to sweeten her again. He couldn't risk anyone digging into his past. He had too much to lose. His throat constricted and he subconsciously massaged his neck with the tips of his fingers.

Malcolm swung out of Duneden and headed for the A92. As soon as he had crossed the Forth Road Bridge, he would stop off at the service station at South Queensferry for a strong coffee and a bacon roll. He had a meeting near Newbridge to discuss the construction of housing and new roads in and around Kirkliston. It was a lucrative contract and would earn his haulage company a lot of money.

Bowden's lorries were well known in and around Fife. The green and gold logos, BHC, on the sides of all their vehicles were instantly recognisable. In memory of his former boss, Malcolm had retained the company's original name – Bowden's. He had worked long and hard to get where he was. Trampled on many toes. He had no intentions of allowing a bitter young woman destroy what he had built.

Unfortunately, Malcolm may have been the big, bold boy in the haulage business but the brain in his dick often had more control than the one in his head.

*

Thirty-eight years ago

Malcolm was only fourteen when he had fled from Gateshead – exactly one month before the Japanese formally surrendered, ending World War Two. His father's sorrowful words rang in his ears and even now he couldn't bear to repeat them or to think about what had unfolded on that dreadful day. His dad had shoved enough money into the young lad's fist to last a few days at most. There was no opportunity to say goodbye to his mam or sisters. No emotional hug from his dad. Only a quick glance at the dirty streets and even grubbier coal miners' cottages.

Penniless, hungry and dishevelled, Davey Bowden discovered him hiding in one of his broken diggers tucked away at the back of his yard near the Kirkcaldy shore line. It was Davey's two useless Alsatians that had alerted him. In reality, two poodles would have been better guard dogs but the dogs were restless and, despite the pouring rain, Davey took a second look around.

'What the fuck?' wailed Davey, holding a foot long wrench above the young Geordie's head.

'I ain't touched nothin',' screamed a weary 'Malcolm' scrambling through sodden, cardboard packaging and sacking. 'I just needed somewhere to sleep. I'm sorry.'

Perhaps it was the dire weather that had dampened the old man's typical, unsympathetic nature but he took pity on the bedraggled boy below him. Davey Bowden never questioned, properly, the young runaway that day or any other about how he ended up in Kirkcaldy. He let the lad sleep in a shed on his premises in return for odd jobs – a decision he never regretted.

Malcolm Patterson, a name Davey found for him, earned every penny and more. He worked hard and learned the haulage business inside out, taking Bowden's from a tin-pot operation to a decent company before Davey handed the business on gratefully to the son he never had.

Malcolm had lost all trace of his North East accent and had deliberately cultivated a Fife brogue. He rarely talked about his youth, intimating it was arduous and one he would rather forget. Davey was the only person that knew of his origins and he had taken that information to the crematorium.

SIX

Earlier that same morning

Mark had heard the apartment door close behind his wife.

'She's keen,' he sighed and rolled on to his back.

His hand slid towards his enormous erection. He thought of Roxie – her fresh, young breasts smothering his face, her round, ample bottom rocking in his hands. He came quickly, suppressing the delight that groaned in his throat. As he reached for some tissues, the three faces of his wife and his two young daughters stared from the photo frame. Mark Cameron winced and closed his eyes guiltily. He should have risen then but he couldn't be arsed. He would have another hour in bed.

He thought back to the time when he and Jen had taken off for France. Her mother and father had actually turned up at his parent's house in Morningside begging for him to leave Jen behind. She was young; she'd get over it. They had been certain. Mark had forgotten how pathetic they had come across.

When the wanderers returned, penniless and pregnant, Mark was taken on by Gordon and Blair Brewery based in Leith in Edinburgh. There was no way he was working for his father's firm. His brother would never be his boss. Mark rose quickly to district manager and a rapid promotion to area manager thereafter. It was through one of his former salesmen, Bob Gregson, that he first heard about The Maltings. Bob had iterated that in the right hands it could do extremely well. The seed had been planted.

The move had not gone well. He had pissed Jen off big time and she'd sulked for the best part of the year (which was most unlike her). She wasn't pulling her weight and she was dragging him down with her.

Mark sighed wearily. How had it come to this? He had presented his parents with the Holy Grail – we told you so!

*

Morningside, Edinburgh

John Cameron released Barney from his leash and the energetic, golden retriever bounded to the open doors of the conservatory.

The Camerons resided in a large 1930s bungalow, a ten minute walk from Morningside Road in Edinburgh; a sought-after area and one that Marjory had long aspired to in her formative years.

John had retired at Christmas handing over the reins of his architect's business to his elder son, Mathew. Against his son's wishes, John popped into his old office most afternoons and dressed accordingly; a flecked tweed jacket, grey flannels, a checked shirt and his signature green, woollen tie. If he was feeling that a little extra was required for a particularly influential client, he tucked a green, silk handkerchief into the top pocket. The rest of the staff had a more casual, modern dress-code. Today, John was minus the handkerchief. Life was good and the Camerons were content; most of the time.

'Uh uh!' warned Marjory. The dog paused, waiting for the all clear. 'Is he clean?' She did not want her cream trousers or her cream cashmere top covered in dog hair.

'As a whistle,' laughed John.

Marjory was an elegant lady. Her clothes were close fitting, complementing her slim waist. She preferred pale pastels or palettes of coffee and cream. Her sister had introduced her to smart slacks whilst visiting her in Vancouver; unusual attire for woman of a certain age in the desirable area of Edinburgh south. Marjory felt a little rebellious in them.

Marjory clapped her hands three times in quick succession. Barney headed straight for his water bowl; it had been a long, thirsty walk over the Braid Hills.

John Cameron kissed his wife on the top of her immaculately coiffeured-head; maintained with a weekly shampoo and set. She was sitting on a bamboo chair easing her foot into her sensible loafers with an elongated shoehorn.

'Where are you off to at this time in the morning?' he enquired. The grandfather clock in their dining room rang out the first of nine chimes.

'The guides are having a coffee morning in the church hall on Saturday and I'm going to lock away our good Royal Albert.'

'Can't it wait?'

'No, it cannot!' Marjory stated indignantly, with her clipped Morningside inflection. 'That crockery is far too expensive for silly little girls to be trusted with. I don't know what possessed that Jean woman to authorise its use last time. It clearly states on the cupboard door GUILD AND BOARD MEETINGS ONLY.'

'Why the hurry?' John had been looking forward to having breakfast with his wife on the patio. The past few weeks had felt like one glorious, continuous holiday.

'The guides are setting up tonight and, as you are fully aware, we will need to set off early to be at that interminable garden party.' The thought of spending time with the uncouth, coarse lot that frequented The Maltings was something that Marjory would normally have preferred to avoid if she were honest. But equally, she would not have given her ungrateful daughter-in-law the opportunity to gloat at their lack of parental support, if they had declined the invitation.

John was only too *fully aware*. Marjory loathed Jen. She blamed her for all Mark's short-comings. What Marjory was reluctant to admit, was that Mark left the family business to spite his father AND he married Jen to spite his mother.

SEVEN

Further down the coast, in Jennifer's home town of Port Seton, her brother, Andrew, was checking his van to make sure he had everything he needed. He was rewiring a second floor flat not far from Musselburgh harbour and not too far from the semi-detached cottage that Andrew and Jennifer owned. The old, neglected cottage had been bequeathed to them by their father's mother, four years previously. Their eldest sibling Morag had been given money and jewellery (something that Jennifer would have preferred if she had been given the choice). Jennifer had warned her family that the bequest should remain a Thomson secret and it was never to be discussed with Mark. Andrew seemed surprised as both his sisters seemed to have solid relationships. Jennifer's dad, Jimmy, intuitively and quietly agreed with his daughter's decision.

There was something about Mark that Jimmy Thomson didn't trust – there were many things about Mark that triggered alarm bells – and Jennifer obviously needed that insurance. Jimmy kept his own countenance. None of his family needed to know about his misgivings.

At twenty-five, Andrew Thomson was the baby of the family and he still stayed at home with Jennifer's Mum and Dad. Although slightly taller, he had the same petite frame as Jennifer. Poor Morag had slavishly tried every diet available in an effort to achieve what nature had gifted to her siblings. Morag, a nursing sister, lived in Glasgow with her GP husband and her baby boy.

Jennifer didn't see as much of her as she would have liked but they kept in touch by phone each week. It amused Jennifer that in spite of her sister and brother-in-law's medical backgrounds, they sought Jennifer's opinion on everything from the colour of poo to what new foods they should try.

Andrew had a boyish, handsome face; a face that made you assume that you knew him from somewhere or that you'd seen him on the telly. Perhaps, it was the way his sandy, blond hair flopped around his face or the cheeky grin he had perfected for the ladies. Whatever it was, people – male and female – found him attractive and endearing.

'Andrew!' yelled Grace Thomson. 'Jennifer's on the phone!'

'I'll be there in a minute!' He hated being interrupted. Andrew found it difficult to focus on mental tasks, like ensuring all his tools were in his van. He couldn't retain too much information at once (lists or simple immediate recall) yet for some strange reason he found complicated electrical work a doddle.

'Gie him a minute. He's been at that bloody van for ages,' moaned Grace. 'If he took as much care wi' his room as he did with that bloody thing then everybody would be happy.'

Grace moaned when she wasn't gossiping.

'I'm sorry mum but this is a quick phone call for Andrew.' explained Jennifer. 'I'll phone you back later when I have more time to talk.'

'Well, we're a long time deid!' Her mother always used that tack when she was miffed.

'How's ma dad?' Jennifer asked hoping the explanation would be brief.

Jimmy Thomson was still recovering from an operation on his varicose veins and that meant her parents wouldn't be able to make it to the barbecue. Jennifer was gutted. She had hoped that Grace would distract Mark's mother and keep her from following them around.

'Och, he's fine. Doctor said he's responding well and should be on his feet in no time. I'm going to ask the doctor to...' The phone was yanked from her hand.

'Jenz? How's it hanging?'

Jennifer loathed that phrase – and he knew it. She paused (always did) then he laughed. Predictably.

'Only kidding. Are we still on for tonight?

The arrangements were agreed. He and Rebecca, the *new* girlfriend, would look after the girls while Mark and Jennifer mingled with the customers. Then, once the girls had had a chance to be part of the evening, they would go upstairs to bed. Around eight would be late enough; it was a school night after all. Neither Mark nor Jennifer were comfortable with their youngsters hanging around the bar. Punters came out to get some peace away from their own children. Plus, there were some very unsavoury characters that frequented The Maltings. Low lives as Mark preferred to call them (out of earshot – naturally) or, when he was in a mean mood, 'retards!' much to Jennifer's disgust.

'Will foxy Roxie be there? Andrew enquired.

Roxanne Patterson worked at The Maltings. On his previous visit, Andrew flirted outrageously with Roxanne. Mark told him to back off. He didn't know why. It wasn't as if Roxanne was complaining.

After her phone call with her brother, Jennifer took the stairs two at a time up to their living quarters. When she opened the flat door, she could hear Mark. She hauled off her trainers.

'Where the fuck is it?' he shouted.

'Daddy said a bad word… again,' boomed little Katie's deep voice.

Katie, with her strawberry blond hair, lay, stretched out on the floor of the family area. Wearing only her pink pants and colouring in a bright, waxy sun, her white ankle socks tapped alternately off her chubby bottom.

The kitchen units shook. Yank, slam! Yank, slam!

'Jen-ni-fer!'

Mark only used his wife's full name if he was truly ticked off or when he was as horny as hell and would rasp it in her ear. It was most definitely not the latter so he must have been pissed off. Again.

'What?' asked Jennifer.

'Where's that fucking cash and carry list?' He demanded.

'Is that really necessary?'

'What?' He looked genuinely perplexed.

'Cursing in front of the girls?'

Jennifer hated Mark swearing in front of her two wee ones. She hated anyone swearing in front of them. At thirty-one years of age, she had never heard her dad swear. Her mum did frequently. Not the stuff you would bawl and shout at the ref at a football match, just the bloody hell and shit kind of thing. But her dad? Never. Actually, he had. Once.

'Like you don't,' he snapped.

Neither of them used to curse but lately it had been creeping into their vocabulary with increasing regularity. Jennifer padded around, bare-footed, in their open-plan kitchen to look for it herself. Anything for an easy life.

The living and kitchen area was directly above the lounge bar. It was a large, bright room. Light poured through the long, sash windows that overlooked the car park at the side of the building and to the large beer garden at the back. Unlike downstairs, their rooms were modern and tastefully decorated – if a little minimalistic.

'It was there on the breakfast bar last night,' explained Jennifer.

He leaned in closer; she could smell his coffee. 'Well, it's not there now!'

For a split second, Jennifer Cameron considered smacking, extremely hard, his sarcastic coffee-breath mouth.

For a split second, Mark could have gladly strangled her.

Jennifer scanned the worktops then the chairs then the wooden flooring. Nothing. She asked their eight-year-old, Emma, who had dragged a pine storage box in front of the mirror above the fireplace so that she could see more easily, if she had seen a large sheet of white paper with Daddy's writing on it? A hairbrush struggled with the maze of knots in her long, brown hair; knots that had engineered a thousand tears and arguments.

'Katie's drawing on something,' she puffed.

'Jesus Christ!' Mark stormed past Emma, leaned over Katie, and snatched the folded paper from beneath a fat, yellow crayon.

'Daddy! That's Fergal's card.'

Mark shook out the drawing. On the back, was a detailed list of everything they had decided they would need for the pub's first birthday bash.

'That was my bestest sun.' Katie's little body began to shudder and the beginnings of heavy sobbing rattled in her little chest.

'You can be such an arse-hole at times!' rasped Jennifer.

Determined to keep the peace, Jennifer steered her youngster through to a small study off the living area where she kept a folder of cream and gold, Macintosh stationery; smart paper stored for extremely important letters. Emma, sniffing out a potential treat, slipped in behind them. The cellophane was still intact and the dust was swiped off.

'Can I have some?' pleaded Emma.

'There's enough for both of you,' said Jennifer

Mark followed them into the large cupboard and offered a weak apology for losing his temper. Everything the girls did, or Jennifer did, annoyed him of late: little things, big things, anything. The four stood, huddled in the tiny room, as if they were waiting for a bus or sheltering from the rain. He squinted at his wife and seemed to be waiting for confirmation that all was forgiven. He was on a hiding to nothing and the girls were too busy planning their next artistic assignment.

He made to skulk off then stopped. 'Why's she making a card for Fergal?' he asked and then looking like a smarmy, school boy gloated, 'Is he ill? Or dying?'

'Not funny,' Jennifer hissed. 'It's his birthday. Next Saturday.'

'I wish you'd stop encouraging the girls to see that bent-shot and his batty old bitch. Why didn't you dump them when you had the chance?' He appeared genuinely aggrieved. 'You know, Jen, you're attracted to misfits.'

'Present company excepted?' she couldn't help sniping back.

The bent-shot, as Mark referred to him, was Fergal, a fifty-nine-year-old accountant who lived in Edinburgh. Hannah, the batty old bitch, was his very elderly but very sharp next-door neighbour. Jennifer had befriended them both when she was pregnant with Emma. Actually, she met Fergal just after she had had Emma. Jennifer used to clean for Hannah and through Hannah she began ironing for Fergal. Both of them had kept

Jennifer sane and solvent. It had been a wrench to leave Hannah behind when they moved to Fife.

'What's a bent-shot?' enquired Emma, who was still teasing out her knotted tresses.

Jennifer swung Emma around, probably too forcefully, by her shoulders. Standing on the box, in her blue gingham, school dress, she was taller than her mother.

'Don't you ever use those words in front of Uncle Fergal. You'll make him cry,' she barked.

Mark began to laugh.

'I won't. Promise.' Her lips began to tremble and her eyes filled with tears.

Emma adored Fergal. The feeling was mutual. Emma only had to tilt her beautiful face and smile and Fergal would have done anything for her. Poor Emma, she looked confused. Jennifer felt rotten as it wasn't her fault. She could have murdered Mark. He'd never even tried to get along with Fergal or Hannah. Although they were too polite to say it, Jennifer was sure they knew how Mark felt about them.

With long, soothing strokes Jennifer brushed Emma's hair. It was far too curly to be left long but when Jennifer was younger, she would have given anything for long hair and she couldn't deny Emma her wish to grow it.

The daughter smiled at her mother in the mirror. That felt better. Everyone thought that Emma looked like Mark. She had the same brown hair, dark eyes and olive complexion. And charming smile. Yet as Jennifer pulled her daughter's hair back into a pony-tail, it was as if she'd come face to face with herself as an eight-year-old.

Her stomach lurched in the way it does when you drive too quickly over a short, humped bridge. She didn't know if it was hunger or nostalgia. It couldn't be PMT and she wasn't pregnant. God! That was all she needed. It would warrant a trip to the Forth Road Bridge. Mark would probably jump first. Ooooh! It happened again. It was definitely hunger. Jennifer hadn't eaten much since yesterday and breakfast would have to wait. But she made a mental note to check the date of her last period; just in case.

'Mummy! Are you listening to me?'

'Sorry, sweetie, what did you say?'

Emma wanted to know if Bethany, Angie's wee girl, was going to the barbecue.

'Only if her granny can pick her up later,' her mother explained.

Angie had been hoping that her own mother would go along to the party for a while to keep an eye on Bethany. She was on a promise with the D.J. and wanted the house free for afterwards. Jennifer didn't know how she did it or had the energy. If only.

Mark helped Katie with the buckles on her sandals and slipped a blue gingham dress over her head so that she could be the same as her big sister. Jennifer pushed the pine chest to the side of the fireplace while Emma ran to fetch her lunch box. Mark whistled; earlier niggles forgotten. He was going to drop the girls off at nursery and school before heading to the Cash and Carry in Cupar to pick up last-minute provisions for the pub's birthday bash.

One full year had passed since they had opened the doors of The Maltings and had become embroiled in the life of Duneden; too many lives for Jennifer's liking.

'You've double-checked the list? I haven't left anything out?' he asked.

'I've checked everything,' his wife assured him, 'I'll pick up the flowers in the afternoon and Angie and Maureen are going to help me with the buffet. Go. Shoo. I'll see you later.' She pushed him jokingly with her finger.

'A year already! Where's the bloody time gone?' He sighed.

He pulled Jennifer towards him and rested his forehead on hers. She inhaled him. It smelt good. They paused for a moment then he kissed her nose. Her green hazel eyes smiled at his – very similar in colour but Mark's had a tinge of golden brown. His strong hands cupped her sides gently as his thumbs brushed over her nipples in small, circular movements. The slightly flushed, red-head checked to see that the girls weren't looking. Mark maintained his fingers could touch when wrapped around his wife's waist. She wasn't that thin!

'Mmmmm.' That was the Mark Jennifer knew and loved.

'We'll be alright, won't we?' He looked sad.

Jennifer vowed there and then, to make more time for her and Mark; on their own. No girls. No interruptions. Her mother was always offering to come through to Fife. Jennifer would phone later and organise something. They deserved it. Hell, they needed it. When they lived in Edinburgh, night outs were a must. Somehow, they'd allowed treats and everything else to slip. Jennifer was reluctant to scupper the moment, but chivvied them out the door.

'Scoot! The three of you.'

She watched from the window as her handsome husband, and former rugby player, swung the two girls, dangling on either arm, high into the air. They squealed hysterically. Jennifer smiled. Fat chance of anyone in Duneden getting a long lie with that racket echoing along the street.

EIGHT

When Angie arrived at The Maltings, Jennifer was already downstairs. 'Morning,' she sang out as she breezed in. Angie always made an entrance whether intentional or not.

The weather forecast had predicted that it would be a Mediterranean summer and it wasn't wrong; the temperature was twenty-three degrees and counting. Angie walked behind the bar, scooped a mound of ice from the ice bucket, threw it into a glass, and poured herself a pint of water. The serving area of the bar could be accessed from the hallway without having to enter the actual lounge. It was an L-shaped bar, skilfully hand-crafted from one, large piece of wood, reclaimed from the bridge of an old ship. Tam Blakeley and his dad were proud to discuss their handiwork every time they frequented the place.

'Want one? Good for the complexion!' Angie was unable to speak quietly; everything she uttered was a few decibels higher than necessary.

Jennifer nodded. With the exception of a few freckles – which had to be expected with her colouring – Jennifer had quite a clear skin, usually. Thank God the girls didn't have her hair. She hated it; always had. It wasn't nearly as orangey as it used to be when she was young! It had darkened greatly during her teens. But once a Ginger Nut, always a Ginger Nut. It blighted her childhood. Perhaps not all of it but it spoiled the important bits.

Jennifer's mother insisted that most girls would have given their right arm to have rich, auburn hair like hers.

'Only if they were blind!' hissed Jennifer.

Jennifer's primary years were spent at a small school, with only two teaching staff, not too far from Port Seton. One boy in her class had his nose burst open at school, by Jennifer, for calling her 'carrot heid' once too often. Mrs Goodall, her teacher, had declared that Miss Thomson was the most despicable girl she had known. 'Me?' Jennifer smirked at the recollection. Her punishment was being banned from attending school camp at Aberfoyle for a team building weekend.

Grace Thomson did not take that news sitting down. No teacher was going to stop one of her bairns from going to school camp. Grace dropped in to see Brenda Goodall, one afternoon after school, to inform Brenda that her husband, Charlie, dressed in women's clothes when he visited the pubs in Rose Street. Some second cousin of Grace knew Charlie well and Grace would be more than happy to share the information with the rest of the parents. Later that month, the unpopular, upper-primary teacher left the school's employ after having had a nervous breakdown. Consequently, Jennifer had a great time at camp that summer term.

Angie had hair to-die-for; thick, cropped, sleek, shiny and black. She wasn't particularly 'pretty' but there was something about Angie that was *very* attractive. Striking in fact. It was her cheek bones. They were so well defined and they accentuated her dark, almond shaped eyes. Women would say they were her best asset but most men would disagree. She had the most enormous tits! Well, they looked enormous on Angie's tall, slim frame. 'If you've got em, flaunt em,' she'd say. And she did. Mark said that it brought in the punters. It certainly didn't put them off. Angie never seemed to be embarrassed by their crude comments. In fact, she had a knack of biting back with equally vulgar retorts.

Jennifer cupped her small breasts in the palms of her hands and pushed them upwards.

"That'll no' fucking work!" shouted Angie, who'd been watching Jen as she prepared their drinks. 'Rubbing them disnae make them bigger!'

Jennifer was mortified; not just at being caught but at the uncouth language that tripped off Angie's tongue on a daily basis. Correction: hourly basis. More than that, it was constant. Jennifer had stopped pointing it out to Angie as she was totally oblivious to it.

'It's worked for you,' cajoled Jen.

Angie looked down on her double F cleavage bulging out of her vest. 'Nah, I had big tits long before any greedy bastard got their hands on them.'

Jennifer found it funny and laughed. She rarely joined in the banter at work. She only had herself to blame. She had deliberately distanced herself from her employees because she hated being there. At the beginning, the staff invited her and Mark to all sorts of things but Jennifer always found an excuse, plus, there was no way she was leaving the girls with some of the oddballs that volunteered to babysit.

The moment wasn't lost on Angie either. It was good to see her boss laughing. Angie had given up explaining to Maureen and to the rest of them that Jen was unhappy. Maureen said that it suited Angie to fight Jen's corner. An element of that was true. Jen often looked after Bethany to give Angie the opportunity to pick up more shifts. It was a mutual arrangement that suited them.

A loud rattling of the door interrupted the congeniality.

'It's open!' Angie yelled.

A female stumbled into the room.

'Shite! I do that every time.' Maureen had not mastered the knack of opening the lounge bar door. Maureen was Angie's older cousin on her mother's side.

Everybody in Duneden was related to someone else in Duneden. The Camerons learned very quickly not to criticise anyone publicly. The most unlikely folk seemed to be related. Mark said it was worse than Port Seton – which said a lot, as he used to claim (unfairly) that it was the in-breeding capital of Scotland. He referred to Duneden as *'Stepford* Geeks'; home to all the ugly people. One day, somebody was going to hear him.

'For fuck's sake, Maureen! How many times have you came through that door and you still cannae open it properly?' scolded Angie.

Maureen was annoyed. She struggled with the bar door every other day. 'It's the bloody handle! It needs UB40.'

'It's WD40, ya twat. UB fuckin' 40's a group!' squealed Angie. Angie, Maureen and Willie had gone to a small UB40 concert the previous summer. 'WD40!' she began to laugh. 'Are we even related?'

Angie dissolved. Jennifer buoyed by her previous fit of the giggles, joined in. Maureen stood: looking vacant. Jennifer's reaction had completely thrown her.

'What?' Maureen swung her head from Angie then back to Jen. 'Wha...at?'

Her incredulity made it worse for Angie and Jennifer. Their laughter quickly descended into hysterics. It was infectious and set Maureen off too. Every time, they seemed to gain control, one of them would start again. It would begin with a muffled snigger then explode into a pack of squealing hyenas. It was intoxicating. Maureen leaned on the bar and crossed her legs in case she peed herself. Jennifer decided to leave the room. Putting distance between them was the only way they would all calm down. The women's belly laughing could be heard from the Ladies.

Angie was in the kitchen busy preparing garnishes when Jennifer entered. A self-taught cook, Angie's dishes were typical pub food – steak pie, lasagne (she'd never heard of it until Jen showed her how to make it), fish and chips, scampi, Cajun chicken and a combination of salads. At Mark's insistence, the menu had been changed several times but the regulars kept asking for the same old staples. To keep everyone happy, Angie suggested having a Daily Specials Board for the more adventurous clientele. It worked. And it helped Angie to research different cuisines.

Mark had put up notices earlier in the week informing the punters that last orders for Thursday lunches would be 1.30pm, instead of the normal 2.00pm cut off. The family barbecue would kick off at 6.00pm. Stevie Wilson would entertain outdoors, weather permitting, until 8.00pm and then set up in the lounge bar to finish off the evening indoors. All children would be expected to vacate the beer garden by 8.30pm at the latest.

'What's up with Mark this mornin'?' Angie asked, as she carefully arranged her side salads on to a tray. 'He's a torn face git!'

'The Cash and Carry had no Lagavulin so he's off to Asda to buy some there. It's an important day for him,' Jennifer felt compelled to explain.

'And for you too,' Angie reminded her. 'God forbid that Malcolm Patterson would have to go without his favourite tipple the night.'

Jennifer flashed Angie a warning look as Roxanne trooped in. Malcolm was her dad. Angie shrugged as if to say, 'SO?'

'The Guinness isn't pouring,' announced Roxanne, in an overtly girly voice.

'I've probably not hooked it up properly,' explained Jennifer. 'I was in a bit of a rush this morning. I'm sure you can manage.'

Roxanne displayed her freshly, manicured nails, 'Sorry, no can do,' and she hung her head to one side like a naughty Labrador pup; her highlighted blonde locks lapped down her back.

'Who has time for bloody manicures?' sighed Jennifer.

Sometimes she could've shaken that girl. She dressed as if she was working at some kind of dolls boutique in Barbie Land instead of a country village pub. She teetered on ridiculously high, red, wedged sandals and looked even more ridiculous because of the red laces that wound around her fat ankles. A red, polka dot, pelmet skirt struggled to cover her rounded bottom and a white, sweet-heart neck top showed off her plump boobs (aided by a push-up bra that was far too small for her). Most girls around Roxanne's age were wearing high-waisted jeans and cheesecloth shirts. Roxanne seemed out of step with other youngsters barely out of their teens. Was Jennifer Cameron jealous? She hoped not. Perhaps if she was as dippy as Roxanne, life would be less stressful.

As Jennifer returned from the cellar, she could hear the chat.

'Angie, you must be roasting in those boots!' squeaked Roxanne.

'I'm not.' Angie growled.

'Don't you have sandals you could wear?'

'Eeehh, now that might be awkward given that I could drop hot food on bare feet.' Angie held up her booted foot and wiggled it aggressively in front of Roxanne's face.

'Could I have a note of today's soup and specials please, Angie?' Roxanne's swift avoidance of confrontation impressed Jennifer. 'Oooh, Jen. Would you like me to do your make up for tonight?'

Although the offer surprised Jennifer, she declined – politely. As Roxanne squeezed past her, she reminded Jennifer, a little, of *Miss Piggy* on the *Muppet Show*. Okay, a prettier version, but the voice was similar; if you could imagine *Miss Piggy* with a broad Fife accent.

'She'd have you looking like a bloody clown,' warned Angie.

Jennifer defended her. 'She was only trying to help.'

'She's a sleekit wee cow that one. Watch her!'

Angie looked hard at Jen trying to detect if she had the teeniest inclination of what Mark and Roxanne had been getting up to. Angie doubted that it was common knowledge. Malcolm obviously didn't know. God help Mark if he ever found out.

Jennifer couldn't blame Angie for being envious of Roxanne. As an only child, Roxanne wanted for nothing. Recently, she'd drifted from one college course to another eventually settling for Beauty Therapy. Once qualified (or not), daddy Malcolm would set her up with her own little salon.

Lunches turned out to be busier than expected. Mark covered the bar while Roxanne served the meals. Maureen, Roxanne and Jennifer prepared the sandwiches for the buffet in between helping Angie. One loaf made ten rounds of sandwiches. They buttered eight loaves and filled them with a variety of fillings.

'Did you tell Jen what Malcolm Patterson said last night?' Maureen nudged Angie and nodded tellingly at Jen.

Normally, Maureen would never have discussed pub gossip in front of Jen but the earlier shared antics had emboldened her and she let her guard drop. She deliberately ignored Angie's glaring eyes. Angie flicked her fingers over her throat in a cutting motion, mouthed 'no' yet Maureen still ignored her.

'Uh ha?' Jennifer was intrigued.

'That he wanted to shag you,' blurted Maureen.

Jennifer glanced quickly over her shoulder in case either Roxanne or Mark were hovering. Maureen had a foghorn on her like Angie.

'Put it into fucking context, Maureen!' snarled Angie whilst concentrating on creaming a cheese sauce for the chicken breast in front of her. 'She was one of many!'

Angie explained that the previous night in the bar, a group of them had been discussing who they thought was shaggable; as you do on a quiet Wednesday night before closing time. The gossiping was put on hold as Roxanne swanned into the kitchen for Haddock Goujons and a Hebridean Chicken. When she'd gone, it resumed.

'Anyway, Malcolm said he wouldn't mind getting into your knickers,' blurted Maureen. Jennifer scrunched her nose. Malcolm was not her type. 'I'm not into older men.'

Angie jumped in, 'He's not that old. There's plenty of mileage left in Malcolm... I'm assuming obviously.' The torch that Angie carried for Malcolm had never fully extinguished.

'And guess who got jealous?' Maureen was now in full flow and enjoying the moment.

Jennifer had no idea.

'Joe Blakeley!' Maureen squealed as if the answer was apparent.

Jennifer felt her face burn. Joe was a good-looking bloke. A bit tame, maybe a little too insular for her, but still, a fit guy.

'Of course,' joked Angie, 'I was everyone's first choice.'

'If they've been there already, how does that count?' Maureen chuckled.

Angie fired salted chips at the giggler sniggering in the corner. Jennifer was intrigued. She resisted pushing Maureen for more information. All the same, she was flattered.

'That's eighty rounds of sandwiches. And roughly a hundred and fifty sausage rolls. If there's not enough, we can rustle up more in the evening.' Jennifer didn't expect a reply. She just wanted to voice her thoughts out loud. 'I'll put them in the function room. It's cooler there.' There wasn't enough room in the fridge. Only Jennifer called it the function room. Everyone else called it the back room.

Angie, Maureen and Roxanne bustled about putting everything away. They wanted home. It had been a busy shift and they were running late.

Neither Angie nor Maureen were prepared to chip in later to help in the kitchen. Once the drinking started nobody would care. Crisps and nuts would eke things out if it got too busy. Anyway, Maureen's oldest son, Martin, was in charge of the barbecue. There would be plenty of food.

Jennifer suppressed the niggling doubts that no-one would turn up. How humiliating would that be? Everyone had gone, except Mark. Like her, he was checking everything twice and was ensuring the shelves were fully stocked.

'I'm going to pick Katie up from Shirley's then I'll pop into the florists for the baskets of flowers for Angie and Maureen, before they close,' Jennifer called to Mark.

'What about Emma?' he asked.

'She's at Angie's mother's house. I'll pick her up later.'

'And your brother?'

'He won't be here until at least seven,' answered Jennifer.

'How long will you be?'

'About an hour or so. I'll be back by half past four, I hope.

Don't worry, I've tidied up and everything's ready. Gotta go. Love you.' And she hurried out the door.

Jennifer turned left onto Eden Road. She cautiously approached the narrow bridge as only one car could cross at a time. It was easier to spot traffic if you were heading into Duneden. The River Eden flowed beneath them separating their beer garden and Malcolm Patterson's orchard. She drove past his ornamental gates and the long driveway that led to Orchard House. About a quarter of a mile further on, she slowed down and peeped the horn. Three large, barking, friendly dogs dodged her nifty reversing and continued to bark until Brian Munro whistled them in. The busy farmer gave Jen a thumbs-up and called on the girls.

'See yous later, I hope. Shirley and the kids will definitely be there. I'll try and mak it later.'

At first, Jennifer was surprised that the Munros would even bother turning up until it dawned on her that Duneden folk (whatever their background) needed little excuse for a booze-up. Life had been quiet before The Maltings reopened and most of the village was looking forward to something different.

Katie skipped out to greet her mother. She was hot and thirsty and wanted a cold drink. Jennifer bribed her with an ice-lolly from the Post Office. She'd some letters to post so she pulled up outside The Maltings' front door and told Katie to wait in the car while she popped into the shop. As she waited in the queue to pay for the stamps, she realised that she'd left her purse in the pub kitchen. 'It never fails. When you are in a hurry everything conspires against you.'

Mrs Cowan allowed Jennifer to take an iced Zoom for Katie who was hanging half way out the window of the car looking like a bedraggled waif. Jennifer promised to hand in the money later. One cold offering was greatly received. The front door of The Maltings was pad-locked and Jennifer assumed that Mark had gone upstairs. She slipped in the back doors and found the purse on the worktop next to the fridge. As she was about to leave, she heard something: a low moaning sound from the lounge bar.

That's when she found them. Mark with the red-wedged slag sprawled over the pool table. Somehow, Jennifer made it to the car.

'Mummy! I'm not fastened proply!' Katie's little voice echoed at the end of the tunnel that used to be normality.

The car raced away. Jennifer's thoughts were racing faster.

NINE

Marjory Cameron asked her husband, John, to fasten her pearls for her. She tilted her head forward. Her grey hair rested on the back of his hand as he skilfully linked the delicate clasps. She turned to face him and he smiled. Marjory had a plain face; very average. One that would be hard to recollect if you had only met her once or twice. What she lacked in the looks department, however, she made up for in her overall appearance. She was immaculately well groomed.

'You look lovely, darling.' He meant it.

Marjory had decided to wear the cream outfit she had been wearing earlier in the day, except for the shoes. She had changed into beige sandals. She handed John her ivory, cabled cardigan to pop on the back seat of their car. Before he left, she fixed his gold cravat, speckled with splashes of navy, and tucked it into his white shirt. 'Very smart,' she said approvingly.

They were a smart couple. They didn't do casual terribly well.

'Mummy and Daddy are going out for a while. There's a little food in your bowl and plenty of water. Give Mummy a kiss before we go.'

On cue, Barney padded up to Marjory and lifted his eyes towards hers, whereupon, she smothered him in kisses and cooed as if he were a little baby. The happy retriever toddled back to his basket. The radio played softly in the background so that he wouldn't feel lonely whilst they were gone.

John opened the car door for his wife. He laid his navy jacket on top of her cardigan. He had the same grey slacks on that he had worn to the office but at Marjory's insistence he changed into a lighter weight shirt.

'Ready?' he asked.

'As I'll ever be,' she replied nervously.

John patted her knee. 'You'll be fine. We'll be fine.'

They drove down Morningside Road then headed towards Haymarket. Rush hour was gearing up but with luck they would reach Duneden within sixty minutes. John had informed Mark that it was their intention to be there for five-thirty. He hated being late.

*

Doreen Patterson prepared Malcolm a long gin and tonic and an extra-large one for herself; it was her third.

'It's my first one of the day!' She answered the question before it was asked.

Malcolm suspected otherwise but said nothing.

Glass in hand, Doreen stretched out on one of the three Chesterfield leather sofas in the music room. It was an exceptionally large drawing room with double French doors that opened on to their lawn and the orchards beyond. Malcolm sat on the one adjacent to his wife. He worried about her fragility. A fuchsia, velour lounge-suit swamped her skeletal frame. Her long black hair had been pulled tightly into a pony-tail, emphasising her painfully thin face. Roxanne had painted her mother's finger nails and toe nails that morning before she set off for The Maltings. They were blood red.

Malcolm pondered how someone who spent the best part of the day in the kitchen could actively avoid eating. At meal times, she rarely finished anything on her plate.

'I pick as I'm preparing! I can't help myself,' was her well-rehearsed response.

Doreen was an adventurous cook and a good one. Her attention to detail was commendable – from the quality of the food, to the presentation of her dishes and her table. The overall effect was lost on Roxanne (although she was a girl that liked her food) but not on Malcolm. Mealtimes at Orchard House, were a dining experience and one which Malcolm loved to share with his family and, when possible, in the company of good friends. Recently, however, he had felt a little cheated. Roxanne gulped her food, stuffing it in with the grace of an oaf, and was just as quick to leave the table without having the courtesy to thank her mother for her efforts. Doreen ate less than a sparrow, leaving Malcolm to finish his food while she watched albeit with a long drink in her hand; to keep him company, of course. Where was the fun in that?

Malcolm knew Doreen was bored. There was not enough for her to do in a day since he cajoled her into giving up working at Bowden's. It was tiring juggling a wife and a mistress in such close proximity and one of them had to go. He kept the one that opened her legs at his behest. Doreen would never have contemplated a quickie in the office: not since Roxanne was a toddler. His secretary, however, often took Malcolm's hand and rubbed it over her bum. 'No knickers,' she'd whisper in his ear. That was a huge turn on for him.

Like Malcolm, Doreen enjoyed a game of golf and had a decent handicap but she felt as if she didn't fit in at the golf club anymore. They only tolerated her because of Malcolm's generous sponsorships.

Their patience at the golf club had decreased as Doreen's drinking had increased. The stewards were used to helping her into a taxi after lunch and popping her car keys into her handbag. Her gold E-type Jag was a common reminder in the otherwise empty car park overnight.

Doreen pottered about in the garden but the size of it was daunting and gardening really wasn't her thing. Anyway, they had a gardener. He was one of Malcolm's drivers, long since retired. He came most days. His conversation was tedious and monotonous but there were times when it was better than nothing.

'Shall I rustle us up a wee something before we go out tonight?' Doreen asked.

'For Christ's sake, mother. D'you not listen to nothin'?' Roxanne had overheard her. 'I've just spent the whole afternoon making hundreds of sandwiches. There'll be plenty to eat. And Martin Ross is on the barbecue. WE DON'T NEED ANY MORE FOOD!'

In the awkward silence, Doreen's stony face willed the tears, close to brimming, to remain firmly behind her eyes.

Roxanne felt rotten for snapping. She knew her mother wouldn't be looking forward to the party.

'Come on. Let me put your hair up into a chignon. You can wear that nice kaftan that dad bought you in Morocco. It's perfect for this weather.'

Roxanne pouted, waited, and then smiled. She put her hand out and pulled Doreen to her feet. She had the knack of winning her mother over quickly. Doreen behaved like a coy lover being led upstairs for a naughty encounter.

Malcolm could hear the two most important people in his life laughing and carrying on; a sound that would normally have cheered him hugely, but he was preoccupied: what to do with Angie Lennie?

*

Emma and Katie trailed behind Jennifer who sprinted up the stairs towards the flat despite being laden with flower baskets and school bags. Adrenalin surged through her veins. She held the door open with her bottom as the girls tumbled in. The building shook as the door slammed behind them causing both girls to shriek. The door closer was lethal.

'That'll be you back then!' joked Mark, grinning. He stood in the hallway with a large, white towel wrapped around his lower torso. His hair and body were still wet.

Washed off the shagging smell? Jennifer wanted to shout.

'Come on, girls, it's party time,' he cried, pretending to tickle the girls as they ran giggling into Emma's room.

You've had your party. You fucking fucker! fumed Jennifer. She stood in the doorway and forced a smile.

'Get everything?' Mark asked. He was ever so cheerful.

She swallowed her words. *Not as much as you did.* God, she was good at holding back.

'You, okay?' He looked worried.

'Yeah, I'm good,' Jen lied.

'Sure?'

Jennifer wanted to scream. She wanted to scream and shout and swear and kick and stab the two-timing bastard. She leaned her head on the door frame. 'Just tired. I'll be fine.'

'Right!' Mark clapped his hands. 'Everyone get their glad rags on. The Camerons are going to partaaayy!'

Mark whipped his towel off once he had passed Jennifer. She watched with disgust as his bare backside disappeared into their bedroom.

Jennifer decided to dress the girls first. She couldn't bear to be alone with Mark. She didn't want to see him naked nor did she want to feel exposed. He would never get that satisfaction again. Also, the temptation to confront him was too strong and the temptation to bash his head in was even greater.

The girls sat quietly on the floor in front of the telly watching *The Wizard of Oz* for the hundredth time. They knew the script and songs off by heart. Mark had gone downstairs to help Stevie Wilson set up his kit in the beer garden.

Jennifer knew she was procrastinating. The girls' school clothes were laid out neatly for the next day. School bags were replenished with a snack and a drink. She tidied up, put clean towels on the futon for Andrew and Rebecca, moved the baskets of flowers from the table to the floor and back again. Anything but get ready. Eventually, she plaited her hair. A French pleat that she could manage without a mirror. Her fingers laced her hair effortlessly as she wandered around the flat daydreaming of what their life would look like without Mark. She felt empty and incredibly lonely. The loud knock at the door jolted her back to the present. The girls ran to the door.

'Leave it!' warned Jennifer. It was too strong for them. It was going to take a finger off one of these days.

Marjory and John stood on the doormat like a pair of Jehovah Witnesses with an expectant – sure to have the door closed on them – smile. Their expressions changed when two delighted grandchildren sprang forward.

'Grandma! Grandpa!' sang Emma.

'Hooray!' cheered Katie.

Both girls embraced their grandparents. Marjory patted Emma on the back. John lifted Katie up for a generous hug. 'Careful, John. Your back!' said Marjory in a softly spoken voice that always had an edge of authority to it.

'We're a little late, old gal. Traffic busier than I anticipated,' John explained.

Jennifer had always encouraged a healthy relationship between her daughters and Mark's parents. It irked her that Mark's brother's boys were the outright favourites; fortunately, the girls were oblivious to the Cameron's league table. To be fair, John Cameron was surprisingly tactile with them. His grandsons had outgrown cuddles and playfulness and John clearly enjoyed these quintessential moments with his granddaughters. Marjory had always played the cautious game. It was as if she just gave enough. It did make Jennifer question her motive. Was it her disdain for her younger daughter-in-law? Jennifer was certain it was more than that. Surely? How would she react to the news when it was eventually broken? Jennifer suspected that somehow, she would be blamed for engineering it. Shit and smelling of roses sprang to mind – for Mark not for her.

'Not ready yet?' Marjory asked. 'Mark seems to be in great demand downstairs.'

Was that a little sneer, Jennifer could detect? 'He's been in great demand all day, Marjory. A little Jack of all trades!' Jennifer replied.

John intervened, as he always did. 'Jen, darling, how about

Mater and I take the girls downstairs. Give you some time to sort yourself out. I'm sure you've had an eventful day too.'

Not as eventful as the slag-shagger downstairs! she was tempted to say. Instead, she said, 'Thank you, John. You're most gracious.'

'Come and see the beer garden, Grandpa. It's beautiful. It has fairy lights and bunting and everything,' cried Emma.

'Everything!' chorused Katie with equal excitement.

Emma led the way. Three of them rushed eagerly downstairs. The fourth one carefully placed one foot at a time on the stairway as if trying to avoid something.

'You're most gracious. Really?' moaned Jennifer. 'Why do I always do that?' It perplexed Jennifer that whenever she was with 'Mater and Pater', she spoke with a pinched and phoney Morningside drawl.

'They are no better than us, Jennifer,' her dad would say.

Jennifer had never felt compelled to change her dialect in front of Hannah or Fergal, her old Edinburgh pals, and they both had a 'posh' accent. Fergal more so than Hannah, who could often drift back to her Portobello colloquialisms. Jennifer was comfortable in the presence of her dear friends, whereas Marjory regularly corrected her pronunciation. Not her grammar. Jennifer had been fortunate in having an excellent Latin teacher at high school. It was Marjory – she brought out the worst in her. Foolishly, Jennifer inadvertently condoned it.

Oddly enough, Marjory had the same thoughts about Jen as she held onto the handrail. She rebuked herself for allowing Jen to goad her. That manipulative upstart brought out the worst in her.

Jennifer couldn't decide what to wear. The bedroom floor was strewn with clothes. She needed confidence. Nothing seemed to suffice. Then she spied it. It was rolled up into a tiny ball and had been pushed to the back of the shelf in her wardrobe. She tried it on. Perfect. She ditched the sparkly silver belt that was part of the original garment and selected a rusty rope version. It made the outfit less formal. Her black, flat sandals replaced the silver, four-inch heels that she would normally have worn with it. The ironing board was standing where Mark had left it, as usual. Jennifer eased out the creases, taking care not to burn her wrists with the hot steam. She quickly tidied the room. Order calmed her.

Jennifer applied an extra layer of mascara, as she rarely wore eye shadow, then a little gloss over her burnt-orange lipstick; a vibrant shade that her oldest and best friend, Fiona, had chosen especially for her. Fiona, an artist, had an eye for colour. 'It's too bright and orangey for me,' protested Jennifer when Fiona had first applied it. 'Nonsense!' Her friend was indignant. 'It has enough brown to take the sting out of the orange.' Jennifer had to agree. The colour was fabulous; it complemented her complexion and hair beautifully.

A dusting of blusher and she was ready.

'Mark Cameron eat your heart out!'

TEN

The Barbecue

Mark balanced precariously, with one foot on a bar stool and the other on the ledge of the long sash–window in the function room; or the back room as Maureen preferred to call it. He draped his arm over the top and grabbed the plug that Stevie had swung up to him. A tad too gung-ho for Mark's liking.

'Don't break the bloody glass!' shouted Mark.

Stevie continued to unwind the extension cable over to the edge of the beer garden where he had positioned a table, a mic, a stereo-unit and two speakers. He covered the cable with cuttings from old carpets as there was a narrow, gravel road that separated the back of The Maltings and the garden. It was a one-way system through the car park; entering from the main road at the left-hand side of the building, around the back then exiting onto Eden Road.

The grassy area at the back of the pub was vast and had panoramic views overlooking the orchards in Malcolm's estate. The River Eden, at the bottom of the garden, added a little romance to the enviable location. Mark joined Stevie.

'I don't want to overload the circuit,' Mark explained as he plugged it in. 'We already have one running to the lights.'

The electrics in The Maltings caused Mark many sleepless nights. A lot of the wiring was dodgy and many areas still had the old, round sockets. It was near the top on his long list of 'things to be done'; a list that was soon to be scrunched up by him and deposited in the nearest bin.

'Nae worries.' laughed Stevie. 'The disco system wi' the lights on, is plugged into the lounge. This lot could run on batteries,'

Joe Blakeley had fashioned a barbecue pit from an old oil drum. The one they had bought from the garden centre was too small. Maureen's oldest son Martin had it fired up and was stirring up onions and butter in a large pan. His brother Ryan had been roped in to cut and butter the rolls. The sausages and burgers were piled high in portable cool boxes. A few were already sizzling above the hot coals. Neither of the boys had been fed and they were starving. Martin reckoned that they were better to eat before the rush. The two boys were taller than their dad, Willie. They looked like a couple of surfing dudes with their sporty build and long, dirty blond hair. All the Ross lads were a clone of their eldest sibling and were often mistaken for each other. Maureen said they took their height from her uncles and their thick mop of hair from her dad. Half of Duneden ribbed Willie that they couldn't possibly be his; too lean, too tall and better looking. They were his alright and his heart burst with pride for each and every one of them. Maureen had covered the trestle table in a brightly patterned, wax cloth so that it could be easily wiped down and kept clean.

'Keep that table spotless,' she had explained to her boys before they left the house. 'Clean, clean and clean again! And keep washing your hands. No bloody lickin' fingers in front of anybody!'

'MUM! We're no' a couple of eejits. We ken how to serve some hamburgers,' grunted Martin.

'Some? You'll be selling hundreds ya wee arsehole! I won't have anybody saying that one of Maureen Ross's gave them food poisoning. Get along that road now and get yerselves organised.'

Behind Maureen's back, Ryan waved his fingers beneath his chin; a gesture that made the rest of her brood cackle.

'Fuck off ya wee sod. I can see ye.' She couldn't but could guess what he was up to.

Ryan ran up behind her, wrapped his arms around his mother in a giant bear hug, lifted her up and birled Maureen around.

'Ahhhhhhh!' she squealed.

'The louder you scream...' he shouted. His brothers joined in, 'The faster we go!'

For the second time that day, Maureen crossed her legs in case she peed herself. Not easy, when you're flying at high speed in circles. Just as well they had a big kitchen.

Many of Duneden's teen boys were gathering in small groups close to the barbecue. As soon as the high school bus had pulled into the village, the bigger ones were pushing past the younger pupils, eager to race home to change out of their uniforms. Families with small children had started to drift in. Bags and jumpers were scattered around the picnic tables to reserve seats for those who would be arriving later. Blankets began to dot the lawn leading down to the river. The Rosses were the centre of attention.

'Everything's fifty pence,' shouted Martin.

'What aboot onions?' a deep voice asked.

'Even wi' onions, its fifty pence,' Martin confirmed. It had been agreed that fifty was an easy round number to work with.

'It's a rip off,' a wee, spotty faced third-year shouted from the back of the crowd.

'You'll no' get better burgers and sausages than McKenzie's Butchers. Better than the cheap shite in The Centre! Tak it or leave it, ya wee wanker.' Martin ignored the school boys and turned his attention to a young dad. 'Can I help you, sir?' He was determined to make the barbecue a success. He would soon be eighteen and wanted a job behind the bar.

'Daddy! Look who's here.' Emma tugged John Cameron along by his sleeve. She stepped back, smiled and gestured approvingly to her grandpa as if he were something she had just finished making.

Mark shook his father's hand vigorously and air-kissed his mother on both cheeks. 'Good to see you both. Thanks for coming.' He looked around. 'Where's Jen?' he asked.

'Still titivating herself, I believe,' replied Marjory. She raised her eyebrows to indicate her displeasure.

Mark frowned. 'Really? Damn! I'm so sorry... Can I ask you to keep an eye on the girls a little longer? I have so much to do and people to greet.'

'Of course, darling. Bash on. Daddy and I will see to them. Won't we, John?' A rhetorical question and one that John understood would not require a response. 'It's hardly surprising,' she said to John when Mark was far enough away. 'Now girls, how about a little tour of the garden?' The girls skipped off in their identical attire; white tee shirts with a large daisy on the front and cute denim shorts. All the Duneden Cameron females were sporting French plaits.

'Evening, everyone,' squeaked Roxanne. She breezed past the barbecue and gave a flirty, little wave to the boys who had worked up a sweat in the heat.

They couldn't take their eyes off her. Her boobs bounced rhythmically in a tight, navy halter neck. She had crimped her hair. Large butterfly clasps, pinned above her temples, stopped her long fringe from falling onto her face, revealing cheeks, lips and eyes that had been heavily made up. Martin and Ryan's eyes fixated on her rear. Ryan cupped his hand over his mouth to ensure that only Martin would hear. 'Need somewhere to park yer bike?'

Roxanne's bright, emerald trousers had disappeared up the crack of her arse.

Roxanne spotted Mark heading towards The Maltings. She caught up with him. 'Evening, gorgeous,' she giggled. Flushed with excitement, she brushed his arm, ever so slightly, with the back of her fingers.

'Keep your voice down!' he hissed. 'You promised to behave tonight.'

'Nobody can hear me.' She glanced around quickly to double check. 'I am behaving but I'm hoping to be *very* naughty later.' She was such a tease.

'I sincerely hope so.' He felt a stirring in his crotch.

Roxanne drew back sharply. 'Jen! Wow. You look lovely.'

Wham! Roxanne's words rounded like a boxing glove and punched Jennifer squarely in her stomach. It didn't matter that her words were complimentary. The sound of Roxanne's voice was enough. The wee slag had the audacity to stand next to HER husband, the father of HER children as if nothing had happened. Jennifer glared at them both. *Not now, Jen,* she said to herself. *Concentrate. Breathe.* Then with unexpected stoicism, she pulled her shoulders back and said, 'Aww thank you, Roxanne. You don't look so bad yourself.' It was a lie. Roxanne's make-up was ridiculously thick and her boobs would take an eye out.

For a brief moment, Mark thought that they had been rumbled. There was something about the way Jen had paused before she spoke; it unnerved him. He recognised her outfit. It was a favourite of his. The last time she had worn it was at his work's regional dance in Glasgow before she was pregnant with

Katie. He had said she was the best-dressed woman there by miles. The silky, grey jumpsuit skimmed his wife's slender curves. The neckline at the front stretched from one shoulder directly to the other and dipped in little folds at the centre. Simple but oh so elegant. The dramatic effect was at the back. The thrill of slipping his hand into that inviting opening was still there.

'What about you, Mark? What do you think?' asked Jennifer calmly.

'Sorry?' he looked perplexed.

'How do I look?'

'You look great, Jen. You really do.' He said it with sincerity.

Mark and Roxanne watched Jen as she sashayed past them and out into the sunshine. A deep V opening slashed from her shoulders to the bottom of her spine. There was no way she could be wearing a bra and Mark guessed correctly that there would be no knickers either. The stirring in his crotch grew.

The beer garden was filling up quickly. A cacophony of laughter, loud voices, and children screaming clamoured to be heard above *The Eye of the Tiger* blaring from the loud speakers. Jennifer was searching for her two girls when she bumped into Maureen and Angie.

'You scrub up well,' screeched Maureen.

Jennifer could tell from the whiff of alcohol on their breaths that they had started the celebrations earlier. She was also pleasantly surprised. Both Angie and Maureen looked really nice; summery and cheerful. Maureen wore a knee length, denim skirt with a pink, flowery blouse that tied at the front. And she didn't look nearly as fat. Angie hadn't strayed much from her signature black tee shirt and jeans except that her satin, turtle-neck top had yellow polka dots on it and she was wearing sandals. No black boots in sight.

'You two look great.' Jennifer nodded approvingly.

There was no way that they were not going to look good when they accepted their flowers. Intentionally or not, Roxanne had let it slip when they were charging around after the lunch shift, that her colleagues were in for a surprise later in the evening. Neither of them would let it drop so Roxanne was forced to admit that she had organised flowers for them on Mark's behalf; a detail that Mark had omitted when he had told Jen that he had ordered the flowers the previous day.

'You look good, Jen.' Angie didn't give compliments unless she meant them. 'You look like the owner for a change.'

'Right, scoop up!' Maureen poured the three of them a generous shot of her home-made sloe gin into three plastic cups. 'In one. On the count of three. One... two... three.'

They threw their heads back and swallowed in one go. Wooooo! It was difficult to laugh and cough at the same time.

'Bloody Nora, Maureen. What's in that?' asked Jennifer.

'Secret recipe.' Maureen winked.

'It doesn't look right if the staff are drinking from bottles they have brought from home,' lectured Jennifer.

'Fucking hell, Jen, who cares? You own the place! Get another one down yer throat,' giggled Maureen. 'On three...'

Before she had time to assess her actions, Jennifer knocked back another large measure. The heat from her belly rushed to her head. She felt tipsy. She wished she hadn't skipped lunch.

Maureen and Angie technically should've been working. They were on 'floating' duty until roughly 9.00pm. Mark had drafted in the bar staff from the bowling club to help behind the bar. Archie Hannigan, one of The Maltings part-time employees, had volunteered to work all night. Angie had promised him some extra shifts in return.

From the corner of her eye, Jennifer could see her in-laws winding their way towards her. 'Excuse me ladies. Here comes sour pus. Do me a favour, if I ever get as sour as her give me a good shake!' With a renewed twinkle in her eye, Jennifer waved enthusiastically as she marched to greet them.

Angie and Maureen squinted at each other as if to imply, 'what does she mean... if?'

ELEVEN

Maureen rushed around picking up plastic tumblers that had been discarded. With unabashed frankness, she reminded the punters that it wasn't a fuckin' fly tip and to use the bins provided: there were plenty of them. They all knew Maureen. She was Duneden born and bred so no offence was taken. Not everyone in Duneden cursed like the Rosses or the Lennies; for some families, like them, it was second nature. Most of the villagers accepted it. Those that didn't, chose to keep their opinions to themselves. A safer choice. Some folk had been living in Duneden for twenty years and were still regarded as incomers. Others, like Mark and Jen, were lucky enough to be inducted sooner because it suited those that mattered most.

Angie was leaning into Stevie Wilson in a provocative manner when Malcolm spied her. He would have to re-evaluate his seduction strategy if he were to make a move before Stevie-boy. Malcolm had to have Angie firmly on board, for as long as was necessary, in order to find out what she really had on him and more importantly what was required to keep her big mouth shut. If he wasn't careful, Angie would mistrust his intentions and revolt. She was nobody's fool.

'Malcolm,' Doreen slurred. 'I can't get near the bar. It's mobbed. I've tried to attract Roxanne's attention. I'm sure she deliberately ignored me.'

'I need a long cool drink anyway. A G&T?' he asked.

'Get me a double. Plenty of ice. Question when you'll get served again.' Doreen perched on the end of a bench with her back to the other revellers. What looked like a rum over ice, nestled close to her elbow. The rest of the table was littered with lager or cider glasses. That little measure seemed to have been forsaken. It had her name on it if nobody had claimed it before Malcolm returned.

Joe Blakeley couldn't take his eyes off Jen. He had followed her every move since she had cat-walked into the beer garden. She was gorgeous. He had never seen her look so good or so happy. He watched as she had hugged her two youngsters, a few feet in front of him. In those few seconds, before she had scooped them up, Joe had interpreted that her warm smile and friendly wave had been directed at him. He should have hesitated. Joe was a betting man. He was on first name terms with all the staff at the bookies and they with him. What were the odds that Jen Cameron, who had hardly acknowledged him since her arrival at The Maltings, would (uncharacteristically) run towards him with open arms? Too late! He had returned the gesture by grinning broadly and throwing his hand high into the air only to withdraw it rapidly when he realised his mistake. He body swerved the family group, fixed his eyes on the back doors and walked purposefully as if someone was actually waiting for him there. His face and cheeks burned long after he had ducked into The Maltings.

Archie Hannigan, the barman, called out Joe's name and signalled that a pint of Guinness had been deposited at the end of the bar for him; a thank you for all the odd jobs that Joe and Willie had done for him. The black liquid barely touched the sides of his throat. In a couple of seconds, less than a fifth remained at the bottom of the glass. Joe needed that.

'Grandpa bought me a burger and Katie sausages!' Emma was dying to tell Jennifer what they had been up to.

'Yummy!' laughed Jennifer. 'Did you have onions? Katie? How did I guess that? No kisses for you tonight.' Jennifer chased her four-year-old in and out and around her grandparents. 'And where's mine? Did Grandma eat it?' Jennifer knew that remark would irritate Marjory. Katie screeched with delight.

Emma was happy to explain, 'Grandma doesn't like grease and gristle and she didn't like the look of the boys who were serving us.'

'The Rosses are lovely boys. Their mother Maureen works for us.' Jennifer had a strong urge to defend them.

'Street food doesn't agree with me. Does it, John? John! I'm saying...'

Jennifer didn't allow her to finish, 'Then you will love our sandwiches. There's bound to be one... out of all the sandwiches that we have made... there must be at least *ONE* of the delicious fillings to your liking. Wouldn't you agree, Marjory?'

Marjory sensed her daughter-in-law's challenging tone and for once remained tight-lipped. She felt that restraint was the admirable option given the circumstances. The girl was full of impudence.

'Hey, you two! How about a cuddle for your favourite uncle?' hollered a familiar voice.

'UNCLE ANDREW!' It was Andrew's turn to chase the girls around everyone.

It must be a family trait, thought Marjory. *Let's whip the girls up into a frenzy then slink off and leave Pater and me to calm the melee.*

'Marjory! You're looking sharp. John, mate, you'll need to be on your toes tonight.' Andrew looked directly at Marjory and gave an exaggerated wink. He shook hands with John and slapped him on the back with genuine affection. 'Good to see you.'

Jennifer wrapped her arms around her younger sibling and held him tightly. It was so good to have a member of her family here. And he always managed to say the right thing at the right time. She pulled back a little, smiled, and embraced him again.

'You okay?' Andrew whispered.

'I am now,' she said, squeezing even tighter.

Marjory liked Andrew. He was a little rough around the edges but a well-meaning young man, nonetheless. More than could be said for his ill-natured sister.

Mark merged with the group. Andrew introduced Rebecca to Mark then left them to chat while he turned his attention to Marjory and John.

Jennifer was fascinated; an ensemble of Duneden spread out around her. There were teenagers sitting in groups on the tables, families picnicking down at the river and babies sleeping in prams. Everyone from the local road sweeper to the biggest landowner in that part of Fife drifted from one chat to another. They were actually enjoying themselves. Each and every one of them. It had the buzz of a mini festival and one that was in full swing.

Bethany, a mini version of Angie, but in black shorts, had dragged the girls off to the dancing space in front of the music table. The *Hokey Cokey* was playing and all the primary kids, as well as the adults, were belting out the lyrics. Someone was screaming 'louder!' every time the chorus rang out – '*Woah-oh the Hokey, Cokey...*' – Jennifer recognised Maureen's wheezy bark.

'Who would have thought?' Mark slid his arm around his

wife's tiny waist. 'Well done. I couldn't have done it without you.' He kissed her tenderly on the shoulder.

Jennifer tensed her body. The sloe gin erupted at the back of her throat. She swallowed hard. 'I'm sure you had everything under control.' She smiled sweetly at her husband. A smile that belied her true sentiments.

'Is it too early to hand out the flowers?' he asked.

Jennifer said she would fetch them from the function room and shrugged off his grip.

The heat in the building was intense but Jennifer was surprised to find the air slightly cooler in the dark, back room. In the hallway, she bumped into Joe. He looked flustered.

'Could you give me a hand?' Jennifer asked nodding towards the basket of flowers.

One of their younger punters had thrust a Pernod and lemonade into the palm of her hand. One of the baskets hung precariously on the same wrist. Joe aimed to take the other basket, not the one that Jennifer had proffered and an awkward game of toing and froing ensued. They both giggled at their confusion.

'Let's start again,' she grinned. Joe blushed which Jennifer found endearing. 'I thought it best to give these out now before Angie and Maureen are totally hammered,' she said as they walked towards Stevie Wilson who had joined in with the *Birdie Dance*.

Bethany, Emma and Katie skipped round with him like starstruck groupies. It was hilarious to witness. When the dance finished, Mark signalled to Stevie to turn down the volume. Stevie yelled for a bit of hush and soon all eyes were on Mark as he stood in front of the music system, mic in hand.

'First of all, I would like to thank you all for coming.' A loud continuous screech pierced the ears of those that had gathered. Mark held the mic further from his mouth and tried again. 'What a fantastic turn out.' A huge cheer rang out followed by a long round of applause and loud whistling. When the rapture died down someone called out that they were only here for the free beer and sandwiches. Once the laughter settled, Mark continued.

'Seriously though, Jen and I are blown away with your well wishes today. When we first came to Duneden, we didn't know what to expect. What if we'd bitten off more than we could chew? Running a pub as big as this, was... is a new ball game. We worried that reopening it would be a waste of time. What if it had had its day? But when I look around at all the regular faces, and many we now regard as good friends, our worries were unfounded.' Another cheer whipped up the spirits of an already animated crowd. 'There are so many people that we need to thank for getting us to this point. To Tam and Joe Blakeley and their fantastic team of workmen... thank you guys.'

'Dinnae forget my Willie!' barked Maureen.

'How could we forget Maureen's Willie?' Mark could work an audience. 'Joking apart. Willie, you are a green-fingered genius! The front of the building is stunning. The baskets, the tubs, the window boxes. And look around us. The beer garden looks great. We are truly grateful. Thank you. I owe you a few beers.' More clapping and cheering ensued; sparked off by Willie's five boys who were standing on empty beer barrels at the back of the barbecue. Mark pointed them out. 'I'd like to thank Martin and Ryan for manning the barbecue and to Stevie behind me for supplying the entertainment. More of that will be heard later in the lounge bar when the kids have been packed off to bed.' Some of the under-agers, many of whom had been sneaking alcohol from their *juice* bottles, started to boo. Mark laughed. 'And a big thanks to the staff at the bowling club for allowing our own staff here at The Maltings a well-earned night off. Talking of which?... Our greatest asset... The Maltings' staff.' Angie started off the whooping and the brief banter that interrupted his flow. 'The Maltings would not be the success it is today without the support from our wonderful staff. Together, this year, we have shared ups and downs... mainly ups I hope and we have come out the other end stronger and better. I thank you all from the bottom of my heart. BUT. There are two ladies who need a special mention. Angie and Maureen would you like to come forward.'

'They ain't no ladies!' came a cheerful retort.

'Feck off!' rasped Maureen with a mischievous twinkle in her eyes.

Marjory cupped her hands over Katie's ears and sneaked a look at John. That was exactly what she had referred to earlier that morning; needless vulgarity.

Both Angie and Maureen feigned surprise at being called up. Emma walked forward with the baskets of flowers. She had been tutored previously by Jennifer. She handed the first basket to Angie and proffered her cheek for a kiss. When it was her turn, Maureen brimmed over with emotion and hugged little Katie; more of a strangle hold than a display of affection. Katie squirmed, managed to twist her head and gasped 'help!' to a bemused Angie. Both 'ladies' kissed and hugged Mark.

'Hey, you!' Angie summoned Jen to come and join the celebrations.

As Stevie played *Congratulations*, the majority of onlookers drifted back to their benches, blankets and conversations. Some remained to shake hands and admire the flowers. Youngsters chased each other, screaming at the tops of their voices, leaving mild irritation in their wake. Mark set off through the throng on his networking journey and Jennifer returned to her brother and Rebecca.

'A drink, Miss Lennie?' asked Malcolm as Angie passed his table.

She hesitated. 'Why not?' and she nudged him along with her bum.

He left her just enough space on the bench to ensure their bodies nuzzled together. He poured a glass of Moet et Chandon for Angie then topped up his own glass. He gazed forlornly at Doreen who was slumped opposite them; the palm of one hand supporting her heavy head. He sighed, looked at Angie and shrugged, deliberately seeking sympathy. 'To friendship' and he clinked her glass. It seemed to have worked. A frown of concern washed over her face. She rested the side of her head on his shoulder. For the next half hour, they were lost in quiet deliberation. At no time was their recent altercation mentioned. He was ever so carefully reeling her in.

TWELVE

The Karaoke

It was eight o'clock. Time had flown by. Andrew and Rebecca joined in the frenetic turnaround of the beer garden. Rebecca held open black bin bags while Andrew shoved a mad collection of rubbish into them. Anything that looked semi-decent was dropped onto a lost property pile. Andrew chased off teenagers who were swigging from dozens of drinks abandoned on the tables and grass. Marjory and John said they would oversee bath time and ushered the over-stimulated twosome up to the flat. The garden emptied surprisingly quickly. School didn't finish for another week and that contributed to the speeding up of farewells. Several folk settled down again outdoors. It was a warm, balmy evening and relaxing in the ambiance of the holiday atmosphere seemed far more preferable to retreating inside where it was hot and stuffy. However, the party diehards certainly disagreed. The merriment had kicked off with *Come on Over to My Place*. Musically, The Maltings clientele were partial to anything remotely connected to R&B or Country and Western. Also, Fifties and Sixties music was as popular as Queen and Madness.

Mark and Jennifer stood side by side accepting and declining drinks in equal measure. Jennifer had lost count of how many drinks she had had.

'Careful, Jen,' purred Mark. 'Don't want to spoil a good

night.' He bumped her playfully with his shoulder and gave her a smouldering wink.

She didn't know whether to laugh or cry. Earlier that morning, she would have found it cheeky: sexy even. Hell, she had been planning mummy and daddy times. Now, she just wanted to knee him hard in the nuts. How had they ended up like this?

*

In the January of 1973, Jennifer met Mark in the middle of her third year at Moray House; the teacher training college on Edinburgh's Royal Mile, after watching rugby at the Peffermill playing fields. Post match, the players and spectators made their way to the Gold Medal pub opposite the Commonwealth Pool. From the moment Mark strolled across the bar with that big, confident grin and whispered in her ear, she was besotted. His wavy, brown hair tickled her cheek and his warm, mellow voice melted her insides all the way down to her toes. He was everything that she was not: edgy, older, sophisticated, interesting and very middle class.

In June 1973, he'd persuaded her to go travelling with him the week before her graduation ceremony. It was wild and wilful. Her parents were distraught, yet, with no consideration, they sailed off into the sunset and spent over a year in Spain and France, living off very little other than love, lust and an awful lot of good luck. It had to be way up there, as the best year of her life.

Mark was undeniably handsome: still is. He had the type of olive skin that even with a smidgen of exposure to sunlight transformed him from a Brit abroad to a tall, Mediterranean

God. Jennifer spent the entire year seeking the shade and slapping on the sunscreen. Still, it was all deliciously bohemian. They returned penniless and pregnant.

During her pregnancy, a friend from college told Jennifer that her mother was giving up a cleaning job. A cushy wee number, she had said and would Jennifer be interested. It was then that Jennifer had her first encounter with feisty Hannah Urquhart and (several months later) her debonair neighbour, Fergal Fitzsimmons; a well-heeled, fifty-year-old businessman. None of them, least of all Jennifer, could have foreseen that their little business arrangement would have blossomed into mutual admiration and an unbreakable friendship. They had been a lifeline for Jennifer: financially and emotionally.

Mark and his family didn't approve of her cleaning but it fitted so well around baby Emma and provided Jennifer with some much-needed personal income. Lack of childcare prevented her from returning to teaching and finishing her parchment. Her own mother was still working and Mark's mother would never have entertained such a notion. Hannah had recommended Jennifer to a couple of other families at her church and none of them objected to Emma being brought along. It was one of Hannah's church cronies that had encouraged Jennifer to become an Avon Lady – an unlikely pursuit for someone who rarely wore make-up. But Jennifer was good at it: so good, she became an area manager, responsible for dozens of other representatives and only gave it up when she moved away from Edinburgh. Jennifer had been loath to leave Hannah behind. Mark had had no such qualms.

*

Andrew nudged his sister and whispered, 'How you doin', Jenz? Everything okay here... with you and Mark, I mean? I dunno, but things seem a wee bit frosty.'

'We're fine. Honestly. It's been manic that's all. We're just tired.' Jennifer reassured him. 'Where's Rebecca?'

'Taking over from Mater and Pater,' sniggered her brother.

'You've a good one there. Look after her.'

As the music faded, Stevie yelled for some order. 'I need a John Travolta. Someone who haaaaas the moves.'

There was some jostling and shoving and suggesting of names when Willie Ross strutted to the front with his arms in the air as if he were the prize contender in a boxing match. His black, aertex shirt reached the bottom of the pockets on his jeans. The crowd reacted as if they were at a huge sporting extravaganza!

'Give it up for Willie!' bawled Stevie. 'Danny Zuko, choose your Sandy!'

Willie scoured the room and with a devilish glint he made for Jen.

'Don't you dare,' Mark warned her and he dug his nails into her wrist.

Willie gyrated in front of her. The punters willed her to accept his crazy challenge. They clapped their hands and stamped their feet. 'Yes! Yes! Yes! Yes! Yes!'

'DON'T!' growled Mark behind a fixed smile.

Then she did. Just like that. She stretched out her hand towards Willie. He dramatically accepted it and he led her to a clear patch in front of the disco. The beginnings of *You're the One That I Want* could just be heard above the noise.

'Does our Sandy know the words?' Stevie asked.

Of course, she did. She knew every word, every move, every pause, everything. In a previous life, Jennifer worked for her friends in their video shop in Dalry Road, in Edinburgh. Every Thursday from nine in the morning until eight at night. *Grease* played on a loop on the giant television provided by Radio Rentals. It was one of the few adult films that could be viewed in the shop without causing offence.

When she mouthed, *'tell me about it, stud,'* and pretended to stamp on her cigarette, the place erupted. The cheers and catcalling were deafening. Jennifer undid her pleat and shook out her long, chestnut hair.

For three and a half minutes she *WAS* Olivia Newton John.

THIRTEEN

Friday 24th June

'Wakey, wakey!'

The echo reverberated in Jennifer's head; it was competing with the painful thud, thudding of the nerve endings in her delicate brain.

'Are you gettin'up?' Angie yelled.

'I can't... I feel terrible,' whimpered Jennifer.

Angie leaned in closer and tried whispering, 'You look like shite!'

Jennifer had neither the strength to moan nor the inclination to attempt even the flimsiest of a smile. She could smell the booze on Angie. Last night? Jennifer wanted to cry, or throw up. Even the teensiest movement was difficult. It was like having the world's most monumental hangover and the most nauseating case of morning sickness all rolled into one. The room was spinning. She felt as if she'd been strapped to one of the rotary blades of a helicopter that was flying at two hundred miles an hour and just for fun, was nose diving into the Grand Canyon. She tried moving on to her back. Whoo-aah! Forget it. The foetal position was resumed.

'Where am I?' her rasp was barely audible. It was a pretty room with dainty, blue flowers on the wallpaper. The white furniture looked solid: not cheap MDF. The bedding was white too. The blue trim on the pillow was soaked with Jennifer's saliva and God knows what else. She hoped it wasn't vomit.

'You're at mine. Can ye no' remember?' Angie drew back the curtains and opened the blinds.

The brightness caused Jennifer to recoil. She tried to concentrate but her mind was blank. 'The last thing I can honestly remember was dancing with Willie. Oh my God! Did I make a complete fool of myself?'

'Nut! Jen, you were pure, dead brilliant.' Angie began laughing, 'Mark's face! It was a fuckin' picture. No-one, not one person there, would ever have imagined that you would of done it. You blew them away! When did you learn to dance like that? I wish I'd had ma camera. Talking about cameras... I think I left mine in the beer garden.'

Jennifer wished she could recall more. She shut her eyes to think but quickly forced them open as closing them only increased the spinning. 'Where are my girls?'

'It's sorted. Your Andy is taking them to school this morning. Ye'll have to pick them up after nursery and at home time. I'd do it but I've got the dentist then I've got a driving lesson.'

Jennifer wanted to say that her brother was not 'Andy' but it really wasn't important nor was it the time to remind Angie to clean her teeth.

'I've asked him tae come here after he's dropped the girls off,' quipped Angie.

'Does he know where you live?'

'Eh... he helped to carry ye here last night!' Angie left the room.

Whatever Jennifer had been drinking, a second fermentation began to bubble in her stomach. She needed to pee and to be sick. She had to move, preferably with haste, but past experience dictated no sudden or jerky movements. She rested her elbows on the mattress, allowing her knees to keel, very, very slowly, to the floor. There was no point praying. She had an inclination that her behaviour last night didn't warrant a smidgen of divine intervention. Angie returned with a cup of tea and a Resolve. Bile seared the back of Jennifer's throat. She swallowed hard to preserve her dignity. Not that Angie would've minded. Jennifer had witnessed Angie spewing on more than one occasion during a drinking session at The Maltings then think nothing of topping up what she had just thrown up. Was it a Fife thing? Or just an Angie thing?

'It'll give you something to heave on,' Angie insisted.

The room listed as Jennifer's shaky hand reached out for the warm cuppa. Heels supported her grateful bottom. She was still wearing her grey jumpsuit and the disgusting deposits on the pillow case confirmed her make-up had not been removed. That was so not her! Jennifer had a strict cleanse, tone and moisturise routine at night. Clean clothes would be looked out the night before, folded over her chair for the following morning and her washing basket was topped up nightly. Jennifer tilted her head meekly to face Angie who flicked straggly, auburn strands away from her employer's lips. She took a few sips of the tea – it was too sweet! On Angie's insistence, Jennifer drained the Resolve while it was still fizzing. The second fermentation reacted violently with the effervescing salts.

'Where's the toilet? I need it now!' She scrambled on all fours towards the bedroom door. She bit her lips with her teeth to seal in the vomit but the burning bile was surging up through her nose. Her cheeks bulged like a hamster's. Angie's cream carpet loomed in her face. Jennifer clamped a hand over both orifices. Angie bolted in front of her and flung open the bathroom door.

'LEFT! Turn LEFT!'

Jennifer's aim was inextricably accurate and the toilet bowl accepted the eruption. Each wave of vomiting was accompanied by unnatural groaning and heaving. She sounded like a wild animal in advanced labour. She felt the same. When it was over, she sobbed with exhaustion and humiliation. 'I am so so sorry. I'll clean it up. Please get me some cloths and bleach.' Her jumpsuit was soaked in piss.

While Angie fetched the cleaning products, Jennifer stripped off. She rinsed her delicate outfit in the bath.

Angie slipped the bits and pieces through the narrow gap in the door. Jennifer asked her for some clothes – anything would do. Angie checked her carpet. It was spotless, thank fuck! It was brand new and she still had fifteen months of payments left on it. She found a pair of tracky bottoms, knickers and the smallest sweatshirt in her chest of drawers. A bra was a waste of time. She knocked on the bathroom door and a pale arm peeked out to receive the grateful offering. Someone was at the door. 'It's open!'

Angie called to Andrew and Rebecca to go into the living room.

They both stood up as Angie entered. She felt like a headmistress who had summoned two naughty children to her office. They could have been twins. Rebecca was a little shorter than her boyfriend but she had the same, bright blue eyes and tousled blonde hair. In their similar khaki outfits, they looked as if they were setting out on safari; a fashion-conscious safari.

'How is she?' asked Andrew.

Angie was touched. None of her brothers would have shown the same concern for her.

'She's a mess. Give her a minute to get back into her bed.

She's not fit for anything else this morning. Can I get yous a coffee?'

Andrew followed Angie into the kitchen. 'What a night! I thought us lot across the water could drink but you lot are somethin' else,' blurted Andrew. 'I watched your vodka bottles on the gantry. One after another, they emptied as quick as that.' He lifted his hand up into the air and brought it down quickly. Each bottle on the optic held three litres of vodka. It was an inordinate amount of alcohol consumption for a small establishment in one evening.

Angie laughed, 'It's no' always like that. It was a special night.' She handed Jen's brother two mugs of coffee and suggested they go upstairs. 'First on the left an' watch my carpet!'

The smell of bleach hit them as they reached the top. It didn't mask the stench in Angie's bedroom.

'Aaaahhhh! Jenz, it stinks in here,' he said.

'Don't make me feel any worse,' pleaded Jennifer feebly.

Andrew sat on the edge of the bed and Rebecca stood at the bottom so as not to intrude too much. Jennifer lay on her side with her legs curled up. Angie's leggings were draped on the bed post at her head.

'What's everyone been saying?' she asked sheepishly.

'Not much.' Andrew was being honest. Everyone was too drunk to notice or care.

'Did the girls not ask where I was?'

'I told them you were at Angie's and they accepted it. Anyway, it was the truth.'

'What happened? I can't remember.' Jennifer's voice faltered and tears trickled down her face. 'Was his mum and dad still there?'

Andrew explained that Marjory and John had left about ten

not long after the Grease histrionics. Jennifer groaned at the embarrassment. Rebecca chipped in to say that Andrew had thought it was fantastic and everyone had swarmed round to congratulate her. Marjory didn't know what to make of it but John had thought that she was a jolly good sport for trying.

'What happened after that? How the hell did I end up here?' Jennifer did want to know but part of her wished she hadn't asked. She braced herself.

Rebecca looked at Andrew. Andrew looked at Rebecca. Rebecca glared at Andrew encouraging him to say something. Andrew made a *give me a second* face.

'For God's sake, please tell me what I did,' insisted Jennifer.

Andrew cleared his throat nervously. 'I'm not sure exactly but I think you pissed Mark off with the way you were sort of dancing with that guy.'

'Willie? He was jealous of Willie?'

Rebecca chipped in, 'No, not him. The tall one... the good looking one. Andrew, what are you looking at me like that for? I'm not saying that I fancy him but... for an older guy, he was alright. What was his name? Joe. Yep, definitely Joe. Was he the same one that was holding the flowers for you, Jennifer?'

'When did I dance with him?'

Andrew sniggered. 'It was when you were Sandy. You were so funny.'

He stood up to demonstrate and used a high-pitched voice to add drama. He exaggerated a sexy gait as he moved towards the imaginary 'Joe' at the window. He pointed to 'Joe' singing, you're *the one that I want*, did an odd skip, turned his back to the window, sang *ooh, ooh, ooh, honey,* bent forward, grabbed his ankles, looked though his legs then wiggled his bum. Andrew stopped and looked up at Jennifer. He did make a formidable Sandy and he had a good memory for recalling actions.

Jennifer flinched. 'Nooooooo!' She pulled the duvet over her head.

'Everybody thought you were great,' he said, hoping it would help. When his sister tentatively emerged, she looked pale. Andrew settled on her bed again. 'About five, maybe ten, minutes later, Mark chummed his mum and dad out to their car. When he came back, he made a beeline for you. You kept ignoring him. I could see he was trying to talk to you but you kept turning away. I was wedged in at the bar. I couldnae get to you. You were arguing. It looked ugly. But... I don't think anyone was paying attention. They were all too busy watching Maureen and Willie on the karaoke belting out *I Want You Babe*. The pair of you made for the door. I couldnae tell if he was shoving you but that's what it looked like. I'm not sure. When I made it to the corridor, I could hear you shouting. Christ Jennifer, you were screaming at the top of your voice. It was coming from the big room near the back door. It was in darkness.

'What was I saying?' Jennifer asked.

'To be honest, I'm no' sure. You were screaming, "I hate you. I hate you." Over and over. That's when I saw Angie. She had her arms around your waist. She was holding you back. You were like a mad woman. Some random man had Mark pinned to the wall by his neck.'

'What? Was Angie in the function room with someone? Stevie Wilson, the DJ?' Jennifer pressed him for an answer.

'I dunno. Naw. He was still doing the disco. It all happened so fast. I think she'd been in the garden. The next thing I ken, Angie says she's taking you to her house. She asked me to make sure the girls got to school. You were sobbing. Mark was saying that everything was fine. That you'd had too much to drink. You came wi' me an Angie. Mark went back to the lounge bar. When I got back, I hung around until closing. Mark wouldn't say anything when I asked him what was going on. That older barman, Archie, he locked up and I went to bed.'

'Where was Mark?'

'I'm no' sure. I don't think he came back last night… but he was downstairs when we took the girls to school.'

Jennifer closed her eyes. Her breathing was heavy. Every outward breath was long and protracted. Nobody spoke. Andrew and Rebecca listened in the awkward silence.

'Jennifer,' Rebecca spoke her name gently. 'We'll go back to the flat and make sure everything is nice and tidy for you. Downstairs looked pretty well organised. Emma has a packed lunch so she won't be home at lunchtime. Me and Andrew were planning to go to St. Andrews for lunch. We'll pick Katie up from nursery and take her with us. Is that okay? That way, you can have a wee sleep and get up when you're feeling better.'

Tears rolled down Jennifer's face. She had neither the energy nor the gumption to protest. She nodded her thanks.

They slipped out the door. Within a few minutes, there was a quiet tap at the door and Angie popped her head round.

'Can I come in?' She entered anyway. 'I've set the alarm clock for quarter past two. That'll give you time to get ready. You'll have to pick Emma and Bethany up from school. It's too late for me to make other arrangements. Sorry. Hopefully yer brother'll be back from St Andrews by then.' Angie put a glass of water and two paracetamols on the bedside cabinet beside the alarm clock. 'Take them later. I have to go to work.'

'Angie?' Jennifer was reluctant to ask. 'Is there anything I need to know about? Please?'

Angie shook her head. 'Nope. Nothin'. Get some sleep, Jen.'

There was plenty of time later to fill in the blanks. As far as Angie was aware, only she, Mark and Malcolm had witnessed Jen's revelation that she'd caught Mark humping Roxanne. Unfortunately, Mark had caught Angie and Malcolm doing the same and, therefore, threatened to tell Doreen if Malcolm or Angie blabbed his predicament to all and sundry. What a carry on! Too many secrets. Too many indiscretions.

FOURTEEN

A naked body rocked rhythmically as the woman straddled her man. Long, red hair billowed in the warm, summer wind.

'Ride me faster you bronco bitch,' he urged.

'Fuck me harder you mad, bad stallion,' she responded, with breasts pointing upwards and arms stretched back in wild abandonment.

A bedroom window was thrown open. Emma looked down on the pair galloping uninhibitedly.

'Mummy! Grandma's ringing the front door bell.'

Jennifer stopped and looked at the formal, stern woman standing on the doorstep. Mark's mother's eyes were fixed on the two of them as the ringing droned on; her forefinger glued to the buzzer. Their king-size bed was in the middle of the front garden. Neighbours, in their Edinburgh cu-de-sac, mowed their lawns, washed their cars and little children played on their tricycles.

Katie came to the window and sang, 'Mummy is squashing Grandpa.'

Jennifer looked down at the grinning face on her pillow. Oh my God! She was shagging John Cameron.

'Get off my husband, filthy whore!' screeched Mark's mother.

Nonchalantly, Jennifer flitted off the bed, shook out the bed sheet which was now no bigger than a large pillow slip and tied it deftly around her upper body as you would a boob-wrap. She was so pleased at how authentic it looked. Mark's 'emergency' boxers were under his pillow and his young wife pulled them on. Ready and dressed appropriately for a hot, summer morning.

'Good morning,' she rejoiced, waving to her neighbours.

'Good morning, Jen,' they regaled.

The mattress was yanked off the bed to reveal a trampoline beneath it and the girls bounced merrily on their new toy. Mark's white BMW swung into the drive. John Cameron clasped his hands in front of his cock.

'Your filthy whore has been bonking my husband,' wailed Marjory Cameron to her son.

'She made me do it,' squeaked his father.

'Liar! You sneaked into my bed pretending to be Mark,' Jennifer shouted.

'I did not.'

'How could you? And with my father?' Mark stared accusingly.

'I thought it was you!'

Mark summoned the girls to his car. Bloody cheek. He was not taking *her* girls. She pushed (with incredible ease) another car in front of Mark's to block the drive and his exit. She had to phone her mother; Grace would know what to do. Fumbling fingers slid over the trim phone. No matter how hard she tried, she couldn't find the correct numbers to press.

John Cameron pressed against his daughter-in-law from behind, fumbling her breasts.

'We could do it again. I won't tell. I'll pay you.' His wheezing breath condensed on her neck.

Jennifer struggled with him, trying to remain focussed on the moving buttons. John had red sandals on his feet. Long red laces trailed behind him. The phone was getting smaller and smaller. Her fingers were too big for the digits. Why couldn't she phone home? Why was a naked John Cameron wearing Roxanne's shoes? His legs were too hairy for red wedges. The phone rang and rang and rang. It wouldn't stop.

Jennifer shook herself from the nightmare.

The palm of her hand slapped the large, pause button on the top of the alarm and it tumbled noisily to the floor as she leapt from the bed. It took several moments for her to work out what had happened and where she was. She felt as if she had just finished a marathon. Her jelly-legs couldn't support her body and so she toppled back on to the bed and melted into the duvet. Reality dawned.

She forced herself to sit up. Two little tablets lay next to a glass which still had a few mouthfuls left in it. She placed them on her tongue and finished the remainder of the water. She pulled on the black jogging bottoms and searched the bedclothes for Angie's sweatshirt. A loud clanging caused her to jump again. That bloody clock! She made sure it wouldn't ring again. Everything was an effort.

The pungency of bleach still lurked in the bathroom. Jennifer splashed the freezing tap water over her face until she felt strong enough to tackle the remainder of the day. She found some hair bobbles in the cupboard beneath the sink. She examined her face in the mirror. Grey semi-circles were wedged between her eyes and cheeks. She looked as bad as she felt. A blob of toothpaste was squeezed onto her finger and she cleaned her teeth as well as she could. The stairs creaked softly as she made her way to the small lobby at the bottom. Her sandals had been stuffed into a woven basket at the front door. It took ages to unbuckle the straps.

An eerie haar hung over the streets of Duneden. The sun was trapped behind layers of orange and grey. The hot air enveloped Jennifer as she closed the door. *Only a good thunderstorm could shift it*, she thought. God! She was beginning to sound like her mother. Jennifer had decided that a walk would help to clear her head before she collected the girls from school.

Angie's house overlooked the swing park. It was empty as Jennifer took a short cut through it and she recalled her first visit there fourteen months earlier. Mark was at a meeting with someone from the brewery while she occupied the girls. Everything seemed so different then; unfamiliar. The grass was longer. The park was empty then too – except for the three of them. She could remember scrutinising the cottages that bordered the park, each one as quaint and different from its neighbours, and she wondered then what the owners were like and if she and her wee family would fit in. She was pretty sure the consensus now would be that she hadn't managed to fit in. Her fault.

She found herself admiring the well-maintained gardens as she trudged to the school. The uncharacteristically warm spring had encouraged the growth of colourful flowers and green shrubbery in abundance. Hanging baskets hung from most of the lampposts in preparation for Fife's Small Villages in Bloom competition but the pleasant surroundings did nothing to lift her bleak mood.

When Jennifer thought no-one was around, she allowed her feet to drag and her shoulders to slump. Her heavy legs felt as if she had just stepped off a trampoline. As soon as anyone approached, she tried to quicken her pace and keep upright. She knew she must have looked a sight from behind. From any angle really. A 'T. Blakeley & Sons' van tooted its horn. Jennifer forced her shoulders back and waved but it was only two of the young lads who were driving. She was relieved it wasn't Joe. She couldn't get the image of Mark and Roxanne out of her head. Every time she thought about them, a speeding truck smacked her in the stomach then stayed there, abandoned, with its wheels churning.

Emma and Bethany sprinted towards her. 'Mummy can we go to Granny Joyce's later? Bethany has a new paddling pool and it's humongous.' Two pleading faces willed her to say yes.

'It depends,' said Jennifer.

'On what?' asked Emma.

'On lots of things,' sighed her mother.

'Like what?

'Grown up things.'

'Pleeeeeeze?'

'EMMA! I am NOT in the mood.'

Even eight-year-olds recognise a certain tone, so Emma decided not to push it.

Katie's nursery teacher called after Jennifer. She handed over a letter to remind parents that the nursery would be visiting the primary one classroom on Monday for their transition visit and the morning nursery group would be taking part in the end of term assembly on Tuesday morning. Jennifer smiled politely; it was all she could manage. Several mums and one dad were helping their offspring change into their outdoor shoes.

Shona Blakeley, Tam's daughter-in-law, was shoe-horning her son's fat, size nine feet into a pair of size eight trainers when she spied Jennifer. 'Hi, Jen, how are you? Sorry daft question. You look like how I feel... well felt. I'm a wee bit better now.'

'I'm a little rough, to be honest,' Jennifer apologised. 'I lost count of the number of drinks people bought for us.'

'If it's any consolation, I think we all had too much to drink. George and me didnae get up until half past nine this morning. Thank God for videos. Just as well this wee bugger's nursery's in the afternoons. It was a great night though. Everybody said so. And, Jen, you were a great sport.'

Jennifer was touched. Shona Blakeley had invited her over for a coffee on several occasions yet she had never accepted and now she was grateful for the friendly words from someone whom she'd actively avoided for most of the year.

'Thank you, Shona. Let's meet up soon for a coffee. I'd like that.' Jennifer didn't linger. She felt her resolve diminishing and her tears were close to watering her cheeks again.

On the way home, Jennifer racked her brain for the millionth time for the clues that must have been missed or misinterpreted. How long had it been going on? Why hadn't she seen it coming? Admittedly, Mark and she had had more arguments since their arrival in Duneden. Bickering over trivial things. Nothing major. Instead of talking it over calmly and truthfully, they'd allowed their resentment to fester. Sex had been quieter; practically non-existent if she was honest. Not always her fault. It had turned into a quick kiss, a quick fumble and an even quicker finale. Was it like that for him and Roxanne? Or was it long, slow and passionate? A juggernaut stole her breath again.

Jennifer had rehearsed what to say to Mark over and over while she had lain in bed all day, but knew it would come out wrong. Surely, he must realise what a stupid, bloody idiot he's been. What possessed him? With Roxanne of all people. Technically, she was young enough to be his daughter. Jennifer knew what she could be like; too unforgiving and holding a grudge way longer than was necessary. She would never let it drop. At every opportunity, she'd regurgitate it, rake it over, and cause an argument. Yet, no mother wants her girls to be without a dad and if she was honest, she didn't want to be without Mark. She loved him – even though she hated him too.

The front door of the pub was padlocked and Jennifer revisited the moment she stumbled from the back doors, through the car park and onto the pavement on Main Street. Salty tears trickled into her mouth. 'Stop it now!' she warned herself.

She didn't know why she was sneaking in like an intruder breaking into someone else's home, though most housebreakers would not have two, chatty youngsters in tow. On reaching the top of the stairs, she eased the silver, Yale key into the lock and pushed the heavy door open with her shoulder. She heard Mark talking on the phone. His voice sapped her courage. She felt as if she had swallowed a sponge: her mouth was so dry.

Mark walked into the square hallway. 'I saw you from the window,' he said in a calm voice. 'Girls, I've left a snack on the table for you. Emma, choose a video for you and Bethany or go and play quietly in your room. That's a good girl.'

'Okay.' Emma was happy to comply. Both her parents had been acting oddly, plus, she was hoping that she would be allowed to visit Granny Joyce later and play in Bethany's new paddling pool. She was sure if they behaved properly then her mum would reward them with that treat.

Jennifer stood face to face with her betrayer.

'We need to talk,' he said.

FIFTEEN

Four days later: Tuesday 28th June

The patio doors of the music room were open wide. Doreen Patterson stepped outside and put the breakfast tray on their garden table. The dreadful storms, weather-wise, over the previous few days had settled and glorious sunshine greeted them once more. Family problems, however, were still rumbling. She poured Malcolm a strong black coffee and topped up her own cup.

'Is she up yet?' Malcolm asked his wife.

Before Doreen could speak, a barefooted and bare-chested Mark sauntered onto the terrace and helped himself to some strawberries from a crystal bowl. 'Morning. Sleep well?' he asked. It seemed a friendly enough question but there was a sinister tone lurking in his cheerfulness. Malcolm could detect it but he hoped that Doreen would be oblivious.

Doreen smiled warily at her most unwelcome visitor and worried why Malcolm was allowing the smarmy buffoon into their house and to sit unchallenged at their breakfast table. There was no way that Malcolm would usually condone such a sloppy dress code at his table. They enjoyed casual dining as much as the next person but, given his background, Mark should have known that sitting shirtless was not acceptable protocol. Shorts were fine, Malcolm wore his most weekends too but Mark's posturing suggested he was taunting them for some reason. Something was amiss and the truth had been deliberately sidestepped. Doreen hoped that Malcolm would break his silence soon and confide in her as he usually did.

'When do you plan to leave?' Doreen asked Mark.

'We're thinking early next week if I can secure a flight. I spoke with a travel agent yesterday so Roxie and I will pop down to Glenrothes today and make a decision. We should be back a few days later.' Mark reached over for the cafetiere and filled a coffee cup with what remained in the ornamental jug.

'Her name is ROXANNE! Doreen wanted to shout but politely enquired about his young wife instead. 'And how is Jen? Now that she's had time to digest all of this.' Doreen's loyalty lay with her only child but that didn't mean she had no sympathy for Jen and her predicament.

'How do you think she feels?' snapped Mark. Then in a more controlled voice added, 'It is what it is, Doreen. Roxie and I didn't set out to hurt anybody, especially my girls, but we love each other... and we want to be with each other. We will be together, regardless of what others think.' Mark was pleased with his performance to date. He genuinely believed in his own justifications. He had convinced, perhaps coerced, Malcolm into part-funding their Spanish project.

Malcolm sat in silence. He had tried in vain to dissuade Roxanne without pointing out the obvious – that Mark Cameron was a selfish, lazy bastard and would stop at nothing to achieve what he wanted; a meal ticket to what he perceived to be an easier lifestyle. It hadn't taken long for Malcolm to fathom out what had been unfolding at The Maltings. Mark had lost momentum. He had lost interest too. Mark had overseen the building of the bar and some minor renovations downstairs and up, then zero. Jen had been the one who had furtively kept going. She cleaned and worked hard behind the scenes as well as working front of house which seemed to have been more frequently of late but Mark had slowed down; buying fancy cars, entertaining futile clients and playing golf.

Malcolm was no saint but Doreen and Roxanne had always been his main priority. His dalliances would never have taken precedence over their well-being.

Neither Roxanne nor Doreen knew about Angie – yet. As long as Mark upheld his agreement, never to disclose what he had seen, at least until Malcolm no longer relied on his silence, Malcolm was prepared to indulge Roxanne. Yet to be fair, Roxanne's hapless plan actually had some credence. She may have been perceived as flighty by many but Roxanne had inherited a work ethic that the majority of her peers would have found difficulty in keeping up with. She had a paper round at twelve years old, worked in the local shop until fifteen then secured a position in the most fashionable hairdressing salon in St Andrews thereafter.

Malcolm was a successful business man. Doreen had been an extremely, efficient office manager. Surely between the two of them, some reasonably reliable genes had filtered through to Roxanne. Her hair-brained idea might actually work. Roxanne had spent a large part of their holidays hanging around the resorts' spas taking it all in. In the evenings, she'd babble on about what she would introduce to improve the overall experience for the guests. Neither of her parents had taken her seriously. Malcolm hoped it would work out for her.

In different circumstances, Malcolm would have been able to smooth things over with Doreen if she had found out about Angie but the problem was... Angie. He hadn't had the time to fix that particular complication. So far, Angie had succeeded in convincing Jen that both Malcolm and she had heard the commotion from the beer garden. She claimed that Malcolm had called a taxi earlier to take Doreen home and Angie had gone outside to tell him that the taxi was waiting on Main Street when they heard the fracas inside. It wasn't a lie – merely that the taxi had been summoned an hour earlier than Angie had implied and the drama had interrupted their love-making. Malcolm had had to pin Mark to the wall because he had gone berserk when Jen had disclosed Mark's dalliance with Roxanne. Admittedly, he had applied additional pressure on his daughter's lover's Adam's apple, with his strong forearm. A wee reminder to Mark of what he was capable of.

Jen was unaware that there was anything going on between Angie and him. Angie wanted it kept that way. Too many people now had a hold over him and Malcolm Patterson was not prepared to sit back and allow others to dictate what he could and could not do.

*

Angie and Maureen had taken to sitting at the back door for their morning break. Too many nosey parkers were lining up, at the front, to get the low down on Mark and Roxanne. It seemed that everyone and their granny wanted to know what would be happening to The Maltings now. Angie and Maureen were reluctant, for once, to share everything they knew. They were both heartbroken at the thought of losing their jobs and discussing the outcome made it all too real. Plus, a part of them felt an obligation to remain loyal to their bosses, especially to Jen.

'I think I'll look for another job,' declared Maureen.

'It'll no' come to that. Just sit tight for a wee while. The next licence renewal date is on the first of July. They can't find a buyer in a week. The earliest they could sell is three months away. A lot can happen in that time. Just sit tight. New owners are going to need us.' Angie sounded more hopeful than she felt.

A van drove through the car park and pulled up on the gravel in front of the two women who were sitting on the doorstep. Willie got out. 'For fuck's sake, nobody's died!' The two cousins attempted to laugh then resumed their glum expressions. 'Any news?'

Maureen answered first. 'Nut. Nuhin. Christ knows where Mark is this morning. Jen is up in the flat, packing. She's going to stay at her mother's for a few days. She's coming wi' me to the school show. Then I think she's leaving straight after.'

'Are they definitely selling?'

Angie took over. 'Not yet but they'll probably have to. What else can they do? According to Roxanne, her and Mark are flying over to Spain next week to find somewhere to stay.'

'Hey, that didnae take long. Had they been planning it?'

'I don't think so. Who knows? All I know is that it's in Murcia, La Manga, wherever the hell that is exactly, and Roxanne is setting up an up-market beauty salon for golfers' wives. A pal of Malcolm's will be her Spanish sleeping partner. Something to do with keeping it legal.'

'She lives in another world that one. How many times can you get yer nails done on one holiday?' quipped Maureen.

Angie decided that it was not the time to lecture Maureen on how bored, affluent women could easily spend a small fortune in a hotel spa.

'An' what aboot Mark?' Willie asked.

'Here's a laugh. Mark is planning to wine and dine corporate groups. To lure them, sorry, he said entice them, into staying at the golf resort. Apparently, it's very exclusive and expensive. Not for the likes of us. Cheeky shite. And wait for it... if that doesn't work, there's a BIG market out there for Time-Share properties. I mean... he is a VERY experienced salesman! It's what he used to do before he bought here. G&B, his previous employers, were bereft when he left.' Angie almost spat out the last sentence.

'Tae think I used to like 'im,' whined Maureen. 'What happened?'

'Folk are saying that Mark and Roxanne have been at it for months. Angie?' Willie knew that Angie must have known. Maureen wouldn't have been able to keep something like that to herself without telling him.

Angie shrugged. 'I guessed. But I never actually saw them. If Roxanne wasn't on the bar, she always had an excuse to come in. Sometimes she would bring in that wee skank from Falkland. She plied him wi' drink but that was just to throw folk off the scent. On other nights, she came in late then Mark would turn up and take over from me. I've clocked her car outside the shop loads of times. I think she slipped in when I left. There were lots of things... if you looked hard enough.'

'Ye never said nu'hin' to me! What for?' asked Maureen.

'It was none o' ma business.'

'It's a waste o' a guid business, that's what.' It saddened Willie to say it. 'I thought Mark would've made something of The Maltings. It could've been a wee goldmine. He should of made more of the rooms. That's where the money is. Looking back, he never tried hard enough. To think I put all that work into the window boxes and everything an' never took a fuckin' penny!... D'you think Jen might take it on?'

'You've got to be jokin'. Wi' her poker face?' scoffed Maureen. 'She's not got it in her.'

'You said that night at the barbeque that you could get to like her,' Angie reminded her cousin.

'Aye, but I was gubbed on sloe gin,' laughed Maureen.

'She could do it wi' you two behind her,' insisted Willie. 'Let's face it, you two practically run the place!'

That wasn't entirely true, as Angie knew, but she had already suggested the very thing to Jen a couple of days ago. Angie put forward a plausible and feasible plan. It was something that Maureen and she had discussed on many occasions, usually when they were pissed-drunk. It was one of those just in case this or that happened scenarios. With Jen on board, it would be a really exciting challenge. Angie had factored in child care arrangements, as that would be Jen's biggest concern. She had considered the workforce – permanent and part-timers; their roles and rotas, and how different members of staff could stay over if Jen was worried about being on her own when the rooms were occupied. The one thing she could not account for, was the funding. If Jen was not able to secure the finance or she totally rejected her proposal… then they were fucked!

SIXTEEN

Jennifer didn't hesitate when her mum demanded that she and the girls head over to Port Seton as soon as. Jennifer desperately longed for some T.L.C. Her mother would be unlikely to fulfil that specific need but her father certainly would. Four long, miserable nights had passed since Mark had made his announcement; that he and Roxanne had decided to go ahead with their plans to move to Spain. SPAIN! Just like THAT. How long, realistically, had these plans been brewing? A decision like that didn't evolve overnight.

'You have no fucking money!' Jennifer had screamed. 'How are you going to live?'

'Malcolm has offered to lend us some money. When we're on our feet, we'll repay him. Anyway, I have enough to get us started.'

'Enough for what? When was this arranged?' Jennifer grabbed his shirt with both hands and shook him roughly. When he didn't answer she pounded his chest with her fists. 'Answer me you big, fucking bastard. How long?' She was howling with rage.

Mark grabbed her firmly by the wrists: too firmly. It made Jennifer wince. 'There's no need for violence. DON'T do that to me again!'

Apparently, big-hearted Malcolm Patterson was prepared

to part-fund the move. 'Well, fuck Malcolm Patterson!' fumed Jennifer. 'Who died and appointed him as Patron Saint of Fornicators?'

'He is someone who is willing to support his only child's dreams,' spluttered Mark.

'Listen to yourself! What about your girls' dreams? I think that might be that their daddy doesn't run off with a young woman not much older than them!'

'Now you're being ridiculous.'

Malcolm and Doreen had felt the move would help Roxanne to grow up: give her a chance to put her life in order away from scornful, prying eyes.

'Tying her bloody legs together would have helped!' cried Jennifer

She had to concede that Mark was a willing and energetic player. Tying his straying dick in a bloody knot might make her feel better. Although, if her mother got her way, there would be nothing left that was worth knotting.

Jennifer would have fled Duneden sooner but the girls had important parts in their school's end of term celebrations. During the performances, Jennifer had been aware of sly glances and comments being made behind hands. Roxanne had taken great delight in sharing her news. Juicy gossip travelled quickly. Others, like Shona Blakeley, avoided any eye contact with her. That made it worse somehow. If either of their teachers knew of the change to their domestic situation, they'd been polite enough to refrain from questioning Jennifer further. Not even the school was exempt from the tom-tom drums. Maureen had sat next to Jennifer throughout, staring out anyone who blatantly scrutinised them. Her loyalty shamed Jennifer. Several times Jennifer squeezed her cleaner's hand apologetically. It was

Maureen's youngest son's last week at Primary School. After summer, he would join two of his older brothers in High School. When the audience was invited to join the children for tea and shortbread, Jennifer slipped away with Emma and Katie.

The girls were desperate to see Fergal as was Jennifer. At least, she could be guaranteed impartial advice. If her mother threatened to cut off Mark's balls once more, she'd swing for her. They couldn't hold a conversation for more than thirty seconds without Jennifer wanting to throttle her. Grace's constant interfering was making an intolerable situation worse. She had even visited Marjory Cameron at her home. Mark was livid. He'd told Marjory nothing of the separation and was furious that Grace had given her version first.

'Look, Katie!' yelled Emma, 'There's a train on the Rail Bridge.'

Two small necks strained from their seats to watch the carriages rumble over the Forth. Three huge, rusty, red diamonds spanned the mile long, watery gap from Fife to South Queensferry. The train sped through them heading north while they were south bound.

'I used to think the train went up and down the humps,' hooted Emma. 'Up and down, up and down.' Her hand dipped and rose as she explained the movements to Katie.

They giggled away for ages and Jennifer joined them. It was the first time she had laughed in days and it made her want to cry again.

They followed the coastal road, from Silverknowes, along past Leith and into Portobello then headed for Duddingston Village. The car could have made the journey on its own; Jennifer had driven that route so many times since moving to Fife.

The car bumped slowly along the cobbled street, past the

church and through the narrow gates that led to Duddingston Loch. If she had continued on this winding road, it would have brought her out to the Halls of Residence where Jennifer had lived for two years as a student before moving into a flat in the Marchmont area with three friends. It was through one of her flatmates that she first met Mark.

For once, luck was on her side. There was one space left in front of the loch and it was the closest to the church as well. They had decided to rendezvous at their usual haunt for lunch: at the Sheep's Heid. Emma ran on ahead, familiar with the way and the destination. She waited at the door and pleaded with her mother to hurry. Fergal must have heard Emma remonstrating and appeared at the entrance.

'Uncle Fergal, happy birthday!' Emma beamed at him, threw her arms around his neck and smothered him in several, dramatic, quick kisses.

''Thank you, Emma,' replied Fergal with bemused decorum but bursting with obvious pride as his little companion explained the great lengths that she and Katie had gone to in making his birthday card. There was a card for Hannah too. Emma insisted that whenever one of them was given anything then the other had to receive a little token as well. She felt sorry that Fergal and Hannah only had each other or the Camerons. That was not the case at all but it appeared that way to her.

Jennifer negotiated her way through the tables: not easy when laden with a dozy four-year-old and several bags. As Emma began reading the menu aloud, Jennifer flopped down beside Hannah.

'I could have carried those for you, if you had come in and asked!' Hannah scolded.

'I know you would have, thank you.' Jennifer planted a kiss on her frail, silvery cheek. She was afraid that one day her old friend's skin would dissolve at her touch, like a moth's wing might. She leaned over Hannah and greeted properly the impeccable but casually tailored gentleman beside her. Fergal had agreed to say nothing about the Mark situation to Hannah. She didn't need to know.

'Happy birthday, Fergal. You don't look a day older than you did a fortnight ago.'

'I don't feel it either,' he joked back.

'Right, you two, give Uncle Fergal his presents.'

Two eager beavers fought over who should hand them over to Fergal. Jennifer encouraged them to give one each but still ten pairs of excited fingers entwined with Fergal's as he grappled to open his gift.

'Girls! You'll break it!' warned Jennifer.

Fergal prized the rectangular package gently from their grip and unwrapped the gold tissue paper.

'I hope you like it. Fiona painted it for you.'

Fergal adored steam trains. It was one of his passions and one which he shared with Jennifer's Dad. Fergal's father and Jimmy Thomson had both been train drivers. Sometimes the pair of anoraks did a little train spotting together. Fergal stared at the painting, smiling and nodding with genuine approval.

'Thank you so much. The Flying Scotsman; a wonderful train and gift of course. Just champion. Your father has driven it. So fortunate. Pass on my regards to Fiona.'

Fiona was Jennifer's artistic, school friend.

'Granny and Grandad got you this. It's a bottle of wine,' declared Emma.

The bottle almost walloped Fergal's skull as neither of the girls were willing to let go first.

'They didn't need to do that,' Fergal protested meekly, pulling his head back to a safer distance.

'Och, they didn't pay for it,' explained Emma, 'Granny won it in a raffle. Grandad said it would do the job nicely.'

'They know you're a wine drunker,' chipped in Katie.' Every night.'

'Sorry, Fergal,' Jennifer apologised. Her parents, particularly her mother, said far too much in front of her ear-wigging offspring.

'Nonsense,' he chortled, 'no offence taken.'

And he meant it. Fergal was a member of a couple of prestigious wine clubs. He enjoyed a glass in the evenings but rarely had more than two a night. He would spend his holidays visiting wine regions all over the world and quietly regarded himself as a wine connoisseur. He joined Jennifer and Fiona on a bender one night. They polished off several of his finest clarets and suffered for it the next day. Fergal missed a day at the office; something he never did. One of the bottles cost thirty quid. That made it worse somehow!

During the meal the girls jostled to be near the birthday boy while Jennifer did her best to ensure that Hannah felt part of their conversation. Jennifer left most of her meal – no appetite. Fergal insisted, politely but firmly, that he would pay. Normally, Jennifer would've put up a good protest but, instead, agreed. Fergal looked concerned. Hannah gave her apologises for having to leave early. She'd booked a local taxi to take her to the Royal Infirmary to visit an old neighbour. The 'old' neighbour turned out to be eight years younger than Hannah. Jennifer waited with Hannah until the taxi arrived. Fergal left his parcels with Jennifer and walked hand in hand with Emma and his little Goddaughter to the duck pond.

'I've missed you,' said Hannah as Jennifer helped her into the taxi.

'And me you.' Jennifer squeezed her hand gently. Her old friend looked so wizened and dejected. 'I'll see you tomorrow, I promise.'

The girls and Fergal were feeding the ducks in front of the car parking area at Duddingston Loch. Katie was clinging to Fergal for grim death, wary of the larger geese mooching for some bread.

'Quick, Uncle Fergal. Throw them some bread,' squealed Emma as the geese sprinted towards her.

Her 'uncle' obliged. The geese squabbled over the meal scattered before them and a relieved Emma managed to shout, 'Thank you. Love you,' through the hysterical laughter.

Fergal's chest burst with pride. Emma looked so like her mother.

*

October 1975

Fergal Fitsimmons was enjoying his first wine of the evening when his doorbell rang; longer than was actually necessary.

He opened his door to a fiery red-head who stood to attention on his Bienvenue mat. She meant business. In fact, she had a proposition for him. An impudent proposition.

'Fergal!' she announced. 'Pleased to meet you at long last. I'm Jennifer. May I come in?' Without waiting for a response, she waltzed through to Fergal's living room and plonked herself on the arm of his leather sofa. (The layout was a mirror image of Hannah's flat.)

Fergal chastised himself for allowing an unknown entity into his home. He was rarely so careless. He did, however know *of* her.

He'd had his doubts about this young woman. She'd begun cleaning for Hannah, his old neighbour, months ago and Hannah seemed to be most taken with her. Full of praise, she was, for the young mother who turned up twice a week. Fergal pondered over what kind of girl takes a new born baby to work with her. And one that Hannah seemed to be showering with gifts. Even the girl's father (Jimmy) had started doing odd jobs around the place. His trusting, elderly neighbour was leaving herself open to abuse and deception.

'Please sit down, Miss...' He'd said most sarcastically.

'Jennifer'll do. And it's Mrs,' interjected Jennifer. 'Fergal. You don't mind me calling you Fergal, do you?' Two could play the sarcastic game. 'I'll get straight to the point. I can't get on with cleaning for Hannah because I'm too busy doing all your shirts.'

'My shirts?' guffawed the startled accountant.

Hannah had badgered her neighbour into allowing her to iron his shirts. Nine times out of ten, he'd had to redo them but it made Hannah feel important. Admittedly, since Jennifer took over, there had been no need to re-iron any of them.

'I don't think they belong to anyone else. Do they? Anyway, sorry, but you'll have to come to another arrangement,' explained Jennifer.

'What kind of arrangement?'

'Get someone else to do them or if you're really stuck, perhaps I might be able to help...'

'Ahh!' he interrupted. 'It's nothing to do with you making some extra dosh for yourself?' He made little attempt to disguise his contempt.

Jennifer glared at him. 'If you'd've let me finish! I was about to say until you find someone else. But... I'll tell you what. Rather than upset Hannah, I'll do your bloody shirts.' And without another word, made for the door.

Fergal couldn't fail to notice the distress on her pretty, young face. What an old fool! He followed her quickly and prevented her from opening the door wide enough to exit.

'I'm so sorry that was despicable of me.' Sincere regret was etched on his face. 'Can we start afresh? Please?'

Half an hour later, they parted as friends. The rest, as they say, is history. The two embarked on a mutual journey of trust and friendship. And payment, of course! Fergal had insisted that Jennifer should be paid for the shirts.

Mark never approved of Jennifer working, especially as a cleaner, and preferred to remain a peripheral observer to the trio's strange alliance.

*

Jennifer heard the shrieking as she hurried towards the duck pond. Fergal, all six foot one of him, towered above Jennifer's two. In many ways, he looked much younger than his fifty-nine-years. You'd never have put him and Jennifer's Dad in the same age bracket but then again, Fergal had no children and was unmarried. Jennifer's mother said children aged you. Huh! Her mother aged her.

Fergal had looked after his own mother for a long time until dementia forced him to put her into a nursing home. Maybe that was why he was so tolerant of Hannah. He had a handsome face. A thick mop of white, almost unruly hair gave him a boyish look.

Jennifer called to him and they brushed cheeks and kissed the air. He smelled of crisp exotic spices.

'Shall we walk?' he suggested.

The four of them crossed the road and tackled the steep steps stretching towards Arthur's Seat.

'Are we going to the top?' asked Emma.

'Not from here, we can't,' her mother replied. 'Take Katie's hand, please. And mind your dresses. You'll need them for the Gala.'

Jennifer's dress was similar to her daughters; cream with green stripes but she wore a short-sleeve, cream cardigan with hers. The girls walked on in front tucking into the sweets that Fergal had given them.

'How are you?' Fergal asked.

'Fine.'

'Fine? Your world has just fallen apart and all you can say is fine.'

Tears hovered on Jennifer's eyelids. She was frightened to blink in case it caused a tsunami again. Fergal stopped, unfolded a pristine, cotton handkerchief, dabbed her eyes, smiled and tucked her arm under his.'

'Do you remember when we first met? I thought you were a bolshie, little madam.'

'When did I lose my bolshieness, Fergal? When did I stop being happy and become so bloody boring? I can't blame Mark for everything. No wonder he was desperate to find someone else.'

'Nonsense. You've never been boring. And as for bolshie... well, I'm sure there's an abundance in reserve for later – especially for Mark,' he was teasing. 'So, Ms Bolshie, what are your intentions?'

'God!' She threw her head back. 'Where do I start? The Maltings is on the market and Mark's desperate for a quick sale. I'll have to move in with my mum and dad. Nightmare. Oh, Fergal, I had great plans for the place but I deliberately held everything back. For what? To spite Mark? To spite me? At least if I'd tried, I could've walked away with my head held high. Now I'll never know.' She was full of self-pity. 'What have I achieved since hooking up with Mark? I don't mean the girls… or you and Hannah… but me? I've done nothing.' She puffed her cheeks and blew out loudly. It was as if she were describing someone else's life and not her own. 'I just want this to be over. Finished. I hate him so much.' Tears flowed freely.

Fergal waited until the sobbing had subsided.

'Have you thought about buying him out?' he asked.

'You're the second person who's asked me that. With what? Plus I couldn't cope. Who would look after the girls?'

'Who looks after them at the moment? Not that dreadful specimen of a man? If you're not with them, you always have someone else organised. Because you cope. Better than you give yourself credit for. Better than that useless bugger back in Duneden.'

Jennifer had never heard Fergal sound so resentful about another person before.

'I don't have enough money. And, I don't want the burden of borrowing extra money either. You know me? I'm not a risk taker. At least I didn't think I was.' Jennifer was referring to her choice of men.

'What about a sleeping partner?' Fergal enquired.

'I don't think I'll have one of them for a long time,' she said, trying to smile at her own expense.

'Actually, I know of someone.' Fergal's smile broadened.

SEVENTEEN

Monday 1st August

'Spain again?' asked Mark's mother. 'It's only a few weeks since your last visit.' Apart from a one-off vacation to Vancouver, Marjory and John didn't holiday abroad preferring annual holidays to Jersey instead.

'I refuse to explain everything over and over again. If it's inaccurate information you want then phone Grace bloody Thomson!' spat Mark.

'Language! We are not in Duneden,' sneered Marjory. 'I did not appreciate Jen's mother turning up on my doorstep spoiling for a fight. It was frightful. Thank goodness your father was here.'

'You wonder why I wanted out.'

'You should never have opted in.' Marjory reminded her son. 'When are Pater and I going to meet this girl properly? I can hardly recall her face.'

'That's because it wasn't the place or the time for formal introductions. Roxie was the *PRETTY* young woman serving behind the bar. She is bright and smart... and this should meet with your approval, Mother, her family are successful and extremely wealthy.'

John Cameron lifted his gaze from his newspaper to study his son more closely. If this information was news to him, its content did not surprise him. Mark was much more ambitious than his brother but, unlike his brother, Mark was content to hitch a ride on the back of someone else's successes and hard work.

'I only want the best for you, Mark. To suggest otherwise is unfair,' huffed Marjory. 'What was so important that she couldn't pop in for five minutes before your flight?'

Mark wondered if he had ever liked his mother. 'I'll say it again. It wasn't possible or she would have done. Roxie is having her hair highlighted and a manicure somewhere on George Street. It's important that she looks her best when she meets with the owners of the resort tomorrow. We are meeting later at the airport. Did she not send you flowers and a card? Her idea, not mine.'

It was actually Doreen Patterson who had suggested that Roxanne send flowers to Marjory, with a card apologising for not having the time to meet before their flight and to insist she was looking forward to catching up with them when she returned.

*

Jennifer had a lot to do in the short time that Mark was in Spain. To give her a chance to fit it all in, the girls had been packed off to Port Seton to their granny and grandad's then they were spending another few days with their Auntie Fiona, who had a wonderful old townhouse overlooking North Berwick harbour; an apt location for two creative souls. Fiona was a reasonably successful artist while her husband, Walter, sold his wooden artefacts for hundreds of pounds apiece and some larger creations could fetch thousands. Although it seemed a lot of money, months of painstaking craft went into the larger pieces. The girls were enthralled when they were allowed to explore in his ground floor workspace. Customary safety rules and regulations were abandoned in North Berwick and Emma, in particular, embraced the freedom they were allowed there.

Jennifer had already met with her brother to discuss selling the cottage they owned together. He had intimated before that he was keen to buy an old flat to renovate and sell on then buy another and so on. There were plenty of properties in Musselburgh and Edinburgh that fell into that category. Some of the flats that he had been rewiring recently had rooms with no electricity at all, only gas. Many were on the market for as little as six thousand pounds. The siblings reckoned that their two-bedroom cottage was worth around seventeen to eighteen thousand pounds and they were hoping to walk away with at least eight thousand pounds each. When they inherited the cottage, Andrew stripped it back to the bare brick and completely rebuilt the inside, with a little help from friends. The finish was of a very high standard. He may have done all the work but Jennifer had provided the funds to do it.

Jennifer had to pinch herself. She was actually going ahead with it. At least, she was going to try. After her walk with Fergal on Arthur's Seat, they spent the next evening poring over their sums to see if Jennifer taking over The Maltings was a viable plan. When Fergal revealed that he would be willing to put in twenty thousand, Jennifer was gobsmacked. Her initial reaction was to refuse his generous offer. It was not up for debate; she would never risk her friend's money. Fergal insisted the risk would be minimal. He wanted nothing in return, only his original investment plus the interest that would have been accrued had he left it in a high interest account. That would happen when the business was sold or when Jennifer had the means to reimburse him: whichever came first. The loan would be drawn up legally to protect them both.

What Jennifer didn't realise was that Fergal's risk was not as great as she had assumed. Fergal was the executor of Hannah's will. Hannah and her husband Leonard, long deceased, had had no offspring and relatives were very distant. Leonard had been a keen dabbler in stocks and shares and he had accumulated a small fortune before he died. Hannah had instructed that a good portion of her estate should go to the two families who were her previous neighbours before she downsized and moved into the modern flat next door to Fergal. A generous sum would be given to her beloved Duddingston Kirk. However, a substantial amount of money had been set aside for Fergal and Jennifer. Jennifer had no clue as to Hannah's true wealth nor would she have ever presumed that Hannah would wish her to have some of it after she had gone. Fergal had been entrusted with this information and, although he would never have dared to divulge it to Jennifer, the least he could do was to help her in her hour of need. Plus, he knew a good business opportunity when he saw one.

The bank manager's first-floor office overlooked Princes Street Gardens and had an uninterrupted view of Edinburgh castle. It was an ornate room, with deep Georgian cornicing on each wall and a large chandelier hanging from the centre of an intricate ceiling rose. The large, old-fashioned desk and furnishings reflected a bygone era. Jennifer had expected a more informal office downstairs but suspected that Fergal's presence may have had something to do with the upgrade. Fergal Fitzsimmons was a senior consultant with Cunningham's, a prestigious accounting firm in the New Town. Fergal had attended a charity event in a much larger room on the same floor, the previous summer.

The evening culminated with everyone gathering outside on the balconies cheering enthusiastically as the spectacular firework display, in and around the castle, signalled the end of another successful Edinburgh International Festival.

Jennifer stood nervously and looked on as the bank manager shook Fergal's hand warmly and welcomed him like an old friend. He was a short, fat man whose suit was more C&A than Austin Reed. Fergal exuded city chic in pinstripe grey. The manager's chubby fingers were clammy to the touch. Jennifer hoped she hadn't grimaced as he gripped her hand. Though to be fair, she had rubbed her sweaty palms on her navy, shift dress before reaching out for his. Fergal explained that he was merely a bystander and was there to offer moral support as a sleeping partner, not that Jennifer would need it.

Jennifer calmly talked through her business plan and shared the history of The Maltings income and expenditure over the past year. They discussed at length how she would expand the business and increase the turnover. Jennifer insisted that her vision was manageable and achievable and at no point had she exaggerated her targets. After all, her personal investment would be almost as much as she was hoping to receive from the bank and she had no intention of squandering her hard-earned money on an ill-conceived plan. The last part had not been rehearsed with Fergal but when she smiled at him, he smiled back and nodded approvingly. When she had finished, she sat upright, crossed her ankles and placed her hands on her lap so as not to fiddle with her pearl earrings or to play with her hair which was styled in a neat up-do and secured with plenty of 'invisible' pins. She did not break eye contact with the man who was contemplating her future. When her confident smile faltered, she thought of her two girls and their happy faces – it helped, a bit.

'I can't believe I did it!' Jennifer stifled her urge to scream as they made their way down the elegant staircase and into the chequered-tiled lobby of the bank. 'At one point, I honestly thought I'd lost it. God, Fergal, did he actually approve the loan? I haven't imagined it? I'm shaking. Feel my hands.'

Although Fergal displayed little emotion during the meeting, he was as jubilant as his young friend. 'If you were not driving, I would propose a celebratory drink but perhaps we should save it for when the final deed has been accomplished. Wouldn't you agree?'

'It's a yes from me. Oh, Fergal, I wish I could go for that drink but I have to get back. But I promise, the next time I'm through we will definitely open a nice bottle of red. My treat.'

'Don't bring Fiona!' he joked. He had barely recuperated from their last encounter.

'Thank you, Fergal. Love you so much.' She hugged him tightly.

'And I you.' Fergal watched Jennifer dodge the crowds as she headed for the multi-storey parking at the east end of Princes Street. He longed for the day when he could publicly embrace his own long-term lover. For the moment, Jennifer and her adorable girls would suffice.

Jennifer dumped her jacket and handbag in the hallway of the flat. She made a quick visit to the loo and changed into comfortable sandals and a short sleeve cardie before heading downstairs. The lounge bar was busy but most diners were on their sweets or sitting with coffees and dwindling glasses of wine or cola. Immediately, she began clearing tables and chatting with her customers. There were a few familiar faces but many were passing trade. St Andrews was only a twenty-minute drive from Duneden and the main road was at the end of the village. The

Maltings had been a popular watering hole for those en-route to or from the historical seaside town: as famous for its university as it was for the golf. Memories of the Mediterranean heat wave were fading and familiar, unpredictable weather was the norm once more. It was a breezy, cool day in Duneden and if it was cold here it was guaranteed to be blustery and freezing in St Andrews.

Maureen looked pleased to see her. Jennifer was delighted to see how efficient Maureen seemed to be. She could clear several plates at a time without contaminating the clean cutlery or anything else on the tables. Perhaps she'd been paying attention after all or perhaps Jennifer hadn't given Maureen enough credit in the past. Angie and Maureen had a bad habit of conducting their own private conversation while serving customers – and not quietly either. They were not deliberately being rude but until Jennifer had flagged it up, they'd been totally oblivious. Jennifer encouraged them to engage more with visitors rather than gossiping with locals all the time.

Archie Hannigan had taken over Roxanne's shifts. Jennifer refused to have her back in The Maltings.

'If she steps over this threshold, I'll have her!' she warned Mark. It was no idle threat. He knew, first hand, how fiery a red-head could be.

Jennifer had taken on board her own misgivings when Angie had pointed out to Jennifer what rattled her and the rest of the staff about their female employer.

'It wouldn't hurt you to praise us where praise is due. Fair's fair. You're no' doin' us a favour by allowing us to be here. Aye, we need the work and sometimes it's bloody hard work for not a lot of money.' Angie had consciously not used the F word as it might have appeared too aggressive. She still wanted to work there, even for a paltry wage.

'Thank you, guys. Much appreciated,' called Jennifer as she closed the door behind Maureen and Archie after their lunchtime shift had finished. Angie was sitting on a stool at the bar when Jennifer returned.

'Well? Spit it out. You've been up to something the day. Is the pub sold?' Angie was keen to know.

'How about a wee drink first?' laughed Jennifer as she walked behind the bar. 'I'm having a large wine. And you?'

'I'll have the same. Medium for me.'

Jennifer filled up their glasses ignoring the 250 ml line. 'Do you have a driving lesson later?'

'Not today. And I'm night off tonight, but I only want the one.' Angie gestured towards her glass. She was meeting with Malcolm later and preferred to be compos mentis for her date.

'Me too. Archie is going to lock up tonight and I'll turn in early. I need to be on the ball for the next few days.'

Jennifer pulled up a stool next to Angie and took a deep breath. 'Remember a few weeks ago when you tried to persuade me to buy Mark out and I said no. Categorically, NO! Well, I've changed my mind.'

'Fucking hell, Jen. I was not expecting that. But how? You said that you couldn't afford it.'

'I know but things have changed. I had a meeting with the bank today and they said yes.' Jennifer clasped her hands in front of her lips as if she were about to pray and giggled. 'Honestly, you could've knocked me down with a feather. I thought the bank manager would laugh me out the door... but he liked my business plan and said the money was mine if I wanted it.' Jennifer omitted that Fergal was there and she withheld other personal details. There was a limit to how much she could entrust them with Angie. 'So how committed would you be if I decided to go ahead with it?'

'I thought it was sorted?' asked Angie.

'I've secured the finance but I have to be sure that everything else is right for me. I have to submit an offer. There will be a generous pay rise for you if you're happy to be the manager and I'll be able to increase Maureen's wages. Not by much. Certainly nothing like yours and I'm aware that we both have young children and we need a life too and it's a big commitment. God, Angie, I'm wavering already.'

Angie could see the initial euphoria draining from her boss's face. She cupped Jen's hands in hers.

'I need a challenge, Jen. I've lived all my life in Duneden and amounted to nothin', except for Bethany of course. This is the biggest opportunity that's come my way. I am so grateful. I'll do everything, I mean it, everything to help you. You'll be great, honestly. Willie will help all he can. He's fuckin' brilliant, by the way. Can turn his hand to anything. If you're asking for my honest opinion then go for it.'

'If I do this then I need an absolute promise from you that you'll tell nobody. Not your mum, not Maureen, especially not Maureen. I can't risk Mark finding out. The sale can only go through on condition that the licence is granted. I can't risk a late objection. PLEASE, Angie, you can't discuss this with anyone,' pleaded Jennifer.

'I won't. I promise.'

'We'll find out a lot about each other, you and I. Private things. Confidential things. We need to trust each other.' Jennifer studied Angie's reaction. Obviously, she would have to hold a lot back.

'I get that. I'm not a blab. Not like Maureen. You can trust me.' Angie hid behind her sincere smile and hoped that Jen hadn't detected any doubt. There was no way that she would be sharing any details about Malcolm and herself to Jen or anyone else.

'Let's sleep on it,' said Jen. 'If we both feel the same tomorrow then I'll put in my offer.'

'What if Mark turns it down?'

'Fat chance. I'll have it signed, sealed and delivered before his plane touches down in Edinburgh,' laughed Jennifer. 'Here's to us,' and she raised her glass high into the air, splashing some of the contents down her wrist.

EIGHTEEN

Friday 5th August

'Do you think we should wait for Mark to return?' asked the selling agent who was at the other end of the phone.

'No, I don't.' Jennifer insisted.

'I would feel more comfortable if I could discuss it with Mr Cameron,' he urged.

'How comfortable would you be if I asked another agency to deal with the sale?' asked Jennifer. There was a very long pause. 'Thought as much. Mark made it perfectly clear at our last meeting that if a reasonable offer was made and he was out of the country, he would trust my judgement. Do you have a record of that instruction?'

'Er... yes, we do... but it is the first offer that we have had. It's early days, Mrs Cameron, I'm sure if we just waited...'

Jennifer interrupted him. 'I appreciate your advice but I want to accept the offer on the table and I want to seal it today. You are fully aware of our circumstances and the sad state of our relationship. I want closure. If you don't want to handle the sale then I shall find someone else who does. Have I made myself perfectly clear?' His exacerbated sigh was tangible but Jennifer sensed that he would have no option but to concede. 'Good. I'll pop in later today to sign any papers.'

Jennifer replaced the receiver quickly; she did not want to dither. She was secretly satisfied with the way she had handled herself. Fergal had made the offer, the previous morning, through his friend Dom, a corporate lawyer and partner with a reputable firm in Atholl Crescent, in the West End of Edinburgh. Fergal had suggested their company name should be F.J&H. Holdings; Fergal, Jennifer and a wee nod to their friendship with Hannah. She liked that. Hopefully, neither Mark nor anyone else would make a connection to Jennifer before the sale. She would have to submit an application to the licensing board and prove that she was a 'fit and proper person' to hold a licence. Mark would have no knowledge of Jennifer's involvement until the licence was actually being granted. If Mark did twig immediately beforehand then it should be too late for him to do anything about it but meantime, she preferred not to disclose anything just in case he was mean enough to thwart her plans.

Jennifer had discussed her intentions with her dad, Jimmy, who was reassured by Fergal's association with the business. There was no need to bring Grace into the loop yet. Jimmy promised to stay over occasionally to give Jennifer a break. His daughter was extremely grateful but would only agree if it meant that she was not taking any of her dad's time away from Hannah. Grace (surprisingly) and Jimmy Thomson took over caring for Hannah when Jennifer moved to Fife. Jennifer felt guilty enough already, although she had spent and intended to spend as much time as she could on the other side of the Forth before October. Even Fergal was keen to stay over the odd weekend.

Knowing there was a credible support rota that could be called upon to stay overnight, should she need it, was a huge relief to her. She was ashamed to admit it but the thought of being in charge at night on her own scared her shitless. An over-active imagination was what her mother Grace would say every time Jennifer crawled into her sister's bed after watching a night time horror film. It was the dreams and nightmares. Jennifer had always had strange dreams.

Jennifer was helping downstairs an hour before lunches kicked off when she bumped into two men around her dad's age hovering at the front entrance. They were like a younger version of *Statler* and *Waldorf*, the two old codgers that shouted abuse from the viewing balcony on *The Muppet Show*: a favourite of Jennifer's. Only, these two were wearing smart, Mackintosh coats.

The smaller man with the white moustache spoke first. 'Good afternoon, Madam, would it be possible to speak to the proprietor if it's convenient?'

'That'll be me,' answered Jennifer. 'Can I help you?'

The taller, slightly younger man smiled. 'We're from the R&A,' he explained, as if the initials would be enough of a clue. 'The Royal and Ancient? We were enquiring about possible accommodation for next year's Open Golf Championship... at St Andrews.'

When it dawned on Jennifer what they were after, she apologised for being slow on the uptake and invited them into the lounge. Jennifer switched on the lights and they all sat around a table. They explained that they were in the area looking for rooms to accommodate golfers who would be participating in the qualifying rounds. Nearby Ladybank Golf Course would be one of the courses used in the qualifying matches and The Maltings would be an ideal base if that were possible. Jennifer established that neither of them were from Fife so reasoned that there was no need to inform them that The Maltings was up for sale as she would be the future owner anyway.

'We haven't been here for long and we do have a substantial renovation programme in the pipe-line as soon as the summer season has finished but I can show you the rooms if you like.'

Jennifer led the way and the two men tagged behind. She called to Archie, who was in the kitchen with Maureen, to keep an eye on things on the ground floor while she was upstairs. Maureen was covering for Angie and they had agreed to run with a reduced menu to help Maureen cope. Maureen and Archie craned their necks to get a good look at the two men. At the top of the staircase, five steps curved to the right and another five curved to the left towards the family's own private quarters. The R&A representatives followed her to the right, through a heavy, swing door and into the residents' corridor.

The guest accommodation was a large, grossly underused area. Mark had not actively encouraged people to stay. He felt that once the rooms had been upgraded, he would advertise The Maltings as an Inn. There were two double rooms, a twin room and two bathrooms – one of which had a separate toilet and bathing area. It meant that the toilet was free if the room with the bath was occupied and vice versa. The other bathroom had a ghastly, avocado suite with an olive, shag-pile carpet. All the rooms were a generous size. A smaller room was being used as storage space but Jennifer planned to clear it and turn it into a single bedroom. None of the bedrooms had been painted since the Camerons moved in but Jennifer had scrubbed them inside out and although they were pretty basic, they were scrupulously clean, as were the bathrooms.

The men were pleasantly surprised when they entered the wide, L-shaped corridor and one of them commented on the unusually long, Victorian sideboard. Jennifer had forgotten how grand it looked and it did add a touch of elegance as you entered the area. Jennifer apologised that she couldn't show them room two as it was occupied and had been for several weeks. She omitted the seedy details: no need to mention that her two-timing bastard of a husband had been kicked out from the family wing to the one opposite. They found the remaining bedrooms acceptable and neither of them commented adversely on the green bathroom. All in all, they seemed to be pleased with what The Maltings had to offer. Nor did the price put them off. When they asked about the cost, Jennifer added another ten pounds per night to each room and neither of them flinched at the price.

Jennifer made them a coffee and they finalised the arrangements. All the rooms were booked from the 14th July until the 18th July 1984. The Royal and Ancient would pay the deposits but the players themselves would be responsible for the balance and their own food and drinks. A cheque was made out to F.J&H Holdings and all future correspondence and enquiries would be conducted through Fergal's home address until further notification. Again, neither queried that request. Before they left, the moustachioed one gave Jennifer some advice.

'Accommodation for The Open is like gold dust. Everything is snapped up quickly. Hoteliers double, some even treble, their normal tariffs. You need to be part of it. Sell the rooms as a package – dinner, bed and breakfast from the 18th to the 22nd all inclusive. Make no allowances. No one will bat an eye. If you can, seek out a company that will take all your rooms over that period. Insist that everything is paid in full, weeks in advance. Trust me. They will be queuing up for your rooms.'

When they left, Jennifer was buzzing. It was too early to discuss it all with Fergal but she had to share it with someone.

Angie wouldn't be in until 6.00pm and so her pal Fiona got the short straw.

Later, Angie listened intently as Jennifer regurgitated everything that had been said and done that day. Every word, pause, look, movement and breath were pored over and shared with her future manager.

'Away upstairs and relax for a while,' Angie insisted. 'Have a long soak in the bath when you're getting the chance. I'll see you later. Don't come down until it's time to lock up.'

Jennifer took her friend's advice.

She felt chilled after her pampering experience and dosed for a couple of hours in front of the T.V.

Ten o'clock crept up quickly and the ritual began. Jennifer walked through all the rooms in the flat before locking the door then made her way to the wing opposite theirs. She tried all the door handles of the bedrooms and the store room to ensure they had not been left open and checked the two bathrooms were empty. When she was satisfied that no-one was there, she fastened the bolt at the top of the swing door. She continued downstairs, checking all the windows then shutting off as many rooms as was possible after making certain that no-one could have been lurking, leaving only the Ladies and Gents open. The long corridor downstairs ran from the front doors to the back doors, splitting the building in two; not equally. If someone stood at the front door facing the back entrance, the Gents and the lounge bar would be to their left. The Ladies, the staircase and the kitchen were on the right. The function suite was at the far right of the building. Jennifer headed up to the flat and waited for Angie to knock on her door.

Normally, when she locked up with whoever was on, she would close up the lounge, secure the back doors and check out the toilets before they left. Once the front doors were double locked and bolted, she would take to her heels and not stop until she was safely in the flat. The flat entrance seemed miles away when the race began. It was an absolute piece of nonsense and one that she was ashamed to admit to.

'I'm not phoning when I get in,' Angie warned her, 'I might pop into my pal's for a wee nightcap.' The pal was Malcolm and they would pop into his little, hideaway cottage tucked away at the end of a dirt track two miles outside Duneden. He called it his but and ben (the shagging shack was what Angie used to call it). Very few people knew of its existence and only a selected few had ever been there. Neither Doreen nor Roxanne had ever been told about it.

*

Angie had begun a heady affair in 1976 with the married Malcolm. She knew he would never leave his wife but she didn't care. She was a single mum and although she loved Bethany, there had to be more to life than watching *Bagpuss* and changing dirty nappies. Malcolm, seventeen years her senior, was a welcome distraction. He wined and dined her and splashed his money. Although she had known of him, it wasn't until she chatted to him at Freuchie Cricket Club, where she worked on a Saturday night, that they had become acquainted. After her shift, Malcolm would give her a lift back to Duneden.

One night they fucked in his car. She straddled him in the driving seat and as he buried his head into her breasts, she guessed he was hooked. For the next ten months they couldn't get enough of each other. Malcolm persuaded her to give up her wee job so that he could have her all to himself on a Saturday night. He had a cosy, secret 'shagging-shack' a short drive from Duneden and away from prying eyes. Angie was more than adequately recompensed. Neither of them discussed their clandestine relationship with another soul and as far as she could tell, it had remained that way. If they had been found out someone would have broadcasted it. However, after they returned from that fateful weekend in Newcastle, Malcolm refused to have anything to do with her and pleaded with (or it might have been threatened) Angie to stay away. She was heartbroken but resilient.

*

Jennifer's feet barely touched the ground as she sprinted upstairs to the sanctuary of the flat. The lights were on and the chat on the television helped to calm her down. She boiled some milk and stirred it into the hot chocolate that she had left on the worktop. She sat on her comfy chair with her feet tucked beneath her, sipping the sweet, milky drink. 'This has to stop!' she called out. Jennifer had contemplated a dog but Emma had always been wary of dogs and it wouldn't be fair. She sat for ages and drifted off to sleep.

She woke with a start. Had she heard something? She switched off the annoying tune replaying on the telly and tiptoed to the flat door. She pressed her ear against it, squeezed the knife handle in her fist and listened. Nothing. Except for the beating of her heart. After several long minutes, she sneaked to all the windows and cautiously peeked out from behind the blue and grey, Paisley patterned curtains: still nothing. The car park and beer garden were ghostly quiet. It was dusky dark, but the dawn chorus had started, indicating it had to be around four thirty.

Next, she lay on the floor in each room, ear to the carpet, straining to hear any noise coming from downstairs. Eventually, she gave up and went to bed. A plan was formulating; she had to break out of the obsessive, compulsive behaviour she was feeding each time she was left in charge on her own or she was never going to make a success of The Maltings.

NINETEEN

Wednesday 10th August

'I am fucking FURIOUS!' wailed Mark as he stood at the entrance of the flat.

'So would I be. Your hair is a disaster zone.' Jennifer was referring to the teenage highlights in his hair. What was he thinking?

'You know exactly what I'm referring to. BITCH!' He stormed past his wife and threw a large, brown envelope on the breakfast bar and began pummelling it with his fist.

'Come in, why don't you,' smirked Jennifer. The flat door slammed as usual.

'Don't get fucking smart with me… you know exactly why I'm here.'

The last thing Mark Cameron had been expecting to hear from the selling agent was that The Maltings had been sold. He had given them a courtesy call first thing in the morning after his late flight the night before.

'Coffee?' asked Jennifer.

'What is this?' he banged his fist on the envelope again. 'Why, Jen? To piss me off? You could have waited.'

His face was almost touching hers. She pointed her finger within millimetres of his nose as if daring him to come any closer. The pause seemed like forever then he took a step back.

'I need to move on,' stated Jennifer. 'It was a good offer and they want in for October.'

'A hundred thousand pounds! We could have got a lot more than that.'

'It's nine thousand more than we paid for it. You said that if a decent offer came in when you were... otherwise engaged...' She used the most derisive tone she could muster. 'Then I was to bite their hand off. Well, I did.'

'Yeeesss! But not the first fucking one. You're not that thick, Jen!'

'Well, I was thick enough when it came to you.'

Mark dropped onto the sofa and rubbed his hands over his head, ruffling his newly dyed mullet. Jennifer fixed him a coffee. She sat opposite him on the pine box next to the fireplace and waited for him to speak.

'Any idea who they are?' Mark asked. When Jennifer shook her head, he took that as a no. 'I think it will be The Longford Consortium... bunch of wee bastards.'

The Longford Consortium was a group of young, fool-hardy builders who had a reputation of being a bunch of bully-boys. They owned the King's Hotel in Longford and pubs in Cupar. Many of them had taken to sniffing around The Maltings before the deal had gone through. They would deny it of course but it was common knowledge that they wanted to tighten their grip on the Howe of Fife.

'I thought it might have been Malcolm.' Jennifer was hoping to deflect any notion that Mark might have an inkling it was her.

Mark raised his eyebrows. 'If that had been the case, I would have made sure that I'd been here.'

Malcolm had seemed relieved when Mark had told him that there was no way that Jen would have tolerated him as a business partner. It was Roxanne who had suggested it. Surely

Malcolm hadn't considered taking on The Maltings as sole owner without consulting him?

'Daddy!' cried Katie and she sprang on to his knee. The girls had been playing in Emma's room.

Emma was less keen. Although Jennifer had tried to shield her from the fallout, it wasn't easy to protect her from all the gossip and all the shouting. Emma sat on her mother's lap and buried her head into Jennifer's chest. Mark and Katie looked on.

Jennifer nudged Emma's chin up with her fingers. 'Just because Daddy and Mummy are having grown up problems, it doesn't mean that we don't love you and Katie. You two are the most important people in the whole wide world to us.' Jennifer did the tickling-trail game all over Emma's body and finished on her tummy. 'We love you... all the way up to the moon... way beyond the stars and sun... and all the way back again.' Emma laughed and Katie jumped off Mark's knee to join in the fun. 'Give Daddy a big cuddle then go and get ready. You two are going to that new burger place in Kirkcaldy. Yeah.'

While the girls gathered their belongings, Jennifer put the finishing touches to her eye lashes and lips as she stood in front of the long mirror in the hallway. Even from behind, she looked fabulous – and sexy, which surprised Mark. Her hair was piled roughly on top of her head and a navy shift dress hugged her waist and hips. He had to admit, there was something different about her. He wondered for a moment if there was another man. Nah. She was too sophisticated for the dickheads around Duneden. Mark's stomach flipped again. The Spanish Project? Nerves or excitement? He tried not to dwell on the answer.

It was not a direction he'd planned; it had just happened. Roxanne was a flirt. He'd flirted back, expecting no more than the odd shag here and there, not a full-blown affair. It was a 'what if' remark that he'd made to Roxie in bed one night that sealed his fate. Jen had been staying over at her mother's in East Lothian with the girls when he'd suggested running off to Spain and starting up a business of their own. He hadn't really meant it. Roxie took it literally. She was like a child who'd been given the keys to Disney. It was all she could talk about for weeks. It had been far too late to backtrack.

*

Ten Years Ago

Mark's godparents owned and lived in a large steading only a twenty-minute walk from the beautiful, historic 'Old Harbour' in La Rochelle on the South West coast of France. Although Mark had taken a two-man tent with them, Aunt Alice had insisted they should stay in the main house with her and Uncle Gilbert.

After a few weeks, Jen suggested they should move on. She'd overheard Alice and Gilbert squabbling over how long the leeches intended to languish under their roof. Mark insisted that Jen had misinterpreted their conversation as he'd always had a close relationship with his godparents but felt it was too early into their trip to argue. At least they had saved ten weeks spending money.

For the next six months, they drifted through France as they made for the southern coast and carried on along into Spain, picking up odd jobs here and there; some fruit picking and bar or café work. On the final leg of their journey, they ended up in Lloret de Mar on Spain's Costa Brava; paradise in the mid-seventies for those Brits who had never been abroad before.

If you looked much more critically, it was no more than an elongated building site that stretched along the Spanish coast in either direction. If they hadn't crossed paths with Stan and Peggy Stokes, they would probably have been back in Edinburgh months earlier and maybe, just maybe, Jen wouldn't have fallen pregnant.

They had arrived in Lloret two days prior to finding Stan's wallet on the beach. Initially, Mark was all for taking the wad of notes before leaving it on the doorstep of the nearest police station. Credit cards etc were of no use to them. However, a prick of conscience (Jen) swayed his decision. The wallet was returned intact to Stan, a retiree from London, who was determined to reward their honesty. Stan and his wife Peggy looked after several of the rented apartments on their small complex close to the beach and next to many of the large hotels that had sprung up all over the area in the last few years. One of the holiday lets would be empty for the next fortnight and as long as the young couple were frugal with the electricity and gas, Stan could see no reason why they couldn't stay there free of charge. The apartment was basic but luxurious compared to some of the places they had dossed down in when they couldn't pitch the tent. They managed to scrounge another four weeks.

When their freebie was almost up, the Stokes had a proposition for them. Peggy would have to return to the U.K soon for an operation (women's problems) and would Mark and Jen be willing to act as temporary caretakers? Rent free and with a small allowance to boot. Stan had originally planned to remain in Spain but if their new friends were willing to run the place, for eight weeks to ten weeks say, then he would catch up with family and friends while Peggy was recuperating. No cleaning would be required as a squad of locals were already in their employ. They would only be responsible for ensuring the properties were fit for purpose and for the handing over and collecting of keys. Caught up in the holiday mood and the prospect of stretching out the adventure at no cost to themselves, they required little coaxing. Jen secured a job at the nearby Flamingo Plaza Hotel as a Kids Klub rep for extra money. All in all, it was an easy call.

The day Peggy and Stan returned; Jen had her pregnancy confirmed.

'Do you love Jen?' Stan had asked Mark.

'Absolutely.' He wasn't one hundred percent sure. A baby didn't fit in to his future plans.

'Then that's it. Peggie will organise the wedding.'

'Whoah! Let's think about this,' replied Mark, choking on his words.

Four weeks later and four days before flying home, one of Peggie's pals conducted the ceremony and the reception was held at The Flamingo on one of their party nights. They selected a ring each from the many that had been left behind at the apartments and had never been reclaimed. Jen had never replaced her ring and Mark rarely wore his, claiming that it could get caught too easily on crates and pallets at his work. Fortunately, the photos showed a happy, contented crowd.

*

'Off anywhere nice?' he asked, as Jennifer slipped on a white denim jacket, and then wished he hadn't.

'No.' Her reply was clipped yet a hint of 'yes, I am actually,' hung in the air.

TWENTY

As Jennifer looked out over the calm waters of the Forth from South Queensferry, the clear blue sky reflected in the glass-like surface. It looked like a photograph – but she wasn't fooled. She knew that beneath the facade, the treacherous currents in the Forth were weaving and twisting towards freedom: the North Sea. Jennifer had always been drawn towards the sea in time of need, probably because at twelve years of age she ended up living in a fishing town. She'd lost her virginity behind the open-air pool in Port Seton to some Danish scout on sabbatical, two days before her sixteenth birthday. She couldn't remember his name only that he was kind, gentle and inexperienced, like her. There was no way that she was returning to school after that summer with her 'ha'penny' intact.

There was a cool, sea breeze and Jennifer was grateful for her jacket and scarf. The white made her arms appear quite brown. In her youth, she used to sport the pink lobster look but the pigmentation of her skin seemed to change with each pregnancy, allowing her to tan a little more easily.

She was pleased with the progress she had made in such a short time. She was referring to her farcical night time carry on. She still locked up all the areas that she could, as that was only sensible, but once she was on her own, after staff and punters had gone, she forced herself to walk slowly around downstairs;

no scurrying. Only a slow pace and keeping her breathing steady.

The night before the girls returned, she did it in the dark. It was terrifying. Once she was back in the flat, she went straight to bed and played a music tape quietly to mask the usual creaking sounds an old building makes in the night. Strangely and thankfully, she wasn't as frightened while the girls were there.

The Rail Bridge towered several hundred feet above her and she decided to turn round and head back towards the promenade where she had arranged to meet Bob Gregson at twelve-thirty. She was lingering at an exhibition set up by the R.N.L.I. when a familiar voice called her name.

'You look bloody fantastic!' announced Bob cheerfully.

'You too,' she fibbed.

'Hardly.' And he patted his expanding midriff somewhat proudly.

Bob Gregson worked for Gordon and Blair Brewery and North East Fife was part of his area. Mark had run their Eastern Division for two years before his promotion to regional manager. Jennifer had met Bob and his wife at numerous G&B outings; the last one had been at Gleneagles. Bob's wife, Ella, was a tall, cheery soul – a female version of Bob, except that Ella had more hair. He dabbed his flushed, sweaty face with a white handkerchief. Wet patches were forming all over his blue and pink striped shirt.

'Is it hot or just me?' he panted as the two of them crossed the road, parallel to the sea front, to a café that Bob frequented regularly.

They sat in a quiet corner. Jennifer ordered a white wine spritzer and Bob a fresh orange and lemonade. Surprisingly for a drink's rep, Bob didn't like alcohol. His wife joked that she made up for it but Ella rarely had more than two during a night out.

'So, you've bought the stupid bastard out then?' asked Bob.

Jennifer had explained the scenario on the phone when she'd contacted him last Friday. 'He doesn't know yet and I'd like to keep it that way.'

'What the hell's got into him? A beautiful wife and two gorgeous bairns. What more does a young man need?' Bob took a huge gulp of his juice. 'He needs a good kick up the arse. Doesn't surprise me though.'

Jennifer was a little flummoxed. She had always presumed that Mark was popular at G&B.

'Why? Did he flirt when he stayed away?'

'No, nothing like that. At least not in front of me. No, your Mark always wanted more. And he was a grasser. Told tales. Who was doing what. Who wasn't where they should have been. Caused a lot of tension and bitterness among us oldies. We were glad to see the back of him when he moved up then moved on.'

'Everybody seemed so friendly. I didn't realise.'

A young girl cleared Bob's drink and he ordered another. Jennifer had hardly touched her glass.

'Oh, don't get me wrong, he was good enough at his job; the master of delegation. And he was a good laugh. Kept us entertained. I don't know how he remembered all those jokes or where he got them from but the young ones liked him.'

'But you didn't?'

'I kept on the right side of him. I can't say I wasn't disappointed when he went to Calsco for his beer. He was getting a really good deal with us. It was like two fingers to his old team and everything the brewery had done for him. Striking a deal with our rivals? Nobody could fathom it.'

'Well, that's why I'm here. I'd like to go with G&B. I trust you to look after me, Bob.'

Although The Maltings was a freehold and would remain one with Jennifer, it was customary to order the majority of the beer and lager through one brewery. Customer loyalty would be well rewarded and that's why Jennifer had chosen Mark's old employers. Bob went over the details. He could give Jennifer an incentive 'loan' of ten thousand pounds for five years. The 'loan' would reduce by two thousand a year as long as all the beer, lager and cider were purchased from G&B. After five years the brewery would consider the loan paid. If the pub was sold within that time, then Jennifer would be expected to repay a percentage of the loan back. Bob threw in the usual accessories: drip mats, bar towels, coasters, ice buckets, glasses, a new sign and some free stock.

'I could do with a new fridge. Oh, and some tables and chairs and umbrellas for our beer garden.'

Bob laughed. Jennifer knew the score and he was happy to oblige. They shook on the deal or at least squeezed on it. Bob held Jennifer so tight she could barely breathe. She thanked him profusely. He would be an asset to her.

*

Doreen Patterson was in her element entertaining Mark's two young girls. They were making cakes and both girls were up to their elbows in flour. Doreen had fashioned aprons from two old tea towels and some safety pins.

'Can we take some for Mummy?' asked Katie.

'Of course, you can,' answered Doreen, 'but we have to measure everything very carefully or there won't be any cakes worth taking.'

'I'm good at measuring,' declared Emma.

Mark, Malcolm and Roxanne sat in the dining room; a long room that had a butler's gallery separating it from the kitchen. In front of the large window, at the far end of the room, was a dining table that could seat twelve people comfortably and at the opposite end of the room was an entertaining space dominated by an enormous black, marble fireplace. Malcolm and Mark sat on Harris Tweed, high-back wing chairs while Roxanne stretched out on a grey chaise longue. Mark had wanted to be in earshot of the girls but, in all fairness to Doreen, the girls were perfectly happy in her company.

'Roxanne was telling us before you arrived that the resort seemed really pleased with her ideas for the place,' said Malcolm.

'They've made her a job offer. Which is a start. Ideally, we would have preferred to have been setting up our own salon but for now, it's a way in. Hopefully, it will give Roxie an insight into what the women out there really want.'

'And what about you, Mark? Any job offers for you?' Malcolm found it difficult not to leap over the coffee table and wring his scrawny neck.

'Things are looking good. I'm really pleased with the contacts I've made in La Manga.'

'Mark was invited to dinner at the professional's house but we couldn't go as it was the day we were leaving. Apparently, Seve Ballesteros's brother was going. We were gutted but he said that we must go the next time we're out,' explained Roxanne.

Malcolm had to concede that Mark had the self-belief to

pull it off. He had an aura about him. His good looks and confidence helped.

'Is it true? Has Jen definitely sold The Maltings without your consent? Can she do that?'

Malcolm's question had Mark rattled. 'That'll be a yes, unfortunately. I honestly thought that Jen had more upstairs.' He stood up. 'Sold for a fucking song!'

Roxanne threw Malcolm a 'don't you dare' look and patted the space next to her for Mark to sit down. 'Forget it babe, we don't need her bloody money.'

'It was my bloody money!'

Malcolm didn't have all the information but from his understanding he assumed that they would have been in it together as a partnership. He doubted that Jen would have had the authority to sell The Maltings without Mark's agreement. Mark had taken his eye off the ball.

'Do you know who's bought it?'

'Jen actually thought it might be you, Malcolm. It's not you, is it?'

'Christ, no!' He laughed. 'What the hell would I want a pub for?'

Malcolm decided that Jen had much more upstairs than Mark had given her credit for. Never underestimate a scorned wife or girlfriend.

TWENTY-ONE

Monday 3rd October: Licence Day

Mark and Roxanne had just finished breakfast at Orchard House.

'Sit down, Mark! You're making me nervous,' scolded Roxanne.

'What time is it?'

'It's five minutes after the last time ye asked.'

Mark sat back down at the dining table. He was on his third cup of coffee. He checked his watch: 8.45am. They didn't have to be there for another hour and fifteen minutes. Malcolm wandered into the room. His hair was still damp from his shower. He'd gone out for a morning jog earlier, something he rarely had time for on a Monday but he had decided to take the rest of the day off to accompany Mark and Roxanne to County Buildings in Cupar. Today was the day the licence was to be transferred.

'Good run?' asked Doreen as she placed two boiled eggs and a rack of toast in front of her husband. Doreen claimed she had already eaten when Malcolm asked if she was joining him. Malcolm kissed the back of her hand and said he'd had a refreshing run. A light drizzle of rain hadn't put him off. 'Has Jen packed yet?' Doreen wanted to know.

'She says as soon as the licence has been granted to the new owners and the money is in the bank, the removal men will move in. With luck, the girls will still be in school when it does kick off.'

'It makes sense in a way. I would hate to have to pack all my belongings only to find it had been a waste of time,' said Doreen.

'It won't come to that,' insisted Malcolm. 'Unless they are known to the local police or have a criminal record there will be no reason to withhold the licence.'

'Or if they don't come up with the money... What?' said Doreen when she caught Malcolm glaring at her. She was only stating the obvious.

Mark was perfectly aware of the licensing laws but he had a bad feeling about it all.

'Was the pub busy last night?' Mark asked.

'Very,' replied Malcolm. 'I think everyone was hoping you would make an appearance. A lot of people were disappointed.'

'More likely, they were hoping to find out who the new owners will be. They'll have to wait. According to Jen, who appears to be privy to information that I'm not, they are planning to open, for drinks only, on Friday evening. Talking of which, did Jen show?'

'She did. For about an hour. She bought everyone a drink and left money behind the bar for anybody she had missed.'

'That was a first.'

'Angie had everyone warned that Jen did not want or expect gifts but a few of the women got her something anyway, I think.'

*

Fergal parked his white Mercedes in Fluther's car park – a five-minute walk from the County Buildings. The large, parking area was exceptionally busy and they were lucky to find a space. Fortunately, they were early. Jennifer sat in the front beside Fergal while Angie sat in the back with a cardboard file of important paper work on her knee.

'Do I need to remind you of what we agreed?' said Fergal. 'Mark might surprise us and be perfectly happy that his estranged wife happened to purchase their property at a very opportune price. Or, as we are expecting he will be...'

'Totally hacked off!' Angie mocked Fergal's accent.

'Indeed,' Fergal agreed. 'And if he is, we must remain calm. No matter what he does or may say to goad Jennifer, we do not retaliate.' He looked over at Angie who was sitting behind Jennifer.

Angie held up three fingers of her right hand and crossed the thumb and pinkie. 'Guide's honour.'

'Right,' said Jennifer. 'Let's do this!'

Angie and Jennifer put up their umbrellas to ward off the light shower and Fergal donned his Trilby. All three set off together.

A young, blonde woman met them at the top of the stairs. 'Good morning, ladies. I'm Anita-Anne Telfer and I'll be your legal representative today should you require my services. Angie thought that Anita-Anne looked like a lawyer in her smart, black suit and crisp, white shirt. It's exactly what Angie would have chosen to wear.

'Fergal, I've to let you know that Dom asks after you.'

Fergal smiled. 'Thank you, Anita. Likewise.' Fergal had organised for his friend's legal firm to be on standby. Anita-Anne had an in-depth knowledge of the hospitality industry.

Anita ushered them to a more private area of the foyer. 'Proceedings should be straight forward. Your licence is twelfth on the list.' She handed them a programme of the proceedings. 'Might be a long wait but I don't foresee anything that would warrant my intervention. The Chairman of the Licensing Board will ensure that there are no objections from say the police or fire service then, Jennifer, you will most likely be asked to make yourself known to everyone. Local councillors will then deliberate and once satisfied the Clerk will grant you your licence. Do you have any questions?... Good. Shall we?'

The four of them entered the hearing.

Angie nudged Jennifer when Mark, Roxanne and Malcolm came in. Mark acknowledged them with a nod and they sat several seats away to Jennifer's right. Both husband and wife knew that the other would be attending. There were about forty people in the Sheriff's Court altogether. The Chairman of the Board sat on the 'stage' area while the Clerk (the council's lawyer) was seated at a table facing him. His table was strewn with folders of legal documentation that he would have to refer to if needed. At a long table to the Clerk's right were the local councillors. Jennifer spotted two of them smile at Malcolm when he entered. At an even longer table situated to his left sat all the applicants' legal representatives; Anita was positioned at the end nearest the Chairman. Two policemen in uniforms sat near the doors at the back along with a Fire Officer. Jennifer prayed that they were not there to pass judgement on The Maltings. All the applicants and others were facing the Chairman in rows at the front of the court. Jennifer knew that Mark would be trying to suss out where the future owners were sitting so she avoided eye contact with him or anyone else. The programme only listed The Maltings and F.J&H. Holdings as item 12: nothing that would implicate Jennifer. Existing licensees and those applying for extensions of some kind were the first groups to be discussed.

The Chairman informed the meeting that they would retire

for a late lunch after the next hearing. Angie dug her nails into her boss's hand when the Clerk called out that The Maltings would be heard next. Fergal gave Jennifer's other hand a reassuring squeeze. One minute she was concentrating on what was being said and the next she was being urged to stand, as the new applicant, to allow the councillors to see her. She hoped her brown trouser suit had been an acceptable choice of clothing – business-like but not overly so. It was then that she stared at Mark. He appeared truly and utterly bewildered.

'What's going on?' asked Roxanne as they pushed their way past the occupied seats. You could only leave court once your application had been granted or refused. 'I don't understand. Who's the new owner?'

'Jen!' hissed Mark and Malcolm in unison.

'Why didn't you object?' Roxanne was confused.

'Trust me. I was so close but we can't risk losing the sale now. Where is the fucking bitch?' snarled Mark.

Mark scrambled after his wife and her companions as they disappeared from the County Buildings. He shouted for her to stop. Jennifer looked over her shoulder but walked on.

He grabbed her roughly by the sleeve of her jacket. Jennifer stumbled. She swung round to face him.

'What just happened in there? You... you played me like a fucking fool and I fell for it. You tricked me. You lied to me.'

Mark's face was puce. He was spitting as he spoke through clenched teeth and more worryingly his index finger was dangerously close to Jennifer's face as he emphasised every word with a short, stabbing motion.

Malcolm intervened. 'It's not the time or place, son. Come on, let's go.'

'All those months, when I was worrying how you and the

girls would cope and all the time you were planning this. How could you, Jen?'

'Worrying? You couldn't give a damn about me or the girls. You have NEVER asked, not once, how we would manage. You were too scared to ask. As soon as I said I would move back in with Mum and Dad that was it. Sorted. So don't you stand there pontificating to me. Mark Cameron is only interested in one person. Mark Cameron!' Jennifer turned away.

'Yeah, off you go with your poncy pal and slag of a mate. This is not the last, Jen,' Mark called after her. 'You'll be hearing from my lawyers!'

'Leave it!' Malcolm had a firm grip on Mark's arm.

Jennifer strode directly to the car and only stopped when she reached it. Fergal opened a door for her then another for Angie. Once they were all inside, Jennifer started to cry, for a good few minutes.

'I'm sorry. I know we should be celebrating but that was hard. Why do I feel so terrible?'

'I'm no' a doctor or anything but I would say it's shock. It does that to you. I was bitten by a dog when I was in my last year at school and I cried all day after it. Couldn't stop. I was told I was in shock,' explained Angie.

Neither Jennifer nor Fergal had an appropriate response to Angie's psychological analogy.

When they pulled up outside The Maltings, Jennifer's good spirits had returned. Fergal fetched his luggage from the boot; he had decided to stay over. Emma and Katie had planned a 'video night' for them all and Bethany had been invited to the sleepover too.

'Can you believe it's yours yet?' asked Angie as she stood shoulder to shoulder with Jennifer facing the black, double doors at the back entrance. An ethereal mist hovered above the trees and shrubbery in the beer garden behind them and settled on the River Eden.

'Not really. Seems surreal now that I'm here.'

'I feel I should offer to carry you over the threshold,' said Fergal with an impish grin.

'Let's walk in together,' said Jennifer and she linked arms with her two friends. 'Oooooh! I feel like *Dorothy* entering the woods with the *tin man* and the *scarecrow*. *Lions and tigers and bears, oh my!*'

'Oh aye! I'll be the fuckin' *scarecrow* nae doot. No' got a brain,' laughed Angie.

*

Malcolm Patterson poured the four of them a stiff whisky each. Doreen was waiting patiently for an explanation. 'Are we celebrating or not?'

'Yes and no,' said Mark.

'Well, I'm bloody celebrating. CHEERS.' cried Roxanne and she raised her glass to toast Mark. 'The Maltings is sold. You will get your share and we are moving to La Manga. It's what we wanted.'

'I wanted my fair share. I deserved a fair share and now that bitch is sitting over there,' Mark stood at the patio doors of the music room and gestured his glass in the direction of The Maltings, 'laughing at me. Conniving bitch!'

'I doubt very much she's laughing. I think she'll be thinking *what the fuck have I done.*' said Malcolm, topping up all the drinks. 'How is she going to run that place properly without you and two youngsters to consider? She can't. No, it's not your problem, Mark. She's dug a hole for herself and she'll have to dig her way out.' Malcolm hated sounding so callous at Jen's expense but he needed Mark to pull himself together – loose cannons were dangerous.

'I agree with Dad. She done it to spite you and ended up spiting herself.'

'Didn't you speak up?' enquired Doreen.

'No licence. No sale. We were too far down the line. She deliberately tricked me out of several thousand pounds and saved herself a small fortune.'

At no time did Mark show concern for his two girls, noted Malcolm. It was all about the money.

The same thought was playing out in Doreen's mind.

'Surely as her husband d'you not benefit from The Maltings, in some way, further down the road?' enquired Roxanne.

'No more than she would from our Spanish project, honey.'

'God, I hope not.' Roxanne looked worried.

'Anyway, that won't happen. We're not married.'

'NOT MARRIED?' squealed Roxanne. A little tune in her brain was already playing *Here Comes the Bride* as her wedding dress wafted in a Caribbean breeze.

'That was a ploy to keep the parents off our backs when we found out Jen was pregnant. We staged a fake ceremony and party. Nobody knew. We had plenty photographs to back it. We thought that we would marry legally when we returned to Edinburgh but never got round to it. Probably for the best.'

TWENTY-TWO

Thursday 6th October

The inside of The Maltings looked like a building site; it wasn't quite but it looked that way to Jennifer.

'Do you think we should postpone the opening until Saturday?' Jennifer asked Willie Ross.

'Jen, dinnae get your knickers in a twist. It looks worse than it is. All the major work is finished. We're just about to clear a' this rubbish,' Willie reassured her.

His workmates began sweeping up the mess in the hallway.

Maureen and Angie had persuaded Jennifer to tear down the wooden, folding panels that separated the lounge and the pool room. Opening up the area had made a huge difference to the natural light; it flooded in, even on a dull day, and it hadn't been the massive task she had envisaged. The pool table would be tucked to the side during service then wheeled out again after food had been served. Willie had made a smart, wooden covering for the top for when it wasn't in use.

Jennifer, Angie and Maureen had been working flat out since Tuesday; painting, cleaning and labouring for Willie and his workmates. Joe Blakeley had insisted that Willie should concentrate solely on The Maltings for the rest of that week and he would help out in the evenings. The majority of the work required was mainly cosmetic but it needed a lot of man power in a very short space of time. Jennifer's brother Andrew had assessed what would be required from him weeks ago and had all the materials in place ready to tackle some rewiring. They would all concentrate on the entrances, corridors, the toilets and the lounge bar for now. Jennifer wanted an immediate visual impact when the locals stepped through the doors tomorrow evening.

Two of Maureen's sons and anyone who had a spare five minutes had helped the women with the painting. Martin and Ryan Ross were both attending local colleges. Every wall had been painted white. All the doors and skirting boards had been sanded down and stained with a light oak. A back breaking task. In the hallway, below the dado rail, Jennifer had reluctantly agreed to Maureen's recommendation of navy. It looked great and complemented the existing, busy blue carpet – a necessary requirement for the footfall walking through the long corridor. A plain carpet would show every speck of dust. Joe Blakeley said that his dad was reasonably sure that there was original flagstone flooring in the lounge and it ought to be in good nick. When Willie and Andrew pulled back the bottle green carpet, sure enough, he had been right. And, it was in excellent condition. The consensus of opinion was to go with it. It had scrubbed up well. The blue theme had been continued into the lounge.

The seating that stretched the length of the long wall and the short wall to the left as you entered would be covered (next week) in navy velvet. The remainder of the stools and chairs would be finished off in the navy or other shades of blue; to be peppered here and there. Ideally, Jennifer wanted to have all the seating in the lounge reupholstered before the launch but that would not have been possible in the time available. A local company in Cupar had agreed to do it the following week. Meanwhile, they were stuck with the original faux leather.

The females voted for a modern version of the navy and white Ramsay tartan for the drapes. Instead of dressing the three slim windows, on the long wall, with a pair each, Maureen suggested hanging one substantial, single curtain at either end of the trio and running a tartan pelmet the full width above them. The large bay window overlooking the beer garden was styled in a similar fashion. Thanks to Maureen and Willie, the effect was stunning and seemed to elongate and widen the room.

Friday 7th October

Jennifer's mum and dad collected the girls from school. Andrew was tightening up the wall lights in the corridor. Maureen and Jennifer were wiping down and polishing the tables. Angie and Archie, the barman, were preparing the bar and gantry for the launch when Hannah, Jennifer's old friend, toddled in. She leant on her stick which emphasised her stoop, hidden beneath a pale, pink twin set. Her sensible walking shoes buckled slightly at the heel and insteps and her burgundy tweed skirt almost touched them as she shuffled along. A fluffy, white cloud of hair softened a well-loved face.

'Is it safe to come in?' she cooed.

'Just in time for a cup of tea,' replied Jennifer. 'Sit down here and admire our handy work while I make the rest of us coffee.'

Hannah marvelled at the transformation; the difference from yesterday was remarkable. When Fergal had called in on Wednesday to say that Jennifer had taken over The Maltings, without that pest of a husband of hers, Hannah couldn't have been more proud; if a little apprehensive. She jumped at the chance to be present at the opening. Jimmy and Grace picked her up on the way across and they were all staying over for another night. Hannah had only been at The Maltings once before with Fergal but Mark had made them most unwelcome. Neither she nor Fergal were in a rush to return.

'Coffee, anyone?' called Jennifer to whoever was within earshot. She placed a tray of mugs on a table and Ryan followed behind with a huge, silver coffee pot. Jennifer handed Hannah her tea in the best mug she could find.

No sooner had they gathered round the table when two excited girls raced into the room.

'Watch the coffees!' Jennifer stood up to shield the table with the pot and mugs on it.

Poor Hannah was forced to abandon her tea to go and inspect the girls' bedrooms; she hadn't had the chance before they had set off for school that morning. Their grandad retrieved Hannah's cup and followed them upstairs to aid his elderly friend. He had so much more energy after recovering from the surgery on his legs.

'What do you think?' Jennifer asked, admiring the decor. 'Ignore the brown seating, obviously! Try and picture the blue.'

'Aww, Jen, it's beautiful,' admitted Maureen. 'It's hard to believe it's the same room.'

'Maureen, you have a gift. You visualise things that I, for one, can't see. Thank you so much.' Jennifer rose from her stool to where Maureen was sitting and wrapped her arms around a valued member of her team.

'Don't get me started. You'll mak me greet.' Maureen rubbed her damp eyes with the tips of her fingers. She thought that Jen looked vulnerable – like a wee girl seeking approval from a grown up and felt guilty about all the rotten things she had said and thought about her in the past.

'Right!' announced Angie. 'Let's give ourselves half an hour to get everything done. Archie and me'll finish stocking the bar. Maureen, you can dust and hoover the corridor and Jen you wander about and see that you're happy with everything. Ryan! Get yer arse in here. I need you to give that flooring a final wash. Put in some Zoflora. It makes it smell nice.'

It was time. No going back now.

Jennifer's family, Hannah and Fergal commandeered a table on the left of the lounge. The staff gathered for a quick pep talk from Jennifer before the doors were opened. Their uniforms gave them a professional edge. Angie had had the final say on the colours: black trousers and white shirts. Three quarter length sleeves for the girls, short sleeves for the men (keeps them cleaner when hands are constantly in and out of water and stops them dipping into food). A small firm in Strathmiglo had embroidered a logo on the front of their shirts. The words, 'The Maltings', were stitched in black in the shape of an arch with a sheaf of golden barley beneath the writing.

Jennifer began her pep talk. 'We agreed no drinking on duty. You can save all your drinks and have them at the end of a shift or keep them for an evening off. However, tonight will be a one-off exception. Please don't abuse it. Try and not eff and blind in front of our customers. Help each other out behind the bar and don't leave one person to do all the work. Martin, it's your first big shift, enjoy it. Ryan, you are on the glasses. Do NOT accept a drink.'

'He better fucking no'! Oops sorry about that,' interjected his mother. He had only just turned seventeen.

Jennifer continued. 'I just want to say a big thank you to all of you for your support this week. It means a lot to me and my girls. Good luck and enjoy your evening. Angie, you are out front with me. No hiding behind that bar. Oh, and before I forget... don't we look smart in our uniforms?' She beamed at her staff. She was genuinely proud of each and every one of them.

Archie volunteered to open the doors. Everybody else had chickened out! Willie and Joe were the first to burst in. By eight o'clock, the place was heaving.

Everything was going really well. Jennifer and Angie were mingling with the crowd, topping up the bowls of nuts and crisps on the tables; by doing so, it gave them an excuse to approach people for a chat. Jennifer looked over at her mother and indicated it was time for them to take the girls and Hannah upstairs. Andrew's girlfriend had driven over from Port Seton to join in this time. Jennifer's friend Fiona and her husband had decided to wait until next week so that they could help out with the girls. All her family and close friends were rallying round her. She knew she was lucky.

'No *Grease*?' Joe poked fun at Jen.

'Not tonight,' laughed Jennifer. 'Got me into a lot of trouble last time.' It was Jennifer's turn to blush.

'Pity, you were good.'

Just then, Brian Munro, a local farmer and husband of Jennifer's friend approached. 'Jen, meet Horse, a good friend of mine.'

'Horse? Why do they call you that?'

'Cos I'm hung like a fucking stallion.'

'More like a miniature Shetland pony,' mocked Brian. 'Jen, this is Alan Clydesdale, gamekeeper for Eden Estate. He wants to put a wee bit business your way.'

It was a much bigger proposition than Brian had indicated. Alan needed bedrooms for the many shooters he entertained on a weekly basis. Some were here to shoot geese others were his gentlemen shooters who were keen to bag some pheasant and partridge.

'What are we talking about? How often and how many?' asked Jennifer.

'I could fill all your rooms most nights now and until the season finishes at the end of January.'

'Bloody hell, I was not expecting that.'

Alan explained that a local hotel had let him down at the last minute and he was desperate for accommodation. All his other hotels were full. Most shooters came for four days but foreign groups would stay for a week. The geese boys went out before daybreak and wouldn't require breakfast but the others were more likely to set off after breakfast.

'They are really good guys all vetted by me. There would be no trouble. They spend a lot and are usually easy to please. What do you think?'

Jennifer didn't hesitate. 'Absolutely. Can we discuss it all properly tomorrow? It's a lot to take in.'

'Nae bother, I'll be in. See you at ten tomorrow morning.' Alan gave Jennifer a broad smile and a cheeky wink. With his crew cut hair, crooked nose and broad stature, Horse did look a little intimidating – he had the look of a gangster's minder; albeit in smart, country farming clothing.

Before walking off, Brian leaned in. 'He's a pussycat really, Jen. He's got a great family. Adores his grandkids. He's a good guy to have on board.'

How about that for a piece of networking! Jennifer was blown away with what had just been offered. Before she had had a chance to process it all, Malcolm and Doreen breezed in, followed by Mark and Roxanne. Jennifer had not considered for one minute that Mark would show his face nor had she prepared for it. She needn't have worried. Within seconds of their arrival, Andrew and her dad were by her side.

'Jennifer,' whispered her dad, 'you can do this. Be pleasant. He is the father of your children... and look around you. Everyone here, is here because of you. Don't give them any gossip for tomorrow.'

Jennifer hugged her father; wise beyond words. Andrew broke the ice and walked up to Mark to ask how he was doing. He deliberately withheld his hand as that might indicate to Mark that all was forgiven. It was not.

Next, Jimmy Thomson sidled up to the four of them. He knew who they were, not personally, but Jennifer had talked about them so often, he felt as if he did. 'Thank you for coming tonight. Can I get anyone a drink? Mark?' Mark visibly squirmed but politely refused as they had already ordered. 'The place looks great, doesn't it? They've been working all the hours. I can't tell you how proud I am of Jennifer but I suppose most dads feel the same. It's Malcolm, isn't it?' Jimmy extended his hand to shake Malcolm's.

Sly, old bastard, thought Malcolm, shaking Jimmy's hand. He had put them all firmly in their places but in a polite manner. Jimmy excused himself and slipped off as quickly as he had appeared.

'What if she says something?' asked Roxanne. 'We should leave.'

'She won't.' Her father assured her.

Malcolm watched Jennifer as she worked the room calmly and efficiently, ensuring that at no time was she near Mark or Roxanne. If she did get close, she always had her back to them. He had to admit, the place had been transformed; it appeared bigger, cleaner and smarter. Jen had done remarkably well in such a short time. Comfortable, smart surroundings made people feel better about themselves. Malcolm felt that life had taken a turn for the better for him too. He had been able to convince Mark that his frolic with Angie had been a one off. Mark had no reason to disbelieve him and it was never mentioned again. Plus, he felt sure that Mark needed him more than he needed Mark Cameron. The loved-up pair were due to fly off to La Manga the day after tomorrow. Malcolm was looking forward to having their house to themselves again. He would miss Roxanne as she was good at occupying her mother but he detested the way that Mark had become too familiar with the ins and outs of Orchard House and those who frequented it.

Angie caught his eye and smiled. It didn't linger but there was warmth behind it. Although Angie must have known about Jen's plans months ago, she had never once let them slip or even hinted that something was in the offing until the evening after the transfer. Angie could be trusted; that was a pleasant and unexpected surprise. There was an air of confidence surrounding Angie these past few weeks, he had noticed. She had passed her driving test and Malcolm had helped fund the yellow Mini she had chosen. She was very animated the previous night when she had shared all her ideas about taking The Maltings forward while lying in a bath with him. Malcolm not only found it endearing but being around Angie made him feel young again. Her sexual appetite more than matched his and he began counting the days, hours even, when he could see her again. With Mark and Roxanne gone, he would be able to arrange more trysts with Angie without the worry of getting caught out. He had deliberately avoided discussing his past with her but felt he had left it long enough. He would choose his moment: soon.

*

December 1976

Everything had been swimming along nicely. Angie had provided Malcolm with everything that his wife, Doreen, could no longer deliver. He'd had other lovers, naturally, but Angie was in a league of her own. The sex was something else. At one point, he actually believed he loved her. She had said it to him so often that he had convinced himself that he felt the same and so when she had pleaded for him to take her to Newcastle, he reluctantly succumbed. He had always promised never to return to that part of the North East in case someone recognised him.

When a carefree Malcom and Angie had been sauntering along Sandhill, arm in arm, near the Swing Bridge, an old ghost from his youth had barked, 'Sid, is that you?'

Malcolm had been yanked unceremoniously to confront the consequences of his past. Then, he bolted, just as he had done all those years ago. The loved-up pair returned immediately to Duneden whereupon Malcolm dumped Angie, on the pretence of his wife's poor health. He never discussed that encounter with Angie ever again. He'd shut it off completely until that night, in the bar, when Angie had called him Sid.

TWENTY-THREE

Sunday 9th October

Cup in hand, Jennifer sauntered to the back door of The Maltings. It was early. Her time. Just as she liked it. The last of her visitors had gone home and the girls were having a lie in. His unexpected appearance as she opened the door startled her and he was lucky that the hot coffee didn't end up all over him.

'Mark!' It took his wife a few seconds to recover. 'What do you want? The girls are still in bed.'

'It's you I'm here to see. I knew you would be here. Can I come in?'

'I'd rather you didn't.' Their altercation outside the courtroom still unnerved her. 'Say what you've come to say then please leave.' She was expecting another woe is me outburst.

'I didn't want to leave it like this. Us like this. I've come to apologise. For my behaviour. For everything.'

His voice was soft, sultry. It threw her. She stared into her husband's eyes. Tears welled up then trickled down her face. She brushed them with the palm of her hand. It was futile. Others replaced them.

'Don't cry, sweetheart. I'm so sorry.' Mark carefully eased the hot drink from her slim hand and placed it on the doorstep. He kissed her wet eyes.

Jennifer melted into him. He wrapped his arms around her and held her tightly. Jennifer's legs buckled. She was done.

Her tears soaked his shoulder as she snuggled in. It seemed like hours but could only have been seconds. A minute at most. His warm mouth found hers. It felt good. Natural and very familiar. Yet somehow, during that delicious embrace, the memories of the past few months hit her. Flooded in. All she could think of was Roxanne's tongue searching for Mark's. She pulled away.

'You hurt me,' she simpered. 'Really hurt me.'

'I know. If I could take it all back, I would. Jen...'

Who knows what might have developed if Maureen hadn't crunched her way round the corner. The moment was gone. Jennifer jumped back.

Maureen looked shocked. 'You okay, Jen?' She flashed Mark a warning glare.

'I'm fine. Thanks, honey. Mark was just leaving.'

He hesitated briefly then shrugged and kissed Jennifer lightly on the cheek.

'Bye, Jen. Take care.'

'You too.'

Maureen slipped past her boss. 'I'll fetch you a fresh coffee and give you a wee bit of peace and quiet,' she said intuitively.

Friday 23rd December

Eleven weeks had passed since Jennifer took over The Maltings. They had been busy. Busier than they could ever have envisaged and they were knackered. At some point during the first few weeks, one of the threesome, Jennifer, Angie or Maureen, would moan about being overwhelmed and overburdened with the amount of work and organisation that they had taken on. It was Maureen's Willie who pointed out the obvious.

'The three of you are here all the time. Nae wonder you're exhausted. Get it sorted!' After lots of tears, hugs and alcohol, an amicable solution was reached and a flexible rota that suited all three of them was agreed.

Maureen and Jennifer took turns to do the cooking at lunchtimes and on Friday and Saturday evenings to give Angie a break. If any of the shooting parties needed a meal in the evening, it was pre-ordered in the morning and prepped, if possible, during the lunchtime shift. Even Archie Hannigan had been coached in a few basic dishes to enable him to step in if required and he was also happy to help with breakfasts. Archie was now a full-time member of staff and along with Angie and Maureen, he plugged any staffing gaps. They were all capable of covering any department. Apart from the cooking shifts and odd bar stints, it was a logical decision to have Jennifer floating. It allowed her to spend quality time with the girls especially at bedtime. A local, responsible sixteen-year-old girl was recruited as chief babysitter. She was able to study while the girls were asleep. Jennifer used the time when her youngsters were at school to work through The Maltings 'to do' list – it never shortened. There were three columns; urgent, soon and maybe. It was amazing how quickly the 'soons' ended up under the urgent heading.

They had agreed not to open at all during the day on a Monday or Tuesday; the winter months were quiet and didn't warrant opening up for the odd passing trade. Although their residents were free to come and go. It gave everyone much needed breathing space and would be reviewed at the end of February. A new cleaner had been taken on to help Maureen and to help Jennifer with the rooms. Some local youngsters (including Ryan Ross who was training to be a chef) helped in the kitchen and to serve food at the weekends. Something that worked really well was the evening bar rota. Several locals had requested the odd bar shift; for one night a week or even one night every fortnight. Many had opted for a set day. When Angie notified them of their shifts for the following fortnight, they could swap with anyone in that pool. So far nobody had let them down. Jennifer made a point of popping downstairs at the end of an evening shift if a younger member of staff was on duty but often Willie or Joe would insist that they would wait and lock up with them to save Jen.

Horse, the Eden Estate gamekeeper, had booked out every bedroom until the end of January. If all the beds were in use, The Maltings could accommodate up to six people. The shooters came from all backgrounds and from every corner of the globe. Jennifer's initial reservations about keeping guns on the premises were quickly allayed. Horse had strict protocols in place and all guns were stored under lock and key.

The Northern Ireland groups were particularly raucous and the Maltese were exceptionally quiet. Four criminal lawyers from Alabama recounted some blood-curdling murderers they had prosecuted.

Two surgeons from Great Ormond Street hospital and their pal Pierre, a celebrity chef, seemed incredibly hard to please or converse with, to the point that Jennifer was going to ask Horse not to allocate them to The Maltings again. Then lo and behold, they turned up with a huge box of Christmas goodies to be shared amongst the staff with a card thanking everyone for the best stay they had ever had in Scotland. And, as with many others, they planned to return before the end of the season.

Horse was particularly pleased with the hospitality that had been shown. The Maltings, he explained, was part of the overall package. If the shooting was poor, either because the geese were not where the guides were expecting them to be or the weather conditions were dire (not that the weather was a huge deterrent for the hardies), the accommodation and food could make or break the experience. The Maltings staff went above and beyond. Jennifer allowed those who were going out before dawn to use the kitchen to make some toast and fill their flasks with coffee or tea. The guns would have to be in position before the geese left the loch at daybreak to seek somewhere to feed for the day. That early morning flurry of flight was the ideal time to take the shot. When the group came back, usually around eleven in the morning, a full breakfast would be waiting for them. For good measure, a free breakfast would be thrown in for any of the guides. Their presence at night meant that Jennifer felt safe enough to be on her own with the girls. Most of them were in bed by eleven-thirty as they had an early start and Horse had asked them to be mindful of Jen and her wee ones.

Willie and Joe had been working behind the scenes since day one. They had reconfigured the hallway inside and outside Jennifer's flat. The bedroom and bathroom that used to be Mark's and hers could now be accessed without having to enter her family space at all, allowing either a member of staff or a guest (paying or otherwise) to have a bedroom outwith her own private area. However, by closing the landing door, the spare bedroom and her family rooms were automatically reconnected.

The girls now had to share a bedroom but that didn't seem to bother them and Jennifer slept in the other one. She preferred being closer to them. A new much smaller bathroom had been installed in a cupboard between their two bedrooms. Jennifer had never seen such a dinky bath. It reminded her of one that had been in a hotel in the Latin Quarter in Paris when she had back-packed through France with Mark. Although, she hadn't intended to rent out the new guest room regularly, there had been several occasions where she had had to use it to accommodate Horse's overspill.

One of the double bedrooms in the residents' wing had been converted into a twin room and an extra single bed had been put in the other larger double room making the rooms more practical and profitable for groups like the shooters. Unfortunately, the bedrooms had not yet had a fresh coat of paint. That would have to wait until the spring.

Tonight, was the last night of opening before Christmas. Everyone was looking forward to their Christmas break; four whole days of relaxation. Five shooters were booked in from the 28th to the 31st. Angie and Maureen had been desperate to host a Hogmanay Ceilidh on old year's night. It would be a great way to end the year. The Edendale Ceilidh Band hadn't been booked by anyone else and Angie claimed that was a coup. Another four days of nothingness would follow. Jennifer and the girls planned to stay with her mum and chill.

Maureen had invited Jennifer and the girls to her house at five for mulled wine and mincemeat pies. Emma and Katie had started referring to Maureen and Willie as Auntie and Uncle because Bethany did. No amount of explaining that Bethany was actually related to Maureen deterred them.

There was one hurdle to jump before that. The meeting of the out-laws.

John and Marjory Cameron had driven over from Edinburgh with Christmas presents for their granddaughters. They made their way into the lounge bar laden with gifts. John apologised and left again to collect more bags from the car. The two women stared at each other. Their exchange of greetings was stiff and awkward. Thankfully, John returned fairly quickly and both Jennifer and Marjory used his presence to reduce the need to interact with each other. John embraced Jennifer as he always had; less of a bear hug more of a tentative squeeze. The bar had quietened down. A few customers sat at the opposite corner chatting over their coffees. Festive songs played softly in the background. The silver and white decorations were the ideal accessories for the navy and white furnishings. The room twinkled – oozing Christmas charm.

'Will you be staying for a coffee?' Jennifer asked.

'We were hoping to see the girls.' Marjory stifled the squeal in her throat.

'They'll be here any minute. Angie's mother's dropping them off.'

'Perhaps the girls shouldn't see their presents,' urged Marjory. 'John could help carry them upstairs for you.'

Jennifer wanted neither of them anywhere near her personal space. Fortunately, Ryan popped his head round the door before she could reply.

'That's Mum and me finished, Jen. See you later.'

'Ryan! Before you go, do me a wee favour. Put these bags through the back for me. I don't want the girls to see them.'

'Aye, nae bother.' He scooped up all the bags, by hooking the straps in between his fingers and carried them out the door.

Maureen sang from the corridor, 'Cheerio. See yous later.'

'We're looking forward to it, honey.' Jennifer tittered – more so at the bemused look on Marjory's face.

'You've done a sterling job with the place and the uniform... very good,' said John.

'I thought you might have gone for something more...'

'More what, Marjory?'

'No matter. There are also parcels from Mathew and Elaine and Mark asked me to buy some special pieces of jewellery for the girls from him. Please make sure they are handled carefully. They're easily identifiable by the wrapping and ribbon.'

Jennifer wanted to shout *FUCK OFF, MARJORY* but grimaced instead. There had been a deafening silence when Jennifer asked if her out-laws had any indication as to when Mark might be back on Scottish soil. Mark had made very little effort to keep in touch. Their emotional encounter before he had set off for Spain had long been erased from her memory.

'How about that coffee?' suggested John.

Jennifer ordered a pot of coffee and some tablet to be brought to them and gave Archie the thumbs up to disappear upstairs for a while. He would open up again while Jennifer was at Maureen's soiree. John helped Marjory with her long, camel coat and brown felt hat. The beige, turtle neck jumper and matching woollen skirt were a typical Marjory outfit. Jennifer thought that Marjory had put on a little weight. *Post menopause,* she grinned. John revealed a grey, Christmas jumper with a snowman on the front when he unbuttoned his heavy, black overcoat. Jennifer had never seen him wear anything as 'frivolous' before.

'For the grandchildren,' he explained when he saw the look of surprise on Jennifer's face.

'They'll love that, John.'

And in they came like Christmas whirlwinds. Both Marjory and John seemed pleased to see their granddaughters. Jennifer reckoned it had been early September since they had last met each other. Marjory had not once condemned Mark's actions preferring to skirt around the issue when the conversation centred on him. It was the girls that were seeking some kind of explanation not Jennifer. The adults' conversation was polite and controlled unlike the youngsters who were full of chatter and high jinks. Marjory reached into her bag for cards. Two large cards were handed over to the girls and a much smaller one was placed on the table for Jennifer.

'It was difficult to choose the right words,' said Marjory, 'now that we know.'

She was obviously referring to the non-marital status of Mark and Jennifer's relationship which had been blabbed to everyone by Roxanne.

'Funny, I thought the same.'

John Cameron could sense the change in atmosphere and decided to end the visit on a high by asking the girls to sing them a Christmas song before they had to go home. They needed little encouragement and blasted out *Rudolf the Red Nose Reindeer* with all the Christmas cheer they could muster. It certainly filled the room with goodwill.

Once the Camerons had gone, Jennifer changed into red jeans and a cream, fluffy jumper. The girls chose red polo necks and black, sparkly skirts and tights.

Their breaths cooled into little, white clouds in the cold, December air as they walked round to Maureen's house. The three of them were well wrapped up in cosy duffle coats and hats, scarves and gloves. Tiny speckles of snow fluttered around them but the ground was too wet for it to lie. Jennifer held their hands tightly. It was the first time in ages, that she felt the Christmas spirit sneak in.

It didn't surprise Jennifer to see that Maureen's garden had lights in the trees and bushes but she was taken aback when she stepped through the front door. In fact, she was awe struck. From the outside, it was a typical stone-built, detached cottage but the inside was like something from a Norwegian interior design magazine. The hallway was huge and spacious. The most beautiful wooden flooring flowed into all the rooms leading off. An unusual knitted troll held a placard reading 'deposit your outdoor shoes here' and a grey basket was positioned to receive them. A real Christmas tree bedecked in white baubles and snowflakes dominated the space. Two separate doors opened from the hallway and two of Maureen's boys shouted, 'Hiya, Jen,' before kicking them shut again. Facing the front entrance were double patio doors that led to the biggest kitchen area that Jennifer had ever seen. White shaker style cabinets filled the wall on the right-hand side. A large rectangular, stand-alone unit, that housed a sink, was in the middle of the room; it was centred more to the right. Maureen referred to it as an island. Deep wooden worktops completed the look perfectly. To the left of the island, was a long, wooden table with benches on either side and beyond that, against the faraway walls, were two light grey, leather sofas festooned with an array of grey and white textured cushions and throws. The back garden could be seen through another pair of patio doors. A well-lit pathway meandered through the shrubs and lawns. It looked like a fairy glen. Magical.

'Shut yer mouth, Jen,' laughed Maureen. 'You might catch a fly.'

'Maureen, you have the most beautiful home. It's absolutely stunning.'

'We don't spend our money on anything else. My passion is my house. Willie's is the garden. Come and see upstairs.'

At the far-left-hand side, an open wooden staircase stretched to the upper level. Glass panelling prevented you from falling off the steps: one of the leather sofas was directly underneath.

The lounge area upstairs was equally impressive. Jennifer walked across a plush, cream carpet to admire the view through the ceiling to floor window.

'You need to see it in daylight. We're so lucky.'

Lucky? thought Jennifer. It was breathtaking. Before they had left Edinburgh, friends of Mark's had bought a new Cala home near to the ski slope that were selling for over one hundred thousand pounds. It was the first time that residential builds, in estates, had crossed that benchmark. That Edinburgh house couldn't hold a candle to this Duneden home.

The hullaballoo downstairs indicated that Bethany and Angie had arrived.

'I'm not stopping,' shouted Angie clumping up the stairs in her stocking soles. Angie was on evening meals and would have to leave shortly. She sank into one of three white, leather sofas. 'Well, what do you think?'

'Gobsmacked. I honestly am!'

'I ken. Everybody's the same when they see it for the first time. It's fuckin' gorgeous. You should see their bedroom.'

Maureen poured some steaming wine into three goblets. The girls were screaming downstairs while Jamie, Maureen's youngest son, chased after them wearing an elf mask.

'Cheers,' said Maureen. 'Here's to us. Wha's like us? Help yourselves to some pies.'

A fluted plate of short-crust pies sat on a long pane of glass supported by a large piece of sculpted wood: it was a piece of art that her friend, Walter, would've been happy to have created.

'Who designed your house, Maureen?'

'I came up wi' the ideas and Willie built it for me. I love the Scandinavian vibe.'

'I'm blown away. It's truly beautiful.'

The craftsmanship was top notch quality. Every inch of the house oozed attention to detail.

'Willie's uncle left us this cottage before we got married. It's taken a long time to get it like this but it was worth it. I love it.'

Jennifer was humbled. It was a true saying; never judge a book by its cover. Jennifer Cameron had judged Maureen on her appearance and everything else that she had taken umbrage with. Yet, here lived a member of her staff, in the most stunning environment, and Jennifer would never have made the connection. She had been unkind; a fool and a snobbish brat.

'Come and see,' beckoned Maureen. 'It's snowing.' Bi-folding doors opened up onto a balcony that overlooked Willie's pride and joy. A garden that would dignify any stately home.

'I wish you the best Christmas ever,' said Jennifer. 'Thank you both so much.'

They chinked their glasses as the snow settled on a winter wonderland.

TWENTY-FOUR

Wednesday 28th December

Angie and Malcolm lay naked, spooning in bed at his but and ben. The silhouette of their long, lithe bodies bathed in the warmth from the coal fire. The shadows of the flames danced on the ceiling and walls. The small cottage was much bigger than Malcolm's nickname for it: it was comfortable and cosy, if a trifle old fashioned. Its function suited them perfectly. Angie was not required at The Maltings until the next day so didn't feel guilty that they were languishing in bed on a dark, cold Wednesday afternoon. What else was there to do?

She pressed against Malcolm and could feel him unfurling behind her. She pushed a little harder until he groaned in her ear. He slipped his hand over her leg and in between her thighs.

'You're wet,' he murmured.

'Always.' It was Angie's turn to moan. She eased her top leg over his.

He swapped hands to enable him to stimulate his lover with one hand and her breast with the other. Her nipple grew hard and lengthened as he gently nurtured it. As the caressing intensified, Angie's body writhed and stiffened as she beckoned him to enter her again.

'Please,' she urged.

Malcolm obliged. His hands gripped her hips tightly as he penetrated deeper. Their grunting and wailing reached a crescendo and somewhere, lost in the moment of the heady thrill, Malcolm blurted out that he loved her. Then, as their moans of gratification abated, they relaxed, exhausted, listening to the inhaling and exhaling of their breaths until they were silent. When Malcolm slipped out to the bathroom, Angie douched with a damp, lavender-smelling face cloth that she kept in a little box by the side of the bed. On his return, Malcolm recognised the perfume and smiled. She was full of considerate surprises.

They lay for a while, neither of them speaking, but both lost in their thoughts. Angie was cooking later: surf n' turf, a rare steak for Malcolm and medium for her. Cooking for her paramour gave Angie a real feeling of belonging.

'Did you mean it?' Angie asked, facing the man with whom she had been meeting secretly for months.

'Mean what?' He knew she would ask.

'That you loved me.'

Malcolm considered his reply. 'Do you know what, Miss Lennie? I actually do.' He kissed her gently on the mouth, neither of them closing their eyes in case the other gave something away. They smiled.

'Would you like to go on holiday with me?' he asked.

'Where?'

'You choose.'

'I can't think. I've never been outside Scotland or England.'

'Somewhere in the Caribbean?'

'You have to be kiddin'. I couldn't afford that.'

'Angie,' Malcolm tilted her nose up with his, 'let me worry about that.'

'How would you explain it to Doreen?'

'Easy. A boys' golfing week. We've gone to Barbados before.'

'It would look conspicuous if we went on holiday at the same time.'

'Not if we each had a plausible reason.'

Angie snuggled in. Perhaps 1984 held more than she could ever have dreamt. She hoped so.

'Can I ask you about something else?' she hesitated. 'When were you Cyril Rose?'

Malcolm should have been prepared for the question but hearing his name mentioned after all those years still brought him out in a cold sweat. Malcolm asked what Angie had remembered about that encounter seven years ago; a week before Christmas. Her response would gauge his reply.

'I know you broke my heart,' she said. 'All the way home in the car when you wouldn't give me an honest answer. I knew it was over.'

'I'm sorry, baby.' He brushed a tear from her cheek. 'I was an arse. I fucked up.'

He coaxed her to recall more.

'When that bloke called out "Sid, is that you?" The colour really did drain from your face. You went white... a terrible white. I was so scared. He was disgusting. I can still smell him – mouldy and wet. Then when he said, "Cyril Rose, Elizabeth Rose's brother?" I thought you were going to pass out.'

Malcolm pictured his favourite sister, Elizabeth; her smiling face and curly fair hair. Roxanne was so like her. It had been such a long time ago but Malcolm recognised that distinctive croak. His front top teeth were missing and those that were remaining were decayed or broken. The effects of alcohol and, Malcolm assumed, sleeping rough had shrivelled his skin and bloated his nose and face. The tramp held on to Malcolm's lapel but through all his rambling, Malcolm soon put a face to the voice: Doug Morris. Back then he was what you might call a smooth operator; something of a dandy. He had been dating Elizabeth around the time that 'Malcolm' had fled. That day, however, he had been begging down at the quayside, sitting on a rotting rug and stinking of drink. But he had been astute enough to recognise Sid after all those years.

Angie winced. 'If you had said that he had made a mistake, I wouldn't have thought any more about it. But... when you got angry... and gave him a completely different name and said that we were from Aberdeen, I knew you were hiding something. Especially when you shoved him and he fell backwards. I think he said something that annoyed you, even more.'

Malcolm had insisted that Doug was mistaken. At first, the Geordie wouldn't drop it but Malcolm thrust some notes into his hand and the beggar apologised. He told Malcolm that he was the double of his girlfriend's dad. If he had left it at that, Malcolm would have walked away but Doug called after him, 'Your da' liked them young too.'

Malcolm lunged at him. A mouthful of rotten teeth laughed at him. 'If you are Cyril Rose,' hissed Doug, grabbing Malcolm by the elbow, 'then you need to come home!' He laughed as he hobbled away, 'Merry Christmas, Sid.'

Malcolm had been reluctant to go to Newcastle that weekend but Angie had begged him to take her there for the night life and the Christmas shopping. Foolishly, he had allowed his cock to overrule common sense. Despite the age gap, Malcolm was besotted with Angie as much then as he was now. He couldn't get enough of her and as a result became careless. After the brush with someone from his past, Malcolm checked out of their expensive hotel and returned home a day earlier than planned. He distanced himself from Angie claiming his wife,

Doreen, was ill and needed him. A few weeks after their trip, a tearful Angie turned up as he was leaving his office, pleading with him to reconsider. He told her that he could not abandon his wife and Angie should forget him.

'So, tell me. Why did you have to leave?' she pleaded.

'My dad killed a young lad.' Malcolm felt Angie tense. 'It was an accident but his father wasn't someone you crossed. He was hard. Hard as nails. A raving lunatic. He said that my dad meant it and it would be an eye for an eye. Two young'uns.'

'You mean you?'

'Aye me. It was different then. You played by different rules. They turned up at our house and dragged my dad outside into the streets for all the neighbours to see. I was hiding in next door's outside toilet. They pummelled his body with iron bars… but not enough to kill him. The lad's father shouted out that if anyone knew where I was then they should hand me over and they would be well paid or if anyone was caught helping me then the same punishment would be meted out. So, I ran.'

'And you never went back?'

'It was safer for everybody.'

'Were you never tempted? Did ye no' write? Would it matter now? He's probably dead. The bloke, I mean. Not yer da.'

'Angie, you can't tell anyone. Not ever. Nobody knows. Not Doreen. Not Roxanne. I can't undo the past. It's too complicated.'

Angie wrapped her arms and legs around him as if she would never let go. There were flaws in Malcolm's story. Why could he not go back now? Who would bother? Surely, his family deserved to know he was alive and well. But Angie dismissed her concerns. As soon as the doubts flooded in, she refused to dwell on them. She had lost him once. She would NOT lose him again.

'How did you get the name Malcolm Patterson?'

'Aahhh, that was our Davey, Davey Bowden, my old boss. His cousin, a farmhand, and his wife had a down-syndrome boy. For whatever reason, they kept him a secret from the local community so when the lad died of scarlet fever, they were too frightened to report it. There was a birth certificate but no death certificate. I was the same age as the lad so Davey got the birth certificate for me... and I became Malcolm Patterson.'

Angie buried her head into Malcolm's chest and promised not to tell a soul. Malcolm relaxed. Angie, it seemed, had believed him. He almost believed it himself. Davey Bowden had indeed managed to get his hands on his cousin's son's birth certificate but the rest was fabrication. His father had killed no one. There was no beating. How could he have told the truth? It was too difficult, even for him, to comprehend.

His father's words rang in his ears, 'There's nowt for it, ye'ull have to gan noo, bonnie lad, or it'll be the hangman's noose for you!' Sid protested that he was too young to hang. 'Deev ye want to spend the rest of your life in prison and have your Mam an' me travel to God knows where to see you. Take this and go. Tell no-one where ye're going and divnae come back. Ever.'

He may have managed to pacify Angie and perhaps convince himself that his account was real but the truth would continue to nag and chip away.

TWENTY-FIVE

Hogmanay: 31st December 1983

Jennifer and Maureen were cleaning after the last departure. Five shooters from Bedfordshire had left after breakfast. They were desperate to stay for the Hogmanay party and partake in a proper Scottish ceilidh especially after Jennifer had explained that it was the name given to a Scottish social gathering of dancing and singing. An excuse for a good knees-up. Severe weather conditions had been forecast for parts of England and Jennifer told them that they wouldn't want to be stuck here in Duneden. The latter warning did not faze them at all.

'How can one dog shed so much hair?' asked Jennifer.

'Cos they're fuckin' hairy!' explained Maureen.

Jennifer laughed but rooms that had dogs in them took much longer to clean. Maureen suggested an additional fee for dogs. Jennifer made a note to discuss it with Horse. The last thing she wanted was to alienate them.

The women chose a bathroom each to clean and that would be them finished: at least upstairs. The old, avocado suite had been replaced with a white one that Joe Blakely had sourced cheaply. Joe was a plumber to trade but like most builders he had a variety of skills. Whatever jobs needed to be done of late, Joe was always happy to oblige. Jennifer felt that she relied on him too often.

The tickets for the family ceilidh had been sold out within

days of advertising it. They had a waiting list of twenty in the event of cancellations but Angie assured Jennifer that nobody would pull out. Angie was making the stovies for the evening dance, her mother's recipe, and everyone in The Maltings' kitchen had a tattie peeler in their hand.

'For fuck's sake, Ryan, what are you doing? You're supposed to be training to be a chef,' yelled Angie.

'I cannae work this wee knife.'

The wee knife was designed to peel potatoes thinly. Martin admitted that he was hopeless too.

'Take these!' Angie swapped them for other vegetable knives. 'Watch yer fingers, they're sharp and I don't want big thick peelings or yous'll find yourselves peeling the peelings... fuck! I sound like my mother.'

There was great camaraderie as everyone commandeered a working space. Stainless steel work surfaces ran along every available wall space ensuring there was plenty elbow room for everyone. Maureen and Jennifer were chopping onions. Jennifer had to stop several times to splash cold water on her nipping eyes.

'They say you should chop them while they are submersed under water but that's shite,' Maureen informed the peelers. 'I've tried it and it doesn't work!'

'Did you have a nice Christmas, Angie?' asked Jennifer as she patted her wet eyes dry.

'We were all at Maureen's... me, my ma and Bethany. It was great. We opened our presents at mine then went to Maureen's for one o' clock. And you?'

'We had a lovely time. Fergal and Hannah arrived on Christmas Eve. We went to the family Christingle Service. How lovely is that?'

'I was at the back wi' Jamie and his wee pal. I saw you. We done that for years here,' blurted Maureen.

'Hannah loved it. Seeing all the wee ones with their oranges and candles. When everyone passed the flame from one candle to the other, I could've cried. Christmas day was really relaxing. Eating, drinking, sleeping and watching telly then more eating and drinking.'

There was a collective groan as they all revisited their excesses. Martin and Ryan emptied their boxes of potatoes into their mother's big bucket and collected more potatoes to peel.

'Martin, you'll need to get the bar ready,' Angie reminded him. 'And use the Brasso to polish up the bar taps.'

'Did the girls miss Mark?' enquired Maureen.

'*Mum!*' Martin chastised her as he dried his hands on the towel tucked into her apron.

'I'm only asking.'

'Not really,' answered Jennifer. They asked about him but they didn't dwell on it. Too much excitement. 'But he's back. With his slag.'

'When did he get back?' choked Angie. 'Did you know he was coming?'

'Turned up yesterday out of the blue. It was Katie's birthday so she thought it was a surprise for her, bless her. The girls are with him now but are coming home for the party then they are spending the next few days with him at Doreen's apparently.'

'I thought you were all going home to your mum's?' Angie was not happy with this news. Roxanne's sudden appearance had completely wrecked the plans that she had made with Malcolm.

'Exactly. I'm not sure what I'll do now.' Although Jennifer didn't want to concede to any of Mark's requests regarding their daughters, she was tired and welcomed the respite.

The atmosphere in the room had definitely changed and nobody could understand why. Angie began banging things unnecessarily and seemed reluctant to join in with the frivolities. Ryan turned up the volume on the radio in the hope that the hits of the seventies might lift the mood again. Once the potatoes and onions were finished, Angie added the other ingredients – some mince and beef dripping, to two large pots and left the traditional Scottish dish to simmer for two hours. Regular stirring would be required to stop it sticking to the bottom of the pan.

Martin supervised Ryan during lunches and Maureen helped Jennifer put the finishing touches to the function room for the ceilidh.

'I wish we'd had the time and the money to do up in here,' said Jennifer.

'It's fine,' said Maureen encouragingly. 'Let's get the tables ready. That'll make a huge difference.'

The tables were covered with thick, white paper that had to be cut from a long roll. Maureen had found some tartan gift wrap in the Kirkcaldy indoor market and it was ideal for adding a bit of colour and Scottish theme to the tables. A lot of the tables were different shapes and sizes but the coverings gave them uniformity. The function suite was big enough to hold around eighty guests and Jennifer conceded that it had been underused since their arrival one and a half years ago. The dark red walls seemed to pull the room in, making it appear smaller. The pattern on the carpet was unrecognisable; it was so worn and grubby. Huge curtains, held together with dust, had been used to close off the staging area that had served as a dumping ground for old chairs and anything else that had no useful purpose. Demolishing the stage was not yet an option but a good clear out and clean had helped. Maureen assured Jennifer that the villagers were grateful for the space and the surroundings would be overlooked for now. Jennifer found it was becoming more and more difficult to prioritise the renovations. She could only do a little at a time now – funds permitting.

'It'll do,' said Jennifer surveying the overall finish. 'Thanks, Maureen. You've come to the rescue again. Away home and get some rest for tonight.'

Jennifer would now seek Maureen's opinion on any refurbishments since witnessing how creative Maureen had been at styling her own home. She was checking the stock behind the function room bar when Angie popped her head round.

'Looking good. Well done. It's gonna be a fab night.'

'Wait a wee minute,' called Jennifer. She swung out from behind the bar to give Angie a hug.

'I stink o' fish n' chips and onions!' grinned Angie, in her kitchen whites.

'Time for a quick one? We might be too busy later.'

'Go on then. It'll have to be quick. The bar's locked up and the stovies are turned off.'

Angie pulled out a chair for them both and she sat staring at the dance floor. She had shared her first kiss with Mitch, only a few feet from where she was sitting, to *I'll be There* by the Jackson 5.

'It's been a quick three months,' said Jennifer as she handed Angie a vodka and coke.

'It's been eventful.'

'Good eventful?' asked her boss.

'Jen, it's been fantastic. Look what we've achieved? What you've achieved? And there's so much more waiting round the corner. Hey, what are the tears for?'

Jennifer swallowed. 'I couldn't have done it without you... and Maureen. I mean this wholeheartedly. You have been such a good friend to me.'

Angie handed her boss a red, paper napkin for her nose. 'Come on, you'll start me off.' The friends laughed and took a swig of their vodkas. 'So, what about you and Joe? Have you done it yet?' Jennifer nearly choked on her drink. 'It's the talk of the bar,' explained Angie. 'Have they? Haven't they?'

'No, we have not! I know he spends too much time here... but honestly, I'm not ready.'

'Fuck off, Jen, it's only sex and we all deserve a bit of that.'

Jennifer sniggered, 'Well you're certainly getting it.' Angie looked taken aback. 'Ah ha, knew it. You've been so happy lately. Spill the beans or am I not allowed to know?' Angie bit her lip and screwed up her face. 'Is he married?... He's married I know that look.'

'It's... complicated. I can't tell you his name. Sorry. But you don't know him and we go way back.'

'He's not Bethany's father, is he? God, I'm so sorry, Angie, that was bang out of order. Scratch that. Absolutely none of my business! Sorry.'

'Forget it. No, he's definitely not. Bethany's dad's long gone.' Angie's mind drifted for a few seconds. 'Mitch, the spineless bastard. I hate him. Loath him with all my being.'

'I've never heard you talking about Mitch. Is he local?'

'From Falkland originally. I loved him. Thought he loved me. But NO. Found out I was pregnant, wanted me to have an abortion. Cunt! Sorry but it's true. Moved away. Abandoned us. Long story. But short version, he knows about Bethany... not really interested. End of. Hate him. Didn't hang around like Mark.'

'And look where that got me. I thought Mark was the best thing since sliced bread. I idolised him. My dad was furious when we went travelling. He wanted me to do my probationary year at a school but Mark wouldn't wait... so I went with him.'

'Were you a teacher?'

'I should've been. Then I fell pregnant. Telling our parents that we got married in Spain didn't go down well. Easier that way.'

'The secrets we keep.'

'Has Mitch ever met Bethany?'

'Once. No, twice. A long time ago. Only cos his mum and dad insisted. They keep in touch... when it suits them'

'I've never ever heard Bethany talk about other grandparents.'

'She doesn't know. That's one of the conditions they get to see her. She thinks they are friends of mine. They live in Broughty Ferry now. Near Dundee. Please don't quiz her about it, Jen. Or mention it to anyone.'

'That's a given.'

'So out with it. What about you and Joe? He's a good catch and I doubt he's after your money.'

'Huh! Fat chance. I haven't got any,' laughed Jennifer.

'So how could you afford this place?' There was no apology from Angie for asking an impertinent question.

'My granny left an old cottage to Andrew and me. He did it up. We sold it and I got half the money... and I got some money from the sale of this place.'

'So, Fergal has nothing to do with here?'

Jennifer was not about to disclose everything. 'Fergal is standing as guarantor for my first year of monthly payments. He suggested it, not me. He said that he had every faith in me.

It must have worked as the bank didn't hesitate in giving me the loan.' It was a plausible explanation if somewhat misleading.

'I'm sure he's loaded anyway. I doubt you were that much of a risk.'

They both sniggered at their logic over each other's predicaments. It was time to part. It would be a busy night and both their girls would need a sleep to see them through the night until the Bells.

'Take care, Angie, see you tonight.'

Jennifer needed her manager to take care. She didn't want an irate wife causing trouble for Angie and more importantly The Maltings. The secrets we keep, right enough.

Jennifer and the girls donned their party dresses. Their little dresses had a navy, velvet bodice with a tartan, taffeta skirt. Jennifer's fitted dress was a similar shade with short, tartan, puff sleeves. Long, loose hair had been their final decision.

'We are looking good, girls. Sit here until I open up. Don't change the channel. Bethany'll join you for a wee while. Wait here until Angie or I come to get you.'

Jennifer heard the voices at the front doors. Bethany had inherited her mother's loud mouth. The door was barely open when Bethany pushed through the gap and raced up the stairs. The merriment of the reunion reverberated throughout the building. Angie opened up the function suite while Jennifer ensured that areas not required were locked up; it would save her later. They met in the kitchen. Angie switched on the gas at low beneath two cooking pots. The stovies had been shared amongst three large pots. The third one was a backup. If it were to be reheated and not used, the contents would end up in the bin; the reheat only-once rule was non-negotiable.

The band had set up their instruments on the stage earlier in the morning and they arrived along with the first guests at eight. The original decision to close off the main bar did not go down well with the regulars so a compromise was reached. It would open at eight and last orders would be called at 10.45pm. The lounge bar would be locked at 11.30pm. Most folk wanted to be back in their own homes or someone else's for midnight anyway, with the exception of the party revellers who would bring in the New Year at The Maltings with family and friends.

The night had been had a huge success so far. From the moment the band struck up *The Gay Gordons* the floor had never been empty. Jennifer was astonished at how many Scottish dances everyone knew, especially her own two wee ones (obviously through the school). The Fifers certainly knew how to party – young and old alike. The stovies and oatcakes had been scoffed, including the third pot, and midnight was fast approaching. The bar regulars had staggered out with less fuss than had been anticipated. One of the young Munros was warming up the bagpipes in the corridor ready to pipe in the Bells. There were so many friends in the room. The Munros shared a table with all the Blakeleys. Unbeknown to Jennifer, Shirley Munro and Shona Blakeley were sisters. Horse and his family sat with them too. He signalled for Jennifer to come over and squeezed her hand.

'You're a braw lass,' he said. 'I wish you all the very best for next year. You deserve it.'

Before Jennifer left, she had to be introduced to all his family members.

The accordionist cried for everyone to charge their glasses. There were only a few minutes of the auld year left. Jennifer made her way across to Maureen and Angie's tables. They were the nearest thing she had to family in Duneden: Mark did not count. A cloud of cigarette smoke enveloped the happy faces. Jennifer tried not to cough. The young piper marched in to *Loch Lomond* then stopped and waited.

The whole room joined in the countdown.

'Five, four, three, two, one. HAPPY NEW YEAR!'

A jubilant roar filled the room, followed by kissing and cuddling, hand shaking and thumping of backs. Jennifer scooped up her two and smothered them with kisses. She worked her way round the group saving her special hugs and thanks for Angie, Maureen and Willie. Within seconds, she was swamped with well-wishers. After a few minutes, the pipes started again and the crowd clapped the beat to a medley of tunes then the young Munro exited to resounding cheers. The ceilidh band chose a couple of waltzes to allow the exuberance to calm down. Jennifer wandered round the hall wishing as many people as she could a Happy New Year. She could feel Joe's eyes on her as she approached his party.

'Happy New Year, Joe.'

'Happy New Year, Jen.'

Awkward. Then Joe leaned in for the kiss. It wasn't long but it wasn't short either. They looked at each other first before looking around them. It seemed as if half of the room had been waiting with great optimism. A wail and a whoop boomed from Joe's table. Even at the age of thirty-five, Joe blushed like a school boy.

'I'll see you at the end of the night,' whispered Jennifer.

TWENTY-SIX

1st January 1984

Malcolm checked his watch again and sighed. It was only twelve thirty; too early to retire to bed. He wondered how the party over at The Maltings was panning out. It had to be better than Orchard House. Everyone had changed into their Christmas pyjamas except him. Doreen only agreed because Roxanne wanted her to. Malcolm refused to comply. Apart from his tie, he still had on his black slacks and the pink shirt he wore to dinner. Roxanne and Mark lay, facing each other, on one of the Chesterfield sofas, whispering and giggling like high school children in heat. Mark's green, Christmas tree socks were tickling Roxanne's white ones with penguins on them. Malcolm could make an exception for his daughter; she had barely left her teens, although they would soon be celebrating her twenty first. But Mark? He was lying there without a care in the world playing silly buggers with a girl almost half his age. I suppose the same could be said about him and Angie.

Malcolm's eyes switched to Doreen. Her cocker spaniel, Henry, was sleeping in his basket beside her. He got up from his sofa and carefully removed the glass that was threatening to slip from her hand. He lifted her legs up to enable her to stretch out and put a cushion beneath her slumbering head, smoothing out her long black hair as he did so. She was still a good-looking woman but she had lost a lot of weight recently and looked haggard. When he lifted her legs, it was like carrying a child. Her feet were cold and Malcolm pulled the sheepskin rug draped over the back of her sofa on to her legs.

The music room was long and difficult to heat as many grand old houses were. He knew Doreen missed Roxanne and felt guilty that he should too, but he didn't. He loved Roxanne and would have done anything for her but she was a young woman and she was determined to live her life in Murcia with Mark. If Roxanne and Mark had remained in Spain then he would have been at the ceilidh and he could have brought the New Year in with Angie: albeit from a distance. Instead, he had to listen to *The Old Grey Whistle Test* and hoped that it would drown out the giggling pair next to him. He was sitting on a quilted throw with a picture of Rudolf prancing on it. He wrapped it around his shoulders and relit his Cuban cigar. He drew on it hard and the smoke filled his lungs. He closed his eyes, held his breath until it nipped a little, then exhaled slowly. He opened his eyes and surveyed the room and his life as he did so.

He was surrounded by the finer things in life: an elegant home, a successful business, a daughter who would find her way, eventually. Everything he possessed had been bought and paid for with his hard-earned cash. He should have been content. Against all the odds, he had survived his past and prospered. Yet something was missing. He poured another Lagavulin 18-year-old and inhaled the peaty aroma. 'Here's to 1984.' Nobody replied. He hadn't expected them to.

*

Auld Lang Syne was still being hummed long after the band had stopped playing. The last of the stragglers shouted their goodbyes to Jennifer as she waved them off and locked the doors. She felt her body sag with relief. It had been an unbelievably good night but she was glad it was over. She checked the toilets and corridors for any strays and any smouldering cigarettes. She was extra vigilant in the function room although Archie and Martin had given the carpet a good sweep as they were tidying up. The band intended to collect their gear in the morning. They were off to the many parties that would still be in full swing when the bacon rolls were being plated at daybreak. When she was satisfied that there was nothing to worry about, she mouthed, 'Thank you,' to Joe who was watching over her two youngsters, sleeping across several chairs that had been pushed together.

'You take Katie,' whispered Jennifer. 'She is less likely to waken.'

Jennifer gathered all the pound coins on the table that had been given to the girls and popped them into her bag. Folk hated the new coins and much preferred the paper notes. Katie looked tiny in Joe's arms. He held the door open as Jennifer turned off all the lights. A beam of light from the hallway was enough for her to see what she was doing. Emma was a dead weight and Jennifer struggled up the stairs with her. Eventually, they managed to lay them on the correct beds. Jennifer quietly undressed her girls while Joe waited in the living area. When she joined him, he was looking out over the beer garden. The curtains were open and the street lamp in the car park shed enough light to create an atmosphere of romantic anticipation or doom and gloom, dependant on the mood.

'Are you happy with this, Jen? Say now if you want me to leave. I won't mind. Well, I would but I'd still go.' His voice was kind and courteous.

He stood statuesque-like with his hands in his jeans. He was a very handsome man. Tall, dark and handsome – the perfect Scottish first foot.

Jennifer put a finger to his lips. 'Shoosh.' She took his hand and led him to her big, comfy chair and gently but firmly pushed him into it. She straddled him and sat on his knees. They kissed, softly to begin with. He pulled Jennifer closer to him and she could feel the strength in the bulge beneath her. It felt good. As the kissing intensified, Jennifer teased him as she lifted her bottom and allowed his strong hands to hold on and pull her in again. Their tongues searched out the other's lips and mouth. The panting became heavier and noisier. Jennifer placed a palm on his chest and sat up. She undid the buttons on his shirt slowly and determinedly. As he arched his back, to pull his shirt from out of his denims, Jennifer moaned at the pressure he put on her bone. Joe unzipped her dress and Jennifer, without taking her eyes off him, eased it up and over her head, revealing a lacy body piece and stockings.

Joe nodded approvingly. She was everything he wanted and more. He had fantasised about this moment but the reality was that Jen was far hornier than he could ever have imagined.

Jennifer moved her head to his chest and teased him with her tongue. His groaning grew louder. She sat back again and ran her fingers provocatively through her long, red hair. Joe pulled the lace down over her breasts and pulled Jen towards him. His mouth covered one of her nipples. Jennifer thought she would burst with wanting. It had been such a long time. She held his head tightly and rocked in his hands. She slipped off the chair and stood up. She unfastened the material covering her crotch and smiled. Joe abandoned any illusion of grace and unceremoniously whipped off his jeans and boxers. Jennifer took him in: his incredible, toned body and the phallic shaft that was waiting to satisfy her. He looked like an Adonis and she felt like a naughty Grecian seductress.

'Sorry, do you mind?' She helped Joe unravel the sheath over his erection and pleasured him briefly with her mouth. Joe threw his head back, dug his nails into the chair as his body contracted and grunted with gratification.

She straddled him again. Their bodies thumped against each other: faster and faster until they stuck like glue, pushing and grating until it was over and their bodies shuddered to a standstill. Neither moved or said anything. Joe broke the silence.

'Fuckin' hell, Jen.'

'Was it that bad?'

They both laughed. 'I forgot to ask,' Jennifer pointed out, 'Did you want a drink?'

She found an old dressing gown of Mark's and tossed it to Joe along with a clean towel.

'Use the bathroom in the hallway and I'll meet you back here in five minutes.'

Jennifer freshened up in the bathroom next to the girls' bedroom, slipped on her cotton robe and checked on the zonked pair before returning to the open-plan lounge. She could hear the shower running. She poured Joe a whisky and a wine for her and waited patiently, curled up on the seat where they had just fucked. And that was what was bothering her. They had fucked. It had been good: better than good but it hadn't felt like love-making. It was entirely her fault of course. She had behaved appallingly. She had used him. For sex! Poor Joe. She scrunched her eyes and covered her face with her hands. What an idiot.

When Joe sauntered in wearing Mark's housecoat, he smiled. 'I look ridiculous.' It was far too small for him.

Jennifer handed him his glass. 'Cheers and Happy New Year.' She did like him. He was a thoroughly decent guy and she felt safe having him around.

'Happy New Year, Jen.' He kissed her tenderly on the lips.

You are such a cow, Jennifer Cameron, she scolded herself. *You don't deserve such a kind man.* Joe was kind and good and undoubtedly attractive and everything most women would want from a partner. Regretfully, he wasn't the man for Jennifer and she wasn't about to change her mind. He didn't deserve to be strung along either. She would have to tell him but not now, not tonight. Selfishly, she wanted to pretend for a little longer.

When he had stood there earlier, framed by the bay window, Jennifer had envisaged four full days of romancing and evenings of passion awaiting them. She had pictured long, happy walks, holding hands and laughing, feeding each other food from their plates and snuggling on the sofa watching T.V. It was only now that she realised, the person she had imagined, had been Mark. It was her and Mark strolling in the woods, wrapped in the hideously long scarves she had knitted for them for their first Christmas. It was Mark who was snatching morsels from her fingertips while watching endearing rubbish on the telly. What possessed him to go off with Roxanne? What possessed her to dupe Joe?

Mark had abandoned his family just like Mitch had abandoned Angie and Bethany. Bastards! The both of them. Jennifer suppressed the urge to weep.

Tomorrow, the girls would stay at Orchard House with their father. Jennifer decided to seek refuge and solace at her parents.

Suddenly, the proprietor of The Maltings felt pitifully lonely and extremely tired. Time for bed.

TWENTY-SEVEN

3rd January 1984

When Jennifer hung the padlock for the front doors in a cabinet in the bar, she shivered. It was as cold in The Maltings as it was outside. She tapped her walking boots against each other to knock off the remaining snow. Fife had got off lightly; the snow had been much heavier in the Lothians, especially over the Braid Hills where she had walked with Fergal yesterday. Horse had warned her that if the ground was covered in snow for more than three weeks then shooting would be suspended. 'Please, God, don't let that happen'. She depended on their business. It had enabled her to do more than she could ever have hoped for.

She switched on the bar lights and everything went black. 'Noooooo!' The lights had tripped. Jennifer had torches placed everywhere for this eventuality. She found one on the floor underneath the beer taps. As she switched it on, there was a loud banging on the front door. Jennifer stood up abruptly banging her head of one off the drip trays. 'Shit!' That was sore.

'Who is it?' she shrieked, reluctant to open the door under the circumstances.

'It's me!' sang a familiar voice. 'I was on the way to the shop when I seen your car and the trail of footsteps. Are you okay?'

Jennifer opened the door to Maureen. 'You are a Godsend, Maureen. I've tripped the lights. Could you give me a hand for a minute?'

'Of course,' she coughed and stubbed her ciggie out before she barged in. 'Brrrr. It's bollock freezing out there... and in here.'

Both women made their way to the electricity box. Andrew had installed a state-of-the-art circuit breaker for Jennifer. All the switches were labelled and there was only one switch down – the one for the bar lights.

'You know you could've turned on the lights in the corridor,' Maureen reminded her.

'I know that now. What a numpty.' Jennifer rubbed her head: it still ached.

'What you up to?'

'I'm just this second back. I knew the building would be cold so the heating needs to be on for tomorrow. It is bloody Baltic though.'

Jennifer had left all the radiators on at '1' as Joe had instructed but it was still cold.

'So, what have you got planned for your tea?'

Jennifer hadn't thought that far ahead.

'Right, you're coming to me... don't argue. I'll see you in an hour. One of the boys or Willie will walk you back and make sure you are settled. See you about seven.'

Before Jennifer had a chance to make an excuse, Maureen had gone and if she was honest, she was grateful for the offer. Jennifer had dreaded coming back. At some point, she would need to discuss things with Joe. Probably tomorrow.

The girls would be saying their goodbyes to Mark. Not that she cared any more. Her lapse of wanting him had diminished. It must have been the alcohol (or her sudden urge for sex) and most definitely feeling sorry for herself that made her wish for her old life again. But that was not going to happen. Neither would the chance of meeting a knight in shining armour. That *would* be shining bright!

Jennifer turned on a tap in each room in case any of them were frozen. They were all running as normal. She set the temperature for downstairs to fifteen and turned the valves in all the guest bedrooms to three. She would increase them tomorrow. The doors downstairs were checked again. She wasn't nearly as paranoid as she used to be but being secure and safe would always be a priority. She closed the curtains in her flat and switched on the gas fire for twenty minutes then set the central heating at twenty. Her upstairs private space was perfect. It wasn't huge but it was comfortable and easy to manage. The wee bathroom between the two bedrooms meant that their area was self-contained and she could hear the girls if they got up during the night. The vibrations from the music playing downstairs at night never seemed to disturb their sleep. In fact, when Emma or Katie slept elsewhere, they complained it was too quiet.

Jennifer left the lights on in the apartment and the long corridor downstairs and headed out to Maureen's. The streets were quiet. The odd car flashed its lights and Jennifer acknowledged them with a wave even though she hadn't a clue as to who the driver might be. Duneden was a picturesque village. There were so many hidden gems of houses, just like Maureen and Willie's, in all the wee nooks and crannies. New builds and old traditional houses blended together making Duneden a very desirable place to live. Although house prices could never compete with St Andrews, the market for Duneden homes remained buoyant.

Maureen's house couldn't be missed. Jennifer looked at the clear night sky and smiled. The stars seemed within touching distance. The tail lights of an aircraft pulsated and Jennifer wondered if anyone on board could spot Maureen's bright house from that distance. She rang the doorbell.

'What the hell are you standing there for? Come in.' Willie reprimanded her from behind the glass door.

Jennifer slipped off her boots and she put them on a large towel at the front door along with several others. The warmth of the home welcomed her.

'Maureen!' yelled Willie. 'It's Jen. Go through, hen.'

Hen? Jennifer thought her granny was the only person who still used that term of endearment. She was met with the appetising smell of garlic bread.

'Sorry. It's only spag bol,' apologised Maureen. 'Willie! Get Jen a drink and round up the boys.'

Within a few minutes, ten bodies were seated at the table. Conversation was loud and animated. No wonder Maureen and Willie were happy. Martin and Ryan's girlfriends had joined them. Jennifer flashed a knowing smile in Ryan's girlfriend's direction. Zoe babysat for the girls at least twice a week.

'I'm punching above my weight, Jen,' jested Ryan as he planted a kiss on Zoe's flushed cheeks.

'Enough o' that at the table... or anywhere else,' laughed Maureen.

'Yer just jealous.'

'Your dad and I have no need to be jealous of you two, I can tell ye.'

Jennifer felt herself blush at the innuendoes batting around the table. Nobody else was remotely embarrassed, except young Zoe. Once the food was gobbled, the boys and girlfriends dissipated to other corners of the house. No sooner had some kind of peace been restored, when Bethany and Angie bounced in.

'You might have said. There's nothing left but I can rustle up something.'

'You're fine. We had fish n' chips at Karlena's,' Angie explained.

Without asking, Angie poured a glass of wine and topped up Jennifer's. Maureen was on cider.

'I can't wait to get back to normal,' announced Angie grabbing at non-existent folds of flesh on her sides.

'Willie and me are joining Scottish Slimmers on Monday,' Maureen informed them proudly.

Angie had heard it all before but she was surprised that Willie had been badgered into going. The three of them sat on the comfy sofas at the far end of the room.

Again, Jennifer marvelled at the expanse and the Scandinavian decor. The garden beyond the glass window twinkled above a blanket of snow. Bethany and Jamie (Maureen's youngest son) were in a T.V. room behind them watching something that sounded wholly inappropriate for youngsters.

'Auntie Maureen, can I stay? Pleeeeeease?' asked Angie's wee girl.

One more made no difference to Maureen and so Bethany skipped away to join her cousin. Jennifer decided to excuse herself and thanked Maureen for the umpteenth time for the invitation.

Angie hoped that Malcolm might be free, now that Bethany was otherwise engaged, and volunteered to chum Jen along the road. Malcolm often phoned around ten at night and if they were able to, they met at the but and ben, although, recently, they had been taking more risks and Malcolm had been sneaking into Angie's under the cover of darkness. Since Malcolm had bought Doreen a dog, a cocker spaniel, it gave him an excuse to walk it around the village. Angie lived near the crossroads only a hundred yards or so from The Maltings and a short walk from Orchard House. It was ideal. Malcolm had no need to deviate from his route.

'Thanks for coming in. You know what I'm like.'

Angie knew only too well but to be fair to Jen, she would be the same. To date, Angie had not been required to stay over on her own and if she had to, she would make sure that one of Maureen's boys stayed with her.

'Jen, would you have any objections to me going on holiday for a week? I was thinking around the end of February or the beginning of March.'

'Not in the slightest. Why d'you think I'd mind? I'm delighted that you're even thinking about it.'

'Will you be alright?... On your own I mean.'

'My dad'll come over. Even Fergal would do it if I asked. Where are you thinking? And who with?' Jennifer poked Angie jokingly with her finger.

'London if you must know and on my own. My best pal from school's there. She moved years ago with her girlfriend. You know what it's like. It would never have been condoned here. Not with her family... too many narrow minds. Anyway, it's been long overdue and for once, I have something interesting to say about me.'

Angie's best friend did live in London with her girlfriend and she had every intention of staying with them... but for two nights only. Then she would fly with Malcolm to Barbados. One whole week of being free, to do what they liked, where they liked, when they liked; twenty-four hours a day without ducking and diving. She couldn't wait.

As Jennifer was about to open the door to let Angie out, someone else knocked. It was Joe.

'Am I interrupting anything?'

'I'm just going,' smirked Angie. 'I'll leave you two to it.'

Jennifer stepped back to allow Angie out and Joe in. As soon as the door closed, he kissed Jennifer. She kissed him back. He pushed her against the outside doors, making the panels shudder then Joe squeezed his hands behind her bottom pulling her into him. She could feel his boner.

Angie swung round quickly as she heard the thump then chuckled, 'Didn't take them long.' The same would be said of her in half an hour. She smirked as she pictured her lover.

Unintentionally, Jennifer inched her knee up the outside of Joe's thigh creating a more inviting space. He kissed her neck and she offered her throat. His breath was hot and she held on to his head as his lips traced her collar bone. He sucked her in and she let him. It was Joe's turn to take her hand and lead her upstairs. Jennifer could hear that voice of caution, 'Say something!' But she chose to ignore it. She was a coward and a tease.

TWENTY-EIGHT

Friday 2nd March

Jennifer thanked her dad before he was forced to pass the phone over to her mother.

'Don't worry about Hannah. Auntie Betty and me are taking her out for her lunch next week. We ken what bus to take and where to get off. We'll do her hoose before we go. We've booked the King James Hotel. You get a cheaper lunch there than you do queuing for hours at British Home Stores' Cafe...'

'Thanks, mum, but we've been over this already. I'm really grateful but I need to go. Love you.'

Grace Thomson didn't know how to give the short version for any story. Her family joked that if she dyed her hair black (it was grey) and changed her glasses to thick black ones, she could stand in for one of Ronnie Corbett's monologues. Nobody would notice; he was Scottish after all. Strangely enough, his brother owned a pub in Strathmiglo, not far from Duneden, and Mark seemed to know him well. Mark had known all the local publicans. Jennifer didn't have the time or the inclination to meet them personally, although she knew she should. She made a mental note to do it soon. On the odd occasion, a couple of them had borrowed a keg of lager or beer but it was always replaced when their own beer delivery arrived. However, there just might be a time when she needed to call in a favour. It was doubtful. Bob Gregson, the G&B rep, had given invaluable advice to Jennifer on stock management. Touch wood, they had never run out of anything yet.

Jimmy Thomson planned to stay the full week with his daughter while Angie was in London, as Jennifer would have to cover a lot of her shifts. Fergal didn't have that week free; he was attending a conference in Blackpool but Jennifer got the feeling that he was telling porkies. She surmised that this Dom fellow was more than just a friend but Fergal had never brought it up for discussion and Jennifer was too polite to ask. Hannah had confided in Jennifer that she thought Fergal had a lady friend and was concerned that she might be married; something that Fergal had let slip several years ago. Plus, Hannah had often heard a car late at night pulling out of one of the parking bays below her window and was sure she had heard Fergal's front door closing shortly before it each time. Hannah may have appeared old and doddery but she didn't miss a trick. It saddened Jennifer to think that Fergal had had a secret lover for such a long time and felt the need to conceal it from her, even now.

Jennifer had dropped Angie off at Ladybank station for the 8.30am Edinburgh train. It would be strange not having her around but Jennifer was genuinely pleased that her manager was taking a well-earned break. Jennifer's dad promised to be in Duneden in time for the girls coming out of school. He would leave directly from Hannah's after having done her shopping and housework.

Archie called out to Jennifer that a brewery boy was in the bar.

'I'm here to have a look at your beer lines.' A young lad, who looked as if he should still be at school, was there to check why the Heavy wasn't pouring properly.

Jennifer showed him where the cellar was and left him to it.

'Do you want a tea or coffee?' she shouted on the way to the kitchen.

'No, thanks.' He even sounded like a wee boy.

Jennifer packed away all the vegetables that had been delivered that morning before preparing a pot of minestrone soup. It was really a cheat's version: a good, quality packet mix with lots of fresh vegetables and chopped bacon added to it. Angie had portioned and frozen enough meals to last for a fortnight. 'We're perfectly able to cook for ourselves,' Maureen had reminded her. Everyone thinks they are indispensable. Jennifer was busy cutting oval pastry tops for the steak pies when the G&B lad popped his head in to say that he had adjusted the pressure and there should be no more problems. Archie had signed the paperwork.

Maureen wandered in; she was helping with lunches. She had left the other cleaner to finish off the bedrooms. Three engineers from the Wirral were staying with them for another few weeks. They were carrying out significant maintenance work at a local paper mill but went home most weekends and would return around teatime on the Monday. Best of all, they paid a sizeable retaining fee for the days they were not there. Jennifer was forever surprised that there was always someone requiring accommodation. Mark's unwillingness to take in residents had cost them a lot of money. Rooms were definitely the most profitable part of the business and for the least input.

'Right, what's going on with you and Joe?' Maureen quizzed Jen, taking the salad vegetables from the fridge.

Jennifer stood and tried to think of how best to explain it.

'He's fuckin' miserable. Willie says his face is tripping him all day long. He won't say anything.'

'Oh, Maureen, I feel terrible... but it wasn't fair on the girls. It was too soon.'

'I said the same to him and Willie. Your bed had hardly got cold when Joe was warming it up again.'

'Thanks for that,' said Jennifer sarcastically.

'Well, it's true.'

'Emma came in from school a few weeks ago and said that boys in her class had told her that Joe was my boyfriend. I was mortified. I thought we had been discreet.'

'You can't keep secrets in Duneden, Jen. As Willie always says, they ken you've wiped your arse before you've taken a shit!'

Jennifer felt that that comment didn't warrant a dignified response. She had explained to Emma that Joe did spend a lot of time working in The Maltings but their Uncle Willie did as well and nobody thought that Willie was a boyfriend. Sometimes people were mean gossips. Emma agreed but Jennifer had taken action quickly and had asked Joe to let things cool for a while.

'My girls are not ready for a new uncle. I asked Joe to slow things down just until the gossiping stops.'

'I never said nothin' to anybody. I know I'm a gossip but not about you or my work.' Maureen knew she had decried Jen in the past but she wouldn't do it now.

Jennifer moved away from the cooker and gave Maureen a friendly squeeze. 'I know that, Maureen. I didn't mean you. But I need some breathing space.' Jennifer wanted more than that. She desperately hoped that the relationship would fizzle out but deep down acknowledged that a direct approach was the most likely solution.

'Anyway, Skinny Malinky, how much weight have you lost now?'

In her eagerness to explain, Maureen took a fit of coughing.

Once it had subsided, she explained that Willie had lost a stone and she had managed a stone and a half. They had wavered now and again but most of the time they had followed the slimming plan.

'Well done, you. You look great.' Jennifer thought that Maureen looked younger too.

'I feel better for it.' Maureen ran the palms of her hands over her midriff. 'Jen, you said if it was quiet, I could get away early? Is that still okay?'

Jennifer had no problem with Maureen leaving before lunches finished as long as all the prep for the evening shift had been done. Both women bashed on.

*

Angie flicked through her copy of the *Cosmopolitan* but was too excited to concentrate. She had picked up the magazine when she changed trains at York before continuing her journey to London. Malcolm was planning to meet her tomorrow at her friend's house and after a night's stay, they would head to Gatwick for their flight to Barbados in the morning. Seven days of bliss awaited them. Her suitcase was full of fashion wear and accessories in sunny, summer hues: a huge deviation from her customary black. Angie attributed her voyage into colour to Malcolm; he made her happy. Malcolm worried that Angie would have to justify her suntan when she returned but she had assured him that she never tanned. Despite having jet black hair and beautiful, dark brown eyes, her skin tone had always been pearly white. Basking in the sun had no appeal for Angie but she enjoyed the heat while sitting in the shade. It's probably the reason why her skin looked so fresh and youthful.

*

Jennifer had switched off the fryers and had begun closing down the kitchen when Archie interrupted her.

'Sorry, Jen. Do we have time for one more? I've persuaded him to go for the soup.'

'Are there many left?'

'No, just him.'

'Go on then. I doubt he'll hang around. By the time I'm finished here, he'll be ready to leave. Could you do the bread and I'll bring his soup through?... And, Archie, get yourself away whenever you're ready.'

Jennifer plated the soup and added some cheesy croutons on top. She double-checked her whites. There was nothing worse than a chef wandering into public areas with grubby clothing. She pushed the door with her bum and looked around the lounge to see where he was seated.

'Whoah! Sorry. My fault. I wasn't looking where I was going.' A bronze arm shot out to steady the bowl in Jennifer's hand. 'I was in the wash room. Sorry.'

Jennifer wasn't sure what took her breath away first. The splash of heat on the back of her hand or the gorgeous bright blue eyes that were smiling back at her.

'You're okay. I'm fine. No harm done,' she lied. Her hand was stinging. Back in the kitchen, the cold water thundered over her hand. She would normally have left it under the tap for at least two minutes but she was desperate to get tidied up and return to her Australian visitor; at least that's what she thought she had detected in his accent. She rubbed some aloe vera into her skin and wandered nonchalantly behind the bar pretending to sort out some bottles on the gantry. Archie had gone.

Her Australian, if that's what he was, supped his soup. 'It's good,' he shouted and signalled with his thumbs up. 'Homemade?'

'Naturally,' she laughed. He was definitely from Down Under.

She grabbed a duster and a tin of polish and started buffing up the tables near the door.

'I think your barman did that earlier.'

'That's good. Saves me. So, what brings you here?' asked Jennifer.

'Visiting family in the area. My sister lives in Cupar,' he explained. 'Scott McIntyre, by the way, but my mates call me Mac.' Mac stretched out a hand.

'Jennifer Cameron but my friends here call me Jen. I prefer Jennifer.' And Jennifer slipped her hand into his. *Keep a firm wrist*, she reminded herself. Mac had a very firm grip. She didn't want to let go.

'I prefer Scott, if that's okay with you.'

His smile warmed Jennifer from the top of her head to the tip of her toes. She sat down at the table next to him and they chatted about where he came from and what he did for a living: a refrigeration engineer. She told him all about Port Seton.

'Are you married?' She was rarely so forward but he was here on holiday so she had nothing to lose.

Scott laughed at her audacity. 'Divorced. And you?'

'Hmmm. Of sorts. Estranged of sorts. It's complicated. Does she live in Australia? Your ex-wife.'

'Adelaide. And yours? The estranger!'

'Spain. Any kids?'

'One. She lives with her mother. And you?'

'Two girls and they live with me.'

'Is the interrogation over? My soup's getting cold.' It was a cheeky remark that made Jennifer laugh.

Jennifer apologised and pottered around behind the bar waiting to clear his table. He *was* good looking. His nose seemed a bit thin and bony; it suited him though. She did like his curly, brown hair. The sun had given him natural highlights unlike Mark's silly, yellow tints. The white shirt and navy jumper emphasised his tanned skin and he had nice teeth. She thought he was as tall as Mark but leaner. Overall, he really did meet with her approval. Jennifer considered tearing up his bill but felt that he might misinterpret her intentions; not that she had any, or had she? Jennifer couldn't remember the last time she had felt this jittery around another man. She must have had the same nervous excitement for Mark when they had first met.

Scott carried his empty bowl and plate over to the bar and Jennifer presented him with his bill. 'Would Jennifer Cameron like a drink?'

'I would love to… under different circumstances. Can I get you one?'

Scott explained that he was driving but he accepted Jennifer's offer of a coffee. As she made the coffees, she tried to check her appearance in the door of the microwave. It was a waste of time. Strands of hair were sticking to her head because of the heat and the fumes from the deep fat fryer. The rest of it was twisted into a tight ball on the top of her head. When she returned with the coffees, they continued sharing their past. They appeared relaxed and comfortable in each other's company and the conversation flowed easily. Jennifer told him how she came to own The Maltings and he explained that his family had come to Scotland from Adelaide when he was twelve years old but he had returned in his mid-twenties after he'd received a good job offer. His father was originally from Fife but his mother was Australian. Scott had dual nationality.

Jennifer's dad and the girls could be heard making their way upstairs. The girls had learned not to barge into the lounge bar while customers were still dining. They had to be as professional as the staff; it made them feel important.

'I'm sorry but I'm going to have to lock up now.' It was futile to try and delay his departure any longer.

'Look, I've enjoyed this. I'd really like to see you again. Dinner maybe? Or a few drinks? I'm planning to be in this part of Scotland for another two weeks. What do you think?'

Scott waited as Jennifer contemplated his request. He searched her face for some clues but was pleased when she agreed: he had expected her to turn him down.

'We can't meet here. Too many prying eyes and loose tongues. Would St Andrews be okay? I'm free all day on Tuesday. We could meet for lunch and make a day of it or cut it short after lunch if you need to be elsewhere.' She didn't want to appear forward or too keen.

They exchanged phone numbers and agreed to talk again on Sunday evening.

Scott McIntyre stepped out on to Main Street. He knew it well. He had been disappointed to learn that Angie was on holiday although he was intrigued to find that she was the manager of The Maltings and even more surprised that Jennifer held her in such high regard. He had not been prepared for a setback but he could wait a little longer; he had no option. And, some inside information might help him weigh up his next steps with more caution, instead of the ambush he had originally considered. He decided against walking past Angie's mother's house even though he was desperate to catch a glimpse of his little girl. It had to be done properly.

TWENTY-NINE

'Hi, Dad and hi, my beautiful girls. Have you had a good day?'

Two pairs of eyes were fixed on the telly screen. The response might have been 'fine' but it was hard to distinguish while their mouths were full of biscuits. They had obviously been to the shop as there was a pile of rental videos on the pine chest. Jennifer gave her dad a scolding look and kissed him on the cheek.

'You spoil them. I need a shower. I'll be back in a jiffy... no more rubbish before tea time!' She would have been better speaking to the four walls.

In the shower, Jennifer played out in her head what had just happened downstairs. It had been surreal. One minute she had been chatting with a customer, a very charming and charismatic customer, and the next she had accepted a date: well, lunch. Not typically exciting but better than nothing. If it hadn't been for the slip of yellow paper with his number on it, lying on her bed, she might have assumed it had been wishful thinking. She sang as she lathered the body wash all over her arms and legs. She was seriously thinking about getting her hair cut shorter; something completely different.

*

'Has Maureen said anything to you about Jen and me?' Joe asked Willie as Willie had his head wedged in a narrow space between a bath and floorboards. He was trying to find the source of a leak in a new extension they had built several weeks ago. Joe had said little about the Jen dilemma up until now. Willie thought that Joe could have picked a better time and place for an intimate discussion. He was grateful that he was facing the other way. Joe would find it difficult to decipher his facial expressions; especially if he had to lie.

'No' much. Only that the two of you had decided to put the brakes on.'

'It was Jen. I couldn't care less what people say. Honestly, Willie, I'm goin off ma heid. I can't stop thinking about her.'

When Willie managed to squeeze his skull out, he sat on the edge of the bath and massaged the purple indentations close to his temples. Joe was sitting on the toilet seat. Two school girls were more likely to be having a girly chat in the loo rather than two grown men in navy boiler suits and obligatory dirty, toe-capped boots. Willie hoped no one would walk in on them.

'Have a quiet word with her, mon, the next time you're in. Explain how you feel... but women and their bairns... tread carefully. I ken what my Maureen's like.'

'I get it. She's only doing it for the girls' sakes.'

Maureen had confided in Willie that she thought it was more than cold feet. Jen had probably been needing a good shag and now that she'd got it out her system, she could move on. Willie was flabbergasted. He thought it was only blokes that behaved like that. At the experienced age of forty-three, he still couldn't fathom women out.

*

Jennifer opened up again for Archie. It was 4.45pm and the workers would be piling in for their end of week celebratory pint. Some of them wouldn't make it home for tea and a few would still be there at last orders; a typical Friday night at the beginning of March. A local girl, Janie Grant, was singing and playing her guitar after evening meals were finished. She was happy to perform for free, as always, but Jennifer insisted she took something for her efforts. It was a token gesture but Jennifer fed her and allowed her free soft drinks all night and most folk would put a few coins or a pound note in her box too.

The place was fairly busy and the evening rush for meals had quietened down. The usual regulars sat on tall stools around the bar as locals from Duneden and from other villages drifted in. Shona Munro, her sister Shirley and three other school mums ordered a bottle of Cava. They chatted with the young singer before finding a table. They had come to support her. Maureen shouted, 'cheerio.' She had decided not to join Willie for a drink before going home. Like Jennifer and Archie, she had extra shifts for the rest of the week and a night in front of the telly, with her baffies on, beckoned. One of the youngsters had stayed behind to sweep and mop the kitchen floor. Jennifer was in the store cupboard checking that they had plenty Cava when she was aware of someone behind her. It was Joe.

'Hi, Jen, how are you?'

Jennifer thought he looked ghastly; pale and drawn. 'So, so I suppose and you?'

Joe smiled a lame smile as if to say, *what do you think?* 'I miss you,' he spoke quietly.

'Miss you too.' She did miss him. He had done so much around The Maltings that she missed his company and her 'to do' list was filling up fast.

Joe gently took her hand and held it. 'Will we be okay, Jen? In a few weeks, I mean. Or am I wasting my time.'

Joe didn't deserve to be kept in limbo. 'You've been so good to me, Joe. I'm so grateful.' The rest of the words were stuck beneath her larynx; the ones that she wished she had the courage to use. 'Do you fancy a walk on Sunday, away from here? We can talk properly.'

Joe instantly perked up. 'How about Falkland Hill? Around two? I'll pick you up.'

'Make it three and I'll meet you there in the car park. Safer that way.'

Joe walked away with a broad grin brightening up his whole demeanour. It had not occurred to him that Jen's intention to take her own car might indicate that she envisaged an early departure in separate vehicles.

As Jennifer was making her way back to the bar, Malcolm was calming down a boisterous dog. He let the inside door swing behind him and a rush of cold air cooled the corridor.

'Evening, Jen. Sit, Henry! Sit!' he called out.

Jennifer laughed. 'Evening, Mr Patterson, you've got your hands full.'

Malcolm and Jennifer had sorted out their differences many months ago. Jennifer had apologised for being stand-offish towards him and Doreen after Mark and Roxanne had declared their love to anyone who cared to listen. Malcolm admitted he had been pig-headed but Roxanne was his only daughter and although his support and loyalty would always be with her, it didn't mean he had condoned or knew of their liaison. He liked Jennifer and enjoyed his visits to The Maltings and wanted to be able to relax when he came in – if he was allowed in, now that Jennifer was officially the owner. Jennifer had decided that Malcolm made a better friend than an enemy. If Mark and Roxanne were to make a go of it, then their paths would inevitably cross. Having Malcolm on board would be to her advantage.

Malcolm found an empty stool beside Willie and Joe at the bar. He ordered a half pint of pale ale and a Laphroaig malt whisky (for a wee change).

'Miss Lennie not working? She's usually on on a Friday.' Malcolm spoke loudly to ensure he could be heard.

'Awa' to London to her pal's,' Willie told him.

'London? You must be paying her too much, Jen.'

'She's worth every penny.'

It was good to hear how much his young lover was appreciated. He ached to be beside her. During the bar banter Malcolm told the others that he was flying to Barbados on Sunday for a golfing holiday and Doreen would be staying with Roxanne for ten days. Willie jested that you couldn't hide money. Malcolm's gardener, a retired driver of his, had volunteered to stay in the house with Henry. On hearing his name, Henry bounded and barked around Malcolm's legs.

Jennifer hoped that no one saw her flinch on hearing about Doreen's trip. It irked her that Mark had shirked his responsibilities to the girls. He'd never paid a penny towards their keep. His parents had phoned only once since Christmas Day and, although she couldn't explain it, that hurt too.

Malcolm left half an hour after he had arrived, explaining that he was driving Doreen to the airport early next morning.

'See you tomorrow night then,' said Joe casually.

'We'll see. I have an early flight myself on Sunday morning.' Malcolm was flying to London a few hours after Doreen's flight but that deception would be easy enough to conceal. He hoped that he'd given enough information to throw anyone off their scent and no one would link Angie's absence to his.

The crowd cheered and clapped as the young folk musician zipped up her guitar. Shona Munro and her cronies were gathering handbags and coats. It appeared as if one of the school mums was related to the singer. They all left together, leaving the two diehards, Willie and Joe, at the bar.

'Needing a hand to lock up, Jen?' Willie asked.

'Not tonight, Willie. My dad's here and he won't go to bed until I'm upstairs. Thanks for asking.'

'Right, Joe, we'll be on our way.'

Joe sheepishly followed Willie out the door. Willie gave Jennifer a reassuring wink as he passed her. Jennifer grinned at Willie's insight. She hadn't the energy to deal with Joe tonight. Everything had been methodically locked up earlier but a noise made her stop on the stairs. She stepped slowly to the bottom and listened: Nothing. It must have come from outside. Lately, a fox had begun rummaging around the bins near the back door but as she turned to go up, she heard it again. She crept along the corridor. Someone was in the function room. She could hear bottles clinking. The door was definitely locked and the only way out was through a window. Jennifer bolted to her flat to alert her dad.

She made a quick phone call to Maureen. Willie hadn't returned but Martin had answered and he and Ryan would be there as soon as. Martin warned Jennifer not to tackle the burglar without them.

Jennifer and her dad could still hear him as they waited outside the function room door. Whoever it was, was fumbling and mumbling around in the dark and by the sounds that were being made, he, it was definitely a male voice, had dropped some of the bottles. They were rolling over the dance floor.

Willie was first to rush in through the back door followed in quick succession by Martin then Ryan; he had met his sons en route. The two boys were carrying baseball bats. They waited with Jennifer and her dad outside the function suite door as Jennifer handed Willie the correct key. He barged in screaming and shouting obscenities as he did so.

On seeing Willie and the baseball bats ready to pound his head, the intruder dropped all the bottles and raised his hands in the air. One of the bottles exploded as it hit the floor. Jennifer switched on the lights.

'Seriously? What the fuck?'

'Jennifer!' Her dad wouldn't tolerate swearing under any circumstances.

'Ya fuckin' knob head,' yelled Willie. 'What are you playin' at?'

A dishevelled David stood in a pool of alcohol and shattered glass. His hoodie was pulled up over his head and his black jeans were sliding over his scrawny hips

'Dinnae move ya skinny wee bastard. You'll tear your feet to shreds.'

'I'm sorry,' he slurred, eyes rolling around in an empty head.

David was in his bare feet. He'd discarded his shoes at the door thinking he could move about silently. He had not expected Jen to lock him in. He was crouched behind the bar when he heard her checking the windows followed by the key turning in the lock. He had planned to sneak in and out before closing time. The booze would be sold on to fund his habit. If it hadn't been so serious it would have been comical.

'Let the druggy fucker cut his feet,' shouted Martin. 'It's what he deserves.'

Jennifer ordered David to stand still while she fetched a brush and pan. Her dad was confused until Jennifer informed him that the pathetic figure before them was Angie's brother and Maureen's cousin. As Jennifer cleaned up around him, David began whimpering.

'What will we do with him?' she asked David's relatives. There was no reason to involve the police, although she suspected that Angie would not have hesitated.

'He can sleep it off at ours,' resigned Willie

'No way!' chorused the boys.

'Aye way. Give me a hand.'

Willie and Ryan hoisted David up by the shoulders. Martin picked up his shoes with the tips of his fingers as if he were going to catch something. Willie apologised and they left.

'Is it always like this?' asked Jimmy Thomson with great concern.

'Never,' laughed his daughter. 'Come on, we could both do with a stiff drink.'

Her father didn't disagree.

THIRTY

Tuesday 6th March

Malcolm prepared a rum punch in the kitchen of their rented villa near Holetown; a small village on the North West coast of Barbados. Mount Gay was his favourite rum and it couldn't be purchased anywhere in the U.K. Malcolm had picked one up, on the day of their arrival, from a local shop near the beach.

He placed their drinks on a small table between their sun beds. 'Cheers, sweetheart and cheers, Frank Ward.' Malcolm took a long sip from his straw.

'Who's Frank?' asked Angie putting down her book.

'I had the fortunate pleasure of meeting him the last time I was on the island. His family own the distillery where this rum is made.'

Angie tasted hers and agreed it was delicious but perhaps anything would taste delicious in paradise. Unlike Malcolm, her lounger was in the shade. A huge blue and orange umbrella shielded her from the sun. It was twenty-nine degrees and Angie felt a pool of moisture gather at the bottom of her back as she sat up.

'God, Angie, you look like a film star sitting there.' Malcolm was sincere.

Angie wore a low cut, high leg, black swimsuit. A black and green sarong was tied around her waist and a large, brimmed straw hat and tortoise-shell sunglasses offered extra protection from the glare of the sun. One knee was bent and the other long, slender leg stretched out in front of her. She had made the effort to paint her finger nails and toe nails a bright pink while she was in London.

'Fuck off!' she giggled. But she felt like a film star.

The secluded villa was everything she had imagined it would be and the views of the turquoise sea and white, sandy beach were breathtaking. A little, green wooden gate at the bottom of the garden opened on to the Caribbean shoreline. She took a large gulp of her punch, removed her hat and lay down beside Malcolm. She whispered that she was going to show him just how grateful she was. She traced her wet tongue from his chest to the waist band of his swim shorts. He lay back with his hands behind his head and moaned. She pulled the material away from his body. His penis reached up to welcome her mouth.

*

The bus drew into St Andrews station. Jennifer had decided to leave her car; not that she was planning to have a lot to drink but was hoping for a glass or two of wine. By the time she wandered down to the Old Course Hotel, hopefully, Scott would be waiting. If he didn't show then she would do some window shopping and head home. She had nothing to lose.

Jennifer loved St Andrews. Not as much as Edinburgh. But there were many similarities. Both had well established Universities and had the same mix of historical buildings and chic bistro pubs – very cosmopolitan. The beaches in St Andrews stretched forever. Jennifer loved the sea. The cold wind made her shiver and she pulled up the collar of her black trench coat and tightened the belt. At least it wasn't raining like it had been on Sunday. She thought back to Sunday, to her and Joe, and shivered again. It had not gone to plan.

*

Before the meeting, Jennifer had driven around the cobbled streets of Falkland, past the twelfth century palace, and stopped at the duck pond to collect her thoughts. She had rehearsed her speech over and over but ran through it again. She would be truthful with Joe. She would explain that it wasn't working and although she was very fond of him, he was not the long-term partner for her. She would not be like her mother and deliver a protracted version. She would keep it brief; it was only fair.

Joe had jumped out of his car as soon as Jennifer pulled up beside him in the East Lomond car park that was Falkland Hill. He hugged her tightly and kissed the top of her head. They walked up the well-worn foot path taking care on the slippery bracken and shingle beneath their feet. Their walking boots certainly helped. A couple of times Joe's strong arms shot out to steady his companion. They had only exchanged pleasantries; it was hard to communicate with a gale force wind in your face. Fifteen minutes into the climb the downpour started. It was relentless. Although they were well wrapped up, neither of them had worn proper waterproof clothing. The stumbling down was arduous and Jennifer's legs were aching when she reached the car. She flopped into the driver's seat, drenched from head to toe. Joe squelched onto the seat beside her. She was cold and miserable. The rain battered her small red Fiesta. A waterfall plunged down her windscreen. Perhaps it was the weather or perhaps it was everything that was weighing her down but Jennifer started to sob; loudly. She held on to the steering wheel for support; her body was losing control. Her knuckles turned white and her shoulders and arms shuddered.

Joe looked at the young, bedraggled soul next to him. She seemed too small for her seat, too small for the car. It was heartbreaking to watch.

'Jen, what's wrong? Tell me what to do.'

Jennifer seemed unable to reply. Gently, he prised her fingers from the wheel and pulled her towards him. Her head slouched on his chest and he cradled her until the crying, then the laboured breathing, subsided. Joe felt her body relax. He waited a little longer. He stroked her hair tenderly, hesitated then spoke.

'What's happened, Jen?'

His kindness made it all the more difficult for Jennifer to tell the truth. 'I'm so sorry, Joe, but I'm still in love with Mark. You must think I'm mad after everything he has done but I can't help it... I'm so sorry, you have been so good to me... and under different circumstances...'

'Hey, don't be sorry.'

'I know he's a bastard... but he's Emma and Katie's daddy and I just want us to be a family again. If he came back, I'd take him back even though he doesn't deserve it. I'm so sorry for giving you false hope. I wish it could be different.'

Jennifer was disgusted with herself. She had no intention of ever welcoming Mark back but how could she tell this gentle giant that she could never love him no matter how kind or helpful he had been and would be. They had nothing in common. There was just no spark. The sex had been great but she suspected that she would have to be the one to maintain momentum and provide the spice. And sex wasn't the real reason either. Conversations were tedious. They had different humour. He didn't make her laugh and she suspected that life with Joe would become mundane and boring. She was entitled to better and so was he.

Joe shook his head and said nothing. That bastard Mark did not deserve her. He loved Jen more than any man could – so he would wait.

'I fully understand that you won't want to help out but please don't stop coming in, Joe. You'll always be welcome at The Maltings.'

'I know. I can't stop how I feel about you, Jen, but I won't make you feel awkward either. I'm happy to help you so please keep asking.' He closed his eyes and buried his face into her hair. He tenderly kissed her head and left.

*

As Jennifer approached a carpark that overlooked the Old Course, a silver Capri slowed down beside her and the passenger wound his window down; a cheeky wolf whistle followed. A pretty brunette leaned over Scott and called from the driver's seat to Jennifer,

'Would you like me to drive on and dump him somewhere?'

She had the same cheery smile as her passenger. Jennifer assumed they must be related. Scott sprang from the car and thanked his sister and reminded her that he would make his own way back. He threw an Auchterlonie's bag on to the back seat. She waved goodbye and cried out, 'Good Luck!' Her sentiments were snatched by the blustering wind.

'Let's go somewhere warmer,' suggested Scott and with an arm resting on her back, they jogged round to the Shoogly Peg, fondly often referred to as the 19th hole.

The warmth from the open-hearth fire met them at the door.

'This is better,' said Scott admitting that he was finding it hard adjusting to the Scottish weather again. 'What are you having?'

'A white wine please. A chardonnay but only if you're having one.'

'A dry, white wine please, preferably a chardonnay and I'll have a Tennent's. Thank you.'

The barman said he would bring the drinks to their table. Scott chose one of the chunky, wooden tables close to the roaring fire.

'I wasn't sure if you'd come,' confessed Jennifer.

'Same here but glad you did.'

They didn't wait long for their drinks and the same barman took their food order. Jennifer rolled up her coat and placed it on the window sill behind her. Scott did the same. She decided to keep her green scarf as it added some colour to her black polo neck and black jeans: she was turning into Angie. Her hair was in a tight pony tail; the last thing she would have wanted Scott to witness was the wind wreaking havoc with her hair. A chestnut, candy floss was not the look for creating an impression unless you wanted to put someone off for life.

Jennifer recounted her visit from the two old guys from the Royal and Ancient. Scott admitted that he'd regretted not booking his stay over the summer season to take in The Open but his work had dictated otherwise. He was a keen golfer and seeing Seve Ballesteros in action would have made his holiday then quickly injected that Jennifer had more than made up for it. Of course. That made her laugh.

They settled into companiable banter over their meals. Scott had chosen steak pie and Jennifer had ordered lasagne. She left the garlic bread. (Just in case!) After three more wines, Jennifer felt the effects of the alcohol and asked Scott if they could go for a walk to help her sober up. He was happy to oblige. Fortunately, the wind had died down but it was still cold. St Andrews had always been subject to strong winds, particularly at this time of year. Jennifer rummaged in her bag for her woollen hat and gloves. Scott zipped up what could have passed for a blue, mountaineering jacket, put on his thermal gloves and a thermal hat with big ear flaps.

Jennifer looked at him and laughed, 'To think I was worried about the state of my hair, Scott of the Antarctic.'

'It's bloody bitter. Enough to freeze the balls of a Roo!' He tried to tickle her but his thick gloves got in the way. They carried on along Old Station Road that ran parallel with the golf course and turned left at Golf Place to head for the great expanse of beach called the West Sands.

'You said you had great staff. That must be a relief.' He tried to sound nonchalant.

'Oh, it is. I couldn't have done it without Angie and Maureen... and you know, I never used to like them much.'

Scott had deliberately held back questioning Jennifer about Angie even though it was at the forefront of his mind the whole time he had been with her. He needed to find out more about the woman who had duped him all those years ago. 'What changed?'

'Me probably. If I'm honest, I never tried hard enough... and now, I can't remember why they irritated me so much.'

'Are they married?'

'Maureen is. Her man, Willie, he's great. He's done all my renovations. You should see their house. I've never seen a house like it. It's absolutely beautiful. They have five boys. Great young men. In fact, you could be a big brother or an uncle. You look like them.'

'I'll settle for the big brother title. I'm too young to be an uncle figure.'

'How old are you?'

'Thirty-five.' He was the same age as Angie: they had hung around with the same crowd from their school days. 'And the other woman, what's her name? Is she married?'

'Angie? Nah! Too sensible. She was hurt a long time ago and I don't think she has moved on.'

'Who hurt her?' Scott tried not to sound too interested.

'The father of her wee girl. Mitch. I think that's what she said. She doesn't discuss it. He dumped her when he found out she was pregnant. What a rat-bag!'

'There's two sides to every story.' Scott was smarting with anger.

How dare Angie make out that he had dumped her? She had known for months that he was moving back to Australia. They had agreed to enjoy the time they had together before he left.

Jennifer detected from his tone that perhaps his own split up had been acrimonious.

'I'm sure you're right. So, tell me, what are your plans for the rest of your stay?' She was anxious to steer the conversation in a more positive direction.

Scott was cross that he'd let his guard drop. He could easily have exposed Angie for the bitch that she was but he would wait until she had returned from her holiday. He sensed that Jennifer was studying his face for some sort of approval that the day hadn't been spoiled. He liked her. He liked her a lot. He sought no pleasure in deceiving her about his association with Angie.

THIRTY-ONE

Thursday 8th March

Malcolm and Angie checked out of the Sandy Lane Hotel. They had enjoyed an overnight stay and were heading back to their villa. Angie had worried that it had been a little extravagant considering the villa was only a short drive from the resort but Malcolm couldn't resist playing the Old Nine Course and he wanted to treat Angie to the best hotel on the island. The holiday was disappearing quickly and she had loved every second of it. They had experienced mouth-watering, Bajan cuisine, dined under a canopy of mahogany trees and sampled the best wines the island had to offer. Never in a million years had Angie envisaged such luxury. They had two full days left and they intended to chill out back at Holetown.

They had crammed a lot in already. On Tuesday, they had visited the Kensington Oval cricket ground in Bridgetown. Unfortunately, the West Indies were playing Australia in Georgetown, Guyana that same week and although Malcolm would have preferred a test match, he was more than delighted to witness the extraordinary skills of the Barbadian National team. Fortunately for Angie, she had been a regular visitor to the cricket clubs of Freuchie and Falkland near Duneden and the rules of the game were familiar to her.

As a non-swimmer, Angie had been happy to paddle at leisure in the tepid sea; trailing her toes through the sand, book in hand, and watch Malcolm take as many swims as he wanted. Liberal lashings of sun creams were dutifully applied each day.

While Sandy Lane Hotel faded in the rear-view mirror, the warm wind cooled her face as their open-top sports car skimmed the surface of the coastal road. Angie whooped and waved as they overtook a ramshackle of a Reggae bus.

*

Jennifer had re-jigged the rota to allow her to have the afternoon and evening off. There were plenty of volunteers eager to swap their weekend shift for a less stressful Thursday night. She had arranged to meet Scott in Dundee. The train was the easier option and she would return to Ladybank station where a taxi was booked to pick her up later that night. She couldn't wait to meet up with her Australian.

Jennifer didn't want to venture out until everything was up to date. She worked her way through the morning list at a frantic pace. Her excitement was tangible. Only once the pipes were done, the bedroom make-ups were finished, all of the downstairs was clean and the vegetables had been prepped in the kitchen, did she feel comfortable leaving her staff to get on with things.

'Stop feeling so guilty,' chastised Maureen. 'It's no big deal. Away an' enjoy yourself with your pal. I'll see to your dad and the bairns.'

Jennifer called in on her dad who was busy painting room 3 in the resident's wing. The present occupier had been temporarily decanted to the room next to Jennifer's flat while her dad freshened up that bedroom. Jimmy was now in Jennifer's bed while his daughter slept on the pull-out sofa in the living room.

'Thank you so much, Dad, for helping me out today. It means such a lot. Maureen will prepare a meal for the three of you before she leaves. Heat it up in the microwave. Don't forget to pick up the girls from school. I won't be too late. Love you lots.'

There was a spring in his daughter's step that had been missing for far too long. He suspected a man was the reason but Jennifer would confide in him when she was ready.

*

Scott checked the arrival board at Dundee train station. He fidgeted nervously as Jennifer's train pulled into the platform. Tuesday had been more than he had expected or wanted: initially. After their long stroll along the beach, they had called into the West Port Bar for a final drink or two. When they spilled out on to the street it was dark but it could have been no later than 8.00pm. The street was busy with students chatting loudly; an array of nationalities mingled with each other. On the way to the bus station, they stopped in the street and kissed. Neither of them had planned the actual moment but somehow it seemed perfectly natural. There had been a great deal of flirting as they had chatted at the bar and the signals were there in their body language yet the enormity of their nuzzle had ambushed them. They stood back to gauge each other's reaction and the answer lay in their eyes and wide grins. Jennifer bit her lower lip with her teeth and Scott was hooked. Like a big fish being reeled in, he was unsure about what had just happened to him.

Jennifer spotted him on the platform. *Behave like an adult. Not a silly schoolgirl*, she thought as a tall Scott walked jauntily towards her. There was something about him that made Jennifer go weak at the knees. They embraced cautiously and were bemused by their initial awkwardness. Within seconds, the barriers were down. Scott kissed her cheek. They linked arms and Jennifer snuggled in as they headed for City Square and the Caird Hall. Scott had ditched his mountaineering jacket for one that was more suited to casual, city dining. They were both wearing denims but Scott's shirt was black and Jennifer had tucked her white, cotton shirt into her jeans. Her black ankle boots had three-inch heels yet she was still shorter than her date. Since she only had one coat, her trench coat made another appearance.

Scott had booked lunch at a small restaurant near the McManus Galleries and because they were running a little late, they didn't linger by having a drink elsewhere. It was more formal than the St Andrews pub where they had eaten on Tuesday and a young woman took their coats before seating them. Large, tinted mirrors stretched along the walls and Jennifer tried not to look at her reflection as she walked through the restaurant. Cream, linen table cloths and large, potted parlour plants in the corners did help to soften the slightly, clinical interior. A huge, leather folder, that was almost as big as their table, was handed to Scott by the sommelier so that he could peruse the wine list. He asked Jennifer if she had a preference.

'I tend to look at the cheapest option then choose one that's a couple of pounds dearer. I'm a skinflint.'

Scott chuckled at her honesty but followed her advice and ordered a bottle of Italian Frascati. Jennifer found him so easy to talk to and when they asked each other questions about their past neither of them appeared to skirt around the details. Although, Scott did say it was painful to talk about his daughter as he hadn't seen her for a very long time and he would rather not discuss it. His reluctance seemed incompatible with his openness to recount everything else about his life. Jennifer was too busy enjoying the present to allow it to niggle.

Scott had been married for three years and divorced for two; irrevocable differences – but that could cover a range of reasons. He communicated with his ex-wife rarely.

They caught up on schooling, jobs, previous relationships and hopes for their futures. When Jennifer asked if he knew people from Duneden, Scott couldn't recall any actual names claiming that he had hung around with boys from Cupar and Ceres. Scott had a very comfortable lifestyle in Adelaide and was about to start up his own refrigeration business with a likeminded friend and colleague.

The waiter asked if they would like coffees. It was that time already. Both of them declined, claiming they had room for nothing else. They'd shared a gigantic seafood platter and oodles of bread. Scott couldn't resist their syrup pudding and so Jennifer had one, teensy ball of vanilla ice-cream. Another long walk was called for. Scott insisted on paying and admonished Jennifer for suggesting they go Dutch.

It was cold and damp but there was no wind. Jennifer was unfamiliar with the city of Dundee and was happy for Scott to lead the way. They walked down to the waterfront on the Firth of Tay. Scott pointed to one of the rigs where his dad used to work and explained how the port provided a range of support for the semi-submersible drilling rigs and vessels for the North Sea oil and gas industry. His parents now lived around the coast and his dad had accepted a less stressful desk job since a recent health scare. It was one of the reasons Scott had decided to visit; to make sure his dad was recovering as well as he had intimated during phone calls.

All the clues were there for Jennifer but because she assumed that Scott's daughter lived in Australia with his ex-wife, although he had never actually stated that, she never made the connection with Angie and Bethany. Nor had Scott ever mentioned that his school friends in Scotland had called him Mitch. He had chosen his words carefully.

Soon they were in The Nethergate area of the city. 'How about a drink in here?' suggested Scott and they entered a bar that led to and was part of the Royal Hotel. 'What do you fancy?'

Jennifer didn't want to mix her drinks as she still felt slightly intoxicated. She was a lightweight when it came to alcohol.

'Could I have a soda water and lime?... just for now, obviously.' She smiled mischievously and found a table while Scott was at the bar.

She knew she would have to pace herself if she didn't want to end up in the toilets speaking to 'Hughie' before boarding the train. It was only four-fifteen and she had planned to catch the nine-thirty back to Fife. Scott had been compliant to her early departure; it was that or nothing.

Halfway through their drinks, Scott informed her that he was actually staying at The Royal for the next three nights. His parents had other visitors and although they had no objections to their son staying with them, Scott felt it would be easier for them if he booked into a hotel for a few nights. He let them think that he was staying with a friend.

'I don't want to you to feel in anyway threatened by my next suggestion... but would you like to have a drink in my room?'

Shit! thought Jennifer, *I was NOT expecting that!*

She must have taken a long time to reply when Scott said, 'We can stay here. It's not a problem.'

Jennifer had to think straight. She had very acceptable underwear on. A given for a just in case scenario. A quick spray with perfume would probably be required. Agreeing to go to his room would lead to other things and was she ready for that? Of course, she was, but she had had her fingers burned on recent occasions and would she feel a proper wee slut if she put herself in this position again? He was going back to Australia, that was inevitable, and the chances of ever seeing him again were slim. What was there to lose?

'It would be cheaper than drinking here, I'm assuming?' It had not been a calculated response and, if Jennifer had been forewarned, she would have delivered a more inspirational retort but her answer had been given.

The climb to Scott's room had felt like an out of body experience. It was as if she were hovering above, scrutinising their every move. Each step on the stairs and every gesture made by them seemed magnified. She was grateful for the soda water.

Scott's room overlooked the busy main road. He closed the heavy drapes and proffered a seat; it was a small, boudoir-type settee, typical of the Victorian era and the original furnishings of the building. It was a spacious room and although clean and cosy, the mix of the old and new didn't quite marry. Maureen would have had a field day redesigning the place.

'Gin and tonic?' asked Scott on opening the self-service bar. 'Or, you can have one of my beers?'

An array of drinks had been left on the top of the small fridge to make room for Scott's own collection.

'As long as it's cold.'

He poured them both a beer and perched on the arm of a chair beside her. A television unit and a coffee table, along with their chair and settee, had created a small living space in the corner of the large room. It was the first time there had been a prolonged lull in the conversation. Jennifer smiled politely and turned the glass around in her hand.

'Would you like some music?' asked Scott.

'Why not?'

He fiddled with the radio and managed to tune into the local station; Renee and Renato's awful song *Save Your Love* filled the room. If nothing else, it curbed the awkwardness and made them laugh. Once the volume was adjusted, Scott switched on some lamps, turned off the main light and sat down next to Jennifer.

He took the glass from her hand and placed it quietly on the coffee table in front of them. He moved his head slowly towards Jennifer and kissed her softly on the lips. His eyes were focussed on her face as his lips traced the contours of her mouth – small, gentle, meaningful pecks from one corner to the other.

Jennifer wanted the gentleness to continue. She rested her forehead on his and asked in a barely audible whisper if he would like to go to bed.

She stood at one side of the bed and Scott at the other. They watched each other undress, in silence. Neither of them rushed. As each item was removed, it lay where it fell. With only their underwear left, Jennifer unfastened her bra and stepped out of her white, lacy pants. She stood naked and looked on as Scott pushed his pants down over his toned thighs. A woman can hide her eagerness but Scott's was there for his lover to see and there was no doubt that he wanted her as much as she longed for him. For a brief moment, he turned from her, reached for the protection they would both need and eased it over him.

They slipped into the cold sheets together seeking warmth as their skin connected and each of them releasing a pleasurable sigh as they did so. They explored each other with hands and tongues, relishing each other's touch. It didn't take long for Scott to pull her on top of him. He entered her immediately. Their rhythm was as new and exciting as it was comfortable and familiar. Jennifer's fingers were entwined in his and he supported her weight: her arms were straight and taut. She arched her back and pushed away from him, causing deeper penetration. Her auburn hair tickled his chest. Scott's body shunted with desire. He rolled her on to her back and she wrapped her legs tightly around his hips. Her wanting groans encouraged him to thrust harder. She felt the power in his arms and shoulders as she ran her palms and fingers over them. As the intensity and adrenalin rushed to their loins, they abandoned themselves as they climaxed and held on. Even in the aftermath, they pushed and squeezed every fleeting arousal until they had nothing left. They lay for several minutes savouring the moment.

'Would you like a bath?' asked Scott. 'There's a huge one in the bathroom.'

Jennifer chose the end with no taps and the two of them lay and chatted with only their heads visible above the soapy bubbles. Scott studied her face. It was perfect. She was perfect. He knew he would have to broach the real reason for his visit. Scott promised himself that he would tell Jennifer about Angie before she left for her train. He dreaded having to say it but it had to be done. Falling for Jennifer had never been part of his plan. Half an hour later, they made love again after topping up with hot water.

They dried off and cuddled down for a short nap. When Jennifer felt his body sag and a purring snore emanated from his throat, she sneaked out of their bed to dress quietly in the darkened room. It was a fitting time to leave. No awkward goodbyes or futile suggestions about keeping in touch. In the dim light, she scribbled a short note, left it on her pillow, and closed the door gently.

Thank you for the best time ever.
Take care and safe journey home.

She signed off with a drawing of a smiley face and several tiny crosses forming the shape of a heart.

THIRTY-TWO

Saturday 10th March

With a heavy heart, Angie prepared a tomato salad for Malcolm and herself. It was the last day of their holiday and it had been idyllic. She didn't want it to end although she knew she was pining for Bethany and longed to be with her again. They'd been apart for a week before but that had been when Bethany had stayed in a caravan in Perthshire with Angie's mother and, for some reason, the separation then had felt less acute.

Malcolm intended to drive to Grantley Adams airport on the South of the island where he would hand over their hired car. The flight was scheduled to depart at 17:20 Barbados time and although the journey normally lasted approximately eight hours, touchdown at Gatwick would probably be around 06:30 British time on Sunday morning; taking account of the five-hour time delay between the two countries.

'Cheers,' said Malcolm and he raised a glass of wine as they sat in the garden looking out to the sea. 'Ah, sweetheart, don't cry.' He rose from his chair and kissed his young mistress's salty tears.

'I'm sorry... but I've had a great time. The best ever.' She mopped her tears with the bottom of her palms taking care not to smudge her mascara.

Malcolm and Angie had discussed at length what their relationship would be like when they returned to Duneden.

Angie accepted that for the foreseeable future Malcolm would not leave Doreen. Actually, that was not a problem for her – the ducking and diving was annoying – but she enjoyed her independence. Angie insisted she got the best bits. Malcolm relished her company, the sex was great, he was generous with his money and Doreen had to deal with the bad moods and the dirty washing. He promised there would be many more weekend breaks and holidays to look forward to.

'And me. I've enjoyed every minute.' Malcolm massaged her shoulders. Her short, jet-black hair brushed his fingers as they made small circular movements behind her ears just above the jaw line.

Angie felt the tension melt away. 'Thank you.' Her time with Malcolm had been so precious and she realised then that she would never love another man as much as she did this one.

*

Jennifer hadn't had much time to dwell on what might have been. The Maltings had been exceptionally busy and both her girls had been unwell on Friday afternoon, especially Emma – tummy bugs. For that reason, Jennifer distanced herself from handling food and took on all the cleaning duties to allow Maureen and Archie to concentrate on the kitchen. Fortunately, the bug had seemed to bypass both Jennifer and her dad but Maureen had heard that Bethany had succumbed too. Scott had tried to speak with Jennifer on Friday night but it was up to her dad to relate the news that she was preoccupied with cleaning up sick and shit. As a precaution, Jennifer had disinfected every surface, door handle and light switch throughout the building every few hours. The last thing she wanted was to be responsible for causing an outbreak amongst her customers although neither of the girls had vomited since midnight last night. Hopefully, it was only a twelve-hour thing. She called into the flat throughout the morning to check they were okay. Two small, pale faces smiled weakly from the duvets that were tucked around them on the sofa. A quiet day in front of the telly and plenty of fluids were dutifully adhered to.

Jimmy had started painting room 2 on Friday and was applying the final coat today. Since all the workers had returned to the Wirral for the weekend, the windows and doors had been left open in the resident's wing to allow the air to circulate. All three bedrooms were ready for the summer season. Beige blackout curtains had been chosen for each room and they had switched to crisp, white bedding throughout after the shooting season had ended. New carpets would have to wait for another year.

Jennifer shouted to her dad to come and join her. Maureen had plated two cheese burgers, salad and chips for them. She felt that the girls would be put off by the smell of hot food and decided to eat over in the resident's area instead. She placed the tray on top of a paint tin that was on a towel on the floor. Jennifer dragged one of the high back chairs from the other side of the long cabinet to face her dad.

'Excuse the posh dining,' she joked as she handed her dad his plate.

'I'm ready for this.'

He was a small, slight man. Her brother, Andrew, looked like him but Jimmy's hair had a reddish tinge to it whereas Andrew was white blond and he was taller than his dad.

'So come on, what happened on Thursday night? You skipped out of this place without a care in the world and returned with the weight of the world on your shoulders. Anything your old dad can do?'

'Nope. Not this time,' and she tried to smile as tears pricked her eyes. She blinked them away and sighed. 'It wasn't to be. Simple as that.'

Jimmy knew if he waited, Jennifer would eventually open up. They were half way through their food when she decided to speak.

'I met this really nice guy. An Aussie. In here actually, last Friday. It was like we'd known each other for years. We just clicked. He made me laugh... but he lives in Australia. End of. We met up again. Twice. But he'll be going back soon. No good wishing for anything else so we said our goodbyes. That's it.'

'An Australian phoned here on Friday night. Same one? He seemed determined to call again.'

'What's the point, Dad? We can't change the inevitable and I'm in deep enough.'

Jimmy tried to think of something reassuring to say but he could see how much his daughter was hurting and any words of wisdom he might have to offer would unlikely make any difference. Unfortunately, time was her best ally now.

By six o'clock, both patients were feeling much better. Heinz cream of chicken soup and a slice of bread each had been quickly devoured. Although they claimed they were still hungry, Jennifer suggested they should wait a little longer before having anything else to eat. By eight o'clock, they had scoffed two rounds of buttered toast. Her dad dozed on the comfy chair while the girls giggled to an *Inspector Gadget* video. Jennifer left them to it.

Evening meals were steady. Last orders had been taken at eight and diners were quickly replaced by the drinking clientele. Angie and Jennifer understood that at some point in the future they would have to discuss extending the hours they served food; The Maltings had become an established and popular eating venue.

The lounge bar was loud and busy and the usual punters were sitting or standing at the bar. Martin Ross and another local were pulling the pints. Jennifer had opted to collect the glasses and to do other chores, such as changing the barrels, further reducing her need to be touching other folk's drinks. She washed her hands as often as she could and gave her tables a good wipe down whenever possible. She laughed at Martin's chit chat with her regulars. He was turning out to be a really good barman and, like his mum and his auntie, he was one hundred per cent reliable. Jennifer hadn't noticed Scott enter as she was busy drying glasses behind the bar and her view was blocked by several young farmers who had gathered near the door.

It was Joe's voice that caused her to swing around quickly.

'Fucking hell! Mitch, ma man, how you doin?'

Jennifer stood on her toes desperate to get a good look at the man who had caused Angie so much grief. It was hopeless; there were too many bodies. She exited the bar and turned into the lounge. She squeezed her way through a group of jocular lads, batting away their flirtatious remarks when their bodies were nudged out of the way by hers. That's when she saw them. Joe was shaking Scott's hand – her Scott, the one she had spent the evening with, had shared a bath with. But Joe had called him Mitch. The enormity of his con engulfed her body and she was unable to move. People say that that can happen and Jennifer would have been the first to scoff at it, but she genuinely could not move; it was as if the pause button had been pushed.

Scott spotted Jennifer before Joe did. He would never forget the look on her face – bewilderment, disbelief and the realisation that she had been betrayed all over again. Before he could say anything, Joe called out to her,

'Jen, come and meet an old mate of mine.'

This was *HER* bar and she would *NOT* cause a scene nor did she want anyone to realise that she knew Scott: especially Joe.

'Jen, this is Mitch an old school pal. Mitch, this is Jen Cameron. She owns The Maltings and she's my... er... the owner.'

Jennifer had no idea what Joe was about to disclose but she knew that Scott had understood by Joe's hesitation that there had been history between them. Joe continued,

'How long has it been? Seven years?'

'Try nine, mate.' Scott couldn't take his eyes off Jennifer.

'Pleased to meet you... Mitch? Is that short for Michael?'

Joe guffawed. He'd had a good drink. 'Mitch as in Michelin Tyres.'

Scott stepped in. His voice was devoid of emotion. 'Tyre as in McIntyre. It was daft then. It's daft now. School boys and nicknames.'

Jennifer would never have made the connection. Angie's bastard Mitch was her bastard, Scott McIntyre. They had both been sucked in and paid the price.

'Nice meeting you, Mitch, but as you can see, I'm very busy.'

Scott held Jennifer by the elbow but she shrugged him off and left the room more quickly than she had entered it. She barged past the animated farmers apologising as she went.

Jennifer sought refuge in the darkened kitchen. The cold steel surface stole the heat from her body as she rested her hands on it.

'I'm an idiot,' she called to the darkness. 'A gullible, stupid, bloody idiot!'

She paced the kitchen, walking in circles around the central preparation station. He was good. Calculating and clever. Worst of all she had never suspected a thing. Scott was waiting in the corridor. She assumed he might be.

'No!' She held her hand up as if stopping the traffic. 'Don't you dare!'

'Please, Jennifer. Let me explain.'

'No need. I've worked it out. You used me and like a fool I fell for it. So, if you don't mind, you can celebrate your victory elsewhere. I don't want you here.'

'It's not like that. I'm sorry. I didn't mean to hurt you. I wouldn't.'

'Well, you did. You had ample opportunity to say something... and... you chose... not to.' She had no fight left and she could feel her voice tremble. 'I would really like you to leave. If you have any feelings for me at all, you'll go. Please.'

Martin popped his head out from the bar. 'Everything okay here? Jen?'

Jennifer smiled at his young face. 'Everything's fine here. Thanks. Mitch is just leaving.' Jennifer returned to drying her glasses. She watched as Scott re-entered the lounge to say his farewells to Joe. Jennifer avoided any eye contact. She knew he'd be back. He obviously had unresolved business with Angie.

THIRTY-THREE

Sunday 11th March

Jennifer had a splitting headache. She had witnessed every passing hour since going to bed and she had snoozed her alarm twice. She had to force herself to get up. Usually, a tepid shower would suffice but that hadn't worked either. The girls were still sleeping as was her dad. According to Jimmy, they were awake until 11.00pm last night; a renewed energy after their lethargic day. As she dried off, she relived the moment when she witnessed Joe shake Scott's hand. It was no use crying; she had done enough of that last night in bed. *Once a fool always a fool.* Maybe there was some truth in the old saying. She didn't see herself as a victim but perhaps she gave off those 'here I am' vibes, unintentionally. And to think she slept with him! He must have loved that. Her staff uniform was hanging on the back of the door. She dressed quickly, tied her hair up and checked her face in the mirror. Her eyes were puffy and her skin was red and blotchy. She splashed her eyes with very cold water. She folded up her bed, smartened up the living room area and tip-toed out of the apartment.

The pace on a Sunday morning was less frantic than the week days. In adherence to the Scottish Licensing Laws, alcohol could not be served until 12.30pm, therefore lunches started later too. Since the day The Maltings had first opened, Jennifer continued to enjoy her morning coffee before anyone or anything could interrupt her day. She wrapped her duffle coat around her and sat on the back doorstep, pulling the coat beneath her bottom to prevent the cold seeping through. At least it wasn't raining. A Scotch mist had settled over the River Eden and the beer garden was green and very peaceful. The weeping willows on her side of the river appeared to touch Malcolm's on the other bank. She sipped her coffee and inhaled the silence.

It was then that she noticed the car in the far-left hand side of the car park. It was parked at an awkward angle and the front wheels were resting on the grass while the back wheels were on the gravel. There were often cars left overnight but she was sure that when she waved Martin Ross off last night that his was the last car to leave. Her curiosity won the battle of should I or shouldn't I investigate and Jennifer wandered over to the stationary vehicle. The windows were steamed up but there was definitely someone stretched out in the driver's seat. The least she could do was to offer him or her a coffee. She tapped lightly on the window. No response. She tapped louder. The occupant jolted, sat up and fingers squeaked on the glass as they formed a circle to peer through the vapour. It was reminiscent of a scene from the movie *Jaws* when a severed head appears through a hole in the boat: only the face that made Jennifer jump back was Scott's.

He opened the car door and eased himself out. He linked the fingers in both hands, reached upwards, arms extended and groaned. He rubbed his back and tilted his head to the right and then to the left. Jennifer thought that he looked bloody awful. Far worse than the blotchy face that had grimaced back at her earlier this morning.

'Sorry, I didn't mean to startle you,' said Scott, apologetically.

His clothes were crumpled and his bed-head hair was not an endearing sight. His light brown, curly hair had been flattened all over.

'You look worse than I feel.' It wasn't a joke.

'Can I talk to you, please? I promise it won't take long but you need to hear me out. Please?'

Jennifer longed for an explanation. The truth had to be better than the scenarios that had tortured her thoughts throughout the night. She wanted to see his face when he confessed to misleading her and only then would she be able to judge if she believed what he had to say.

'I don't want you here when the staff arrive, so you've got half an hour max.'

He could have had much longer than half an hour but Jennifer reckoned that if he needed more than that then he was most likely to be conjuring up lies. She made him a coffee and a fresh one for herself. They sat in the lounge bar. She had her back to the wall and he sat at the table facing her. Jennifer would have liked to open the windows to dilute the smell of stale cigarettes but the heating bills were astronomical. She stared at Scott willing him to speak. The atmosphere was nauseatingly tense – for her at least.

'I know you won't believe me but I wanted to tell you the truth so many times.'

'Why didn't you say who you were right at the beginning?'

'Not many people know that I'm Bethany's dad. It wasn't my place to tell you.'

'But you knew I knew about Mitch... I mean you. Christ! Why does everything need to be so complicated?'

Scott smiled.

Jennifer continued, 'Don't! This is not funny. I would never have entertained the notion of us, if I had known who you were. My friendship with Angie means more to me than...'

'Me?'

It's not what she meant but at this time in her life, she needed Angie and that was difficult to admit out loud. It was a cowardly confession.

Jennifer sighed. 'I never expected to meet someone like you. That sounds corny but it's true. It felt right. You felt right... but it was a lie. And now I don't know what to believe.'

It was beginning to dawn on Jennifer that the definition of what was a lie and what was the truth was blurred. If she had known that Scott was Angie's ex-lover, would she have dismissed his advances based on what Angie had said about him or because the alternative was to risk upsetting Angie and jeopardising their business relationship?

'I admit, when I found out that Angie worked here and that she was on holiday – your barman told me – I was prepared to do anything to get some inside information for leverage. You seemed the obvious way in.'

Jennifer visibly cringed at his frankness.

'But that was before I got to know you,' he chipped in quickly. 'That day in St Andrews changed everything. It's the same for me, Jennifer. I'm comfortable around you. We fit. And that night in Dundee, that was for real. It had nothing to do with Angie.'

'You abandoned her, Scott. You turned your back on her and your baby.'

'It wasn't like that!'

'Then how was it? Tell me.'

Scott put his cup on the table. He rubbed his face with his hands – distorting the skin with the force.

'Angie knew for months that I was going back to Australia. All our friends knew. We were going out but it wasn't heavy. Okay, we were having sex but I liked Angie and she liked me. I really liked her. We had been mates for a long time but we agreed that we were having fun. That was all.'

'It takes two. You had responsibilities. Even Mark knew that.'

Scott was clearly exacerbated. 'She was supposed to be on the pill.'

'So was I but accidents happen and you were part of that accident!'

His neck was reddening. 'I had a job to go to. A really good job. It was a great opportunity for me. My grandfather had gone to a lot of trouble to secure the position for me.'

'You were having a baby!'

'A baby was never part of the deal!' shouted Scott. He banged the table, got up abruptly and paced the room. When he had garnered his thoughts, he sat back down again. He spoke more measurably. 'I liked Angie but I didn't love her, not like... but I did ask her to come to Australia. I would've tried to give her and the baby a decent life but she wanted to be near her mum in Duneden.'

There was a very long pause before Jennifer replied. She was calmer too.

'You gave up on them, Scott.'

He threw his head back in frustration. 'I suppose I did.'

Jennifer could see that tears were not far away. 'So why are you here?'

'I want to be part of Bethany's life. If Angie will let me. I just want my wee girl to know that I think about her every day and any communication is better than nothing.'

'You've left it a bit late in the day.'

'Yeah. Well, I've tried before and was kicked in the teeth so I'm back for more.'

'Did you try hard enough?' Jennifer was determined not to make it easy for him.

'I came over when Bethany was three months old. I had to ask my work for compassionate leave to attend a funeral. Angie let me see her once. ONCE. All that way for one hold. What else could I do? I came back a year later. That time, Angie dropped her off at my mum and dad's for a few hours. My mum cried the whole time but at least Angie agreed to let them see Bethany again as long as they never told her who they really were. I decided not to return. It hurt too much and I wasn't getting a chance to save any money.'

Jennifer scoffed loudly.

'I'd just finished my probationary year! I didn't get paid a lot... so I set up a trust fund instead.'

'For Bethany?' That was not the impression Angie had given to Jennifer. She'd intimated that Mitch had been unsupportive.

'Who else would it be for? I'm not trying to pretend that I'm blameless and I don't know how things would have worked out if I'd stayed but I'm here now and I'm desperate. You know Angie well. What d'you think of my chances?'

Jennifer genuinely couldn't guess. The last time (the only time) that Angie had mentioned Mitch, she was undeniably scathing; she had called him a c**t! Jennifer chose not to disclose the fact that Angie claimed he'd asked her to have an abortion. Mark had suggested the very same to her.

'I wish I could give you some words of wisdom but I'd be frightened they'd backfire and make things worse. Please do me a huge favour. Would you, please, leave me out of your discussions with Angie? She can't know about us. Please don't say anything.'

'You don't have to worry about that; I think I've done enough damage. I'm sorry.'

Jennifer leant back and rested her head on the wall. The past year had been one long roller coaster ride. Some thrill seekers find them exhilarating yet terrifying at the same time. Jennifer just wanted to get off!

'So, what now?' she asked.

'Now?... I'll have to face Angie.'

THIRTY-FOUR

Monday 12th March

'Good morning, baby,' whispered Angie.

'Mummy!' squealed Bethany. 'How did you get here?'

Angie laughed. As soon as she had arrived home on Sunday night, she dumped everything and scooted over to her mother's house hoping to catch Bethany before her bedtime but her eight-year-old was fast asleep. Bethany would have said that she was eight and a half: that half makes all the difference when you are young. Angie nipped back to her own house to unpack and to gather all the gifts she had bought Bethany and her mother in London. She sorted her washing into two different piles: the Barbados bundle and her everyday clothes that she could wear at home. The colourful, summer clothes were loaded first. As she tucked her passport at the back of the drawer of her bedside cabinet, she revisited the moment she kissed Malcolm goodbye at Kings Cross Station in London – it had been so emotional for both of them. They had clung on as if they would never see each other again.

'I climbed in beside you last night so that I'd be here when you woke up. Is that alright?' Angie snuggled down under the covers as her giggling daughter wrapped her arms around her neck and kissed her mummy on the lips. Angie gazed at her perfect, innocent face and mop of black hair; she really was a wee *Snow White*.

'Guess what I got you?' teased Angie.

'Can I have it now?'

They hurried downstairs as if it was Christmas morning. Angie had deliberately wrapped up lots of little gifts separately to increase the anticipation of guessing what they might be. It was a game that mother and daughter loved to play. There were all sorts of things from a tiny teddy bear to bracelets, London trinkets, Carnaby Street tee shirts, stationery and sparkly hair accessories. Angie's mother, Joyce, had made a large plate of French toast, a favourite of all three of them, and along with her granddaughter joined in the guessing game.

There were more big hugs and cuddles when the Lennies and the Camerons met at the school gates on Monday morning. Emma and Katie were as excited as Bethany had been to see Angie again.

'It's so good to see you. I've missed you,' confessed Jennifer.

'I'd like to say that I've missed you lot. But can't tell a lie.' Angie pulled a funny face. 'Only joking. I had a fantastic holiday. Really relaxing.'

'Huh! You must be the only person I know who has found trailing around London relaxing!'

Angie noted Jen's comment and would have to concentrate before blabbing next time. She'd bought a pocket sized 'London Tourist Attractions' guide book and devoured it on the train. Although Angie had stayed with her friend in Clapham before, it had been more of a drunken fest rather than a cultural experience. She had to be more careful. No flippancies.

When the school bell sounded, the girls ran to their lines; Emma and Bethany were in the same class as there were only eleven weeks between their two birthdays. Jennifer and Angie walked together. Angie was popping into the shop for her mother's morning paper and rolls.

'See you later,' she called to Jennifer as she breezed into the family grocer's.

Jennifer had no idea what the day might bring. Scott had asked to meet with her again before his vacation ended. Jennifer would have to think long and hard about that request and was unable to give him an immediate response. 'Let's wait and see,' she'd said. Thank goodness he'd not surprised Angie on her doorstep last night. What an ending to a long-awaited break that would've been for her friend. Angie looked refreshingly well after her holiday and Jennifer was a little envious. There was no time to plan or take a holiday before August – The Maltings was too busy. Jennifer was grateful that Mark was taking the girls to Murcia for a week during the Easter Holidays, despite worrying that Roxanne seemed incapable of taking care of herself never mind Jennifer's precious twosome. She tried not to dwell on it. Perhaps when the girls were away, she would manage a couple of days through in North Berwick where Fiona and Walter would thoroughly spoil her. Jennifer felt she'd neglected her close friendships lately, especially Hannah, even though she rang her old companion every other day for a catch up. Fergal had reminded Jennifer that she had her own life to lead and that Hannah had a social diary that most energetic sixty-year-olds couldn't compete with.

Maureen was waiting at the back door when Jennifer swung round the corner. She took a last puff of her cigarette and stubbed it out on the bin before dropping it through the hole in the top.

'It's a disgusting habit. I ken, but one naughty thing at a time,' said Maureen patting her decreasing waist line. 'And I don't mean Willie.'

Jennifer gave Maureen a jokey shove; knocking her off her feet. 'Sorry, are you okay? I don't know my own strength. Or it's all that weight you've lost?'

The two colleagues giggled their way into the kitchen. Maureen piled all her cleaning products into her caddy while Jennifer gave the kitchen work surfaces their first disinfection of the day. Maureen began her well-practised routine while Jennifer sprang upstairs to catch up with her dad. He had pushed all the furniture back into place in room 2.

'A quick hoover and I'll be out of your hair,' he yelled above the wailing.

Jennifer switched the vacuum cleaner off at the wall and waited for the droning to abate. 'I can finish that off.' She admired his handiwork. 'Thanks, Dad. The rooms are looking great.'

'Can you still smell the paint? I've become that accustomed to it that I can't tell anymore.' Jimmy had finished all the decorating on Saturday.

'Only in here... slightly. If the guest wants to move, he can sleep in our wing for a night. They won't be back until six thirty so plenty of time for it to disappear completely.'

The Wirral boys were usually very accommodating and Jennifer was sure there would be no complaints. She double-checked that all their belongings were where they ought to be. The workers usually left some clothing and other personal property behind when they went home for the weekend. When her dad was organised, she walked him to his car.

'If you ever need me, you know where I am.' And they both chorused together, 'If you need me thingmy, ring me!' She waved until his car turned out on to Eden Road.

'Hey! Is the kettle on?' It was Angie and she looked radiant.

'I need a holiday,' huffed Jennifer. 'You're early.'

'I only popped back to my ma's with her paper and left.'

Jennifer shouted on Maureen to join them and they listened to Angie enthuse about her week in London. Angie had studied her pocket book well. Neither of her two pals seemed to suspect what she'd really been up to. Her skin had a hint of colour but Angie claimed she and her friends had walked everywhere and the London temperatures were always higher. When she'd enquired about their week both Jennifer and Maureen had shrugged; there was nothing interesting to report. The David incident was not to be mentioned to Angie and Jennifer was waiting until the end of the lunch shift before disclosing what she knew about Mitch – only the parts about him visiting The Maltings twice. Fortunately, Willie had not been in on Saturday night or Maureen would have forewarned Angie straight away of his presence.

The lunches were almost over when an ashen face Maureen walked in to the kitchen.

'Angie, you've a visitor. It's Mitch.'

'What the fuck? Maureen, you'll have to cover the kitchen. Where's Jen?'

Maureen ran to fetch Jennifer who was busy pricing up what it would cost to spruce up the function suite. Jennifer guessed what was unfolding by the anxious way that Maureen was leading her by the hand. Angie was at the sink washing her hands.

'It's Mitch, isn't it?'

'How the fuck did you guess that?' asked Angie.

'He was in here on Saturday night. Joe introduced me. We spoke very briefly. I was going to tell you at the end of your shift.

Sorry. I had no idea that he would turn up here today.' That was a half-truth. Scott had indicated that he was going to visit Angie at her home.

'Can we use the back room?'

'Of course,' confirmed Jennifer, 'or you're more than welcome to sit in the flat. You do whatever you're comfortable with.'

Angie left, leaving Maureen and Jennifer unsure of what they should do next. Maureen hovered at the kitchen door and as soon as she saw Angie and Mitch walk down the corridor towards the function room, she gave the thumbs up to Jen. Maureen followed Jennifer to the bar.

'When did she tell you about Mitch?' asked Maureen in a whisper.

'Around New Year.'

'You're privileged. He'll be wanting to see Bethany, no doubt.'

The wait was excruciatingly painful. Jennifer could barely concentrate. She cleaned everything behind the bar in record time. Tables were wiped down and ashtrays were emptied and washed. A little brush and pan swept up crumbs of food that had fallen on to the floor during service. The last two diners were putting on their coats when Maureen appeared.

'Anything?'

Jennifer shook her head.

'That's me finished. I'll make us a coffee. I'm no' going until I can see that Angie's okay.'

As Maureen placed the coffees on the bar, Angie opened the lounge door.

'Me and Mitch are going for a walk. Jen, will you collect Bethany if I'm not at the school gates?' Angie looked crestfallen.

'Absolutely.'

'Are ye going to be alright?' asked Maureen

'I'll be fine. I'll tell you all about it later.'

Maureen slurped her coffee. 'I expected her to be screamin' and shoutin.''

Jennifer's mug was visibly shaking in her hand. She was praying that it worked out well for both of them. She couldn't afford to lose Angie and as much as she had been disappointed in Scott, she hoped he'd be given an opportunity to build bridges with Bethany and Angie.

'Mitch McIntyre was a nice guy, you know,' said Maureen. 'They were never oot o' our house. Angie should of went wi' him to Australia when she had the chance. Maybe she'll go now.'

That option had never occurred to Jennifer and it was one that filled her with dread. Not only would she lose Angie but she would lose her to the man that she had begun to fall in love with.

Angie and Mitch were standing at the school gates when Jennifer turned the corner. She felt her knees wobble. They looked like a normal couple waiting to collect their child after school. It made Jennifer want to weep.

'Jen, this is Mitch. Mitch, this is Jen, my boss and my very good friend.' Angie looked so happy.

Mitch leant in for an embrace as Jennifer's hand shot out to shake his. After the short confusion, they settled for a courteous handshake and a tentative smile. There were so many questions buzzing about in Jennifer's brain but the answers would have to wait.

'How long are you here for, Mitch? Sorry, I was so busy the other night that I didn't ask. I'm assuming that's an Aussie accent? '

'I'm going home next week.'

As the school bell rang, one of the dads recognised Mitch and

Jennifer stood back to allow them to chat. Emma ran up puffing and asked if Bethany could come for tea. Angie mouthed 'NO!'

'Let Bethany have the rest of the day with her mummy. She hasn't seen her for a long time.'

Jennifer watched as Bethany skipped off hand in hand with Angie as Scott flanked her other side. Before they disappeared from view, Bethany slipped her hand into Scott's.

THIRTY-FIVE

Easter Sunday: 22nd April

Emma, Bethany and Katie were poised with their chocolate Easter eggs.

'One, two, three... go!' shouted Fergal and the girls rolled their eggs down the lower slopes of Falkland Hill. Squeals and laughter swirled around the grassy hillside.

Emma and Bethany's eggs fell at the first hurdle – they bounced off a large turf and landed in a hollow, inches apart. Katie's egg made its bid for freedom but in doing so lost all the tin foil and the chocolate broke off in large sections. Jennifer and her dad scrambled after it trying to pick up the pieces that were strewn over the grass and heather.

'Yeah! Katie's the winner,' proclaimed her mother.

'Can we eat ours now? They're definitely cracked,' Emma informed the group.

It was customary to eat your egg only after it had been broken: symbolic of the rolling away of the rock from Christ's tomb before the resurrection.

The two losers tucked in but poor Katie had to be given another egg as her one had rolled over rabbit droppings and God knows what else. Fergal had to judge the painted boiled eggs before the adults could roll their eggs. Angie's punk rocker was declared the winner. Once the rolling had finished, the two grannies, Grace and Joyce, found a flat area for the picnic. Two large rugs were spread out to accommodate the large gathering of Jennifer's family (including Fergal) and Angie's mum and Bethany. Six hungry adults and three not so hungry, chocolate-stuffed children started passing around sandwiches and sausage rolls. Jimmy Thomson poured coffees and tea from two flasks. It was another glorious day and arguably the sunniest Easter Sunday that any of the grown-ups could recall. Everyone was in short sleeves – even Fergal had pushed up the sleeves of his yellow cashmere jumper.

'That's a beautiful top,' said Jennifer. 'Purple really suits you.'

'Makes a change from black,' laughed Angie. She'd bought the floaty blouse, in pastel shades of pinks and purples, for her Barbadian holiday. Her purple, corded jeans partnered it perfectly.

Jennifer felt dull in comparison and wished she'd chosen something smarter than a white tee shirt and jeans. However, it gave her great pleasure to see how at ease everyone was with each other.

Jimmy stood tall and pointed to the south-east across the Forth estuary to the coastal line directly opposite Fife. 'See those two tall chimneys? That's Cockenzie Power Station, near Port Seton, where your granny and I bide. And that tiny wee island is The Bass Rock. Look, Emma, I can see Hannah waving to us from Arthur's Seat.'

'Let me see,' demanded Katie, jumping into her grandad's arms for a better view.

The two grannies enquired about each other's families. Jimmy and Fergal discussed Fergal's latest visit to the Museum of Transport in East Anglia. The girls were playing with their My Little Ponies and Angie had stretched out to bask in the sunshine. Jennifer leaned back on her arms and thought about the last time she had been with Scott.

*

Scott's meeting with Angie had surpassed everything he had hoped for. Apparently, Bethany had told her Granny Joyce in February that after Mark had left and gone to Spain that she suspected that her daddy had done the same, except that her daddy had gone to Australia. When Angie had pushed Bethany further, her little girl had told her that Brenda and Bob, Scott's parents in Broughty Ferry, had pictures of her all over their house and most of them were next to Scott's. Brenda and Bob were always so kind to her that she didn't want to upset them or Angie by asking awkward questions and so she had told her granny instead. If Brenda and Bob's son was her daddy then Bethany wanted to know. Jennifer had to agree that her deductions had been pretty astute for such a little girl but Bethany had spent so much time in adult company that she often talked like one. Angie's decision to re-establish contact between father and daughter had been a relatively easy one to make.

Understandably, Scott had spent every spare moment with Bethany but on his last evening he'd asked Jennifer to meet with him. They met once again at the Shoogly Peg for drinks and Scott had organised a taxi to take him to Cupar to his sister's house and Jennifer on to The Maltings.

The St Andrews pub was as warm and cosy as it had been on their first encounter. The smell of burning logs filled the room. Jennifer wore the same black polo neck and black jeans as she had done on their first date but had a different scarf to add some colour; blue and black. Scott ordered the drinks at the bar and brought a lager and wine to their table.

'Chardonnay for the lady.'

'Your patter stinks,' jested Jennifer. 'Here's to new beginnings... for you and Bethany.' Jennifer would have liked to have toasted to something exciting for them but couldn't find anything witty to say. 'And to friendship,' she added.

Before their glasses had touched, Jennifer's lips began to tremble and she had to blink away her tears. Scott stood up and squeezed in behind the table to sit next to her. He dabbed her eyes with his own hankie and kissed her nose.

'I'm so sorry, Scott. I promised myself I wouldn't do this.' Then she laughed, trying to make light of it.

They told each other how they wished things could have been different. If only they had met earlier in life or had known each other longer. Or if they could change where they lived but the inevitable couldn't be avoided. Scott had to return to Australia and Jennifer had a business to run. Both admitted that they'd never expected to feel the way they did. Neither of them used the word love: it would have been too painful. They sat for a long time in silence with Scott's arms wrapped around her and Jennifer's head resting on his shoulder – each lost in their daydreams. Every now and then, they would stare at each other, smile and kiss. Their next kiss would last longer than the previous one. After two hours had passed, Scott asked if she would like another drink but Jennifer reluctantly suggested it was time to go home. There was nothing left to say. Scott summoned the taxi earlier than planned. Their parting kiss was unbelievably heartbreaking for Jennifer. She sobbed all the way from Cupar to Duneden. The poor taxi driver didn't know what to do. He kept glancing at Jennifer in his rear-view mirror. She was so grateful that she had been able to sneak upstairs without anyone seeing her. She had called to Zoe, her babysitter, from the hallway that she was desperate for the toilet and would she let herself out.

*

'Wake up, sleeping beauty!' Jennifer's dad kicked her white trainer with his foot.

Jennifer woke with a start and Angie stirred too. The two young mums sat up and laughed that they had dozed off in front of everyone. Jennifer felt her face tingle and applied some sun lotion. It was hot for April and she wondered if they would be lucky enough to have another heat wave this year. Probably not. The girls fidgeted as she rubbed some cream over their pink arms and faces. Jimmy and Fergal carried the heavier bags downhill as the rest of the entourage followed. Jennifer and Angie lagged behind them.

'Did the girls have a good time in Spain?' asked Angie.

'I think so. They didn't say much. There was a lot of sitting in cars waiting for Mark.'

Angie coughed and cleared her throat. 'There's something I'd like to tell you.'

Jennifer hoped that it wasn't something to do with Angie and Scott.

'You know that married man I've been seeing? Well... it's Malcolm.'

'MALCOLM PATTERSON? Bloody hell, Angie.'

'Sssshhh. Keep your voice down. I can't keep it to myself any longer. I had to tell someone. You're not mad, are you?'

Jennifer was so relieved that it wasn't Scott. Not that it really mattered with him being on the other side of the world.

'Why should I be? If he makes you happy and I can see that you have been happy, so good on you. But is it worth the risk?'

'Aww, Jen, he's the best thing that's happened to me since Bethany. I am honestly and truly head over heels in love with the guy... and him wi' me.' Angie clocked Jen's anxious expression. 'I know what you're thinking. He'll move on when he's had enough or feels he's about to be found out. But he won't.'

'So, what's in it for you?'

'Everything. He won't leave Doreen yet. I can live wi' that. He will eventually. We went to Barbados in March.'

'I thought you went to London to your pal's?'

'I did. For a couple of nights. Then Malcolm came down and we flew to The Caribbean together. Oh, Jen, it was beyond luxurious. It was heavenly. Magical.'

Jennifer observed Angie closely. Angie wholeheartedly believed that she and Malcolm would run off into the sunset and live happily ever after. Well, she would not be the friend who would shatter her illusions or happiness.

'If he makes you happy then good luck to the pair of you. Only,... you will be careful. I don't want to see you getting hurt.'

Angie hugged her friend and colleague. She was a bag of bones; she needed fattening up. 'Don't tell anyone, please. I mean it. Not even Maureen has an inkling.' Angie linked arms with Jen. 'I've been bursting to tell you.'

Jennifer felt privileged that Angie had chosen to share this confidence with her although her dalliance with Scott would remain her secret for a long time. If not forever.

Angie and Jennifer were taking over from Maureen and Archie at three o'clock. The Maltings had started serving High Teas on a Sunday until six in the evening; a popular and cheaper alternative to a three-course meal. In Scotland, most High Teas began with tea and toast, followed by a main meal then scones and cakes to round off the feast. The Maltings maintained that tradition. With it being Easter, they were fully booked. Everyone who had been on the picnic, plus Maureen's brood, had a table reserved at 5.30pm. Under Maureen's guidance, the function suite had been transformed into an elegant space fit for weddings and any other form of gatherings. Navy and cream with hints of lemon had been chosen for the decor, allowing the blue colour scheme to flow seamlessly throughout all areas downstairs. Today was the official opening of the refurbished room and Jennifer hoped that word would soon spread that it was a desirable setting for special celebrations.

The two friends caught up with their families in the car park. As Jennifer waved to the three Lennies in Angie's car, she sincerely hoped that her friend's liaison with Malcolm wouldn't be The Maltings undoing.

THIRTY-SIX

The day everything changed: Wednesday 13th June

It was the middle of June and the school holidays were hurtling towards them; only two weeks to go. The anniversary of the pool table escapade was also fast approaching but Jennifer was determined not to dignify its significance by dwelling on it. Despite the downturn in the economy due to the miner's strike, The Maltings had faired reasonably well. The bedrooms were rarely empty and the food side of the business was increasing weekly.

The stock taker, who visited quarterly, had told Jennifer yesterday morning that she was one of the lucky ones: her business was thriving. Jennifer hoped it had more to do with hard work and sheer determination than good luck. Function bookings were rolling in too since the Eden Suite, as it was now referred to, had been successfully refurbished. They had had their first wedding a few weeks ago, albeit a small event, and the feedback had given all the staff a boost. Maureen and Jennifer had attended a Wedding Fair several weeks beforehand in Glasgow to garner ideas for the setting up. Maureen revelled in the experience. Fergal stressed over and again that Jennifer's business acumen had exceeded his expectations. Praise from Fergal was not given without justification.

Willie was busy planting the window boxes and the tubs at the front and back of the hotel. He had three greenhouses in his acre of a garden; one for vegetable plants and two for his precious flowers and shrubs. Jennifer was given a tour of his lawns and allotments last month. His knowledge of plants was formidable for someone who was self-taught and Jennifer had asked him if he had ever considered doing it for a living. Willie had said that he had thought about it but was frightened that the worry would kill his passion.

'Once I get enough moss to line the bottoms, I'll get started on your hanging baskets,' he informed her.

'Your man is trying to line my bottom, Maureen!'

'Get in line behind the queue,' laughed Maureen as she slopped her bucket of dirty water down the drain at the back door.

Jennifer had finished the bedrooms; one depart and two make-ups. The German couple who had stayed one night were on a whisky tour and two Americans in rooms two and three were keen to try out The Old Course. Jennifer informed them that they would have to put their names in a daily ballot if they wanted a chance to play. They had left well before breakfast with unrealistic expectations. If guests required an evening meal on a Monday, Tuesday or Wednesday the staff would recommend a number of pubs or restaurants in the vicinity. Shooters were the exception to that rule.

Wednesdays were unpredictable days with regards to lunches. It was often difficult to gauge what was required but tourists were aplenty; thanks to the forthcoming Open Championship. Jennifer had begun prepping for Maureen who was cooking later when Malcolm popped his head in the kitchen.

'Jen, can I have a quick word?'

Malcolm had never been in her kitchen before but Jennifer invited him in and offered him a coffee.

'No thanks, I'm not stopping.'

Did Jennifer detect a squirm?

'Doreen asked me to call in. For Christ's sake, I'm sorry about this, Jen, but Doreen has invited John and Marjory Cameron for afternoon tea tomorrow and they have asked if Emma and Katie could join them. I could pick them up and walk them round after school if that's okay with you. Why I have to be the bloody lap dog defeats me.'

'Oh, did they now? She's a sly bitch that one... I'm referring to my ex mother-in-law who never was, not Doreen by the way.' Jennifer guffawed loudly. 'Tell the Camerons that Emma and Katie would be delighted to accept Doreen's invitation but they'll have to be the ones to pick my girls up if they want them to go.'

It was Malcolm's turn to laugh. 'Remind me not to cross you, Jen. I'll report back forthwith. Have a good day.' And he was gone.

Jennifer couldn't wait to see Marjory and John. They had never set foot in Fife since the last time Mark was here. Actually, if you disregarded his one-day visit to collect the girls in April, his mother and father had not seen the girls since January. They had the cheek to post Emma's parcel for her birthday in May then phone a week later to enquire if she had received it. A phone call on her actual birthday would have made Emma feel more special. Jennifer had been spoiling to release some of her pent-up anger since Scott left. She relished a little spat with Marjory.

Scott and Jennifer had agreed not to call each other but letters were part of the bargain. Nothing soppy just general chit-chat about their day to day lives. Scott's were sent via Fergal as Jennifer preferred to keep their friendship under wraps for the foreseeable future. She wrote once a fortnight; sometimes it was just a postcard with a couple of sentences. Scott had sent her two letters to date and she would reread them when she was in need of a little lift or if she felt lonely.

When Maureen was ready to take over in the kitchen, they ran through what was required at the cash and carry. Jennifer double-checked that Archie was satisfied with the brewery order. G&B usually phoned on a Wednesday to confirm the delivery for the Friday and she left her two trusted staff in charge while she caught up with some much-needed shopping for The Maltings and for her own household.

*

It was Angie's day off and she had planned to treat herself to a day out in Dundee: a thirty-minute drive from Duneden. There was a new hair salon that had recently opened in Reform Street and she had made an appointment to have her hair restyled. She tended to park near the swimming pool down at the riverside and walk into the city centre from there. City driving freaked her out and negotiating tight parking spaces was even more testing so the spacious parking in front of the Leisure Pool was the easier option. Angie knew that she ought to start taking Bethany swimming as she didn't want Bethany to be wary of the water like she was. She had longed to join Malcolm on his daily swims rather than watch while she paddled.

Angie could sense that people were staring at her as she strutted confidently towards the Wellgate Shopping Centre. Her black leather trousers elongated her already long, slim legs. Black ankle boots gave her extra height but it was her red, leather biker jacket that caused most of the sideways glances. She looked stunning. Since her trip to Barbados, she'd taken to wearing sunglasses whenever she could and they added an edge of sophistication too. After some shopping and a quick burger and chips (she had skipped breakfast; couldn't face it), she headed to the hairdressers.

The salon staff fussed over her as though she was someone who deserved their undivided attention. It was all mirrors and monochrome. The floor and walls were white. The swivel chairs, gowns and towels were black. The staff were all androgynous Duran Duran wannabees with white suits and black shirts. Angie found it hard to distinguish who was male or female so said nothing and smiled politely. When she was asked if she would like a head massage, Angie nodded, unsure of what it entailed. It had not been unknown to have to wash your own hair in Duneden. The hairdresser's there was a shoddy, converted garage attached to someone's house. Her hair was given a 'chopped' cut which was brushed forward during the drying process towards her face. An expensive styling lotion, which she felt obliged to buy, set the fashionable messy creation. She felt fantastic and couldn't wait to show Malcolm her new look.

The route from Dundee passed close to Malcolm's golf club. Less than a minute after she had passed the entrance, Angie spotted a female crouching on the grass verge and she looked distressed; she was resting her head on her knees. She pulled over. As Angie approached the woman, she realised it was Doreen and she could tell immediately that she was drunk. Her mascara had left black streaks all down her tear-stained cheeks. Some of her long hair was still tied up; the rest of it hung precariously around her face. She had cuts and grazes on her hands and the elbows and knees of her clothing were covered in dirt. A large tear on one of the knees of her grey, golfing trousers revealed a nasty gash that looked as if it might require some stitches.

'Are you okay, Doreen? What are ye doing here?'

'Oh, it's you. Leave me alone.'

'How did ye get here? Where's your car? Did you have a bag wi' ye?'

A lorry thundered past. A rush of wind almost blew Angie over.

'Those bastards at the golf club stole my keys. They hate me, you know.' Doreen began to wail – loud, moaning bellows that sounded false yet her tears were very real. 'Look at me! I'm a mess. No wonder Malcolm wants to leave me. Would you want to stay with me?'

'Come on, Doreen. It's not safe here. I'll take you home.'

'He doesn't love me, Angie. He's got someone else. Do you know who it is?' She tugged on the sleeve of Angie's red jacket and looked her in the eye.

Doreen's words had the same effect as the lorry that had just rushed past.

'No, I don't. I'm sure that's not true.' Angie knelt down beside her. 'Malcolm's always singing your praises in the pub. Everybody knows that.'

Doreen wiped her snot on her sleeves. 'I thought it was that Jen from The Maltings but even Malcolm wouldn't stoop that low.'

Angie wasn't sure what to make of that strange retort.

'He's had women before but it's different this time. I think he's going to leave me.' She flopped sideways on to the grass and began to wail again.

No matter how hard Angie tried to coax her, Doreen wouldn't budge. Angie had never considered Doreen properly before today. She had always regarded her as Malcolm's problem. But witnessing Doreen's distress was a sharp reminder that she had contributed to reducing this woman to a malfunctioning wreck.

'Please, Doreen. You're scaring me. I'm not leaving you here. Please, get into my car.'

A black, saloon-type car pulled in behind Angie's distinctive, yellow mini and a young lad in his early twenties jumped out of the passenger's side.

'Do you need any help? My dad and I saw you. Have you had an accident?'

Doreen pushed herself up into a sitting position. 'Roxanne's a good girl. She'll know what to do. She loves her daddy.'

Angie explained to the young man that she knew Doreen and was trying to get her home. Angie straightened Doreen's white body warmer and tied the laces of the golfing shoes she was still wearing. 'Up you get.' They heaved Doreen up into a standing position and supported her sagging body to Angie's car. With considerable difficulty, they lowered an uncooperative Doreen into the passenger's seat. As Angie was fastening the seat belt, around her lover's wife's frail frame, Doreen placed her hand on Angie's arm.

'He's the only man I've ever loved. Will ever love.'

'I know, Doreen.' Angie walked round to the driver's door and thanked her Good Samaritan as he waited at his dad's car. 'What a fuckin' nightmare,' she sighed. She slid into her seat and exhaled loudly.

When she felt that Doreen was settled, Angie continued on her journey. She didn't know if she should drive straight to Orchard House or swing by The Maltings for some moral support from Jen. The blood around Doreen's wound had begun to congeal but she felt that it would still need stitches. Doreen stared straight ahead. Angie kept looking to see if she was alright.

'Do you love him, Angie?' Doreen asked calmly

Angie's heart missed a beat. 'What are you talking about?'

'It's a simple question. Do you love Malcolm? Yes or No?'

'You've lost me, Doreen.' Angie tried to hold her nerve.

Doreen sneered. 'I've seen the photographs. The ones with you on the beach, with your big hat and sunglasses and your young, fit body.'

Before Angie had a chance to reply, Doreen slowly raised her right hand and put her fingers on the steering wheel pushing it to the right. An articulated lorry travelling over sixty miles an hour in the opposite direction had no time to hit the brakes. The impact was immediate and devastating.

When the emergency services arrived at the scene, they were dealing with two fatalities and a seriously injured lorry driver. No other vehicles were involved in the collision.

THIRTY-SEVEN

Malcolm had no need to guess where Doreen was. Her car was missing and his wife only ever drove to the golf club these days. Either someone from the club would drop her off or a taxi would be organised for her. He'd give her another hour. Henry, Doreen's spaniel, began to mooch around Malcolm's feet. He opened the patio doors and the dog rushed out to pee. Malcolm cursed at the number of burnt patches on the lawn. He had been training the dog to use a designated area but Doreen lacked the same dedication. The dog required a firmer hand. Malcolm's stomach rumbled. He would have to make his own dinner – again.

*

Emma, Bethany and Katie tucked into Maureen's homemade macaroni and some garlic bread.

'Switch that off right now, young lady,' Jennifer scolded her elder daughter. 'No telly while we're eating.'

The girls were sitting at the breakfast bar while Jennifer was eating hers at the ironing board. Emma had slithered off her stool to turn on the T.V. hoping that her mother was otherwise preoccupied and wouldn't notice.

'Uh Uh! When you've finished your tea... and that includes

Katie, you can put your programme back on. Bethany will be going home shortly so you don't have all night.'

Emma grumbled that it took Katie ages to finish her food and they would never get a chance to watch anything. The two conniving school chums made nasty faces at Katie while they polished off their cheesy pasta before disappearing to the bedroom.

When Jennifer had finished her food, that had gone cold, she hid the hot iron behind the breadbin out of harm's way. She called to the girls who were now all playing in the bedroom that she was popping downstairs to open up. One of Martin Ross's pals was covering the bar tonight. Jennifer switched on all the lights including the ones for her beer taps. She opened some of the windows slightly to allow some fresh air in and she would close them later on during the shift. Clean beer mats and towels were spread out over the bar top and the water jug and ice bucket were replenished. Her barman was late.

'Sorry, Jen, I was held up on my way home from work. A serious accident on the Cupar Road. It's completely blocked off in both directions.' Young Nathan took off his jacket and tucked it underneath the bar.

'Hope it's not someone we know. Have you had your tea if you were in a rush?'

'Ach, yer fine. A couple of packets of crisps will do.'

'Nonsense. There's loads of Maureen's macaroni left. I'll heat some up for you.'

Jennifer was warming up Nathan's pasta in the microwave when Maureen appeared at the kitchen door.

'Hi, Jen, is Angie here by any chance?'

'No, and I haven't heard from her. She was getting her hair cut in Dundee then going shopping, I think. She'll be here soon. Bethany's up the stairs... Christ, Maureen are you okay?'

Maureen's legs literally gave way and she grabbed hold of the sink to stop her from falling. Through hers tears she explained that she was probably worrying unnecessarily but her neighbour had knocked on her door to say that his son thought that the car in the accident along the road looked awfully like Angie's yellow mini. Maureen took a deep breath.

'Willie's awa' to find out more. Oh, Jen, what if it's our Angie?'

Jennifer took several seconds to process what had been said and selfishly thought about the implications for The Maltings if it were true. She tried to reassure Maureen it was highly unlikely and ushered her tearful friend through to the lounge. She asked Nathan to pour Maureen a brandy.

'Have you spoken with Joyce?' asked Jennifer.

'I popped in in case Angie was there but I didn't say anything. I didn't want to worry her.'

The two women sat in silence for a few minutes. Neither wanted to voice what they were thinking out loud for fear of making it come true. The lounge door opened. Three pairs of eyes were fixed on the tall figure. It was Joe Blakeley. He had heard the rumour that Angie's car had been involved in a crash. Maureen started to cry. Jennifer remembered that she hadn't given Nathan his food and ran to fetch it. Nobody was thinking straight. As she was returning with the hot dish, Maureen's Ryan barged in.

'Mum! You've to come now! There's a cop car outside Auntie Joyce's house.'

Maureen let out an agonising scream and followed her son out the door. Jennifer was aware that she was sobbing in Joe's chest. The room was spinning and the next she thing she knew was that her head was wedged between her legs.

'What happened?' she groaned.

Young Nathan was kneeling in front of her and Joe was standing behind, supporting her upper body with his arms – a chair was beneath her bottom. Jennifer was aware that she still had her slippers on; silly, bulky, green dinosaur slippers. What must Nathan and Joe be thinking?

'I think you fainted,' claimed the concerned voice holding her up.

Jennifer whimpered, 'I'm so sorry.'

Joe held Jen while Nathan, on Joe's instruction, made her a cup of very sweet tea. She took tiny sips. 'I'll have to see to the girls.'

'In a minute,' Joe advised her. 'They'll be fine.'

Jennifer tried to comprehend the enormity of her predicament and the impact it would have now and in the future. Poor Angie. She didn't deserve such a narcissistic friend.

'Jen,' said Joe, 'you'll have to get more staff in.'

'More staff. Why?'

'Because when word gets out everyone will flock here. It's what'll happen. Everybody will want to talk about it. Phone Archie.'

Jennifer called Archie. He didn't hesitate. He was on his way. She decided to call Zoe, her babysitter, then stopped.

'What if we're all assuming that Angie's dead and all the time she's fine?'

Jennifer searched the two male faces for confirmation. Joe held her face in his huge hands.

'There's no way that anyone survived that crash. It was smashed to smithereens.'

That's exactly how Jennifer felt – smashed to smithereens. Somewhere in the distance she could hear a woman howl; she recognised her own screams.

The next half an hour was conducted in a haze. Jennifer managed to call her dad and Fergal and Fiona. Nathan tracked down Zoe who was now sitting with all three girls; they were oblivious to the melee downstairs. Zoe was warned to say nothing. A big ask for someone so young.

When Jennifer ventured upstairs, the wee ones were indifferent to her presence – they were ensconced in a cartoon version of *The Fonz* from their video collection. Zoe was flicking through a pile of magazines. Jennifer asked her babysitter to supervise bath time while she found pyjamas for Bethany who was beyond excited at the prospect of having a sleepover on a school night. It choked Jennifer to watch the three of them giggling cheerfully as they piled clouds of bubbles over their heads and faces and then challenged each other to be the first to blow them away. For the time being, Bethany was better off at The Maltings. Her little life would be shattered soon enough.

Just as Joe had predicted, there was a constant stream of Duneden residents wandering into the building seeking confirmation and solace in familiar faces. Jennifer floundered several times but was aware that she had to be strong, for Angie's sake if nothing else. That confirmation came in the form of a despondent Willie. He could barely deliver the harrowing news to the crowd of friends and neighbours waiting nervously. At first, the words refused to come out and then he spoke; his voice was quivering,

'It's definitely Angie.'

An eerie silence descended, followed by gasps of disbelief.

Then the crying began: muffles from some, sobbing from others and those like Jennifer found it too difficult to hide their pain nor did they care.

Jennifer and Willie hugged for a long time. They found a table at the door and sat down. Those nearest to them respectfully gave them some space to talk.

'Is the bairn okay?' Willie asked.

'She's upstairs, totally unaware.' Jennifer gulped and blew her nose. She tucked the sodden tissue up her sleeve. 'Are they expecting her at Joyce's?'

'Joyce wanted to see her but if she's settled here then leave her be. Maureen'll collect her in the morning. She'll stay the night wi' her Auntie Joyce.'

'How are they?'

'Devastated. And you?'

'Numb. I don't know what I'm going to do without her, Willie.' The tears started again. 'What a bitch! Thinking about myself when poor Bethany's up there without a mum.'

Willie judged when it was appropriate to comment. 'Me and Maureen will be watching your back. Don't you worry.'

'Do they know what happened?'

'According to the police there were no signs of braking from the lorry or Angie's car. But, first impressions were that Angie's car ran headlong into the lorry... an' another thing, someone else was in the car. A woman.'

'Who?'

'Fuck knows. They were hoping that we would know. There was nothin' in the wreckage to identify the other person. No nothin''

The word wreckage made Jennifer want to throw up.

A dog barking reined Jennifer back in. It was Henry and he

was straining at the lead as Malcolm held the door and scoured the room. Jennifer sprang forward all in a flurry.

'You're busy tonight. Has Doreen been in at all?' asked Malcolm.

Jennifer pushed him roughly into the corridor. Malcolm looked disconcerted.

'I'm sorry about Henry. He was overexcited that's all. He's not used to crowds. I thought that Doreen might have popped in earlier.'

'It's not Henry. Oh, Malcolm, can you come with me a minute?'

For the second time in his life, Malcolm found himself in Jen's kitchen. He was still in his smart working suit but he'd removed his tie before leaving the house. His frown turned to concern when he saw how distressed Jen appeared. Henry, perhaps sensing something was amiss, lay at Malcolm's feet.

'I am so, so sorry to be the one to tell you.' Jennifer began to shake. 'It's Angie... she's been killed in a car crash.'

Malcolm was confused. He assumed that Jen was going to tell him that Doreen had thrown a tantrum or such like and she'd been put out. But Angie?

'Malcolm, do you understand what I've just said? Angie...'

'NO! You've made a mistake!' he was furious.

He walked in one direction, turned abruptly and walked in another. He repeated this several times then he crouched down on her red flooring and began to cry. There was no sound, only the violent agitation of his body. The silence in her empty, clean, stainless steel kitchen frightened Jennifer. Malcolm frightened her. He looked up, pain etched on his face.

'When? How?'

'Late this afternoon. A head on collision with a big lorry.'

'You knew about us?'

Jennifer nodded.

'Then you'll know that I loved her. Adored her and she loved me.' He inhaled deeply and closed his eyes.

'I know you made her very, very happy. I'm so sorry, Malcolm.'

He explained that he had to go. Doreen hadn't come home from the golf club and he'd checked all her usual haunts but there were still a couple of places where she might be. Once she was safely at home, he would return. He thanked Jennifer for her discretion and asked that his relationship with Angie should never be disclosed to anyone else but he would appreciate it if he could talk about her with Jennifer sometime soon. Jennifer said she would be happy to oblige.

She followed Malcolm to the back door. It was his preferred entrance and exit probably because it seemed closer to his house. He kissed her politely on the cheek and Henry tugged him on to the gravel path.

'Malcolm! This sounds so silly and it's probably nothing... No, forget it on you go. We'll see you later.'

Malcolm walked the few paces back to the doorstep. 'What's wrong, Jen?'

Jennifer could hardly comprehend what she was about to say especially to the man who had just lost the woman he claimed to have loved.

'Angie wasn't alone in the car. Another woman was with her... and... the police don't know who she is.'

THIRTY-EIGHT

Malcolm half staggered, half ran, over the Duneden Bridge to Orchard House. Henry reacted as if he were having a whale of a time – no one had ever moved at such a daring rate before. Jen couldn't have been thinking rationally. There was no way that the other person in Angie's car could conceivably be Doreen. How could it be possible? Nevertheless, Malcolm felt obligated to verify the possibility, however improbable.

The officer at Cupar Police Station insisted that Malcolm was not wasting their time and a patrol car would be despatched immediately. Malcolm wandered aimlessly from room to room tidying up as he went as if he were expecting an estate agent rather than a policeman. The phone rang and he darted from the dining room to the kitchen.

'Doreen?'

'It's Jen. I'm so sorry for what I said earlier. It was crass and you dashed off before I could say anything else. Are you okay?'

Malcolm told Jen to forget it and that he had made a call to the station at Cupar. They were sending someone out to take more details.

'Is there someone with you? I can't leave here. Sorry.'

Malcolm had called his gardener just in case he had to leave the dog. Jennifer offered to have Henry if it would help but Malcolm declined her kind gesture. He promised he would phone if he had more news – one way or another.

Malcolm sat down on one of the stools at their breakfast bar. He and Doreen had lots of friends yet in a crisis he hadn't a clue who to phone and who he would actually want to contact. There was no one he would confide in either. Their friends, on reflection, were no more than acquaintances that were happy to be wined and dined at Malcolm's expense. Ron Bayne, an old driver at Bowden's, and now Malcolm's gardener, had proven on many occasions that he was discreet and trustworthy as regards to Malcolm's infidelities and Malcolm found it disconcerting that, during such a desperate time, Ron was the only person he felt comfortable with. Over time, Doreen's friends had evaporated as quickly as a drink in her hand had.

*

Malcolm and Doreen had first met at the Glasgow Plaza Ballroom at Eglinton Toll, in the winter of 1956. He'd fancied himself as a bit of a dancer in those days. He and a bunch of his mates had piled into an old Bedford truck, from the yard, and had driven from Kirkcaldy to Glasgow. Three of them squeezed into the front seats of the cabin but the rest of the lads had lain under some tarpaulin in the back to keep warm. (It was like a trailer with a roof and glassless windows.) After the dancing, they slept overnight on the floor of someone's auntie.

The Glasgow Plaza had the reputation of being the place to be seen; it was where Glasgow's best dancers went and the women were exceptionally snappy dressers. Doreen epitomised both categories. She was glamorous and glided over the dance floor effortlessly whether it was a slow waltz or a quick step. Malcolm had thought that she was the most beautiful girl he had ever seen with her long, jet black hair and tiny waist. He was smitten immediately. Doreen had kept him at arm's length for a long time, both on the dance floor and off, but his pursuit of her had been relentless. When she did eventually succumb, she was as infatuated with Malcolm as he was with her. Their courtship was brief and they married in the summer of 1957. She left her native Glasgow and set up home with Malcolm in a room and kitchen in Kirkcaldy. She was twenty-two. After too many miscarriages, Doreen eventually gave birth to Roxanne. It was a difficult birth – the doctor blamed her delicate hips – and she was advised not to have any more babies. Malcolm wondered if it was his fear of making Doreen pregnant that had caused him to look for pleasure elsewhere or was it true what Doug had called out to him in Newcastle, that he liked them young just like his dad.

*

The chiming of the doorbell brought Malcolm back from his reverie. Two uniformed policemen stood on his doorstep and Malcolm invited them in. They listened carefully as Malcolm explained that Doreen hadn't returned from playing golf and that her car keys were still hanging in the steward's office. Malcolm reluctantly disclosed that his wife had a problem with alcohol. She had last been seen stomping out of the car park shouting obscenities at other players waiting to tee-off on the first hole. He had exhausted all of the other places where she might have gone.

They asked Malcolm to describe Doreen: her height, her hair and what she had been wearing. And did she have any items of jewellery that might be of significance. Malcolm tried to picture Doreen that morning but it was Angie's smiling face that had flooded the cognitive part of his brain. He was asked to take his time.

'I think she had on a body-warmer, maybe cream, a short sleeved white shirt and her golfing trousers. Greyish, I think, with small checks. She always wore her wedding band and her engagement ring... it has three diamonds. On her right hand, she has her father's wedding band. It's thick and chunky but she had it resized to fit her finger. She has very long, thin fingers. Beautiful hands.'

The enormity of what was unfolding had become too much. With his hands resting on his knees and with his chin digging into his chest, Malcolm felt the room and the world pressing in on him and he began to weep. Very quickly, he found it difficult to breathe. No matter how hard he tried, air wouldn't go into his lungs.

*

The longest day, the summer solstice, was only a week away and the sky was not yet dark when at ten-thirty Jennifer's friend, Fiona, poked her head in the bar to announce her arrival. It was impossible to be heard above the noise. Not only was it packed with people inside but she had squeezed through a throng of drinkers and smoke at the back door. She signalled to Jennifer that she'd be back in five minutes. The door to the apartment upstairs was locked so Fiona tapped quietly. Ryan Ross looked quizzically at her. And only once he was satisfied, did he let her in. Fiona smiled at him and his girlfriend Zoe, left her suitcase in Jennifer's bedroom, enquired about all the girls and left to seek out her childhood friend downstairs.

'Thanks so much for coming,' said Jennifer before finding comfort in the familiar embrace of her oldest friend.

Fiona would be staying until Saturday morning, when Fergal would take over until the Monday morning. Between Jennifer's family and friends, it had been agreed that someone would be with her for the following week at least. Apart from attending a small art exhibition at the weekend, Fiona had agreed to cover most of the remaining week.

'I'm ready for a very large G&T. What about you, Jennifer?'

Before Jennifer had a chance to reply and Fiona had opened her purse, a gin and tonic and a large wine were handed to them by Joe. It was Jennifer's first drink of the night. She'd refused countless others and it was the first kiss Joe had given her in a long time. It was a tender kiss on her forehead but it had not gone unnoticed by those mourning in the lounge. Fiona rolled her eyes as if to say, 'what was that all about?' and followed Jennifer out into the fresh air.

'Are you and Joe back on?'

'No. I'm not sure. I don't think so. I've got too much going on for anything else. Give me a hand out here.'

Jennifer and Fiona picked up empty glasses from the beer garden tables and quite a few that were on window sills at the back door. Jennifer thanked those that were outside but asked them to be considerate to her neighbours and to come indoors. A small gang of sixteen and seventeen-year-olds were sitting down at the banking chatting but thankfully moved on without any back chat. The darkness was settling over her lawns and it was too dangerous to be near the edge of the river so late at night. Just as they were going in, Jennifer spied a solitary shadow enter the exit area of the car park. It had to be Malcolm. She waited until he was nearer. His face said all she needed to know. She asked Fiona to bring a large Lagavulin out to the beer garden. She sat next to Malcolm on a bench and squeezed his hand. He held on tightly. The only indication that Malcolm was crying was the shuddering of his shoulders. Jennifer wept quietly too.

It was Willie who appeared with a tray of drinks: two large malts and a wine for Jennifer. Willie had surmised something was up when Fiona requested a large Lagavulin for outside. There was only one person who drank that malt. He'd remembered how quickly Jen had reacted when Malcolm had come in earlier and he knew that Malcolm had been searching for Doreen. Doreen had to be the mystery passenger. Malcolm's grief was as tangible as Jen's.

Willie sat opposite them at the picnic bench and placed a glass in front of each of them. Their salty tears diluted their drinks.

'Have the police any idea how they were both in the same car?' asked Willie.

Malcolm was as bamboozled as Willie. He assumed that Angie had stopped to pick Doreen up. It was the only rational explanation he could give to the police. A death in Duneden was a big deal in a small community like theirs. A huge turnout at a funeral was the norm. But two deaths were unprecedented. Willie and Malcolm agreed regretfully that the funerals would have to take place on different days to allow the villagers to pay their respects properly to both women.

'Would you tell the others, Willie? I can't face anyone at the moment. I'm only here because I promised Jen I'd tell her if I had any news.' Malcolm also wanted to be with the only other person that would understand how he was truly feeling.

Willie struggled to his feet. He looked how the other two

felt. Absolutely washed out. Jennifer watched Malcolm take his drink. His trembling hand could barely find his lips. He had aged by about twenty years in a few short hours.

'It's my fault entirely,' he rasped. 'Karma. That's what happens to bad bastards like me.' He sobbed again.

Jennifer placed her hand on his forearm. 'Don't torture yourself. It was a tragic, tragic accident.'

'What if it wasn't, Jen? What if Doreen had found out about us and they had argued in the car? Fought even?'

'Don't go there, Malcolm. We'll never know. But we do know it was instantaneous. They couldn't have suffered.'

'But the two of them, Jen? My two beautiful girls.' His head slumped on to his arms. Jennifer had never heard or witnessed such grief from a man. His roars literally shook her to her core; vibrating through the wood and up through her thin body.

Joe Blakeley walked towards them with more drinks and sat where Willie had been. He stared at Malcolm and then at Jennifer who shrugged helplessly.

'Get this down ye man and then I'll tak ye home,' said Joe.

Jennifer cuddled Malcolm's slouched body and thanked Joe. She lifted one leg over the bench, then the other and stood up.

The black sky was clear and a multitude of stars seemed to hover above them – large, bright and shining, as if they had they had come to pay their respects to a grieving village.

THIRTY-NINE

Thursday 14th June

Jennifer felt a draught on her face and without opening her eyes knew it would be Fiona. Blowing on each other's faces had been something they had done since childhood. She smiled.

'Here. A cup of coffee to get you started. The girls are up. I've given them breakfast... and before you ask it is not biscuits. How's the head?' asked Fiona as she climbed back into bed.

'Surprisingly, fine. I didn't have that much to drink last night. Shit! What time is it?'

'Half past seven. Don't panic. I spoke with your Americans last night and they don't want breakfast until 9.00 am.'

'Thank God. Thanks for being here. What a night! I'm just so tired.'

'Hmmm! This sharing a bed malarkey is getting a bit of a habit. Poor Walter,' giggled Fiona.

'Sorry. You were supposed to sleep in Katie's bed. I forgot to shift her.'

Almost a year ago, after the Mark fiasco, Jennifer crawled into bed beside Fiona and Walter after too many wines, pleading for a cuddle from her best pal. Walter had been given no choice in the matter. 'At least, you were in the middle,' Jennifer tried to justify her intrusion.

'I don't think he could cope with two!... talking of two, I wonder how Malcolm is?'

'Fiona, you can't say anything. Ever!'

'I know, I know. Guide's honour.' Fiona held up four fingers.

'It's three, ya div! You were a lousy guide.'

Jennifer remembered Angie saying *Guide's Honour* to Fergal and bit her lip.

Fiona leaned into her friend, 'I don't recall those Danish scouts complaining.'

They both laughed. Fiona had been much more promiscuous in her youth than prissy Jennifer had ever been.

'It's so surreal. Yesterday I was planning ahead for the school holidays and The Open and everything else... and now? It's mind blowing. I can't get my head round it.'

Jennifer was still drying her hair when the phone rang. Maureen was on her way to collect Bethany. Jennifer braced herself for another round of emotions. Ding, Ding, round ten!

Neither Bethany nor Jennifer's two were going into school that morning: it would be too emotional and after consulting with Archie last night, she had agreed not to open the doors of The Maltings for lunches for the next two days either. They would open at six and five respectively in the evenings as normal, although on a Friday they were lucky if there was an hour between closing for lunches and opening again. Jennifer and Archie had planned to reorganise the rota for the next seven days. There had been so many offers of help that Jennifer was humbled by the generosity of her regulars. Archie had noted their names and phone numbers but assumed that in the cold light of day some of them would renege.

Jennifer and Maureen bubbled in the corridor but regained composure before ascending the stairs that curved to the left to Jennifer's home. Bethany had chosen one of Emma's summer dresses to wear. She had long, willowy limbs like her mother and the pink dress that normally skimmed Emma's knees looked like a mini on Bethany. Neither Maureen nor Jennifer could summon the courage to speak and so it was left to Fiona to cajole Bethany out of the apartment and down onto the path in front of the beer garden. Blissfully unaware, Angie's little girl bade farewell to Jennifer and Fiona and skipped merrily off with her Auntie Maureen. The two despairing onlookers wiped away more tears. Jennifer took a deep breath and trudged up the stairs to break the news to her girls.

Fiona served the two American residents their Scottish breakfast in a jaunty fashion whilst Jennifer remained in the kitchen. She asked about their day at St Andrews and listened politely about their disappointment at not being selected for The Old Course. Undeterred, they had played at one of the nearby qualifying courses for an extortionate fee. Fiona apologised for the golfing fraternity's greed. After breakfast they would be heading to the west coast to try some of the courses there. They thanked Fiona for an excellent stay and asked for their condolences to be passed on to the wonderful staff.

After breakfast, Jennifer walked with Emma and Katie to the park for some light relief. They had not bargained on Willie and Bethany being there. Emma and Bethany hugged then went off to play as if it was the most appropriate thing to do. Jennifer plonked herself on the grass next to Willie.

'I don't think it's sunk in yet,' he said staring at Bethany. 'She's hardly shed a tear.'

'It'll happen when you least expect it,' Jennifer acknowledged. 'She'll kick off with the most God almighty tantrum. How's Joyce?'

'Christ, Jen, it's creepy. She keeps talking aboot Angie as if she's still alive.'

'Probably shock.' Jennifer thought again about the time when Angie had used the very same term to describe her reaction to buying The Maltings out from Mark. It seemed a lifetime ago.

Jennifer smiled as the girls played tig on the witch's hat. Angie's house was only a short walk from the park. Jennifer could see her front door from where she was sitting. 'What's going to happen with Bethany?'

'She'll probably stay wi' Joyce but me and Maureen will help out,' confirmed Willie.

'She can come any time to The Maltings.' Jennifer felt her emotions surface. She'd thought about Scott and what he might make of it all but she refrained from calling him. She didn't want to interfere. 'I'm going to head off now, Willie. Tell Maureen that I'm not expecting her in today or tomorrow. If she can't face Saturday, will you let me know? And I'll pop in to see Joyce later.'

Willie and Maureen had made an appointment with the funeral directors. As soon as they had confirmation that Angie's body could be released from the mortuary, the final arrangements would be made. Jennifer insisted that The Maltings would cover the costs of the funeral tea. She could scarcely believe that they were discussing Angie in such a matter-of-fact way. All the way home, Angie dominated her thoughts. She raked over every conversation, every laugh and every gesture they had shared. It was indeed surreal.

*

Ron Bayne had walked Henry around the grounds of Orchard House and the tired dog slept at his master's feet on the terrace outside the music room. Malcolm looked much better than the dishevelled mess he had been during breakfast. He had showered and changed into dusky pink chinos and a pale blue, short-sleeved shirt. Even although, he, too, would be making preliminary funeral arrangements, he had no desire to dress formally. Fortunately, he would have to liaise with Willie before a definite date could be confirmed. He had to be at Angie's funeral. He poured himself a strong coffee and scrutinised everything he had written down – something he had never had to do before. He had a vast memory bank for storing minute details but at this moment in time he couldn't concentrate on two things at once. He jotted down some points he had remembered for Bowden's and what he still had to organise for Doreen. He had an excellent office team, including his manager, and knew that his business, for the time being, was the least of his worries. His mistress at the office was long gone and the young female he had promoted to take her place was shit hot at her job.

Telling Roxanne had been the third hardest thing he had had to do in his life. The first was leaving Gateshead and the second was identifying Doreen's battered body. Seeing Angie would never have been an option but he had longed to tell her how much he had loved her. He would never forget his daughter's agonising screams last night when he had phoned Spain. Roxanne had secured an early morning flight and Malcolm would pick her up later at Glasgow airport – all flights to Edinburgh were full. Mark was staying behind for an urgent business meeting but would catch the first available flight out. *What could be more fucking important that his partner's mother's death?* Malcolm had wanted to shout when told. *Who would allow a bereft, young girl to fly home alone? He's a fucking tit!*

He had a few other calls to make to family and friends. Both of Doreen's parents were dead but she had a sister in Doncaster that she visited occasionally and vice versa. Malcolm prepared himself for more emotional discussions.

*

Archie and Jennifer were sifting through the names of potential workers when there was a loud rap on the front door. It was Angus Campbell, one of her older regulars, and he had a proposition for her. Angus hobbled in on his walking stick. Jennifer was intrigued.

'Firstly, may I offer my sincere condolences?' Angus spoke ever so slowly and precisely, as if he were giving a lecture to those who had difficulty grasping the most logical understandings of everyday life. 'As you may know, or may not, I am a chef, albeit a retired one... yet I have come to offer my assistance, for a short time only. To see you through this crisis.' Angus looked directly at Jennifer, nodded slowly and smiled, 'Angie was a dear, dear friend and confidante and if I can help in any way, I am at your disposal.'

Jennifer didn't know whether to laugh or cry at his ludicrous suggestion. Angus's portly belly which was hidden by a crisply ironed yellow and white checked shirt, hung over his cream, track suit bottoms He wore an odd-looking white cap.

'I can detect by your hesitancy that my proposal has thrown you. I may not be able to get around as well as one used to but I am perfectly capable of standing at a stove to cook. It's not so long ago that I was preparing banquets for hundreds of guests. Please don't think me disrespectful but, Jen, darling, this would be a walk in the park.'

Before Jennifer had the opportunity to say, 'Thanks but no thanks,' Archie butted in.

'What were you thinking? Hours wise.'

'I don't do breakfasts or Sundays, my Wee Free values, but I will do anything else that is required. Shall we say until the middle of August at most? That will give you ample time to interview other applicants.'

Despite having grave reservations, Jennifer found herself agreeing to his terms.

'The going rate will suffice. I do this for my darling Angie. I can't believe she has gone.'

Angus doffed his odd hat and took his leave.

'What the hell was that all about? Did I just agree to employ him? I must be off my rocker.'

Archie laughed but a good friend of his knew all about Angus and according to him, Angus had worked on luxury cruise ships for most of his career. Archie had every confidence that he would fit in perfectly – for the time being.

Out of all the volunteers, there were only five that Jennifer and Archie would be happy to have and trust to be behind the bar. Archie would contact them as soon as possible.

The bar takings, last night, had surpassed any other wet-sales income: excluding Hogmanay. Jennifer knew that Angie would have been proud of that. They expected a busy weekend and Archie warned Jennifer that the days of both funerals would exceed anything they had taken in last night. Plenty of additional staff would be needed on those days.

Jennifer felt incredibly guilty and exploitative. The Maltings was making money out of other people's misery.

FORTY

The Funerals: Tuesday 26th and Thursday 28th June

Every seat in Kirkcaldy Crematorium was occupied and just as many more people stood outside. Jennifer was several rows from the front but she had a clear view of Malcolm, Roxanne and Mark. Mark's hair was longer and lighter than the last time she had seen him and his skin was a golden brown. He had nurtured a plausible Spanish look. And as much as Jennifer loathed to admit it, she still found him devilishly handsome. Roxanne had her hair up. Perhaps it was her black, short-sleeved dress but she appeared less tarty than her usual tasteless look. Formal dressing suited her. Malcolm looked broken.

The service was very acceptable. The minister told the congregation everything he had been told about Doreen – her love of cooking, golf, dancing and ultimately her family. He shared how Malcolm had wooed her and how, after many years of longing for a baby, Roxanne was born.

Jennifer squirmed at the mention of 'longing for'. Only a few days ago, Joyce, Angie's mother, had called into The Maltings before picking Bethany up from school. She wanted to speak privately with Jennifer. It was the first time Joyce had ventured out of her house and her presence had caught Jennifer unawares. They sat in the apartment in The Maltings and Jennifer prepared a pot of tea – strong, just to Joyce's liking.

'Was Angela seeing anyone?' Joyce asked rather abruptly.

'Why do you ask?' Jennifer wasn't sure how to respond.

'I asked Maureen and she said that as far as she knew Angela wasn't seeing anyone.'

'What's wrong, Joyce?'

'I know Angela trusted you, Jen, so if Angela had a lover, then you probably knew.' Joyce twisted her hands. 'The post mortem showed that Angela was eight to nine weeks pregnant.'

The revelation hit Jennifer like a sledgehammer.

'Do you know who the father might be? I can't tell our Maureen or the whole bleeding place will know!' admitted Angie's mother.

'He's married and it's complicated,' Jennifer confessed.

Joyce laughed. 'Angela could certainly pick them. Bad uns, I mean. Do you think she knew or he knows?'

If Angie knew, and Jennifer doubted that she did, Malcolm definitely didn't.

'I don't think so.' Jennifer knelt in front of Joyce and took her hands. 'What I do know is that your Angela loved this man and he adored her in return and if this baby had been fortunate to have been born, then both of them would have lavished this baby with love. And Angie didn't choose bad men, in fact, she chose very admirable ones. But... for whatever reason, life dealt her an unjust hand. Angela was a wonderful woman and she brought so much joy to others, especially me. You should be so proud of her.'

Jennifer laid her head on Joyce's lap and wept. Joyce stroked Angela's friend's hair as her own tears disappeared into a bundle of chestnut curls.

The curtains closed to Malcolm's and Doreen's favourite song; it was the one that had made them realise they were destined to be together – *Only You* by the Platters.

Jennifer filed out of the crematorium as Willie, Maureen and

Joe followed closely behind. The minister had requested that because it was so busy, those who were heading for the funeral tea should go out the front entrance but the rest who were unable to go to the hotel, close by, should meet the family at the exit. Jennifer was expecting a huge exodus to take over The Maltings therefore she had to return as quickly as possible.

The family lined up in the foyer to thank those who had come. Several in front of Jennifer were Malcolm's employees. They were wearing Bowden's colours; green and gold with the BHC logos embroidered on their clothing. Many more were Duneden residents who turned round to acknowledge Jennifer and Maureen. Jennifer was aghast at Mark's audacity. He stood next to Roxanne shaking hands with those who were leaving as if he had every right to be there. She deliberately passed him by but did stop to comfort Roxanne. Her embrace with Malcolm was as heartwarming as it was heartbreaking. They hugged for an exceedingly long time. She apologised that she couldn't join him but Malcolm understood fully that many of the mourners would be locating to The Maltings for the rest of the night and no doubt he would be joining them later. He had left a substantial kitty behind the bar and had paid for sandwiches and sausage rolls to be handed out in the early evening.

Just as Archie had predicted, it was a busy, backbreaking night.

*

Thursday

The morning of Angie's funeral was full on; rush, rush, rush. Maureen wanted the Eden Suite to be perfect. The room was festooned with flowers – an abundance of colour and textures in every corner. The table centre baskets were a real credit to Willie's gardening skills and creativity. Any bride would have been proud to have them on her wedding tables. Jennifer thought that perhaps that was Maureen's intention; to give Angie the wedding day she would never have. Their fragrances infused every area of the room. The baskets were to be handed out to close family and friends after the buffet.

Angus Campbell, The Maltings temporary chef, broke one of his cardinal rules and volunteered to cover the breakfast shift as there would be no evening meals that Friday night: The Maltings would be too busy. Angie's eldest brother Kevin and his wife had flown up from London on the Thursday night. Angie's best friend, Lindsay, and her partner had flown up on the same flight but they were returning at different times. Jennifer found Kevin and his wife to be a very pleasant couple. Jennifer sat down, after the last breakfast had been served, with the Clapham girls and grabbed a quick coffee to chat about what to say and what not to say about Angie's 'London holiday' should anyone ask. Lindsay was dreading having to face Malcolm later. She would have to remember that they had 'never' met before.

The scene in the kitchen was reminiscent of the one on New Year's Eve when every available workspace had been commandeered by a member of staff – only instead of peeling onions and potatoes, they were preparing a sumptuous finger buffet for Angie. The fillings looked amazing; Angus had deviated hugely from the usual egg and cress, cheese, ham and corned beef, although, Jennifer had insisted on some plainer options for the less discerning palate.

Finally, after everything was ready, a very reluctant and weary

Jennifer climbed the stairs to change into her funeral outfit. Her black shift dress did nothing for her; she'd lost too much weight. Not intentionally. She ate like a horse but burned it off as quickly as a thoroughbred. She pinned her hair back off her face; not quite a ponytail but something that looked like she had made an effort. Perhaps her black heels would give her a little boost.

When she descended the stairs, Fergal was waiting for her. He looked terribly smart in his black suit. Jennifer's parents had also arrived. They were going to collect the girls immediately from school, including Bethany, as no one wanted Bethany to see the coffin being carried into the church. The school playground overlooked the church gates and the mourners would be arriving during the lunchtime break. A picnic had been prepared for them and Jennifer's parents had decided that Falkland Hill was as good a place as any. There was a lovely wee cafe in Falkland village and an ice-cream would be their final treat.

Jennifer held Fergal's hand as they walked to the church. The hearse was parked at the gates. A huge display with the word 'Mummy' spelled out with flowers dominated the side facing the church. Jennifer's eyes welled up. She knew mascara had been a foolhardy choice but she had wanted to look her best for her friend. The sun burst through the clouds and shone down on the large, black car as they turned into the gates. Duneden church was postcard perfect. It was a beautiful building, surrounded by well maintained, mature gardens on either side of the long path from the gates to the church doors. There were dozens and dozens of chairs in the gardens in front of the church and all around for the inevitable overspill. A set of speakers sat on either side of the church doors. They were anticipating a large turnout. Jennifer hoped she had enough sandwiches. The squeals and laughter from children playing seemed at odds with the solemn adults filtering through the church gates.

The first few rows were reserved for family. Fergal and Jennifer sat on the end of a pew a few rows further back. Within a few minutes, the church had filled up with those wishing to pay their respects to one of their own. The church officers were urging everyone to budge up or to give up their seats for the elderly. It was very hot and stuffy. Angie's elegant face smiled from the order of service. She looked so happy; it made Jennifer smile too. On the back was a lovely photograph of Angie gazing adoringly at Bethany as a toddler posing in front of a Christmas tree.

Jennifer had decided to keep Angie's little secret just that – a secret. Malcolm had had enough harrowing news and she wasn't going to be the one to push him over the edge; he was teetering pretty close already.

When the main mourners were being shown to their seats, a hand squeezed Jennifer's shoulder: it was Maureen who sat down next to Joyce. A strong, authoritative voice instructed the congregation to stand. Only the soft footsteps of the pallbearers could be heard above the deafening hush. Then the sniffling started followed by heavy sobbing emanating from a sorrowful Joyce. Her only daughter lay in an oak coffin within touching distance. No one was immune to her grief.

The service, however, was poignant and uplifting. The minister had come out of retirement at Joyce's behest to conduct the sermon. There was no doubt that Angie and her family were well known to this man. He had a hearty laugh and cackled at his own jokes. In another life he could have been a stand-up comic; his delivery was so witty. Yet, he spoke so eloquently and graciously about Angie as a small girl attending his Sunday school and as a teenager getting up to all sorts outside the church youth club and discos. He captured the essence of the well-loved, Duneden woman who had been a loyal friend and colleague to Jennifer.

The walk to the cemetery lasted more than fifteen minutes. It was baking hot and many of the mourners shed their coats and jackets as they followed the hearse. The burial was brief and formal. Angie's three brothers, two of her uncles, a cousin, Willie and young Martin were summoned to take a cord. As Willie and Martin stepped forward, Maureen could be heard crying above everyone else. After the benediction, the mourners quietly dispersed. A few stayed behind to speak with the family and the minister.

On entering the Eden Suite, visitors were offered a choice of whisky or a sherry. The round tables could seat ten comfortably but twelve chairs had been squeezed around each of the eight tables. Each setting consisted of a white side plate, topped with a paper napkin, cup and saucer. Platters of sausage rolls and sandwiches were carried to every table. Coffee and tea were offered until everyone had had enough. The building was a sea of black and white clothing. Jennifer mused at the mismatch of the outfits and how this was deemed acceptable for funerals. As long as black was worn, no one gave a fudge about how ridiculous they looked.

Two young members of staff wandered through every room with surplus platters of food and tablet; that Maureen's mum had made. Jennifer chatted with every table and with as many guests who were scattered throughout The Maltings and the beer garden as she possibly could. She reckoned that around one hundred and fifty people were milling around, both inside and out. When she finally made it to the kitchen, Fergal had his sleeves rolled up and was loading the dishwasher.

'You did her proud, Jennifer. A magnificent effort. Just champion'

'I hope so, Fergal. It's been a long day and it's not over by a long shot.'

Jennifer mucked in to help put things away in their proper place. Many of her regulars were doing the same – collecting glasses, washing and drying dishes and tidying tables once other guests had left. Ryan Ross could be heard asking if anyone had seen Jennifer. There were people asking for her. An older couple stood in the corridor: Jennifer had spotted them in the beer garden earlier.

'Are you Jennifer?' the woman asked as she approached them. 'We're Scott's mum and dad. We just wanted to thank you for letting us know.'

Jennifer had decided to call them a few days ago. It would've been most unfair if they'd not been given the opportunity to represent Bethany's father.

'I would say it's a pleasure but that would be inappropriate today. Did you see Bethany? She's here somewhere.'

They had seen her but only briefly. They intended to call on Joyce in a few days' time and introduce themselves properly. Jennifer agreed that that would be a good plan. Before leaving, Scott's mum took her hand and told Jennifer that Scott had intimated that he was very fond of her.

'Bad timing, unfortunately,' said Jennifer. There was nothing more to be said. The McIntyres smiled politely and left.

After she had contacted his parents, Scott had phoned Jennifer to find out what had happened. The conversation was strained and he seemed distant. Perhaps she had bombarded him with too many chatty letters. On reflection, Scott's two pieces now seemed superficial and insignificant.

The wake was descending into a very boisterous party, as most Scottish funerals tended to do. It's probably a release mechanism. Maureen and Willie smothered Jennifer with kisses and cuddles and promised to help out as much as they could. She continued patrolling her property ensuring that everyone was safe and clearing up as she went. Malcolm was in deep conversation with Angie's Clapham friends and Roxanne was flirting with Joe. Bitch! As if one of Jennifer's men was not enough for her. Fergal said his farewells and intimated he would return within a few days to discuss Jennifer's future plans. Jennifer suggested that they go out for lunch somewhere in Edinburgh. Her treat for his birthday. Her mum ushered the girls upstairs as Joyce had decided that it was time for her and Bethany to go home. Jennifer's dad mirrored his daughter; picking up after everyone, especially black ties.

'Jen?' That voice was very familiar to her so it was not unexpected to find Mark at her back.

'Mark. What can I do for you?' She tried not to be sarcastic.

'It's so good see you. The place is looking great and I hear things are looking up too.'

'If you call doubling last year's turnover looking up, then yes, it is.'

Jennifer knew she was listing and that she must look a sight but she was past caring what Mark thought about her.

'You're looking good, Jen,'

'Hardly,' she snorted. 'I'm knackered,

'I've missed you.' Mark searched her eyes for something. Reciprocation perhaps?

'No, you haven't. You'd just like to think you have.'

Sounding slightly rebuffed, he continued. 'Actually, I was hoping to put some business your way. It would be very profitable and a great marketing tool for you. I know it's probably not the right time... but when is?'

Jennifer wanted to sock him in the face but let him carry on.

'I've some well-connected clients who are looking for cheaper end accommodation for their employees during The Open and I was hoping that it would be of mutual benefit to us. What are your thoughts?'

Her thoughts were that he could shove his mutual benefits right up his arse. 'I'm fully booked for The Open. Ages ago. Sorry. The R&A have reserved all my rooms for the qualifying rounds and a Swedish TV company have agreed to my package terms over The Open weekend. But thanks for the offer.'

'Wow... Good for you. I mean it, Jen. Well done. I wish you well.'

He did mean it. And he missed her. If it wasn't for his good fortune in La Manga, he might have been tempted to make a move. Maybe later. Mark smiled, hovered for a moment then walked away without saying another word – never mentioning his daughters or anything else.

It must be the night for awkward conversations, pondered Jennifer or, perhaps, she was unintentionally giving off illnatured vibes. Scratch that. She knew fine well that she had meant to shut down Mark and the McIntyres. AND, she already knew that she would regret not having been more forthcoming. Not with Mark.

As she was heading out for some much-needed air, Malcolm caught up with her.

'Jen, do you have a minute?'

There was a picnic table near the river that was unoccupied. It was cooler near the water and further away from anyone else. No chance of anyone eavesdropping. Malcolm sat down opposite her.

'I've thought long and hard about this and you are the only person I can discuss it with and... I value your opinion.'

Jennifer prepared herself for Malcolm to disclose Angie's pregnancy. She would feign surprise.

'Malcolm Patterson is not my real name. It's Cyril Rose. I assumed someone else's identity years ago,' he blurted.

Jennifer's eyes widened and she looked around to ensure that no one could overhear their conversation but everyone was busy with their own chat.

'Say something,' urged Malcolm.

Her stunned surprise was for real.

'I arrived in Scotland, from Gateshead during the war and Davey Bowden rescued me in every sense of the word.'

Jennifer heard herself stammer. 'Hhhow?... when?... why? I don't know what to say.'

Malcolm could feel a sense of calm creep in. It was a relief to unburden his guilt and finally tell the truth.

'I killed a man. A good man, with a young family.'

'Christ! Malcolm! What happened?'

'I was young; only fourteen. I had just started working down at the docks. I was keen to fit in. Two of my mates, well I thought they were, knew how we could make a lot of money. It would be easy, they said.' Malcolm squirmed on his seat. 'One of them used to deliver bits and pieces to the Post Office at the end of our street. Security was lax and the Postmaster would be a walk over. No violence, they said, yet we brought heavy sticks. We went in around the back and down some steps. The door was unlocked. We had our faces covered. It was easy. Just like they said it would be.' He was racing now as he spilled his recollections. 'I stood at the back, unsure of what to do. The Postmaster stuffed money and things into a bag but as we were leaving, he grabbed me from behind. There was a struggle and I shoved him back. He fell. Only a few steps.' Malcolm stared for a minute into the pale, cloudless sky before continuing.

'The oldest bloke, Dan Morris, he'd only have been seventeen at the time, checked him. He was dead. I'd broken his neck. We scarpered and ran. When we eventually stopped, they blamed me. They said that they were not going down for something I had done and if the police asked, then they would say it was me on my own. A murderer. I told my dad who immediately sent me away and I ended up in Kirkcaldy. I've never been back.'

'Never? Not even for a sneaky peak?'

'I was too scared. Life in prison is not something I was keen to rush back to. Then as time went on, it was easier to pretend it never happened.'

'And you're sure he was dead?'

Malcolm nodded his head. 'I saw him, Jen. It was awful.' He scrunched his eyes as if he were trying to block the memory.

Malcolm told Jennifer about his trip to Newcastle with Angie and about the tramp, Doug Morris, who was the lad on the robbery's brother. Malcolm scooped Jennifer's hands into his.

'Jen, I have a huge favour to ask of you.'

FORTY-ONE

Tuesday 24th July

Jennifer lay on the sofa. Her legs and bare feet were dangling over one of the arms. She had her eyes closed. 'Please let me not be so tiiii... rrrred!' Her old jeans had been cut above the knee to make a pair of shorts. A red vest was tucked in the jeans – not a good colour as it clashed with her hair but she didn't give a shit. 'Please God, if you are up there then give me a teensy boost of energy. Pleeeeeze!... I can't hear you!' Obviously, there was no reply as she was alone in the flat. If there had been a response, there would definitely have been a little splash of shit in her pants.

Grudgingly, she forced herself to get up. What a week! The week had actually been a great success and not the hard work they had envisaged but the nights were very late – especially for her – as her guests enjoyed drinking into the wee hours. Two days ago, The Open Championship in St Andrews had finished on a high. Seve Ballesteros had won his second Open, two strokes ahead of Bernard Langer and Tom Watson.

When the Swedish T.V. presenters eventually arrived back in The Maltings on Sunday night, they were in the mood to party. It was a hoot. Of course, Jennifer had to remind everyone that she had actually met Seve four years previously while working at a tent in Gullane. The Maltings had been mentioned every day during their broadcasts but she doubted there would be a huge rush for bookings from Sweden in the foreseeable future.

Emma and Katie had spent most of the previous week at Port Seton. Yesterday, Jennifer had packed two little suitcases for a week in La Manga. They should be half way there by now. They flew out with Roxanne and would return with their Edinburgh grandparents who, apparently, were already holidaying in Spain. Before their journey, the girls had spent all day with Bethany who had missed the girls last week and was upset that they were going to Spain without her. Maureen and Joyce had a caravan booked in Perthshire for five days. It was something to look forward to. Bethany had spent a lot of her time with Jennifer and the girls since Angie's death.

Five weeks had flown by since both funerals and Malcolm's jaw dropping confession, followed by his strange request. Today was the day that Jennifer was assisting with the favour that had been asked of her. She was accompanying Malcolm to Gateshead.

He wanted to face his demons, accept the consequences of his terrible crime, but had asked Jennifer along for moral support. With both Angie and Doreen gone and Roxanne leading her own life, he had nothing to lose. He was hoping that a female presence might placate those who sought revenge. Jennifer suggested that he tell Roxanne everything and take her instead but Malcolm refused to consider it, insisting that Roxanne's presence would be a liability. He needed a sensible head with him. Jennifer felt he had inadvertently settled for another airhead. If in the event that he was apprehended and prevented from returning, Jennifer had been instructed to take a folder to his solicitors. Ron Bayne would let her into his house and she knew where to locate it.

'Surely, it won't come to that?'

'It might. My affairs are in order. I've written a lengthy letter for Roxanne.'

'You haven't told her about Angie?'

'No. Never. That can never happen!' was his steely reply.

Malcolm had been keen to return to Gateshead shortly after the funerals but The Maltings was too busy and with hindsight it was the right decision. His absence while Roxanne was staying in the family home would have aroused suspicion.

The plan was to head south around 11.00am. Jennifer would drive round to Orchard House and leave her car there, then head off with Malcolm in his car. Archie was left in charge. The Maltings didn't open until 6.00pm on Tuesdays and Jennifer deliberately chose not to take reservations for rooms while she was away to make life a little easier for Archie and Maureen. In the unlikely event that the golf competition overran, the Swedish company had booked all the rooms for the Monday night too but they were not required. Bonus for Jennifer, because not only was she paid for an extra day, it meant that all the housekeeping duties were completed on Monday and she had less to do on the Tuesday morning. She had forewarned Malcolm that she would probably sleep most of the journey.

At 10.50am Jennifer parked her car on the white gravel at the side of Malcolm's house. He was waiting at the door. She transferred her belongings into the back of his Range Rover. Malcolm wasted no time. They were driving up his long drive to the entrance of his grounds as the church clock struck the final 'dong' for 11.00am.

Jennifer hadn't a clue what to wear – casual or formal? Neither of them knew who they would actually meet. Malcolm had no idea if any of his immediate family still lived in the area but reckoned some relatives had to. They would knock on doors and ask. Jennifer plumped for white trousers and a short-sleeved, navy blouse. A white head band prevented her hair from falling into her face. Although she was wearing white mules for the car journey (to keep her feet cool), she intended to put on a pair of white canvas shoes later in case she had to make a quick getaway. God, she hoped not: she was hopeless at running. Malcolm wore a pair of dark blue cotton trousers and a light blue cotton shirt. It reminded her of something a policeman in warmer climes might wear. Now was not the time to pass comment – he was jumpy enough.

At the beginning of the journey, they talked about the girls staying in Spain with Mark and Roxanne and about the golf. Mark had crossed paths with the Ballesteros family due to his connections in La Manga and had introduced Malcolm to them. Jennifer vaguely remembered seeing the tops of the towers on the Forth Road Bridge from the dual carriageway. The next thing she knew, Malcolm was gently shaking her awake.

'Time to stretch our legs, sleepy head.' She could hear his voice in the distance but struggled to shake herself from her slumber.

'Sorry, I must have drifted off. Where are we?'

'Berwick. You've been sleeping for well over an hour.' Malcolm was mocking her.

They had stopped at a garden centre; a short distance from the Berwick by-pass, on the A1.

'We can grab a bite to eat and freshen up before we set off again. I reckon we are an hour and a half at most from Gateshead.'

Both of them moaned as they stretched off their stiff bodies. Jennifer joked that they were like a couple of old crocks. It was a large, dusty car park but Malcolm had found a parking spot close to the shop entrance. Jennifer thought about Mark and how much he used to annoy her. He would drive around for ages until he found the nearest parking space to wherever they were going.

After a quick visit to the loos, they'd agreed to meet at the cafe. They both had soup, cake and a coffee. Jennifer picked the largest slice of lemon drizzle cake on the display and a piece of millionaire's shortbread: she needed fattening up. Within fifteen minutes of sitting down, they were off again. Malcolm was visibly agitated. He calmed down once they were on the move.

Malcolm spoke about his family; his parents and three sisters. His dad had been a coal miner at Dunston Colliery but Malcolm had wanted a job at the docks instead. He wanted to be an apprentice welder but accepted a job as a rivet catcher. Jennifer was losing interest at this part but refocused when he spoke with affection about his sister, Elizabeth, who was a year older than Malcolm. They had been close and looked out for each other. His sister, Marion, was six years older and his younger sister Jane was only nine when he left. They had another quick toilet stop near Morpeth and were driving over the Tyne Bridge just after three in the afternoon. Malcolm had really gone for it after leaving Berwick.

Everything had changed. There was a huge new shopping centre being built on the Gateshead side of the bridge – tipped to be the largest in the U.K. Malcolm thought of the money that Bowden's could be making from it. The houses in the Staithes area where Malcolm had lived had been knocked down and a new development had replaced them. Malcolm drove around some other areas and streets in the Teams where he thought some relatives had lived. Jennifer had knocked on doors pretending to be a cousin of his sister Elizabeth but to no avail. Nobody could remember the Roses. Malcolm was about to admit defeat when Jennifer persuaded him to return to the original area where he had grown up. Perhaps some of the residents had remained behind.

At the first door Jennifer tried, an old woman answered. A musty, unwashed smell penetrated Jennifer's nostrils. The stooped pensioner was wearing a long, faded-green apron with the straps wrapped around her back and tied at the front – not unlike something Jennifer's own granny would have worn. She claimed to have known a family with the surname Rose. She had lived in the same street as them until 1950. A Marion Rose had assisted her with her daughter's home birth. She'd not been aware her daughter had been pregnant until her waters broke in the front room. She was only fifteen.

Jennifer called on Malcolm to join them. It was established that the Marion in question had been Malcolm's mother and as far as the woman knew, Marion was still alive and living with one of her daughters. She didn't know where. They had bumped into each other at a local supermarket a couple of years ago. A despondent Malcolm headed back to his car. He was about to drive off when the woman waved to them to return. She asked them to knock on the door four doors down as the family there also lived in Malcolm's old street.

Jennifer went first but she was not optimistic. The small garden was in better condition than the old neighbour's. A young man called loudly to his mother who, it turned out, was an auxiliary nurse at Dunston Hill Hospital where Elizabeth also worked as a nurse. As girls, they had attended the same school. Although she didn't have the actual number of Elizabeth's house, she was able to tell Jennifer that she lived in a small cul-de-sac in nearby Whickham called Juniper Grove, off the Orchard Road. Malcolm looked away when the woman on the doorstep strained to see who was in the car. He did not want to be recognised.

Jennifer jumped into the car and beamed. 'Whickham, James, and don't spare the horses!'

Malcolm was jubilant. 'Are you sure?'

'Your sister Elizabeth lives in a cul-de-sac off Orchard Road. Do you know it?'

Malcolm knew Orchard Road. If he recalled correctly, it was fairly long but it had been a long time ago and his memory was fuzzy. After scouring for two and a half hours, the search could finally be reaching a conclusion. Surely Orchard Road was a good omen: Orchard House and Orchard Road? It had to be.

'Nervous?' Jennifer asked.

'Bricking it!'

After twenty-five minutes, Malcolm pulled up outside a semi-detached house. It had a small, well-maintained garden with a small, apple tree. That had to be a good omen too, he hoped. A black Hillman Imp was parked in the narrow drive. There was a chill in the air and Jennifer slipped on a navy and white striped jumper. After five minutes of composing himself, Malcolm gave her the nod to go to the door.

Jennifer rang the doorbell. She could see the figure of a woman appear through the frosted glass. A chubby woman, about Malcolm's height, smiled when she opened the door. It was like staring at a female version of Malcolm.

'I'm so sorry to bother you but I'm looking for Elizabeth Rose.'

The woman laughed, 'I haven't gone by that name for a very long time, pet.'

'Are you the sister of Cyril Rose?' Jennifer thought the woman was going to collapse.

She struggled to give a reply. 'Who wants to know?'

Jennifer signalled for Malcolm to come. It seemed ages until he was by her side.

'Hello, our Elizabeth. It's good to see you, pet.' Malcolm had lost all trace of his Fife accent.

FORTY-TWO

Elizabeth stood mesmerised trying to take him in. She shook her head.

'Is it really you, Cyril?' and without waiting for a reply walked into her little brother's arms.

They both cried tears of joy, both frightened to let go. Jennifer wiped away her own tears. Elizabeth took his hand and led him through the small hallway: pink walls and a burgundy carpet. She stopped short at another opaque, glass door.

'I hope you're ready for this.'

When the door opened an old, grey-haired woman could be seen sitting in a chair in front of the window facing the telly, in her brown trousers and a brown and red, diamond checked jumper. Pink fluffy slippers overwhelmed her tiny feet. An interview with Arthur Scargill, the leader of the miner's union, was blaring from the box. Elizabeth turned down the volume and bent down to her mother's ear and shouted,

'A visitor for you, mam.'

Without speaking, Malcolm knelt down in front of his mother. Her pale, alabaster hands traced every inch of his face. Her sad eyes looked deep into his soul. She cupped his chin and cheeks in the palms of her hands and placed her forehead on his,

'Cyril, my boy, you've come back.'

Everyone in the room was crying. Everyone in the room could feel the weight he was carrying. Malcolm pulled a small pouffe towards him so that he could be near his mother. He sat on it, never releasing his grip on her hand.

'Where did you go?' his sister asked. 'We looked everywhere for you, especially Dad. Weeks and months and years. It took him in the end.'

'What did?' Malcolm was keen to know.

'Not being able to find you.'

'He told me to run, so I did.'

'Oh, Cyril. It was all a big mistake. A terrible mistake.'

Elizabeth in her denim, tunic dress and flip flops, perched on the arm of a big chair where Jennifer was sitting and recalled everything that had unfolded after Malcolm had flown.

Her dad had told the family about Cyril's heinous crime and that Cyril had not meant to kill the sub postmaster. It had been a tragic accident. Jack Rose had persuaded his only son to run and more importantly, to never return. Malcolm nodded in agreement then Elizabeth's eyes filled with different tears.

'Tommy Hall wasn't dead,' sobbed Elizabeth. 'Tommy was out cold, that's all. He must have struck his head and was knocked out.'

Malcolm couldn't make sense of it all. The anger was building up. 'No!' he shouted. 'Dan checked him. He said his neck was broken... they said they would blame me. They didn't want to hang so they blamed me.'

Malcolm was now on his feet. He patrolled the living room like a wild animal captured in a cage.

'He told me that his eyes were empty and that his neck was definitely broken.'

Elizabeth grabbed Malcolm by the shoulders. 'He was wrong.

HE WAS WRONG! That fool, Dan Morris! What the hell did he know about vital signs?'

Malcolm flopped onto the spare chair and stared at the ceiling. He spoke as if speaking to a higher being. 'Thirty-nine wasted years. Wasted!' He began to cry. He had thought that he had no tears left after Doreen and Angie but he had – in buckets.

Elizabeth raised the palm of her hand high above her head and silently ordered everyone to give him time. The observers watched and waited. When Malcolm regained his composure, he apologised to the women and asked Elizabeth to explain more.

'When Dad found out that the Postmaster hadn't been seriously hurt, he hunted down Dan Morris and his equally dim mate and marched them to the police station. I thought he was going to kill them. The Postmaster had been unable to identify them so it was Dad's word against theirs. However, Tommy said that the youngest lad, which must have been you, had stood at the back and did nothing but watch. The police said that if you did turn up, they would have to consider charging you with armed robbery because they knew you had been there.'

'We had a stick not guns.'

'You were still armed. Anyway, Dad threatened to break their legs if they didn't hand the stuff they had stolen back to the Post Office. I think they'd spent some of the money but a bag was left anonymously at the back door of the Post Office. Dad looked everywhere for you.'

It was almost too much to comprehend. 'I went to Scotland,' he sighed.

'Why didn't you come back? All those years, Cyril. Not knowing if you were alive or dead.'

Angie and Jennifer had asked the same question. 'I believed he was dead. I had nightmares about checking the body myself. I convinced myself that I'd seen him lying with his eyes wide open, his neck all twisted and his tongue dangling at the side of his mouth. I thought that you all hated me. I hated myself so why not you. After a while, it was easier to pretend that it never happened.'

Elizabeth had worked with trauma patients and understood why Malcolm had believed it. The brain was a powerful instrument. It could store the most painful or pleasant of memories yet distort them as it saw fit.

Malcolm told them all about Davey Bowden and his new name, about Doreen and Orchard House. He took huge pride in talking about Roxanne. He flicked through his wallet for some photographs – he had more in the car. Only Jennifer could sense his regret about not disclosing his love for Angie. In exchange, Elizabeth explained she was widowed but had two strapping sons; one a doctor no less and the other was training to be a paramedic. Both of their sisters lived in Durham and she would call them later.

Malcolm's mother had said nothing. She had listened with her eyes closed. Jennifer wasn't sure if she had fallen asleep but she had heard everything as later conversations confirmed. His mother smiled at Jennifer and asked her why she was there. She told the old woman about Angie and how she had been in the car with Doreen. 'Cyril' and she had bonded in their grief and she explained that 'Cyril' knew he could rely on her discretion. Malcolm's mother looked directly at her and smiled again. Did she suspect more? Jennifer presumed that she probably did.

There were forty years of catching up to unravel. Jennifer realised she was starving and was delighted when Elizabeth insisted that they stay for supper. After four hours, Jennifer couldn't stop yawning. Her legs were jumpy and she just couldn't settle. Reluctantly, Malcolm tore himself away from his mother and his sister and they drove to the Gosforth Park Hotel in Newcastle where Malcolm had secured a reservation a few weeks ago. Before bed, they had a quick drink in the hotel bar. Like the rest of the hotel, the decor was smart and the carpets were springy. They sat in large, comfortable bucket chairs. It was there that Jennifer suggested she travel back to Fife alone by train and that Malcolm should stay on with his family. He didn't hesitate, not for a second, and graciously accepted his companion's offer.

'I'll never forget this, Jen. I owe you.' He kissed her hand. It was a kiss of friendship and nothing else.

Jennifer went to bed as Malcolm ordered another malt whisky.

What a day. What a week. What a month. What a year.

Jennifer lay in the king size bed swathed in crisp, white Egyptian cotton and cast her mind back to the afternoon she caught Mark and Roxanne on the pool table. At times, it seemed like a lifetime ago and at others only yesterday yet it triggered a tidal wave. She never envisaged in a million years that she would have bought The Maltings from under Mark's nose. Nor that The Maltings would have gone from strength to strength. Before she had moved to Fife, she had known nothing about running a pub, shooting seasons or the income it would generate for her, thanks to Horse. The Wirral boys had occupied her rooms for around fourteen weeks – easy money, only vacating them for The Open. She had never heard of the R&A until the two *Muppet* gents waltzed through her doors. It had been a huge learning curve and she had loved every minute.

And Mark? Why had she never seen him for what he was; a great big, lazy, two-timing twat? As a young girl, she had been seduced by his age. He'd seemed so sophisticated and he had a sense of adventure that she'd found intoxicating. At least that's what she thought he had. It turned out that he just couldn't face reality or hard work. With his inflated promises, he had enticed her to travel the week before her graduation ceremony. She'd asked him to wait, not for her, but her parents were so excited. They'd never been in such a grand building as the McEwen Hall before. Mark, but ultimately Jennifer, had robbed them of the opportunity. Her dad was more disappointed in Jennifer for kowtowing to Mark than the actual 'bloody graduation!' The only time her dad had sworn in front of her. She had been truly infatuated by Mark, yet there must have been tiny alarm bells ringing somewhere at the back of her besotted brain. It was her idea to fake a wedding in Spain and even although Mark had suggested on more than one occasion to legalise their lie, Jennifer had wriggled out of it. Then there was her gran's cottage: she had kept that a secret too. Mark was equally as guilty. Apart from his biggie with Roxanne, he had had the audacity to purchase The Maltings without her consent.

Perhaps her need to snatch back The Maltings from Mark had been more for revenge than setting out to prove to herself that she could do it without him: and she had, albeit with the help of the wonderful Angie and Maureen. Jennifer was convinced that after Angie, everything would fall apart but so far it hadn't. Maureen and Archie had stepped up and even the young members of staff assumed a new professional approach to their duties.

She wondered again if Scott would come back to rescue them all, especially Bethany. It was doubtful. Her last conversation before Angie's funeral had been awkward. He insisted over and over again that returning to Scotland was not an option. He'd sunk all his money into his new business and having Bethany to live in Australia wasn't viable either as he had no time to give her the dedication that would be required. Jennifer had ended the conversation abruptly. He had whinged enough.

And then there was Joe: dependable, reliable, kind but... so boring. What was wrong with her? All the other 'exciting' men had let her down yet she knew that Joe would love her and her girls if given the chance.

She was ashamed to recall it – they had had sex again on the Saturday night of The Open.

It was late, in fact four in the morning, when all the residents and some locals had finally gone to bed leaving just Joe and Jennifer. Joe had insisted on locking up with Jennifer as he felt it would be safer with all those men in the rooms. He had a right to be concerned. The boss man, a good-looking Swede with short, blond, spiky hair and glasses had slobbered over Jennifer since his arrival. That evening he had asked her if Joe was her lover. 'A very, dear friend,' had been her reply.

'I think your friend wants to get into your pants,' he said, and then leaned towards her. She felt the warm breath on her ear. 'But don't we all.'

'Will you be safe on your own, Jen?' Joe had asked as all the lights were being switched off in the lounge bar.

'I think they think you stay here,' she reassured him.

'I could.'

In the dark room, Jennifer thanked him with a friendly kiss on the lips. There is no such thing. Within seconds, he had lifted her on to a high stool and his mouth was sucking her breasts. She rubbed her hands through his black hair and pulled his head into her. Within another few seconds, her black skirt was up around her waist and her pants had been discarded on the floor. Joe fumbled in his pocket for a condom (bless him, forever hopeful), undid his zip and slipped it on effortlessly. Then they did it. She wanted it, needed it. Duneden had unleashed an inner desperate-for-sex maniac that she never knew had existed. What had she done? Again? It was not her finest moment.

She drifted off to sleep in her luxurious, comfy bed.

The next morning, Malcolm was sipping a coffee on a long sofa facing the breakfast room. He stood up to greet her. He had old fashioned manners. He escorted his young companion to their table and asked if she had slept well.

'I had such a good sleep,' she informed him. 'I need a new mattress.'

'Then get one.'

Jennifer raised her eyebrows. 'All the bedrooms need one. I'll be last in the queue.'

'The absolute professional,' laughed Malcolm.

After a leisurely breakfast of smoked salmon and scrambled eggs, Malcolm drove Jennifer to the station and bought a first-class ticket to Ladybank. She had objected as it was a short journey but Malcolm ignored her protestations. He had paid for everything since leaving Duneden.

Jennifer hugged her friend goodbye and they both knew it was a friendship that each of them could depend on.

During her train journey, Jennifer tried to map out her future – not that that had ever panned out the way she had hoped. Joe would have to be her first, hopefully only, casualty. There was no real connection on her part, on which to base a solid relationship. Sex and being grateful was not enough.

Jennifer Cameron did not need a man in her life. She had to be the master of her own happiness and that of her two beautiful girls. The moving train rocked her to sleep.

FORTY-THREE

Sunday 11th November

Jennifer looked at her watch. 9.00pm. It had been a long day.

High Teas were busy earlier. Usually, trade slows down in November as people gear up for the cost of Christmas. Not this Sunday. Next week would probably see a significant dip.

All the shooters ate together at 6 o'clock and were happy with a High Tea. Since there's no shooting on a Sunday, they had taken up Jennifer's suggestion to visit the House of Bruar near Pitlochry and the spectacular Queen's View en route. Two guns had their wives with them. They, too, were happy with Jennifer's recommendations and by all accounts had spent a small fortune on country clothing. Jennifer contemplated if she would ever be as frivolous as to spend five hundred pounds on next to nothing. One could dream.

Willie had offered to lock up tonight. As soon as the last two residents drifted through to the bar, she would secure all the areas downstairs and turn in.

'Jen.' It was one of her guests. 'There's a guy dozing on the sofa upstairs. He was there earlier. Do you want to check him out?'

Jennifer thought about calling out to Willie and Joe but decided against it. She followed Evan Adamson (one of her surgeons) up to the resident's lounge. Right enough, there was a man zonked on the chaise longue; a large canvas bag lodged between his immaculately polished brown shoes.

'Thanks, Evan. I'll take it from here.'

'You sure?'

'Positive.'

'We're in room three if you need us.' Evan had brought his wife along on this trip.

Jennifer looked at her unexpected (and uninvited) intruder and kicked his shoes with her foot. She had no idea what he was up to.

'Mark. MARK!'

Mark's eyes flickered behind closed lids then he opened them. 'Good to see you, buttercup.'

It took her not to laugh or visibly cringe. John Cameron often addressed Marjorie in the same way.

'What do you want?' She was in no mood for games.

'Can we discuss this somewhere more private? Please?'

'Wait here!'

When Jennifer entered her open-plan room, books and note paper littered the floor. The owner of which was fast asleep.

'Wakey, wakey.' Zoe stirred and apologised for nodding off. 'That's me finished for the night. Thanks again, honey. Get yourself off home.'

Without hesitation, Zoe gathered her belongings and was out the door in less than five minutes. Jennifer didn't want Zoe to meet Mark. The less folk that knew he had dropped in the better. That included Joe and Willie.

'Make it quick,' warned Jennifer. The last time she and Mark had spoken on the phone, they were arguing over maintenance. A pittance followed. It hardly covered the girls' school shoes and a winter jacket each.

Mark sat on the wooden box, clamped his hands over his face, then hid behind them for several seconds.

'Can I stay here for a night?' he asked. There was more than a hint of pleading in his tone.

'Can't you stay with Malcolm?'

'He doesn't know I'm here,' he admitted. 'Neither does Roxie.'

Jennifer looked at him quizzically. She was still standing. 'Have you had a fall out?'

'No, nothing like that.'

'What then?' urged his once-upon-a-time 'wife'.

Mark rose up slowly. 'I miss you, Jen. Every minute of every day. It's painful.' His eyes penetrated Jennifer's. 'It's eating me up.' He took her hands and squeezed them.

Jennifer didn't know whether to laugh or cry. But she was angry. Seething.

'You cannot be serious. You walked away, no, ran away, without a backwards glance. You dumped us. Me and the girls.' Jennifer thumped their hands off his chest.

Mark threw his arms wide apart. 'Go for it. As hard as you can. I deserve it.'

For a few seconds, she contemplated it; beating the shit out of him. Instead, she cried. The memory of him on the pool table with Roxanne floored her all over again. She cried for herself. For her girls. For Angie. For Bethany. For Scott. For Joe and even for Malcolm. She truly missed Angie. Running The Maltings without her had not been as easy as she had often made it out to be.

Mark half ushered, half carried, her to the big chair. He knelt in front of his former partner and held her tightly. Jennifer had no idea how long they had remained like that; too long. She sat up abruptly. Mark had to dodge her head.

'Coffee?' She needed to occupy herself.

'A stiff whisky would be better.'

Jennifer poured them both a drink – a whisky for Mark and a Cointreau for her.

'Cheers,' said Mark.

Jennifer refused to acknowledge his gesture. She studied him for a while, trying hard to gauge what was up.

'What's really going on, Mark?' she sighed.

'I couldn't keep up the pretence any longer. I know you'll say I'm bullshitting but that day when we stood on the doorstep, the day before Spain, I wanted you to take me back. I never wanted to go to La Manga. It was never part of my plan.'

'What were your plans, Mark? From where I'm standing, the girls and I were never part of them.'

Mark sat back in the big chair and spread his knees. 'Coming here was a mistake. I get that now. I'm not making excuses, Jen. I got bored. Not of you and the girls. Of me. I thought.' There was a dramatic pause. 'I thought we needed a challenge. A reboot. But deep down, it was me. I think I was trying to prove myself. I dunno.' His head slumped back and he closed his eyes.

Jennifer was too tired to concentrate. 'Let's talk in the morning. My head's pounding. You can have my bed. I'll squeeze in with Katie.'

She wandered through to her bedroom. She chose the things she would need for the following morning: her uniform, clean underwear. Her nightie was tucked under her pillow and as she fumbled to retrieve it, she sensed Mark was behind her.

Be strong. Be firm. Too late. The heat from his body derailed her.

She turned to face him. The orange glow from the lights, on Duneden's Main Street, seeped through the blinds. He looked unbelievably handsome. Her Mark. The father of her children.

'God, Jen. You look great.' He cupped the side of her face and kissed her softly. She kissed him back. Her gentle Mark. In that moment, the enormity of coping with The Maltings on her own became too much. She wanted to share the burden. She wanted to share it with Mark.

'Sorry. I have to lock the Eden Suite. I'll be straight back,' she assured him.

'Leave it. I'll do it later,' and he began unbuttoning her blouse.

'No. Willie'll be expecting me. I'll be five minutes.'

She'd barely reached the bottom stair when an enthusiastic Henry barked his greeting.

'Where's the fire?' laughed Malcolm.

Shit!! She rubbed Henry's back. 'Ha, ha. No fire. Watching something on the telly and rushing during the ads. You, okay?' She could feel the cold air from Henry and his master slap her embarrassed cheeks. Without waiting for a response, Jennifer skipped into the Eden Suite.

A quick recce of the room confirmed that it was empty and the last of the chairs were piled on top of the tables. Jennifer had checked the floor earlier for cigarettes. As she was about to leave and lock the door, Henry bounded in, followed by Malcolm who seemed more excited than his dog.

'A quick word?' Won't keep you.' Malcolm was grinning from ear to ear. 'I'm going to be a granddad,' he blurted.

Jennifer froze.

On witnessing his young friend's incredulity, he apologised immediately for being so insensitive. 'Sorry, Jen. Not good news for you but I'm over the moon. Don't say anything to anyone yet. I've been sworn to secrecy. I can't believe it. A granddad.'

Being hit by a sledgehammer wouldn't suffice. A huge, walloping wrecking ball might just about make it. Jennifer couldn't spoil the moment for Malcolm as he spilled the gory details.

'I'm made up for you. Really, I am. Let's celebrate properly tomorrow. I'll pop round.' How Jennifer managed to sound so cheerful was beyond her. Numbness had replaced the blood in her veins. And full-on, fucking loathing for the bastard waiting for her!

She climbed the stairs and paused at the turning to the left. How and why had she ever loved this complete and utter waste of space?

He was actually lying naked on top of her bed. The glare from the ceiling light blinded him for a second. The thud of clothes on his face momentarily blocked the brightness.

'Sling your fucking hook!' she yelled.

A shocked Mark sprang from the bed.

'When were you going to fess up? The ONLY reason that you are here is because your dozy cow of a girlfriend is pregnant. Definitely not part of Mark Cameron's BIG plan. I mean it, Mark. FUCK OFF! NOW!' She was determined not to shed a tear. She wouldn't give him the satisfaction.

'That's not why I'm here. You have to believe me. It was deliberate. On her part. She knew I wasn't happy She tricked me. Look at me, Jen. I love you.'

'Pathetic! You DIS...GUST me. Get dressed,' demanded Jennifer, 'before I shout on Willie and whoever else is downstairs.'

Jennifer stood outside on the landing and waited. When a sheepish Mark appeared, he slunk past. She had no idea where he would go. Morningside probably. She was past caring.

FORTY-FOUR

Christmas Eve 1984

It was a cold, damp, Monday morning and Jennifer was enjoying her usual constitutional – a coffee in solitude at the back door of The Maltings; a little later than normal. It was exceptionally quiet apart from the flowing waters of the Eden at the bottom of her garden. The girls were still in bed having a long lie on the first day of the school holidays. The Maltings staff unanimously agreed to close today and open up again on the 28th. They could have filled the Eden Suite thrice over for Christmas dinners. Maybe next year. Jennifer, however, would have to be around on the 27th as four shooters were arriving for three days. She had warned Horse that the bar would be closed on their first night but they were welcome to use the lounge to meet socially and to drink their own drink. A hot supper would be provided on their arrival.

Many of the locals had wanted the bar to remain open on Christmas Eve but there had been something on nearly every day in December and a well-earned break was required to recharge all staff batteries. Between Christmas party nights and group lunches aplenty, The Maltings had had another successful Christmas season.

Jennifer was alerted to someone creeping along the corridor. She knew who it would be.

'Good morning, Mr Blakeley. Were you about to sneak off without saying goodbye?' she laughed.

A sheepish Joe apologised.

'Time for a quick coffee?'

Joe declined. He had a job to finish off.

'Shall we see you tonight?'

'Er… probably but Louisa is spending Christmas at mine's.' He smiled.

Jennifer was genuinely pleased for him. Explaining to Joe, that she would not be taking their relationship forward, had been hard for her. As usual, he took it on the chin which was far more than she deserved. For several weeks, he avoided The Maltings but eventually drifted back. At first, their conversations were brief and polite but gradually became easier and friendlier.

Then one day, a damsel in distress came to stay at The Maltings. Halleluiah! Louisa Fleming's ground floor flat had been flooded during an exceptionally heavy rainstorm and her insurance company had asked The Maltings to accommodate her – three months later, she was still there. She was English, thirty, single, shy and utterly delightful. She worked at an estate agent's in Cupar. She had followed her boyfriend to Scotland because he had been posted to the R.A.F. base in Leuchars, near St Andrews, then six months later, he dumped her.

'What a cad!' she had said.

Jennifer insisted 'bastard!' was more appropriate.

In the beginning, Louisa had remained in her room most evenings but Jennifer encouraged her to sit in the bar more often. She'd asked Jennifer if she knew of any workmen that could help her out with general repairs. Cue her knight in shining armour, in the form of Joe. They clicked instantly. Within weeks, Joe was regularly staying over in her room.

Jennifer was about to go in when she heard the familiar barking from Henry, followed by the heavy crunching of footsteps on her gravel. Malcolm was taking a short cut through the car park to his house. He had a paper under his arm and a large carton of milk in his hand.

'Don't you look every inch the country gent,' she teased.

'One has to try,' he laughed. He kissed Jennifer on the cheek.

Malcolm looked swell in his brown, Barbour coat and green, Hunter wellies. The strain of July had melted from his face and a cheerier one had replaced it.

'Thank you for coming over yesterday. Everyone was pleased to see you and the girls, especially my mother.'

Malcolm was having a big family Christmas this year. His mother, his sister Elizabeth and his youngest sister Jane and some of her family had arrived on Saturday to spend Christmas and New Year with Malcolm. Roxanne and Mark had flown in specially to meet them for the first time. When Malcolm invited Jennifer and the girls over, she had politely declined but he would not take no for an answer. Surprisingly, it had been a very pleasant afternoon. She successfully avoided having to chat with either Mark or Roxanne. Malcolm was ecstatically joyful; it had been a pleasure to witness.

Not long after he returned from his first visit to Gateshead, Malcolm began taking Emma and Katie once a fortnight to the cinema. Bethany would often tag along too which was an added bonus. Emma and Katie were very fond of him, so much so, that they asked if they could start calling him Papa Malc. Apparently, Roxanne used to refer to Doreen's father as Papa and the girls thought that the name suited Malcolm.

Malcolm explained to The Maltings clientele one night that he had tracked down his mother after having been adopted during the war by the Patterson family. No one had any reason to doubt what he had told them. Why would they? So many families had been separated during those bleak years for a variety of different reasons. They shared in his delight that his family would be reunited at Christmas at Orchard House.

'Did you open your early Christmas presents?' asked Malcolm dancing with laughter as if he were *Scrooge* on the morning he had discovered it was still Christmas.

'What were you thinking about? It was far too extravagant!'

On Sunday evening while she was at Orchard House, a lorry from Deep Slumber parked at the back door and unloaded a new mattress for Jennifer and three more for her to put in some of her guest bedrooms. Malcolm had arranged it with the owner of the bed company, whom he knew well. The mattresses had been left in the Eden Suite with a huge pink ribbon wrapped around the one earmarked for Jennifer. There was a postcard from the Gosforth Park Hotel attached to it. The message read, *Sleep well my dear friend. Merry Christmas xx.*

Malcolm strutted off, whistling as he went, with Henry straining at the lead.

There wasn't much to do downstairs. Jennifer had done most of the cleaning last night before closing and Archie had washed everything thoroughly at the end of his bar shift. She had a mountain of presents still to wrap. The girls were spending Christmas afternoon and night at Malcolm's, and Jennifer had bought small gifts for everyone that would be there, including Roxanne and Mark – with little Christmas grace, obviously.

She was having Christmas dinner at Fergal's with Hannah. However, there would be four of them. Fergal gave no further information and told a curious Jennifer that she would just have to wait and see. The suspense was eating away at her.

Later in the evening after the Christingle service, they were going to open some early Christmas presents at Maureen and Willie's house. Jennifer would be eternally grateful to them and their boys. Both had supported her when she needed them despite struggling with their own grief. Maureen had blossomed in her role as manager. Her second son, Ryan, had started catering college last summer and under the skilful guidance of Angus Campbell, was turning out to be an excellent chef. Angus had enjoyed his stint at The Maltings so much that he stayed on to do two nights a week; a Thursday and a Saturday. Maureen, Jennifer and Archie had been coached in how to prepare some of his signature dishes for a Friday night, although Ryan was more than capable of running the kitchen on his own. Another local lady helped out with breakfasts.

Jennifer began wrapping some presents for the girls. She hadn't bought them much as they would receive an inordinate number of generous gifts from other people; last year's quota was as good a benchmark as any. Her parents, Fergal, Hannah, her brother Andrew and her friend Fiona spent a small fortune on them. Not forgetting Morag. Although Jennifer didn't see a lot of her sister, giving gifts at Christmas had always been a big deal in their family.

The noise from the T.V in the living area let Jennifer know that the girls were up. She hid their presents on the high shelves in her bedroom and began breakfast – plain cereal and toast. They would consume more than enough sugary treats over the next two weeks. As the girls munched away, Jennifer spread out several small gifts for Maureen's family on the worktops and wrote the tags. She placed them on or beside each gift. As she began cutting the glossy wrapping paper, she thought she could hear a knock at the back door. She stood at the top of the stairs and listened. Sure enough, it started again. On the way downstairs, it sounded as if the door was about to cave in.

'I'm coming!' she roared as she reached the corridor.

She unbolted the door from the top and unlocked it with the big key. She half expected it to be Maureen or Willie or even Mark.

'I know I'm the last person you probably want to see but can I come in?'

'Bloody hell. What are you doing here?'

'Can I come in... please?' Scott took a step back as Jennifer opened the door properly.

'Of course you can.'

Jennifer asked him to wait in the hallway while she nipped upstairs to let the girls know where she would be and to fetch the keys to unlock the lounge door. She checked herself in the mirror. Not the most attractive look – a purple jogging suit that had seen better days and her hair resembled a squashed bowling ball on the top of her head. Scott found a seat as Jennifer made them a coffee. She thought about the first time she had met him and how she had spilled hot soup on her hand. He was holding the door for her as she carried the two coffee mugs.

'I don't want you burning yourself.' His thin smile indicated that he was unsure of saying the wrong thing.

'Are you here for long?' enquired Jennifer, terrified that her tone implied that she wanted him to be.

'I hope so. I owe it to Bethany. To make up for not being here when she needed me.'

Jennifer racked her brains for a suitable response but she couldn't find the right words.

'Our last phone call didn't end well,' he said.

'My fault probably. It was a very emotional time.'

The silence was excruciating.

'I should have written. I'm rotten at writing letters. Not like you. I've missed them,' confessed Scott.

'Truthfully? I thought that you... sorry, I didn't know what you were thinking that was the problem.'

Scott rubbed his gloved hands together to warm them up. He had his thick, blue jacket on again and a very thick, knitted hat. 'Trying to acclimatise.'

'Cold enough to freeze the balls off a kangaroo? Or something like that.'

Scott laughed. 'I would probably have said roo but you're close enough.'

The awkwardness had begun to thaw.

'So, how come you managed to tear yourself away now?' Jennifer regretted her sarcastic comment the moment she said it. 'Sorry. That came out all wrong.'

'Nah, I deserved that one. I had a frank discussion with my business partner and he is going to run things until I get back. I couldn't leave any quicker. He had invested a lot of money too. It wouldn't have been fair. But we've built up a reasonable client base, enough to sustain us for the foreseeable future so he's given me three months before I have to get my arse back.'

'Three months? Wow.' Jennifer was lost for words again.

'I'm not expecting much but it'll give me time to get to know Bethany better.'

'Does she know you're coming?'

'I phoned Maureen last night. We had a long, long chat. She's going to talk things over with Joyce and if her granny's okay with it, I'm going to surprise her tonight at Maureen's.'

'Oh, we're going too.' Jennifer was aware that she sounded more than pleased.

'Will Joe be there?' he asked despondently.

'Joe? Joe Blakeley? Why do you ask that?'

Scott gave his neck and shoulders a little shake and straightened up in his seat. 'Because I saw him leave earlier.'

Jennifer guffawed, 'Were you spying on me?' Scott's face actually turned pink. 'Joe left earlier after spending the night with *his girlfriend* who happens to be living in one of my bedrooms.' She began filling in some unnecessary details about flooding and Louisa needing workmen.

'A "no" was what I was hoping for,' he said as he rose from his seat and walked around the table to Jennifer. 'Can we start again?' He pulled Jennifer to her feet. His face was within kissing distance.

'Hi, Jennifer, it's good to see you.'

'It's good to see you too.' She smiled.

'Merry Christmas, Jennifer.'

'Merry Christmas...' He didn't let her finish.

His mouth had found hers and for several moments they were lost in future hopes and dreams.

When they finally stopped, Scott looked very serious. 'Can I ask you something?'

'Yes.' Although, she wasn't exactly sure what her reply might be.

'Can we go upstairs? It's bloody freezing in here.'

FORTY-FIVE

10th August 1985

The sun made its first appearance of the day just as the bride stepped out of the black Bentley classic car; white ribbons stretched from the side windows to the B mascot on the end of the bonnet. A loud cheer went up from the large, Duneden crowd who had gathered to watch the beautiful young woman being escorted into the church by her dad. As is customary, the bride's 'poor oot' was the biggest. Other guests had thrown money already. Dozens of youngsters scrambled to catch the many handfuls of mixed coins that had been scattered by the father of the bride who then walked with his daughter up the long pathway to the church door to more cheers and thunderous applause.

Willie, who was best man, stood beside the serious looking groom and nudged him when he knew the bride had arrived. 'Last chance to bail oot,' he joked.

'Fuck off, Willie.' The groom was too nervous to laugh.

Jennifer fixed the girls' underskirts and reminded them that it was important to behave as the bride walked down the aisle. They looked like little angels in their short dresses and their white socks and shoes. Masses of grips secured their hair and little white flowers peppered the beehive style on top of their pretty heads. Jennifer was so proud. She gave Bethany, who was standing beside an agitated Maureen, and wearing a similar dress to Emma's, a reassuring wave.

As the first notes of Wagner's *Bridal Chorus* resounded throughout the church, the congregation stood to welcome the bride. There were oohs and aahs aplenty as the radiant bride progressed gracefully down the aisle with her beaming father. Tears pricked Jennifer's eyes as Louisa mouthed thank you to her then took her place beside her handsome groom in his red and white kilt; the Dress Stewart tartan. Joe looked as if he was about to burst with happiness as Louisa lifted her veil.

After the ceremony, friends and family gathered in the church grounds for photos. Kilts in all colours and tartans swished as the men strutted around. The photographer had agreed earlier that the snaps that required Maureen in them were to be taken first to allow her to slip away to organise everything at The Maltings for the champagne reception and the meal. Joyce kept an eye on all the girls as Maureen and Jennifer scurried along the road for the last-minute preparations.

'I'm so nervous, Jen. This is the first wedding where I'm officially in charge and Willie has to be the fu… bloody best man.'

'That was nearly fifty pence in the swear box,' Jennifer warned her.

Poor Maureen, she had been trying really hard to address her cursing habit but at the rate that she and Willie had been popping the money in, they would soon have enough cash for a decent family holiday: not that holidays were their thing, nor would they be for a very long time.

A small marquee had been erected in the beer garden the previous day, by Willie and Joe. It could probably seat around forty people in theatre style but its function today was to serve champagne to standing guests. A large linen clad table was set at the covered end and eighty champagne flutes were lined up ready to be filled.

The two women put the finishing touches to the long top table and all the round ones. They double-checked all the place settings for the third time and ensured that nothing was missing from the tables.

Jennifer stood back to admire the room. 'It's perfect, Maureen. If it were my wedding, I'd be truly happy.'

'Your time will come, honey.' And the two friends embraced.

Maureen checked that the kitchen was on schedule. Chef Ryan was in charge but under the watchful eye of Angus. All the staff uniforms were clean and pressed and those serving the meal had already been briefed by Chef. Archie had everything prepped behind the bar. They were good to go.

'Can I just say that you look fabulous? Elegantly understated,' remarked Jennifer.

Maureen was wearing a fitted ivory dress with black trimming on the collar, on the short sleeves and on the pockets. She had maintained her weight loss and was comfortable with her size fourteen figure. Her hair was cut in a neat bob.

'Aww, thank you. You don't look blooming bad either.'

It was strange not wearing her staff uniform but it was rather nice to be dressed up for a change. Jennifer had chosen a brown, sleeveless dress with cream polka dots on it but she was grateful for the cream wrap around her shoulders. She was feeling the cold.

Guests were already milling outside when Maureen and Jennifer stepped outdoors. They were praying that the rain would stay off long enough for the champagne to be served and more photographs to be taken. Willie had built a pergola at the bottom of the beer garden and for weeks had been training sweet peas and honeysuckle to climb up and over the frame. A sturdy bench sat in the middle and was an ideal setting for romantic photographs.

Jennifer inhaled her surroundings. Everything looked amazing and she had engineered all of it; from refurbishing the building to raising the status of her business. She realised that, at long last, she actually fitted in here. It felt good. Did she have any regrets? Maybe.

'Jen, darling.' Malcolm gave Jennifer a fatherly squeeze. 'How was the holiday?'

'We had a fantastic time. So relaxing. It was just what we were needing. The girls loved it. I can't believe it's been over a week already.'

'And Bethany?'

'She had a ball. As did Joyce, believe it or not.'

Jennifer, the three girls and Joyce had flown out to Adelaide a week before the schools broke off for the holidays. Joyce had taken a great deal of persuasion but both Scott and Jennifer wanted her to be part of the big adventure. Joyce returned two weeks earlier than Jennifer and the girls insisting that Scott and Jennifer have some proper family time together. Scott had a lovely three bed house; a five-minute drive from St Kilda beach. Although it wasn't huge inside, the outdoor space and swimming pool more than made up for it.

'And your little passenger?'

Jennifer rubbed her expanding bump. 'He or she is just fine.'

'And your wee granddaughter?'

Malcom lit up. 'Absolutely adorable. She looks like Doreen. Must be the black hair.'

Roxanne, the little minx, had been playing away behind Mark's back; with a Spanish semi-pro at a nearby golf course.

Oh, to have been a fly on the wall during that confession, mused Jennifer. According to mater and pater, Mark is very happily ensconced in Florida. Selling time-shares!

Suddenly, there was a loud banging with a spoon on the table. It was Willie.

'Can I have your attention for a moment?' He waited until there was enough hush.

'Ladies and gentlemen, and especially to Mr and Mrs Blakeley, I would like to say a few words before we go inside. Don't worry, Joe, it's not the best man's speech yet. I'll be saving the best bit 'til last.' A loud roar went up. Joe toasted him with his pint glass in hand and rolled his eyes as if to say that he was dreading it.

'This is Maureen and me's first wedding as the new owners of The Maltings Hotel. Sorry, Jen, we've renamed it slightly.' It was Jennifer that started the cheering and loud clapping at that announcement. 'We'd like to thank Jen for encouragin' us to make this move and to Joe and Louisa for having the confidence and courage to take a chance on us to host oor first wedding.' Willie was getting a wee bit emotional. He cleared his throat and held his champagne flute above his head. 'Here's to guid friends and we are lucky to have loads of yous here today.'

Somebody shouted out that they were Maureen's friends. The jovial audience appreciated the joke.

'Fuck off!' laughed Willie.

'That's fifty pence in the swear box!' hollered Maureen.

The girls ran up to Jennifer and to grab a quick cuddle with Papa Malc. They were dying to tell him about their holiday.

'I believe there's something else special about today,' said Malcolm, pulling a quizzical face.

'It's Bethany's birthday!' screamed Emma and Katie together. 'She's ten!'

'So, it is.' And he reached into his jacket pocket and handed Bethany a gift-wrapped box.

'Can I open it now?' Two little faces eagerly watched as Bethany carefully unpicked the paper. 'Mum loved to buy me lots of little presents and I would guess what they would be. Is it sparkly?' she asked Malcolm staring up into his eyes.

Malcolm thought she looked so much like her mother. Bethany held up the gold locket. Jennifer helped her to open it. Inside was a beautiful photo of a smiling Angie wearing a beach hat and another that Malcolm had taken of Bethany at Christmas.

'Thank you, Papa Malc. It's beautiful.'

Jennifer could hardly see through her tears to fasten it around Bethany's slim neck. The girls ran off to find Joyce.

'You, okay?' asked Malcolm.

'I am now,' she said blinking away the last of her tears. 'And you?'

'Just,' he said. 'Have you decided what to do?'

*

After Christmas, Jennifer's relationship with Scott had gained momentum more quickly than either of them could have predicted. He spent so much time in Duneden that within five weeks he had moved into The Maltings and into Jennifer's bed full time. To them, it hadn't felt at all rushed but the most natural thing in the world to do. Bethany worshipped her daddy yet he was careful to explain constantly that he would have to go back to Australia at the end of March. No one wanted his return to be a shock to his daughter. Jennifer's girls accepted the situation too. Although, remaining in Scotland was not an option for Scott, he desperately wanted to be with Jennifer and her with him. The holiday was his idea. They were really worried that Joyce wouldn't comply but perhaps if they invited her too then it might work. Joyce was the least of their headaches. What to do with The Maltings? Jennifer asked Maureen and Willie if they would be prepared to look after The Maltings for six weeks. As well as Maureen's wages, they could keep the profits once all the outgoings had been paid.

It was during a boozy night at Maureen's that a seed was planted – dropped into the conversation by Willie. What if they, Maureen and he, bought The Maltings? If they could run it for six weeks, then why not for longer? He reckoned that they had more than enough collateral in their house to borrow against it and they had always been thrifty, so had a healthy savings account. If the bank refused them the money, they were still willing to give Jennifer the holiday.

Although totally unexpected, and probably influenced by copious amounts of alcohol, Jennifer and Scott thought it was a great idea. It was settled. On the first Monday of July, Anita-Anne Telfer sat in the Licensing Court with Maureen and Willie. The transaction was concluded while Jennifer sipped a virgin cocktail in Scott's garden, in Adelaide. It was only after Scott had returned to Australia that Jennifer discovered she was pregnant. Another unexpected shock – but a very happy one.

*

'This little bundle wasn't planned, obviously, but it kind of completes us... as a family. Running this place without Angie,' she lifted her hands and looked around her, 'wasn't the same. It was bloody hard and it wasn't fair on the girls. I would have sold it anyway. My dad worries that history is repeating itself. That I'm dancing to a different man's tune. But I love Scott and I truly believe that he loves me. Does that sound ridiculous?' Jennifer really needed to know.

'I'm the last person to give advice, except grab happiness when you can, as long as it doesn't destroy everything and everyone else. Where does Bethany fit in?' Malcolm felt responsible for her in some small way.

'Scott's trying so hard to make it work, especially for Bethany. It's a waiting game, unfortunately, and I miss him. But you know what? If it doesn't work out, I'll dust myself off and start again.'

Malcolm didn't doubt that for a minute. 'That's my girl.' He sensed a change of mood was required. 'How's my but and ben treating you? There's plenty of room in my house for the three of you. The offer's still open.'

Jennifer slipped her arm into his. 'The but and ben is great. It's quaint and quiet and when I know what I'm doing, I'll be out of your hair.'

Malcolm rubbed his thinning hairline, 'Not much left to get out of,' he joked.

'I took my mattress with me. I wasn't leaving that.'

They sat at a picnic bench and watched the happy couple posing for their wedding album. They marvelled at everything that had happened to both of them over the past two years and how a very unlikely friendship had evolved.

Jennifer had no idea what the future held for her. It was unnerving. Everything had happened so quickly. Perhaps *too* hastily. She truly hoped it would be a future with Scott in it. One thing was for certain, with a new baby on the way, successfully running The Maltings on her own would have been unsustainable.

'It's a beautiful view from this vantage point,' said Malcolm staring out over the lawns and the River Eden towards all the trees on his small estate.

'Do you miss Angie?' asked Jennifer, studying Malcolm's melancholy gaze.

'I absolutely do but oddly enough, I miss Doreen more. It's a funny old world.'

'I can honestly say, I don't miss Mark one single bit,' giggled Jennifer.

Jennifer felt a gentle tap on her shoulder. 'Fergal.' She jumped up to greet him. 'What on earth are you doing here? Have you met Malcolm properly? Malcolm this is my very dear friend, Fergal Fitzsimmons. Fergal... Malcolm.'

The two men shook hands in mutual admiration because Jennifer had extolled their virtues to each of them. They had met in the past but only briefly and it had never seemed to be the appropriate moment to exchange more than a nod of acknowledgement.

'Oh, how could I forget? Malcolm this is Dominique Geroldi, my lawyer, and a good friend of Fergal's.'

*

When Jennifer turned up at Fergal's house for Christmas dinner, the last person she was expecting to greet in Fergal's living room was a tall, attractive, graceful Italian who exuded the elegance befitting a mature, professional woman. She could hear Maureen shouting, 'shut yer mouth, Jen, you'll catch a fly!' She wore a white, woollen, polo-neck dress and soft, suede, grey boots. Jennifer felt decidedly underdressed. She had the same outfit that she had worn last year at Maureen's – red jeans and her cream, fluffy jumper. She really needed to upgrade her wardrobe.

'No wonder Fergal kept you to himself all those years. You look wonderful.' Jennifer meant it and hugged Fergal's mystery friend.

'I like you already,' laughed the older woman who, it turned out, had recently separated from her husband after having conducted a secret affair with Fergal for sixteen years.

Both Fergal and Dom were devout Catholics and divorce had never been considered as an option until now. Dom and her husband were business partners; a divorce would have complicated things. Plus, Dom had put the well-being of her sons first. She did not want them growing up in a home that their parents did not share. Both her boys left home after they graduated from university and now lived their own lives, leaving Dom free to live hers.

Fergal clearly adored her and their body language suggested that they were effortlessly comfortable with each other. Jennifer was so happy for them both.

*

'We were passing through. I have a gift for the birthday girl and, as is customary, a small gift for my nieces.'

'That makes you sound so much younger than me,' cajoled Malcolm. 'I've been given the honorary title of Papa Malc.'

As if they had mastered the art of sniffing out gifts, it hadn't taken the girls long to retrace their steps and find everyone. Fergal handed over the bag of gifts; several colouring books, a sticker book, paints and pens for Bethany plus two small sticker books for the non-birthday girls. The bag was left with Jennifer and the three sticker books went off to play at a neighbouring bench.

Maureen struck a small gong and asked the guests to make their way into the Eden Suite. Jennifer gave a big thumbs up to let her know that the event had been a huge success so far. They were saying their farewells to Fergal and Dom when a shriek echoed over the garden.

'DADDY!' Bethany charged towards Scott and jumped into his arms.

'Happy Birthday, sweetheart. I couldn't miss my little girl's big day.'

Jennifer got up and joined in the big hug. 'How on earth did you manage to get here?'

'I've been juggling so many balls for weeks. I didn't dare say anything in case it didn't work out. I am now, officially, temporarily, a sleeping partner in the business. I'll explain it all later. I'm here for a short visit only, then I'll return before this little one is born.'

Scott knew everyone in the group and wandered around shaking hands. He was looking thoroughly bedraggled as he had been travelling for two days.

'Oi! Are you lot coming in?' yelled Maureen.

Jennifer asked the girls to put their gifts back in the bag and stopped.

'Whoa! It just kicked. Scott! Girls! The baby just moved. Feel.'

So many hands were rubbing Jennifer's belly.

'I can't wait to be a big sister,' announced Bethany.

'But you're already a big sister to me,' Katie reminded her.

On that happy note, they kissed Fergal and Dom goodbye and made their way into the Eden Suite to celebrate.

ACKNOWLEDGEMENTS

I am so grateful to my loyal band of readers who have given up their time, once again, to read *Sleeping Partners*. Your constructive feedback is greatly appreciated. Sandra and Val, your warm words of encouragement keep me going.

I read with envy, the acknowledgements that other authors write. They seem to have dozens of people reading their work, editing, researching and advising. It's a very lonely journey for a self-publisher. I don't have the luxury to employ others to proofread or do research for me. So, thank you Maureen and Linda, for your diligence and help. Both have been my friends since day one of High School.

Many thanks to my husband, Ronnie, for his patience, male perspective and for never moaning when lumbered with the cooking and household chores while I write. Ronnie's knowledge of the licensed trade is extensive and I really did have to pick his brains throughout.

Our friend, Dougie Morris, provided me with the information I needed about Gateshead in the forties and early eighties. He allowed me to use his name for my down-and-out. (His wife found that hilarious!)

A hearty thank-you to my nephew, Mark Stevenson, for the outstanding photograph on the front cover:
www.markstevensonphotography.com

I am extremely fortunate to have Duncan at Lumphanan Press who, once again, guided me through the process of self-publishing on a tight budget. His advice is invaluable. Thank you so much. Honestly, some of the questions I asked!

HOWEVER, a huge thank you is reserved for all you readers who bought and read *Take Me Instead*. Sales and your wonderful comments exceeded all my expectations. So chuffed and very humbled that readers from all over the world took the time to contact me.

And for those of you who have purchased Sleeping Partners. THANK YOU!

Please look out for future books. *The Estranged Wife* should be with you next spring.

Faye grew up in an East Lothian mining community. She graduated with a teaching diploma at Moray House College, Edinburgh. As well as teaching, she helped her husband run the family businesses in hospitality for over thirty years. Now in semi-retirement, she has returned to her love of writing.

Her next book, *The Estranged Wife,* is forthcoming.

Printed in Great Britain
by Amazon